BY THE SHARP AND SHADOWED WINGS

RACHEL N. HARKER

To those who bear the weight of the world...
and still search for their place within it.

Content Warning

Take care, dear reader. Please read the following content warnings carefully and make the best decision for your mental health and well-being. This book contains the following sensitive material:

- Graphic Violence: Including combat scenes and past-tense mentions of physical abuse, torture, and food deprivation.

- Captivity/Slavery: Past-tense mentions of characters experiencing abusive and exploitative situations while held in captivity.

- Self-Sacrifice and Self-Harm: Themes of self-sacrificing tendencies which may be interpreted as self-harm and self-destructive decision making.

- Mental Health Struggles: Includes grief, loss, and themes of depression, anxiety, and emotional trauma.

- Explicit Sexual Content: Detailed and explicit depictions of sexual activity.

Please take care of yourself as you make the decision to continue, and know that you are not alone in navigating difficult themes. If you have any further concerns or questions, please don't hesitate to reach out to me at rachel@authorrachelnharker.com

REALMS

Alfheim (AHLF-hyme): Home of the elves
Asgard (AZ-gahrd): Home of the Aesir
Helheim (HEL-hyme): Realm of the disgraced dead
Jotunheim (YOH-tuhn-hyme): Home of the giants
Muspelheim (MUSS-puhl-hyme): Home of the fire beings
Myddheim (MID-hyme): Home of the mortals
Nidavellir (NID-uh-VEL-leer): Home of the dwarves
Niflheim (NIFL-hyme): Realm of lost souls
Vanaheim (VAN-uh-hyme): Home of the Vanir

CHARACTERS

Angrboda (AHNG-ger-bo-duh): Giantess Witch
Fenrir (FEN-reer): God of Destruction
Freyja (FRAY-yuh): Goddess of Love, War, Sex, Beauty, and Life
Hel (Hell): Goddess of Death
Jormun (YOR-mun): The Realms Serpent
Loki (LOW-kee): God of Mischief, Trickery, and Deception
Revna (REV-na): Commander of the Myddheim Maidens
Tyr (Teer): God of Love and War

OTHER

Aesir (AH-seer): Pantheon of Gods that inhabit Asgard
Galdrloka (GAHL-dr-loka): Power-sharing bind with unknown potential
Hjarta (YAR-tah): Marriage bind of the heart and soul
Seiðr (SAY-der): A form of magic
Skyldu (SKUHL-du): Bind of service and obligation
Vanir (VAH-neer): Second pantheon of Gods that inhabit Vanaheim
Yggdrasil (IG-dra-sil): The World Tree that connects all Nine realms

Asgard
Vanaheim
Muspelheim
Alfheim
Myddheim
Jotunheim
Nidavellir
Niflheim
Helheim

Prologue

T HE TREE BRANCHES GROANED under the weighty pull of the wind, crying out and whispering his failure—hundreds of failures. Half-eaten limbs and time-smoothed skulls pocked the tree's infinite height. Bones stripped of their meat and coated in dark, sappy blood protruded at odd angles. Each a mark of disappointment.

"Perhaps it's time to try a different approach." Her voice caused his grip to tighten on his spear. He tore his gaze away from the tree to face her.

The woman standing before him had her shoulders thrown back in pride, proof he'd yet to make them curve inward in submission. But her eyes proved his work had not gone to waste, the bright brown muted and weary. Nor could her pride hide his mark on the center of her chest—a reminder that she was bound to serve him. 'Til death.

Gods did not bow to things like time and death, but looking upon their many failed attempts, he felt its looming threat. He would not cease his hunt. He would not fail.

He slowly approached and cupped her cheek, her eyes flashing warily. "Just because you have failed me again, does not mean we stop. This pursuit is vital. The balance and fate of the nine realms depend on it."

Many ages had passed since the sisters had bestowed their prophecy and left him to sift through the words and images planted in his mind's eye. A raven whose moon-white feathers bled to black as it landed on

Yggdrasil's limb. Winter opening its jaw and letting coldness devour the lands. Blackened sunbeams and scorched ground. Three monsters standing over the wreckage. They left him to search for the cure to this curse of knowledge. But what he knew with certainty ...

Darkness came on swift wings. Darkness was coming for the realms. *Darkness was coming for him.*

But not if he came for it first.

"And lest you forget," he said, as he slid his hand into her hair and gave it a sharp yank, baring her throat. "You are bound to me. To serve me. Do you need reminding of what would happen should you break the bind?"

"No." The word was firm but coated in desperation.

He thought as much. He released her and she stumbled away, resuming her position to await his next command. For one fleeting moment, her gaze flashed with such fire he could nearly taste the ash on his tongue. It wouldn't do well to forget who she was. What she was.

He wasn't entirely sure what she'd be capable of if he pushed her too far, so he would continue to coat his words in honey and veil his truths.

"I know you do not mean to disappoint me. We both want to find—"

The rasp of volant wings on the wind and warning caws of his returning ravens cut his words short. They flew overhead in frantic circles. He could not make sense of their tangled words and croaked calls in his mind.

"Come!" He slammed his spear into the earth, his voice echoing off root, limb, and bone.

The two ravens finally settled, one on his shoulder, the other on the top of his spear. Before he could focus on their words, he noticed the small twitch of a smile on the chooser of the slain's lips. The expression caused boiling anger to thin his blood.

"What are you not telling me?" he demanded of her.

"*Master—*"

"*We come with great tellings.*"

"*Terrible tellings.*"

The ravens' voices came through clearly in his mind. It shouldn't have surprised him—what they spoke of next. He had known for many haunted ages. But the time was nigh, and it took all his power to craft his expression to disinterest and compel his heartbeat to remain steady.

"Out with it!" he boomed.

Stillness crept into the area surrounding the tree. The branches ceased their groaning sway. As if waiting.

Listening.

Exhaling.

"*The wolf has returned.*"

ONE

I F ONE MORE FOUL-SMELLING drunkard pinched her ass, Revna was going to make a necklace of his fingers. One too many ales and they lost what little sense the Gods gave them. Pathetic. Her eyes narrowed on a man trying to reach up Ingrid's skirt as she refilled his ale horn. Revna took one step forward, hand itching to reach for one of her knives, but caught herself.

Not yet. Ingrid could handle herself. And this was all part of the plan: keep the men distracted.

Carefully resuming the mask of an obedient servant, Revna tried to force a soft smile, only to feel a maddened half-snarl quickly take its place.

A bracelet of teeth. That's what she would gift Ingrid with when this night was over. An eyeball ring for Asta. Earlobe armbands for Hildi. A circlet of toe bones would look fearsome on Brynn. And something matching made of fingernails for Torsten and Haesten ...

A gift for each of the Maidens.

Revna no longer had to fake her smile. The thought of butchering these vile, unworthy slave traders settled something inside of her—a peace that she had been battling for nine long years. Though she knew she couldn't deliver dead enslavers to the king, they needn't arrive whole.

Sinking into the role of both bait and snare, she tugged the bodice of her dress down and gave her breasts a little lift, trying to take a deep breath in the restricting garment. Ale jug secured in hand, Revna moved to follow Ingrid back behind the divider for refills, accidentally knocking her pitcher into the head of the man who'd reached up Ingrid's skirts. He turned, throwing her a glossy-eyed glare. Revna cooed a fake apology and slapped his cheek a couple of times, leaving him to boil.

"They'll be pleased by this lot—even if some arrive a little *worn* in," a foul man said as Revna passed by.

Fingers. Toes. Eyeballs. Earlobes. Teeth ...

"Girl!" another yelled from across the long table. He raised his ale-horn and shook it while the other men laughed. Trying to appear meek and timid, Revna tucked her chin in a subservient gesture and rounded the table. After filling his horn, she found Ingrid behind the divider, red faced and huffing deeply.

"It will be over soon," Revna told her second.

"Much longer and I am going to remove that one's hand," she replied, tilting her chin toward the man sitting at the head of the center table. Ingrid's rising temper made Revna's brow furrow. She decided this would be the last time she would ask Ingrid to play distraction. While Revna loathed this part, she could and would bear it.

"I will happily hold him down while you do." A loud outburst of laughing and the rumble of feet stomping on the meeting house floor interrupted those delightful thoughts. "Keep your eyes on the rafters."

With a squeeze to Ingrid's shoulder, Revna braved the tables again, the smell of ale, sweat, and piss wafting in eye-burning plumes. Several gazes followed her with unabashed hunger—her appearance playing right into what they thought she was: vulnerable, a prize for the taking. This far south, her hair, black as a raven's feather, was something of a curiosity. Revna made sure it was on display, trying to bear the brunt of unwanted attention. The simple braid crown with the rest hanging loose to her mid-back, paired with her gray eyes, made most people look twice.

Unfortunately for them.

The main door to the meeting house opened, bringing with it a taste of the ending summer. Two men stumbled back in through the door left ajar, undoubtedly returning from checking on their *wares*. Still, Revna smiled. Ten men now sat within the hall, the snare ready to be sprung.

Throwing a tendril of her hair over her shoulder, she leaned far enough over the center table that her breasts were nearly spilling from her top. With a coy glance up, the snare sprung. Her eyes caught and snagged on the poacher—a name he had given himself with pride—sitting at the head of the table. He drained his horn with unflinching eye contact, ale dripping and coating his gnarled beard.

Revna and her Maidens had been tracking him for months, and tonight they finally got the opportunity to confront him and his cohorts. They would no longer be taking women and children from their homes while the men and maidens were off raiding. A violent and dishonorable end awaited them.

No Skalds would tell tales of their bravery in this life.

No Valkyrs would carry them to Odin's hall, Valhalla.

No boar would appear to grant them acceptance to Freyja's embrace.

Even Helheim was too good for them.

Their only flicker of hope would be to wander the endless wastelands of Niflheim, hoping to go unnoticed by the Goddess of Death herself.

A cold gust at Revna's backside had her breaking her stare with the poacher and turning toward the still open door. Asta slid in, keeping to the wall, tucking her short blond hair back into the shadows of her hood, and gave her the nod.

Finally.

"Girl!" The unmistakable tenor of the poacher made her spine stiffen. "Come refill my cup. Then sit on my lap and put your tits in my face."

Revna glanced at Ingrid, who came out from behind the partition, twisting her long red braid into a tight bun at the nape of her neck, preparing to break bones. Asta, who was now leaning against a wooden pillar, cocked an eyebrow and gave Revna a smirk. At her relaxed stance, Revna knew that if she glanced up to the rafters she would see more of the Maidens at the ready.

She smiled and made her way to oblige the poacher, first by filling his ale-horn and then by perching on his knee, setting the jug of ale down to free her hands.

"If you're good, maybe I'll fuck you later." He gave her ass a rough pat, then his hand moved its way down her thigh while he tried to bury his head into her breasts. "Or maybe I'll let you watch as I bed your little red-headed friend."

Revna's smile faltered into a sneer. *Fuck this.*

She grabbed the poor excuse for a man's braided hair and gave it a painful yank. He hissed, tightening his grip on her thigh.

The man tried to laugh it off since all eyes had turned to their display. "Go on, girl. I like it when they fight." His hand trailed higher, until it stopped on the unmistakable hardness of blade sheathed at her thigh.

"Oh, the *meyla* has teeth." Meyla—little girl.

She was far from a little girl, but if he wanted to see her teeth ... well, how could she refuse?

More laughter came from the surrounding men, completely unaware of what was about to happen. "C'mon then, show me your little woman's blade. Maybe I'll brand you with it so you will never forget your night with me."

Revna had done her time as a branded woman. Could still feel the burn of its raised edges on the back of her neck.

Never again.

She adjusted slightly, lifting her skirt, and his eyes snapped to the exposed skin. As she pulled the little blade from its sheath, the flash of metal had him ripping it from her hand.

She let him have it. *For now.*

Ingrid came to stand behind the men to Revna's right. Asta still stood by the pillar, looking slightly shocked that her commander was letting this man keep his tongue. Her head jerked to the door as Hildi walked through, looking slightly out of breath. Once the door was shut to the elements, Hildi tapped her knuckles twice against the wood, signaling to bar them in from the outside. All the men were too drunk and distracted to notice the air shifting about them.

"Where shall I carve my name?" the poacher asked, tracing the knife across the tops of her breasts. Revna grabbed his wrist and clucked her tongue at him. Clearly not used to being scolded, his face reddened at the admonishment.

"Did no one ever teach you it's rude to touch someone without their permission?" she asked, batting her lashes.

With the oaf distracted by her sweet tone, Revna was able to reach for the bigger knife sheathed in the leather just below her breast. Leaning in, she held his gaze as she slammed his hand down on the table and stabbed the knife through it, pinning him to the wood. Before he could scream, she twisted out of his lap and slammed his face into the table for good measure, admiring the beautiful cracking sound of his nose on wood.

There was a brief moment of shocked silence, then the meeting house broke into chaos. Cloaked women dropped from the rafters above onto the tables and bore down on the unsuspecting men.

Ingrid bashed her jug into the man in front of her before he could lunge at Revna. She threw her second a grateful look, mentally adding more accessories she'd gift to Ingrid. Perhaps a new herb sack made of a slavers—

"Commander!"

Revna whipped her head to the call. Brynn stood in the middle of the table, jumping over reaching hands, thumping the butt of her spear into the forehead of one of their targets, rendering him unconscious. Once slumped to the ground, she tossed Revna the weapon with a nod.

Normally she preferred her specialty-made twin daggers and battle-axe, but those didn't hide well under such a thin dress. She couldn't wait to change back into her leathers.

She turned back to rejoin the fray, but a quick glance told her most of her Maidens were at no risk of harm. Drunkenness had been in their favor. Ingrid had removed her apron and was cutting off a man's air supply, while several others were in the process of hog-tying their new captives.

A fine haul to deliver to the king of Nantahalla.

"You *fucking* bitch!" a strained voice said from her left. The poacher, now awake from his short nap, stood, yanking the knife from his impaled hand. Several Maidens advanced, but Revna held up her hand.

"Let the commander have her fun," Ingrid chimed in, untangling her apron from around an unconscious neck and pushing the body over with her foot. "She needs it."

The meeting house fell quiet, save for the grunting of trussed up men and the labored breathing of the beast twisting her knife back and forth in his undamaged hand. Blood ran in great gushes from his nose, staining teeth and beard in bright crimson. An improvement, as far as Revna was concerned.

She pointed her spear at the knife in his hand. "I'll be needing that back."

"Come and get it then." He spit on the ground between them then lunged, slightly off kilter from too much ale and blood loss, no doubt. Revna stepped aside and watched him stumble forward as the knife slashed through the space she had just vacated. He turned quickly, swinging in ungraceful arcs.

It was more like dancing with a terrible partner than fighting, his movements slow and erratic. She stepped and weaved and tried to withhold the monstrous laugh that was rising from her belly. Revna had been itching for a fight, but this? This was just boring and embarrassing. She wanted it done.

Revna twirled the spear in her hands, resting it on her neck in a defensive position—the dizzying movement enough to make the poacher sick. He heaved all the contents of his stomach onto the floor at her feet.

Disgusted, she spun, whipping her spear from her neck and slicing the backs of his knees. He fell with a satisfying thud, face first into his own filth. She called for ropes, and two Maidens moved forward and bound him, righting him to a kneeling position.

"I demand to speak to the man in charge!" the poacher said, struggling like an exposed worm in the baking sun. A chorus of chuckles echoed around the meeting house as Revna squatted to his eye level.

"You're looking at her."

She smiled at his obvious disgust. It had taken her nine long years to lose the urge to flinch at the glint of hatred in his eyes, in the eyes of so many others like him. That look that said how little they cared for life.

"The king will have your head for this," he hissed.

"The king and I have a deal," she said, informing him of his error. "He outlawed slavery, and we deliver those who seek to disobey him."

His blue eyes sharpened, lighting again on her hair, her eyes, and a slow smile spread, showing bloodied teeth. "I know who you are. *Revna.*"

That sludgy mixture of guilt and rage boiled just under her skin at the poacher's realization. She resisted the urge to swallow or blink, to show any kind of reaction. The way he slurred her name wasn't in recognition of her being the Commander of the Myddheim Maidens. No, he'd recognized the name, and the story of the girl she'd been before the Maidens. The past that stalked her dreams and haunted her days.

Fenrick. The boat. Sacrificed. Gone.

"Then you should know what happens next," she responded coolly.

His smile turned venomous. "The girl who disobeyed the Gods. The girl responsible for the Gods abandoning Myddheim. The girl responsible for our suffering—"

She shouldn't have done it. She knew she really shouldn't, but the sharpened end of her spear somehow found itself burying into his gut. She was going to kill him.

Asta cleared her throat from beside her, and Revna looked over to see her old friend extending her belt, hung with her two favorite daggers. Smiling, she pulled them from their sheath and sighed at the rightness in her grip.

"Would you like the honors?" she asked Ingrid. After all, it was her who'd received most of the scum's attention that evening.

Ingrid shook her head, then lifted her chin. "Send him to the beasts of Helheim."

Revna smile and looked back to her prey.

"Do you know why I prefer these daggers over a longsword or bow?" She traced one of their pointed edges along the curve of his throat. "They're more intimate. I can get closer. See the heartbeat in the throat, the fear in the eyes. You all even have a certain foul *smell* about you."

The poacher started thrashing about, trying to escape the searing kiss of Revna's blade. Asta moved forward and planted her feet on either side of his kneeling form and gripped his hair, yanking it back to expose his throat to her commander. The most beautiful gift she'd received in a long time.

"The king said I had to bring him to you, but he didn't specify in how many pieces."

"Odin *curse* you—"

Revna plunged her daggers into the sides of his neck. Leaning in close, she whispered, "He already has."

His eyes widened a fraction and then dimmed as she brought the blades through muscle and tendon, hot blood staining her fingers.

All was quiet then, save for the satisfying thud as his body fell forward, dead.

Two

T HE LONG HOUSE WAS cleared out and reorganized into makeshift healing and sleeping areas. Women and children sat around the fire with the Maidens, spooning broth between their cracked lips. Some clung and cried softly to one another. Others darted their gaze around, ever vigilant, flinching at the cracks and hisses of the fire. No doubt wondering if they'd gone from one nightmare to another.

Thirteen.

The Maidens had saved thirteen women and children that night, bound for servitude or worse. While the men had been getting drunk, they were being liberated from the tiny wagons they'd been locked up in—collared and chained to the wagon's inner walls like animals. Revna had made sure the favor was returned to the men.

She ladled a hearty helping of broth and handed it to the youngest among the group, currently being cradled in the embrace of Hildi. The little girl couldn't have been more than five summers old. Revna couldn't stop staring at her. Couldn't stop remembering when she was young and terrified and alone in the world. Couldn't stop the memory of men ripping her from her mother's cold, lifeless body. Of the searing sting of a brand being placed on the back of her neck ...

She grazed her fingers over the raised skin where the mark of her former life sat, the brand now covered by inked runes, climbing like ivy down her spine, strengthening her. Reminding her. All the Maidens that bore scars from their former lives sheltered them within ink and blood—a reclamation of self, they called it. But there were some scars so deep that no ink could reach.

Fenrick.

Revna shook her head, willing that thread of memory to stay carefully knotted. No matter how many times they did this, Revna couldn't battle the inevitable crash from the high of a fight. The thoughts and memories that came bursting in like a blade breaking through a shield wall. Breath would stay stalled within her ribcage even when there was finally space to exhale.

Ingrid tended to a twig-thin girl, her age made indiscernible by the bruises and muck covering her pale face. A long, festering gash was being covered in a salve of the healer's making, Ingrid talking the girl through every step as she was treated.

Revna had never mastered Ingrid's calm and serene voice. Never mastered gentleness. No, she preferred to show her care with actions. With being both the cutting blade and the steady shield. Protecting with all that she could. It's what made them a great commander and second—Revna being the burn and Ingrid the balm. Asta, as the Maidens' third, sat somewhere between the other two in temperament, creating perfect balance.

Revna didn't thank the Gods for much, but she would relent to immense gratitude for the home she'd found with Ingrid, Asta, and the rest of Maidens over the last nine years.

"Thank you," the young girl being held by Hildi rasped as Revna tore off a crust of bread, placing it gently on the side of the girl's bowl. Her young, dirt-covered brow lifted as she tore off another hunk, placing it on the other side of the bowl, doubling the serving. Revna threw the youngling a wink when bright blue eyes met hers in surprise.

Hildi threw a grateful look her way as well, continuing to rub a gentle hand across the girl's back as she slurped great gulps right from the bowl. Turning, Revna found a large pelt draped across one of the benches and wrapped it around the pair. She knew that Hildi would not leave the little girl's side and wanted to make sure they were comfortable as the night's cold grew sharper teeth.

She took in the scene, trying to feel like the night was a success. Like she was doing enough. Every day this was happening, women and children being taken, and sometimes Revna and her Maidens were too late. They pulled one weed and ten more popped up in its place.

A choking, dark grip had plagued Myddheim these last years. Fighting was constant and fatal. Crops that normally thrived under the Gods' blessed summer suns had instead rotted and withered from their roots, as if the very land had been poisoned. Goodness could only be found in a few corners of the realm.

Revna and her Maidens did all that they could. Even when the endless grip of darkness felt tight and unrelenting. She often wondered if Myddheim was the only realm being punished by the Gods or if they found the mortal's plight particularly amusing.

The ever-present weight in her chest thrummed as she looked around the meeting house. She shoved down the feeling that she should still be doing more.

At least she'd been able to convince the king to outlaw slavery five years before. She was grateful for that.

At the time, Revna and her Maidens had been fewer, but were quickly becoming known. Feared. People had sought them out, begging them to help find and return their wives, children, sisters. One day, a summons from the king brought Revna to the heart of Myddheim. His daughter, while on a journey to pay tribute to the Gods at their most sacred temple, had been taken. The search took weeks. It took metal and blood. But

Revna had returned with his daughter, and he'd granted her a request of her time and choosing. She hadn't hesitated to ask him to outlaw slavery. To allow her and her Maidens to seek out those who disobeyed him, with an agreement to bring the slavers to him for justice.

She'd left with the king's blessing and seven new Maidens—including the king's own daughter, Hildi.

Seeing that the women and children were being tended to, Revna stepped outside to check if the others were ready to set off with their newly acquired prisoners. Torsten and Haesten, the only two men in her crew, were guarding the wagons—one sitting and sharpening a sword, the other staring daggers at the men who were currently pleading to whichever God would listen to their plight.

"Commander." Torsten greeted her with a nod. "Do they need anything?"

"No, they have it well in hand."

"We do have some more herbs and linen, if Ingrid needs extra. I can go get them …"

Revna gave him a soft smile. Torsten had been training with Ingrid in the healing arts over the whole summer season. However, they'd found it was easier for the women and children to feel safe without the presence of the men in the moments after liberation. "I believe she's all set. You did well preparing everything for her."

Haesten leaned forward and gave Torsten's shoulder a squeeze, knowing how badly his partner wanted to help—to assure the women they were no threat. Sure, the two men were as strong and intimidating as any warrior, but Revna trusted them completely with her life and that of those they rescued. They would rather die without a blade in their hand, forfeiting their place in Valhalla, than hurt a suffering person.

When the pair had approached Revna, she'd liked them immediately. They'd begged to do the grunt work: sharpen weapons, cook meals, or deliver messages to the other bands of Maidens currently stationed throughout the kingdom. All for the chance to become Myddheim Maidens themselves—a title they'd insisted on earning. To help, and to maybe one day find Haesten's missing sister and mother.

The sound of a sniffle had her turning away from the men. Sitting against a tree was a woman, her forehead leaning on her knees, causing light brown hair to cover her face.

"What is she doing out here? Has she been tended to?" Revna asked.

Haesten sighed. "She wanted to be outside—under the stars."

Revna nodded in understanding. Her former enslaver would punish her by throwing her in a hole in the ground for weeks. No sun, little food, and even less hope. "Torsten, Asta is standing near the hall's door. Have her get Ingrid."

Slowly approaching, Revna greeted the woman, but kept a distance that would make her feel safe. "Hello ..."

The woman slowly lifted her head and Revna was overcome with a sharp wave of recognition, her mind slipping back into memory.

When she'd fled into the night after killing her enslaver, she'd found Fenrick, bound and bloodied, in a cave so remote no one could hear him scream. No one had known he was there. But fate had conspired for her to find him. Revna swallowed as she thought on the way his eyes looked as they first met hers. He'd barely been able to lift his head, but his stare ... it had burned with warning. One she'd ignored as she unbound him from his chains.

Shaking off her reverie, Revna realized she'd been staring and cleared her throat.

"I've asked my healer to come check on you, if that's alright."

It was hard to guess the woman's age. Those who age from pain present differently than those who age by time alone.

The woman continued to stare, so Revna squatted down to sit, hitting the ground with a groan. She was still wearing the thin dress, and the woman's eyes strayed to the blood soaking the front. "Don't worry, it's not mine. It's the poacher's."

Dark eyes flicked to Revna's face, searching.

"Good," the woman croaked, her throat sounding dry, either from screaming or lack of use.

"I agree." Revna gave her a small smile. "My name is Revna. I am the Commander of the Myddheim Maid—"

"I know who you are."

"Asta said you needed me—oh, hello." Ingrid approached with her basket in tow but slowed upon seeing the woman against the tree. Bypassing Revna, she asked, "May I come sit by you? Treat that cut on your cheek?"

The woman ran wary eyes over Ingrid, but nodded. "My shoulder is out of place again," she added quietly.

Revna swallowed against the tightness in her throat as she noticed the way the woman cradled her arm.

Again. She'd said again. That one word would haunt Revna for days to come. How many times had it been out? Maybe if they'd caught up to the poachers sooner ...

"Let's tend to your shoulder and then your cut. I have a tonic that will help with the pain, but it will make you want to sleep—"

"No," the woman immediately replied.

"Of course. It's your choice. Always. But put this between your teeth." Ingrid handed the woman a folded strip of leather, gesturing her to sit forward to get the right angle to put the shoulder back.

"Thank you, but I don't need it."

Ingrid glanced at Revna, lips pulling into a frown. They both knew this state, when it felt like you were immune to any kind of pain because you had already suffered every type imaginable.

"Will you tell me your name?" Ingrid asked, softening her voice.

"Ellika"

Ellika—unbroken one. Revna nodded. Fitting.

"Alright Ellika, on the count of three." Revna knew Ingrid's trick, as it had been used on her many times, and after the count of two, a sickening pop, and Ellika's hiss, the shoulder was back in its place.

Arm secured in a sling, Ingrid started cleaning the gash on Ellika's cheek. It had just missed her eye. The quiet felt heavy, and Revna could sense that Ellika wouldn't ask questions, so she went ahead and explained what would come next.

"After Ingrid takes care of you, you are more than welcome to join the others inside. Or you may sleep out here under the stars—either way I will have someone watch over you. All night." Revna paused to make sure that she wasn't overwhelming the hurting woman, continuing when she got a small nod. "Tomorrow, you will have a choice."

"A choice?"

Revna wanted to tell her that she was free, but it wasn't that simple. She would have to fight against the invisible chains that still held tight. Grieve for all that was lost. Mourn for the person she'd have been and life she might have had, unburdened by this hurt.

"What you want to do next is up to you. We can take you home. We can set you up somewhere safe, we can—"

"I want to join the Myddheim Maidens," Ellika interrupted.

Ingrid paused her tending and studied Ellika's face, then turned to Revna with raised brows.

"I want—no *need*—to do this. I have nothing to return to and nowhere to go. But I want to do what you do. I want to fight. I want to help." Revna didn't respond, letting Ellika solidify her decision. "You said I have a choice. This is my choice."

She considered the woman, then asked, "How long?"

"I'm not exactly sure, but at least three winters," Ellika said, not needing an explanation of what Revna was asking her—how long she'd been with the men. "I saw dozens of women and children being put on ships, and each time, he kept me."

"Why?" Ingrid threw her a look that implored her to be gentle, but she asked anyway. She was pushing Ellika, but it was not without reason. Again, the other woman responded without asking for elaboration.

"I was ... defiant in the beginning. And I think he saw that as a challenge, something to conquer—he did, for a time." She trailed off, eyes going far away as she stared at the dirt between them. "But I couldn't help it. Maybe if I had made myself smaller. Maybe if I'd practiced obedience, he wouldn't have—"

Ellika choked on her words. Ingrid tentatively put a hand on her uninjured arm. Revna stood up and approached the pair, taking out a knife in the process—not one of her twin daggers, but still sharp enough to cut through skin. She squatted down directly in front of Ellika and waited for her to do what she needed. Cry, scream, laugh, go numb—she'd seen it all—each a valid response.

Ellika blinked and let the tears she was withholding fall freely down her face, the act its own kind of strength.

"In my experience, it wouldn't have made a difference whether you were one thing or another. Good and obedient. Loud and defiant. All he saw was a light to snuff out, something to break. But Ellika? Look at me," Revna said firmly, waiting until those pain-filled eyes found hers. "He did *not* succeed. We may burn, but we do not break."

Revna saw it then. The fire reignited in Ellika's eyes, the small ember of hope and determination.

She would fit right in.

"Besides," Revna said, as she quirked an impish smile, "the smarter the woman, the more easily offended the man."

Ellika didn't laugh, but her lips twitched. Putting her knees in the dirt and leaning back on her heels, Revna took the knife in one hand and sliced her palm on the other. She'd never done this with any of the others, save for Ingrid in the beginning, but it felt important—to share this pact with this woman.

She held the handle out, gesturing for Ellika to take the knife and do the same, forgetting one arm was bound. To Revna's surprise, the injured woman took the knife and sliced into her already bound hand.

Ellika shrugged. "It's already hurt."

"Repeat after me."

Revna gently clasped Ellika's hand with her own, careful not to pull on her tender shoulder. She could feel the weakness in the young woman's grip. Instinctually, she wanted to protect her. Let her live a life without threat or fear. But this was Ellika's choice, and Revna would not take that lightly. She would embolden and stoke the embers that Ellika had kept alive through so much darkness.

"Freyja, hear this oath," Revna said, and Ellika responded in kind. "By the salt and earth, by my blood and bones, with these warriors, I make my home. Shield at my back, sword at my side. Through winter's bite and summer's rise. We are the voice that speaks in the dark. The hand that reaches, the flame that sparks. From this day, for all my nights, I do so swear."

Finally, Ellika gave a tear-lined smile.

"Welcome to the Myddheim Maidens."

After some protest on Revna's part, she begrudgingly found herself in a bath. The jarl of this village had insisted that he set her up with a private room and provide whatever she and the Maidens needed, most likely to ensure that word got back to the king about his cooperation and hospitality after allowing the slavers to feast in his hall. Ingrid, knowing that Revna would be presenting to the king in two days, insisted she take the rest—and the bath—saying she smelled, "Like death and whatever shit her horse rolled in." She wasn't wrong.

Heat lulled her body into a false calm, but she still felt as if she was standing on the edge of a blade. One misstep away from crashing down. It seemed like the slavers were getting more and more desperate and striking without fear. Though the Maidens numbered in the dozens, it was never enough to save everyone. Some were stationed within villages, choosing to remain in one place as protection. Some roamed and followed the leads of suspicious bands moving through villages. Others, like the ones accompanying Revna, were the axe bringing down swift justice.

They were headed to Nantahalla at dawn—the seat and heart of Myddheim. A few of the Maidens would stay behind to rest and prepare the liberated for the next steps, whether they had homes to return to or needed to be relocated. But that's not what caused Revna's mind to continue spinning.

Sacrifice Day loomed large and heavy. The Gods had not called forth an offering in nine years, but that didn't mean the day came without burden. One she would always bear.

A knock on the door disrupted her circling thoughts.

"Are you decent, Commander?" Ingrid's voice called from the other side.

"Rarely."

Ingrid pushed open the door, shaking her head at Revna. Kicking off her boots, she pulled a tall stool over to the edge of the tub. "Let me see your hand."

"It's fine."

"I wasn't asking, *Commander*." Ingrid grabbed Revna's hand, which had been resting on the side of the tub, wrapped in shitty linen that she'd ripped off the bottom of her dress. She scowled at Ingrid. The title of Commander wasn't something Revna had sought, but it provided her Maidens a certain protection. Everyone would want Revna's head over anyone else's.

"Fine, *Second*."

Clucking her tongue, Ingrid gave a half-hearted glare. "You know a festering wound can kill you. And I speak for everyone when I say it would be embarrassing for you to die that way."

Revna chuckled and splashed some water in her friend's direction. This wasn't the first time she'd heard this argument, her Maidens often listing all the embarrassing ways she could die by being reckless and proud. Satisfied with her work, Ingrid leaned back against the wall and lifted her feet into the tub, sighing. No one worked harder than Ingrid, who constantly walked the line between warrior and healer—and no one had more blood on their hands.

Except maybe Revna.

"Heading out at first light?" Ingrid asked, closing her eyes.

"Yes. Did the escorts already leave with the slavers?"

"They did. They'll probably be about half a day's ride ahead of us, with the wagon slowing them a bit. Should make it to Nantahalla the morning after tomorrow."

"After we leave the king, we'll make way to Krussa. I want whoever remains to meet us there for a respite."

At the mention of Krussa, Ingrid opened her eyes and met Revna's. Krussa held so much history for them both—good and bad. It's where Ingrid grew up. Where Revna found herself after enduring a life of pain and suffering.

"I know," Ingrid whispered after several moments of silence. By now, Revna should have known what came next, but she couldn't help but feel the sting of Ingrid's words anyway. "When are you going to stop blaming yourself? He made his choice."

"And in doing so, took mine away," she snapped. Revna closed her eyes to the pity that crossed Ingrid's face, waiting for the final blow.

A gentle hand squeezed her forearm. "It isn't your fault."

Like every time before, Revna let the reassuring words slide off her before they could take root.

Fenrick wasn't coming back.

The Gods had abandoned Myddheim.

And it was all her fault.

THREE

T HE MEETING WITH THE king went about as well as expected. He
was not pleased that Revna had let her temper get the better of
her. Again.

King Haarald had stared at the proffered head of the poacher and
sighed in a way that only a long-suffering royal could—lamenting that
another man had lost his life at the hands of her sharpened anger.

Revna disagreed, of course. The poacher had only experienced the
consequences of his actions. The king would have killed him anyway,
as he did with all those who disobeyed him. What did it matter if she
bloodied her hands? The end result was the same. If anything, she'd done
him a favor.

He'd dismissed her with orders to deliver a message to the Jarl of
Krussa with the wave of a hand.

Revna and the Maidens didn't spend the night in Nantahalla, instead
riding back out into the night and making camp on the road. Too many
people in the city. Too many glaring eyes. Too many under-the-breath
insults thrown her way. Especially this close to Sacrifice Day ...

Revna could handle the comments, the bitter glares. In a way, she understood. The sadness and fury that soured their words and face—wondering how she'd dodged her fate when perhaps members of their own
family hadn't. But the Maidens, on more than one occasion, had brawled
with the more daring and cruel insulters.

Of course, the insults always came to a halt when they needed something from the Myddheim Maidens. Amusing how that worked.

Muted sunlight danced from the underbelly of the tree canopy as she and a handful of Maidens progressed toward the village that made her stomach twist in furious knots. Revna reached down and gave her horse a pat on his neck, focusing on the gentle sway of his body under her legs and the smell of the clean forest air, willing herself to breathe deeply. Fighting and moving forward, she could do. But pausing, looking her past in the eye? That was more difficult.

"So, what did the king have to say about the state of the poacher?" Asta called from somewhere behind her.

Revna smiled and turned slightly in her saddle. "I simply explained to the king that I put the poacher's mind at ease."

"Didn't you cut his head off?" Ellika asked.

"Is there a difference?" The Maidens erupted into laughter—even Ellika produced a sound somewhere between disbelief and humor.

But the laughter died in their throats when they exited the tree line and looked upon the diseased and burned fields of a farm. A place they had often stopped by on their route from Nantahalla to Krussa. Land once verdant and full of crop now sat blackened and ruined.

"By the Gods," Ingrid whispered from beside Revna.

Revna pushed her heels into the side of her mount and took off across the field toward the farm's longhouse. A soft whisp of smoke curled from the chimney, but even that looked weak. Once close enough, she called out to the farmer and his family and dismounted her horse.

The farmer opened the door and sighed a little when he saw Revna and the rest of the Maidens close behind. "We tried everything. But nothing will grow—no seed will root. And my little girl ..." He cast his eyes down and took a deep breath. "She grows sicker by the day. The cough won't abate."

Revna turned to meet the eyes of Ingrid, that feeling of a knot pulling tighter in her chest.

"We even sacrificed all our livestock to Frey begging him to bless our fields. But ..."

He didn't need to finish his thought. Revna knew. The Gods no longer answered the call from Myddheim.

Revna approached the farmer and placed a hand on his shoulder. "Gather your family and what you can carry. You are coming with us to Krussa."

"We have nothing left to give—" he started.

"Jarl Gunnilda will welcome you and your family. You will find your place there, I promise. Hopefully, in time, you can return and reclaim your land."

With a defeated sigh and a nod, he turned toward his home to collect his family and what they had left. Revna called for a few of the Maidens to assist and to double-up on horses to accommodate the family. Throughout all of it, Revna felt the burn of Ingrid's eyes. At last, she turned to meet her stare.

"Revna—" Ingrid tried.

"Don't, Ingrid. Not now. Just let me sit in it."

Ingrid narrowed her eyes and looked like she was about to argue when the cough of the sickly child snagged her attention. Grabbing her healers kit from her horse, she left.

The farmer stood away from the gathered party, staring out at his blackened fields. It had likely been in his family for generations. Now it would die with him. Revna wanted to apologize, to beg for his forgiveness. If she could make it right, she would. If she could go back ... she'd do anything to make the suffering stop.

She made her way to stand next to the farmer and gave him what silent support she could. They stared out at the cursed soil, watching as even the birds avoided landing on it. Absentmindedly, she rubbed at the spot in the middle of her chest, as though the large knot could be displaced by muscle and sheer force.

"Fate is cruel," the man murmured, barely loud enough to hear. He tore a carved rendition of Thor's hammer from his neck and tossed it on the soil, leaving it to be eaten by weather and time.

Revna didn't say anything as he turned his back and went to join his family.

Fate is cruel, she thought. *But the Gods are vicious.*

⇥————⇤

They arrived in Krussa on the eve of Sacrifice Day.

The gate groaned open revealing Jarl Gunnilda standing with her arms crossed, waiting. As she had every year since the last sacrifice.

Since Fenrick.

Jarl Gunnilda was currently the only female jarl in all Myddheim, her place won and taken by blood, but more importantly, by the love of the people. She was a fierce warrior with the favor of the Gods. Or so it seemed to most. Her village never went hungry, and her people were never restless.

"It's about time," Jarl Gunnilda greeted. Her ash-colored hair was pulled back tightly, accentuating the ink markings covering her neck. She gave the group a smile, then her eyes landed on the farmer and his family. "What do we have here?"

"New residents of your fine village, Jarl," Revna said, giving the jarl a look that promised to explain later.

Jarl Gunnilda walked around Revna's horse and greeted the farmer and his family. "You are most welcome. For tonight, you will stay within the longhouse with me. Tomorrow, we will find you more permanent lodgings."

The family said their thanks and followed as one of the jarl's warriors showed them their new home. Revna watched them taking it all in—their eyes darting from the walls enclosing the small but mighty village, to the fjord that lay straight ahead, glistening in the setting sun.

Revna turned her gaze from the fjord and swallowed thickly, trying not to think of what those waters had once eaten. Later. She would allow herself to think on it later. Instead, she focused her mind on swinging her legs over her horse and untying her small pack. Ingrid had already dismounted and was giving the jarl a quick hug before following the farmer and his family, no doubt wanting to tend to their sick child.

"Leave that and come walk with me," Gunnilda said to Revna as the last strap came unraveled. Asta came around the backside and patted the horse on his rump before taking Revna's pack and gesturing her chin to go.

"Ellika—"

"I've got her," Asta assured. "Go ahead."

As she approached the jarl, Revna couldn't help but smile. Gunnilda, though old enough to be her mother, was so full of fierceness and energy that Revna knew the older woman could still easily lay her on her ass in the sparring ring.

Gunnilda swung an arm around Revna's neck and directed them toward the water's edge. "Welcome home."

Home.

The jarl said this every time she came to Krussa, and Revna still wasn't sure what the word meant. She'd never felt as if home was a place. Too much stillness. As far as she was concerned, her home would always be with the Maidens. No matter where they roamed, no matter how much distance and time separated them.

"The king sends his regards and a *request*," Revna said as they walked down the path that led to the docks. Residents were gathered in small groups, slowly making their way toward the longhouse, drinking mead and laughing. Reveling, as if it were just another celebration.

It left Revna feeling conflicted. She knew Gunnilda started this as a way to honor Fenrick. To acknowledge that because of his sacrifice, the boat hadn't returned and demanded more lives. But Revna never felt like celebrating the day someone she had trusted—someone she'd begun to care for—had given himself to the Gods to save her.

"And what is this *request*?" The jarl asked, understanding that request was a polite way to say demand.

Revna put one foot in front of the other as they walked down the dock, feeling Gunnilda's arm tighten just a bit. "A large sacrifice is to be made to the Gods."

She didn't need to explain further. They came to the end of the dock and Gunnilda finally removed her arm from around Revna, letting her stand on her own and stare out at the fjord.

She knew exactly what these waters felt like, their taste and texture. The way they had invaded her throat when she'd jumped in after the longboat that had taken Fenrick to his demise. How his name had echoed off the stone walls of the fjord as she'd screamed it over and over.

Until Ingrid and Gunnilda had pulled her out.

"How fortuitous that we kept the pig's blood from tonight's feast. A fitting sacrifice, I should think," Gunnilda said, responding to her previous statement. "And how long can I expect you and yours to stay this time?"

The question was innocent, but one that caused Revna's stomach to clench with worry. The longer they stayed, the more at-risk others were of getting taken. She couldn't be everywhere at once, clearly, but sitting still for too long felt a lot like failing.

"Don't worry," Revna teased. "We won't eat all of your winter stores. We should be gone by the new moon."

The jarl turned to face her, the stare scalding Revna's profile as she continued to watch the water.

"Don't," Revna warned.

Gunnilda held up a hand and a warning brow. "I'm going to say my piece and then be done with it."

Revna crossed her arms over her chest and turned to face the jarl and waited.

"I know what tomorrow means to you. It's been nine years, and you are still trying to prove something. You don't need to."

Nine years she'd carried this guilt. Nine years of fighting her way to worthiness. And it still felt just as raw as if it were yesterday—a wound that she had picked at so incessantly that it never healed.

"I've already received the same speech from Ingrid—"

"Then take heed and listen to those who love you, Revna." The jarl placed her hands firmly on Revna's shoulders. "You are the heart and shield of Myddheim. You have given so many their lives back. And it's enough. *You* are enough."

Revna saw the sincerity shining in the jarl's eyes. The kinship she felt with the other woman went beyond the laws of blood. It was a choice. After Fenrick, Gunnilda was the one who'd put a blade into Revna's hand, any and every kind of blade imaginable, and told her to fight. And she had. A number of the scars decorating Revna's body were placed there by the grueling training Gunnilda had put her through, and she wore them proudly.

She could never repay Gunnilda for the kindness and protection, and the position she'd helped her to gain. Revna was once lost in those waves, but with Gunnilda's help, she'd fought her way back up to a purpose, and to herself.

And she knew she couldn't—wouldn't—slow down. If she did, she was afraid she'd sink and never resurface.

An unseasonably cool breeze whipped over the water, causing Revna's skin to pebble. She turned her gaze to the center of the fjord, and, just for a moment, she was back in that day.

The boat rising from the fog-coated water, heralding her name. Waking up tied to a tree. Ingrid finding her. Running, hoping to make it in time. Diving into the violent waters after the boat, while Fenrick's face stared at her from the deck, and then disappeared into the water's hungry maw.

Word had spread throughout Myddheim about a girl who had thwarted the Gods and their demanded sacrifice. Then, as the seasons continued, and the boat never returned, people began to panic. And with each year, as the fighting increased, the crops withered, the weather worsened, Revna became the reason why.

Perhaps she was.

And that's why she would continue to fight. Not because of the disdain some people felt toward her, but because Fenrick's sacrifice had to mean something. She would be worthy of it. She would fight until her dying breath.

"Come." Gunnilda put her arm around Revna's shoulders again and turned her back toward the village. "Let's go join the feast, get drunk, and then shout at the Gods."

Revna snorted and let herself be pulled toward the smell of burning cedar fires and roasting meats—the latter making her stomach gurgle in impatience.

As they reached the longhouse, Gunnilda left her side and made her way to the center of the hall—taking her place as the beating heart of her people.

Asta was leaning against the door, staring into the hall. Revna joined her, taking up post on the other side of the frame, and peered into the hall where most of the village had gathered.

In the center stood a skald on a table, staff in hand, varying fabrics draped across their body. The keeper of stories captivating the young and old alike. Within moments, Revna was drawn in by the skald's story.

"... and though the Allfather's ravens—Huginn and Muninn—brought with them great and terrible tellings, he craved more, hungry for wisdom and knowledge. And so, he ventured to a sacred well that feeds and nourishes the great world's tree: Yggdrasil. The tree connects all things and *is* all things. Life and death. Order and chaos. Memory and knowledge. A conduit and vessel for all the light and dark of the nine realms. Odin sacrificed his eye to the tree for the power to see. He hung from the tree's branches for nine days and nine nights, absorbing all the tree could give him ..."

Revna secretly loved the skalds. The way they wove stories with just words, creating bridges between time, people, and places. They were an undervalued and underestimated part of the realm in her opinion. What could be a finer tribute than to share stories with the world?

Despite that, she couldn't concentrate on what the skald was saying. Her body felt restless. She pushed off the doorframe and turned to walk away, pausing when Asta's hand shot out and gripped her forearm, brows furrowed in question. Revna gave her smile and squeezed her hand, and her third relented, dropping her arm.

Revna wandered as darkness settled, blanketing her from the many who took to the streets in revelry of Sacrifice Day. As she approached the end of the dock for the second time that evening, she paused, watching the way the moon lit a path on the water.

Nine years.

She couldn't let it go. What Fenrick had done. What he had sacrificed for her. Being here only resurrected the memory in the worst way.

She sat at the end of the dock, feet dangling toward the dark water, eyes unmoving from where the chasm had swallowed him whole. Constantly moving was the only way she'd survived all these years, but on this day, this night, she allowed that slumbering darkness to wake and consume her. Come the rising sun, she'd push it back into that pocket of her being and let it rest again.

Two sets of footsteps sounded on the dock behind her, one pausing, the other continuing until it was right behind her. Ingrid sat down beside her, but said nothing, just gently rested her head on Revna's shoulder. Time passed, the moon continuing its lazy path, and breathing became a little easier.

She eventually looked over her shoulder to see who the other pair of steps had belonged to, unsurprised when she saw Ellika sitting close by, lost in her own thoughts. Ingrid lifted her head and followed Revna's gaze, smiling softly in their newest recruit's direction. Ellika had been their shadow since they'd left the village a few days before. But Revna didn't mind. She would keep the new Maiden in her shade until she was ready to face the light.

Revna cleared her throat so that her voice didn't startle. "How's your shoulder, Ellika?"

"Tender, but healing. Commander," she added as an afterthought. Revna nearly snorted at the formality.

She ran her eyes up and down Ellika, taking in her posture and the set of her jaw—now slightly more relaxed. "Would you like your first fighting lesson?"

"What about my shoulder?"

Revna shrugged. "You have another arm and two legs. And Ingrid is here to patch us up if need be." She grunted as Ingrid's elbow found her side with a huff. "More importantly, you have a mind."

Ellika pushed herself off the dock, stood, and nodded. "I'm ready."

Revna gestured for her to make her way back to the beach. Her second followed in Ellika's wake. She turned for one last look at the water. A layer of clouds obscured the moon, distorting its reflection. Something rippled across the surface, and Revna squinted, heartbeat stuttering, then sighed as she saw a faint glint of scales. *Just a fish.*

Ingrid and Ellika were waiting for her on the beach, talking quietly, giving Revna her privacy. She reeled in the thoughts and memories darkening her mind, sealing them back into that entombed cavern of her heart.

Keep moving, the voice in her head whispered.

When another splash of water sounded from behind her, she didn't dare look. She just moved forward.

FOUR

*W*AKE. *WAKE. WAKE.*

A low snaking whisper wrested Revna from a fitful sleep. She pushed herself up to a sitting position on the stretch of beach she'd fallen asleep on.

In the darkest part of the night, she'd found herself drawn back to the water. She'd sat with the low lapping waves until exhaustion had pulled her under.

Sand clung to her leathers and an early morning frost pebbled her skin, but that wasn't what woke her.

Revna pushed herself to a standing position as a low, keening wail echoed off the imposing stone of the fjord walls—as if a hundred voices were lamenting an unfathomable loss. Her stomach climbed her throat with a familiar sense of dread as a roiling and creeping fog coated the bay.

No.

People started gathering behind her on the beach, but Revna held out a hand to stop them from coming too close as the tide grew higher. Out of the corner of her eye, Revna saw Jarl Gunnilda, axe in hand, make her way to the end of the dock with a handful of warriors. But Revna knew there was no blade or shield that could stop what hunted the village.

The chorus of wails grew increasingly frantic. The lapping water on the shore came faster and higher until Revna's boots were completely submerged. Still, she didn't take her eyes off the fog. It was impossibly dense, as if she could grab it with bare hands and move it aside. But instead of moving toward the shore, it grew higher, until it was nearly level with the sharp incline of the fjord walls.

Revna.

The whisper of her name had her head whipping around, searching for the source. It sounded from all around her, echoing through every corner of her mind. Reverberating against her bones, gripping her muscles.

Come see, come see.

The voice hissed and curled—completely unidentifiable, completely other. It was spine-shivering temptation and knee-buckling demand.

She wanted to see.

She wanted to defy.

Both options left her rooted to the spot.

Water that had once reached her ankles retreated at a rapid pace, and a gasp sounded somewhere from behind Revna just as she saw it.

A great chasm opened in the middle of the bay, water and fog flowing down, feeding the great gaping ingress. The sound of the rushing water and wails of the unknown were enough to make people cover their ears. The sudden cessation of sound that came next was just as jarring. It left behind a silence that had the hairs on the back of her neck standing in alarm.

Revna.

Come see, Revna. Come see what lies beyond the realm.

He waits and waits.

Great gurgling started from the gorge. As the water started to rise once again, Revna felt the people at her back retreat, but against every warning from her body and mind, she waded farther into the water. It was to mid-thigh when something started rising from the roiling hole.

A mast came into view, and the unmistakable carved head of a dragon and curved keel of a longship. The sail was completely sodden and useless, shredded by great claws or teeth. No shields, oars, or seats could be seen, and yet the decimated sail pulled taut, and the longship advanced toward the shore.

Revna could feel dozens of eyes burning into her back, but she couldn't look anywhere but at the boat.

It had returned.

The years had done nothing to alter its appearance. The wooden planks still appeared blackened by fire, cracked by ice, and shrouded with an impenetrable otherworldliness, as if the ship had been forged by parts of all nine realms.

"It is time, mortals of Myddheim," the voice said. But this time it was not in her head. This time everyone flinched as it spoke. *"A sacrifice is demanded, from nine years past left empty-handed."*

Revna swallowed as the ship made its slow progress, feeling frozen in place in the whirling water.

"Send her, the woman of raven hair.
Send her, the woman who frees the fair.
Send her and let this slight repair."

It had come for her nine years ago and was thwarted by the actions of Fenrick. And for nine long, dark years, surely a blink for the Gods, Myddheim had been punished …

But now she could do something about it.

Icy panic melted into fastened resolve. Today, the Gods only demanded her. Tomorrow it could be anyone—or everyone—should she refuse. Revna thought of her Maidens, unwilling to let harm befall them.

The ship was nearly within her reach, its dragon carved hull casting a shadow over her body. With a deep breath, Revna pulled out a dagger from her hip and reopened the healing wound on her palm. Her blood dripped into the cold water as she closed the distance between her and the looming ship.

"No!" She heard from somewhere behind her. Revna turned for a moment, only to wish she hadn't. Ingrid, Asta, Ellika, and the rest of her Maidens were wading their way through the water toward her—fear making their eyes wide, anger furrowing their brows. Somewhere off to the side she knew the splash and even pulls of arms through water were from Jarl Gunnilda jumping from her spot on the dock, making her way toward Revna.

She drank them in, memorizing their features, the faces of her family, and then, before they could reach her, she turned back to the boat. Revna took her bloodied palm and slapped it against the center of the curved hull.

"I give myself willingly," she whispered, wondering if Gods even cared for her acceptance.

The anguished sound of Ingrid screaming had her turning back in panic. Her oldest friend, the one who'd been with her since that fateful day nine years before, was reaching toward her, but unable to move. All the Maidens and Jarl Gunnilda were frozen within the waves, as if it had instantly hardened into ice, though the water appeared as it had before.

"Revna, don't! *Please*!" Ingrid's plea shot through her body. Revna knew the agony Ingrid and the Maidens were about to experience, and she hated that she had to hurt them in order to protect them. But she would do it.

She pushed back through the hold of the water, thighs burning against the resistance. With arms reached out, Ingrid pulled her tight, as if she could rip this fate from her.

Revna stroked her friend's back with one hand, the other securing the dagger back in her hip. With both arms free, she wrapped Ingrid in a hug that stole the breath from even her own lungs. Reluctantly, she pulled herself back and gripped Ingrid's face with her hands, coating one side with unstaunched blood. Sharp grief swept through Revna as she realized Ingrid would no longer be there to chide her for getting herself hurt.

"Listen to me, Ingrid. You are commander now ..."

"No," Ingrid seethed, anger quickly replacing sorrow on her face.

"Yes." Revna gripped Ingrid's face tightly between her hands. "You must. You must continue what we've built."

"I can't—I don't want to do this without you."

"You won't be alone," she assured her friend, looking over Ingrid's shoulder toward Asta, Hildi, Ellika, and the others. With one hand still on Ingrid's face, she reached the other toward Asta, giving her fingers a squeeze as soon as they gripped hers. "Besides, this is the least embarrassing way to die."

Ingrid's eyes flared in shock before she started sobbing anew.

"Asta—"

"I know, Commander." Her stony expression faltered for just a moment as a single tear trailed down Asta's cheek, but she didn't move to wipe it away.

Revna nodded at the new Second and scanned her eyes over the other Maidens gathered in the water.

Hildi, Brynn, Tovi, Runa, Gyda, Sassa, Liv—they all stood with expressions ranging from shock to anger, from sorrow to disbelief. Haesten and Torsten stood close by, feet barely in the water, wide-eyed and jaws clenched.

And Ellika ...

Revna dropped Asta's hand, gently lifted Ingrid's head from her shoulder, and made her way over to where Ellika stood.

"*Fight*, Ellika," Revna said, placing gentle hands on her shoulders. "Fight anything that dares to try to break you. Fight for yourself—fight your way forward because the Maidens will watch your back. Do you understand me?"

"I understand, Commander." Ellika placed a hand on top of Revna's. "We do not break."

Revna used those words as mortar on her crumbling heart as she made her way around to the other Maidens. She pulled them into breath-stealing hugs, saying the goodbyes she had never wanted to make. When she finally made her way back to Ingrid, her throat burned with restrained tears.

"Take care of one another. It's been ..." Revna trailed off, swallowing back the growing lump in her throat. "It's been the great honor of my life to serve with and know you all."

She wasn't worried about her legacy, or whether the work would continue. Revna knew that it would—that these Maidens, these warriors, were her legacy. Nothing could have made her prouder or more ready to face what awaited her.

Ingrid curbed her emotions and met Revna's eyes, speaking loudly for all to hear: "By the salt and the earth, by my blood and bones ..."

The other Maidens joined in, saying the oath together, voices rising as if trying to ensure the Gods heard their devotion and heartache. Revna could no longer hold back her sorrow, so she held her chin high, letting the storm of tears roll down her cheeks. She could count the number of times she had cried in front of the Maidens on one hand, but this—this moment, this grief, broke that final wall. She let them see what they meant to her.

Ingrid reached for a dagger at Revna's waist and ran the blade edge over the long-healed scar on her palm, gripping her hand with Revna's still bleeding one, like they had so many years before. Their eyes meet, Revna's gray meeting Ingrid's green, and let all the unspoken words, all the memories, pass between them.

Revna saw it all in Ingrid's eyes, saw them as young women, when Ingrid had saved Revna's life more than once. First, by fishing her out of that very bay as she'd tried to swim her way down to where that very same boat had disappeared with Fenrick. Then again and again, by not giving up on her, by not letting Revna's wariness deter her from friendship, her hardness deter her from love.

Ingrid had given Revna the kind of love that exceeds that of blood—they were family down to the very marrow of their bones.

The earth trembled beneath their feet, and people back on shore let out cries of fear.

It was time to go.

Ingrid secured the blade back at Revna's side and then leaned her forehead against hers for one last moment.

Without another word, Revna turned and waded toward the boat. Each step heavier than the last.

Jarl Gunnilda was still frozen between the dock and the gathered Maidens. Revna pushed through the water until she pulled the jarl into a hug. Neither of them said a word, and for that, Revna was thankful. She didn't think she could speak another goodbye, and there was too much to say, anyway.

The water grew colder as she approached the boat. Once under its shadow, she gripped the side and heaved herself up onto the deck. There were no seats, no ropes, nothing to grab onto, so Revna made her way to the prow to look upon her life one last time.

The boat lurched and made its way through the growing fog, but instead of returning to the chasm, it headed toward the steep cliffside.

Maybe this was an embarrassing way to die.

Somewhere from the shore, Revna heard the steady and unmistakable rhythm of blade on shield. She turned to look as the sound grew, finding her Maidens saluting her departure with whatever weapons they held.

The whole village joined in as she watched, fists on chests, feet stomping on the dock—sending her off in honor. She watched a moment longer, then turned to face her fate.

They were going to hit the rocks. She braced herself for the impact, chin still held high.

But as the ship approached the cliffside at an alarming speed, glowing runes appeared on the stone. Revna backed away from the dragonhead prow until her back hit the mast at the center of the deck, watching as the front of the ship disappeared, the stone eating it bit by bit. She felt like throwing up, she felt like holding her breath, but before she could decide on either, she, too, was eaten by the stone.

The last thing she heard was the sound of many blades on shields matching the frantic beating of her heart.

FIVE

T HERE WAS ONLY DARK.

So dark that Revna could not see her own fingers as she waved them in front of her face. Either she had gone blind, or she was dead. Awaiting the Gods' will.

A soft tremor traveled up her legs. Stepping, she felt the boat, still solid under her feet, and sensed that it was pulling through the fast-moving tide. The only sound was that of rushing, hungry waters …

Only one thing could make that sound—*a waterfall.*

Feeling for the axe belt strapped to her back, Revna made quick work of removing it and backed up until she was flush against the mast once again, using the belt to anchor her body to the sturdy wood.

Axe gripped in her hands, she held her breath, ears pricked for the sound of the impending drop.

Between one breath and the next, the air from her lungs left in a great gust—her stomach roiling up after it. Water beat down from all around, drenching her, causing her to choke on the cold saltiness.

Revna hated this feeling—this tangled mixture of fear and frustration when there was nothing to fight. Nothing to control. Nothing she could do but hold on and hope that it passed without harm.

She could hardly breathe past the wall of water and near suffocation when the boat gave one more violent tip and settled on even waters. The frantic beat of her heart felt as though it would crack her chest from the inside.

But she was alive.

Dots sparked in her vision as the darkness started to soften. A faint blue-green glow came awake, alighting the cave, and as her eyes adjusted, Revna noticed the great gnarled tree roots running through the cavernous space, some wider than the longboat. They reached up through the ceiling and down through the waters, creating a labyrinth of moss-covered wood.

Revna unhooked herself from the mast. She walked over to the side of the ship where it passed precariously close to a root and the ship paused, as if sensing her curiosity. With a tentative hand, she reached out and placed her palm flat against the root. Vibrant blues and greens whipped out from where her hand rested, tracing every root within the space, as if the dark cave was filled with hundreds of dancing lights. One side of her mouth lifted in a small smile, marveling at the otherworldly beauty.

Otherworldly.

She knew she had to reconcile with the fact that she was no longer in Myddheim, but the thought was so raw that touching it stung—thinking about what she had left behind.

Slowly, she pulled her hand away, and it felt as though the root leaned into her palm for one last caress. Her eyes flared as the blood from her cut palm absorbed into the wood— the bark drinking her very life force. The boat resumed its slow glide through the water.

When it stopped again it was before another wall, this one of solid rock. Runes appeared on the stone, glowing and pulsing in time with the moss on the roots, a strange and frenzied heartbeat. The rock melted and blurred until an opening appeared and soft sunlight filtered in. Through the opening, Revna could make out more water, a rocky shoreline, and beyond that, a lush forest. She shivered as a gentle breeze wound through the cave and hit her cold, soaked body.

The groaning creak of waterlogged boards sounded from behind her, and Revna whipped toward the sound. The stern of the boat lifted, the dragonhead prow plunging headfirst into the water, sending Revna gripping for any kind of purchase. Even the sharpened heel of her axe wouldn't pierce the deck as she slid and struggled. The ship gave a violent lurch, and Revna was launched into the water. As she broke the surface the boat righted itself, creating a small wave.

"You could have given me a little warning," she mumbled to no one.

The cavernous space went still. A slow, creeping darkness dimmed the moss, as if it was waiting. Listening. Hiding. The only light source came from the rune-adorned opening in the stone, and the world beyond it.

The boat gave a lurch toward her, as if it was telling her to move, but she didn't. She had not the faintest idea what waited for her through the runed doorway, but she had a gut-deep feeling that once she passed through, she could never go back. So she stayed where she was, treading water while she secured her axe in its resting place.

The boat lurched again, aggressively so, and she relented rather than be drowned by a boat, turning to kick half-heartedly toward the opening. She could see the shore in the distance, but it was a long swim. Especially weighed down by leather and blade.

She suddenly felt exhausted. The sodden weight of her clothes and weapons weren't the only thing causing her body to feel heavy. She was alone. A realization that somehow made her both relieved and devastated.

Apparently tired of her trepidation, the boat picked up speed toward her wake, herding her to the opening. Revna started to backstroke, barely out-swimming the possessed ship.

"Oh, piss off you fucking piece of rotting wood."

A deep, reverberating growl sounded from somewhere in the darkness.

Revna froze.

So did the ship.

Another warning growl sounded, echoing off every nook in the stone walls. Revna needed no further motivation—she turned for the opening and swam for her life.

The shore was far, but she kept her breathing even, her arms pulling. A fist squeezed her heart as she heard a voice in her head urging her to kick her damn feet, remembering Ingrid teaching her to swim in the early dawn light for weeks after Fenrick was taken.

She'd said she didn't want Revna to sink again.

Revna grunted in frustration and willed the fist to release its hold in her chest. She could mourn later. When a monster wasn't—

Something nudged her feet. Her blood ran cold.

Unknown waters meant unknown beasts. She steeled herself. No matter the kind, no beast would like a blade to the eye. To continue swimming would only encourage it to give chase, like she was prey.

She was nothing and no one's fucking prey.

Revna paused and grabbed a dagger from her hip, looking around the choppy water for signs of a fin or tail. Reluctantly, she dipped her head underwater and opened her eyes, the burning of salt blurring her vision.

After a moment the haze released ... and Revna's body froze. She floated utterly still, trapped under the stare of a giant—beyond giant—serpentine creature. Its eyes, yellow and slit vertically like a snake, stared unwaveringly. When her chest started to burn with unreleased breath, she broke her stare, regaining enough control over her shaking body to give a small kick and push back to the surface, heart beating like the blades on a shield.

She gulped in air, but the relief was gone in an instant, as the serpent's head broke the surface just a body length away. Screaming wouldn't do her any good—nor would the dagger in her hand.

The great monster regarded her for a moment, looming so tall that her neck was fully extended in trying to meet its gaze above a dripping maw. Fangs as long as her arm protruded from a thick, wedge-shaped head. Storm cloud gray scales covered its spiked, serpentine body. Revna swallowed thickly, meeting the creatures aware gaze. They stayed like that for a heartbeat, two, and then the monster slithered, snake-quick, and slammed its tail down, creating a massive wave that sent Revna surging down into the water.

Searing panic burst in Revna's chest, and she flailed in the rushing water. She couldn't find the surface, couldn't tell which direction she faced, where the sky was, or, most importantly, where the monster waited. Another rolling wave pushed her until she hit something solid.

She grasped for purchase. Hard scales slid under her fingertips. With a battle scream unheard beneath the roiling water, she plunged her dagger down. A noise that could only be described as irritation sounded from the beast as its body thrashed, pushing her through the water until she broke the surface, and sent her flying through the air.

Revna landed on her back on a hard, unmoving surface, knocking all the breath from her body. She rolled over, violently purging seawater, and stared down at the sand covering her wet hands.

She'd made it to shore.

Revna turned her head toward the water and watched as the great serpent's eyes met hers for a single breath before disappearing below the surface.

By the fucking Gods ...

No sooner did she roll onto her back to catch her breath than the point of a sword was pressed at her throat.

"And who might you be, little one?" a deep voice asked, face obscured by the sun.

"Am I dead?" Revna replied.

"That's a terrible name, *Am-I-Dead*. What are you doing here?"

Revna might have laughed at the absurdity of the response, but she couldn't muster the energy. "I don't know where *here* is. Perhaps you can inform me."

The man's head cocked to the left above her as if he considered her words. "I think I'll take you to the leader of these lands instead, and he can tell you. Or not. Depends on what kind of mood he's in."

He wanted to move her to another location, but she knew better. "I think the fuck not."

He barked out a laugh, the tip of his sword moving the barest inch on her neck. She tried not to flinch. "Oh, I beg of you, please accompany me and direct your attitude toward Fenrir. It'll do the old boy some good."

Fenrir. The name gave her pause. It was not uncommon for someone to be named after one of the many Gods and Goddesses as a kind of tribute. But never in her life has she met someone named after the most hated and feared God.

The God of Destruction—Fenrir, the wolf. No one would willingly keep the name who did not also relate with the qualities of its forbearer—which meant this Fenrir was likely dangerous and brutal.

And Revna had made it her life's work to eliminate dangerous men.

"Look," he continued. "It would do you well to come with me willingly. I could knock you unconscious, but then I'd have to carry you, and my back is feeling delicate today."

He removed the sword from her throat and circled her, finally coming out of the glaring sun's path.

Revna wasn't sure what she'd expected, but it wasn't the man standing above her.

He was tall, with deeply tanned skin and hair braided and gathered at the back of his head. His face held no derision, and his eyes no malice that she could read. Strangest of all, he was giving her what appeared to be a genuine smile. One that reached his warm brown eyes. He reminded her so much of Haesten that it sent icy spikes into her heart.

She would never see him, or any of the Maidens, again.

"Come along, up you get," he said, sheathing his sword, reaching an arm toward her. Disorientation was the only explanation she had for reaching a hand up to the offered arm, but she did just that, disarmed by the kindness in those brown eyes. She unconsciously outstretched her hand to grip his, but only found part of a forearm leading up to a heavily muscled bicep. With a slight adjustment, she reached instead for the crook of his arm and was hauled easily to her feet.

"Follow me, fiery one."

"Wait—" She turned around in panic, searching for her other dagger, then sighed in relief as the sun reflected off its metal surface near the water. The man didn't protest as she sheathed it back at her hip. Not wanting to disarm her was a good sign, but there were many other ways for people to do harm. Worse ways.

"What was that thing?" Revna gestured her chin toward the fjord.

"Oh, don't mind him." He waved his hand in the direction of the water. "He's ornery on his best days."

With that non-answer, he turned and headed to a trail leading up toward the forest. Hesitantly, and with no other option but to stay stranded on the beach by a sea monster, she followed him.

As her heart rate calmed to normal, her sense of awareness returned, and suddenly her eyes and ears seemed to open to all that surrounded her. Everything was bigger, more vibrant. Trees reached high as though they ached to kiss the sun. Leaves of varying shades of green and threaded with golden veins gave off a shimmer as they rustled in the breeze. The forest floor was lush with thick layers of moss and dirt, cushioning each step. And the smell—the smell tugged at something buried deep in her memory that she couldn't quite place. A mixture of pine, smoke, and the forest after a crisp snow.

She turned to look at the water one last time before it disappeared in the thick vegetation. The fjord met the side of the sheer cliff where she'd passed through, the only similarity to the waters of the land she'd left behind. There was no sign of the monster beneath.

Revna waited for panic to trap her breath, as it was clear she was no longer in Krussa, let alone Myddheim. But after years of remaining calm and clearheaded in tense situations, she'd learned to deal with one thing at a time. She felt her body grip onto that familiar tension, preparing to handle whatever came next. When she turned back to the path, the barrel-chested man was still smiling at her.

What the fuck is his problem?

"Am I a prisoner?" Revna asked flatly.

He turned to continue up the path, calling back, "Too soon to tell!"

With a huff, she trudged after him, clothes sodden and starting to chafe in all the wrong places. She scanned her body for injuries as she walked, but found none other than a slight ache in her lungs and throat from her ordeal in the water. Revna rolled her shoulders and contemplated ways to overpower the man whistling in front of her and get the information she needed out of him.

See if he still smiles freely then.

Before she could decide, the path widened and disappeared over a steep edge. Revna approached the edge warily and saw that it gently snaked down, leading to a small cave opening in the side of the cliffside they had just climbed.

"Hurry along now. I don't want to be out here when the sun sets and the draugr wake."

Revna tilted her head. "Draugr?"

"The undead that spring up from the ground like morbid little flowers, hunting at night and hoping to feast on blood and marrow. Nasty things."

"You can't be serious."

He turned and met her eyes. "Deadly."

They held each other's gaze, Revna's eyes narrowed, and his mouth finally quivered, unable to hold back laughter at his own cheap joke.

"In all seriousness, they are bitey fuckers, so we should move along." With that, he started down the winding path and disappeared through the stone arch.

Questioning her sanity, but reminding herself that she was just biding her time, she followed. The small tunnel was aglow with the blue-green moss she'd seen within the cave, and she was momentarily struck again by the sight. Her strength wavered. She wanted to stay in that beauty, suspend the moment, and take stock. To hide from the hollowness of losing everything she ever cared for rather than face whatever would come next.

We do not break.

She went on, following the huge man until the tunnel came to an end, and she couldn't help the slight intake of breath as a new wonder unfolded before her.

Built within the mountainside, carved from its very stone, was a large keep. The multi-layered levels of stone fortification was surely carved out by man, but that seemed an impossible task. The detail ...

Tower-like shapes and windowed openings. Wood and stone and nature molded together in both captivating beauty and alluring darkness.

Creeping vines lined paths with glowing moss, waterfalls cascaded and fed a heavily flowing river that wound its way through the forest surrounding the keep. A large bridge provided safe passage across the river, leading to an intricately carved door just below a stone parapet.

Revna was still memorizing every detail—including escape routes—when a body-rumbling crack of thunder and a whip of lighting snapped her to attention. She looked at the sky, but saw nothing but the fading pinks of the day's sun. The man stopped suddenly and whispered a curse, then turned to her.

"I'm going to need to tie you up."

Revna reached for one of her daggers. "I'd like to see you try."

"I swear on my sword it will just be for show—just until an unwanted visitor leaves. Unless you mean us harm, you are free here."

"Who do you swear to?" He gave her a quizzical look. "Your God," she clarified.

What God someone dedicated themself to said more about them than their words.

"I swear on myself." He bowed his head to her, as if that answer should have some significance. Whoever this man was, he surely thought mightily of himself.

She stared at him, reading the honesty clear in his eyes, and then sheathed her dagger and held out her wrists to the rope awaiting in his hands. She could practically hear Ingrid and Asta shouting in her head at the idiocy. But no one had ever called Revna cautious, and she had, more than once, let herself get taken by slavers just to take them down from the inside. This wasn't much different.

She had no idea where she was and who she was dealing with. But, though his constant smile was bewildering, her would-be-captor had yet to harm her. She had decided to let things play out.

It's not like she hadn't practiced freeing herself from ropes.

The big boulder of a man took the rope and placed the small noose around both wrists. He leaned forward and grabbed part of the rope in his teeth and pulled it tight, but not enough to keep her from escaping, even without her knives, should she choose to.

"Play along and we shouldn't have a problem. Just act as though I brought you here with brute force and not by my charm."

Revna's gave him an irritated look.

"Perfect!" he said. Placing a hand on her shoulder, he turned her around and gave her a gentle nudge toward the awaiting door.

As they crossed the threshold, he whispered a reminder to play along, and then his face morphed. No more was the man with an easy smile and awful jokes. The man before her now radiated warning—a threat that any who dared to challenge him in battle would surely lose. His expression hardened to stone, and he gave the rope a sharp yank. She wondered fleetingly if this was his true self, and she'd walked right into his trap. But then she glanced down at the loosely tied hands within reach of her daggers. Either he was earnest in what he'd told her, or he was the most arrogant person she'd ever met.

Revna could barely note the vine covered stone walls of the entry hall before she was pulled toward a set of double doors. Her pretend captor kicked the thick wood, the metal hinges crying out loudly under his assault.

Inside the room were two men. One had his back to her—dark haired, broad shouldered, tall, and looking out a window. The other, a red-headed, red-bearded man, turned to look at the intrusion, face masked in irritation.

"Leave us. We are busy," he said, dismissing them.

"I don't take orders from you," her captor responded, voice laced in challenge.

"Who's this?" the man by the window asked without turning, voice deep and spine-shivering.

Familiar.

"Found her down by the water. Figured I would bring her here for questioning."

Revna didn't say a word. She just stared at the back of the man by the window, ice running down her spine as something in her body cried out in warning.

"By all means, question her now. I would be happy to help," the red-bearded man taunted.

Revna bared her teeth and made a noise somewhere between a hiss and a snarl. Her captor yanked on the rope, as if she was a wild thing to bring to heel.

"Take her to the dungeon. If we don't forget about her, we'll deal with it later." The man at the window sighed as if he were bored, and finally turned toward her.

Everything inside of Revna stopped.

Her heart, her breath, her blood.

The man's eyes found hers momentarily—a deep gold she still saw in her dreams and nightmares. There was no recognition in that gaze. Just cold aloofness.

It took everything in Revna not to react. Not to scream or lunge at him as her captor grabbed her shoulders and shoved her back to the door.

Her long-lost friend, Fenrick, just sent her to the dungeons.

Six

Fenrir

HE'D SMELLED HER THE moment Tyr kicked the door open.

Fenrir had endured a lot in his long life. From spending the better part of his childhood hidden in caves, to being taken from his mother and siblings and imprisoned. Beaten, tricked, banished. Being called a monster before fully understanding what the word meant.

But nothing could have prepared him to see her here.

Revna.

Revna was here. In Vanaheim.

He had resisted as long as he could, but when he'd finally turned and confirmed what his body already knew, it had taken every bit of control he possessed not to react. Not to show any kind of recognition. Not while Thor was there. If he reported back to Odin that a mortal woman from Myddheim was brought to Vanaheim ...

Let me out, the wolf under his skin begged.

Thor spouted nonsense, his face nearly as crimson as the hair on his head and beard. But Fenrir couldn't hear a word he was saying. Something about doing his duty and remembering the deal that Fenrir had struck with Odin.

His jaw twitched with how hard he was clenching his teeth—barely holding back the urge to let his canines elongate.

Perhaps she hadn't recognized him. His hair, once cut above his ears, now touched the tops of his shoulders. Being back in the land of Gods had allowed his body to regain the strength lost in his time banished and bound to the realm of Myddheim. He had a bit of scruff on his face and new ink decorated his body—not that she could see that. But the look on her face when they had made eye contact was indecipherable. Somewhere between sharp irritation and complete boredom.

And, by the runes, that one look had sent his body thrumming. Called his wolf so close to the surface, he'd felt his skin prickle.

Thor snapped his fingers twice in front of Fenrir's face and he suppressed a warning growl that built high in his chest.

"Did you hear a word I said, dog?"

Fenrir took a deep breath and repressed the lengthening of his fangs. On another day he wouldn't mind pushing Thor and going a few rounds, but Revna was here and he needed Thor far away from her.

The other Gods could never learn who she was.

"Yes. I am to sniff out any burgeoning disobedience on Jotunheim."

"You are to do your duty as guard dog and attack *who* we say, *when* we say."

"I am doing my duty," Fenrir replied through clenched teeth. "I have not forgotten the deal."

"Good. Should you need another reminder, it may come in the form of my hammer meeting your jaw."

Fenrir remained silent.

"I will see myself out. I can't stand the smell of this rotten, overgrown place." Thor scrunched his face in disgust.

The smell he was referring to—trees, rich soil, and a slight brininess from the nearby sea—was one Fenrir loved.

Without a backwards glance, the God of Thunder walked out of the room.

The moment Fenrir could no longer hear his heavy gait, he placed his hands on the table and let his head fall. Within the span of several moments, everything had changed. Yet everything remained the same.

Revna was here, and he had no idea what to do with that.

When the boat appeared in Myddheim all those years ago demanding her as a sacrifice to Asgard, he'd taken one look at her and made a choice. Despite his attempts to scare her away, she had freed him from his chains and helped him regain his strength. They had only traveled together for two months, but they had built a kind of trust that was edging into friendship. Companionship. And, for him at least, the start of something much more dangerous.

Then the boat appeared, and he had watched as something in her cracked. The anger she'd used as a shield had slipped, and he'd seen pained defeat.

He had owed her a life-debt.

Her being here …

"Rough meeting?" Tyr's jovial voice sounded from the doorway.

Fenrir lifted his head. "Where is she?"

"The dungeons." Fenrir cocked an eyebrow at Tyr knowingly. "I put her in a room nearby."

"Did you at least lock the room?" At his question, Tyr tossed him a key. "I'm sure she was pleased about that."

His old friend studied him with that too-discerning gaze. Tyr was a lot of things, but his most overlooked strength was reading and deciphering a person's thoughts and feelings. On missions, his skill was invaluable, but Fenrir didn't care for the gaze being directed at him.

"You know her." Tyr cocked his head. "How? She's mor—*wait*."

Fenrir crossed back to the arched open window and gazed out. Tyr's purposeful steps followed.

"She cannot be *the* girl. The one from Myddheim?"

"Woman." Fenrir corrected.

Tyr nodded his head. "Yes, woman. But, *by the runes*, Fen."

Silence fell between them, questions trapped behind clenched teeth.

When Fenrir had returned from the mortal realm and made his deal with Odin, Tyr had volunteered to reside in Vanaheim with him and assist. Even after Fenrir, in a fit of rage, bit the other God's hand off, Tyr had still wanted to be his friend. Insisted on it.

Fenrir had never had a friend, aside from his siblings, and hadn't known what to do with the offered companionship. But Tyr had taken the lead and, after much trial and error, they were just that. Friends. They had fought side by side and earned each other's trust. They'd confided in one another.

Tyr knew exactly who Revna was. He probably knew too much.

"How is she here?" Fenrir asked, his voice loud in the quiet that had settled between them.

"I found her on the banks of the fjord. Your brother—"

Fenrir spun and faced Tyr. "What about my brother?"

"I saw him toss her on the shore. In his *other* form."

He didn't say it, but Fenrir knew he meant his *monster* form.

He used to hate being called a monster. He couldn't help that he was born with a big terrifying wolf as half of himself. He hadn't asked to be capable of destroying worlds, or for a power that called to the earth. But now he didn't mind being a monster. Not if it protected the people he cared for.

"I can't begin to guess what Jormun was doing in that fjord, but I will check in with him soon," Fenrir assured Tyr, pinching the bridge of his nose. He would need to make time before returning to Jotunheim to seek out Jor. Maybe he would drag Hel, their sister, with him.

"If you want, I can bring her some food and a dry set of clothes." Tyr offered.

"No," Fenrir snapped a little too quickly. "Thank you, but I need to talk to her."

"Alright, I'll be in the kitchens if you need me," Tyr said, not pushing the subject, just patting his stomach and leaving the room.

With the key gripped firmly in his hand, Fenrir made his way to the room where Revna waited. Tyr didn't need to tell him where; he could smell her—the sweet earthiness and mountain air that brought him back to nine years before. The cool stone halls did nothing to temper the way his blood started to heat. She shouldn't be here. He was confused. He was also wary, and he was ...

Angry.

Yes, that's it. Angry.

Passing behind the waterfall, he took a deep breath, trying to quell the arising urge to go in and demand answers. He knew that wouldn't accomplish anything. She may not even be here willingly. She may not yet know who he was. But she was about to find out and Fenrir felt hesitant.

Fuck.

A couple of residents passed him, and he dipped his chin in a cursory nod. Sensing his mood, they returned his wordless greeting and continued on their way.

Her scent stopped at a small wooden door, but he found his hand unable to put the key in the lock. The uncertainty of what he would find when he entered the room gave him pause. Maybe he should have sent Tyr.

Rolling out his shoulders and neck, trying and failing to rid the tension, he turned the key.

The door squeaked open but she was nowhere to be found. He couldn't see her, but he could smell her. Random chairs, tables and dividers occupied the space, and Fenrir suddenly worried she was hurt or unconscious somewhere.

He took a few steps into the room, ready to search for her, when the door slammed shut and his knees were kicked out from behind him. The sharp point of a knife pricked his throat, but only for a moment. He grabbed the wrist, twisted, and heard a sharp intake of breath. Using this distraction, he pivoted, just as a knee hit him square in the nose with a sickening crack.

Alright, that's quite the fuck enough.

Revna lunged, rolling in attempt to sweep his legs out—which he anticipated because he'd fucking taught her that move.

"It is you," she snarled, lunging again.

Fenrir absorbed her movement, using the momentum to thread his arm across the front of her body, spinning her so that her back was to his front. They hit a wall and Revna planted a foot between his braced feet, pushing them off, using the leverage to take his body to the ground. But he took her with him, until they were rolling on the stone floor, scrabbling for dominance.

To his utter surprise, she wound up on top, straddling him, knife back at his throat, the other braced on the side of his head. Their faces were inches apart, and her hair hung around them like a dark curtain.

He gave her a wolfish grin. "Hello Revna."

"Hello liar."

Seven

Revna

Hearing her name come out of his mouth had her pushing the blade a little harder to his throat.

He fucking knew her. Remembered her.

Blood still flowed from his nose, creating trails of crimson to his ears, his hair. She hoped it was broken.

"Hello *liar*." She emphasized the word and watched when it hit. His nostrils flared and his jaw clenched, but he didn't refute her. They regarded one another for a few more moments, his amber eyes tracing over her face, until Revna realized she was still straddling him. A low heat crept up her neck as she pushed away from him, standing, and backed up a few paces. She decided to keep the dagger out, though, in case he wanted another bout.

He pushed up, but remained sitting, draping his arms across his bent knees. "What are you doing here, Revna?"

She scoffed and pointed her dagger at him. "What are *you* doing here?"

"I live here. This is my home." He shrugged as if that explained everything.

She let that digest and it settled into her stomach like a rock. Revna looked at him—truly looked at him. He appeared the same ... and yet completely different. Long gone was the man she had found bound and broken in that cave. This man—he was darker, wilder. His hair was longer, falling to his shoulders and half bound back. The familiar golden eyes seemed sharper and more aware, tracking her every movement. His face was covered in a light shadow, but still didn't hide that slight dip in his chin. Even from a sitting position, he felt taller, more imposing. She surmised that the only reason she'd been able to take him down was because he'd let her.

He appeared like the Fenrick she'd known ... but something *other* lingered underneath.

His eyes narrowed and Revna's body thrummed in warning.

"Ask me," he said, his voice lower than it had been moments before.

She paused, just for a breath. Did she want to know? But then Revna steeled herself and lifted her chin. "Who are you? Truly?"

"Fenrir. And you are in the realm of Vanaheim."

Revna let the truth hang there for a moment, unsure if she could grasp it.

"You're Fenrir?" she asked, unbelieving. "The God of Destruction, son of Loki and—"

Fenrick—Fenrir—pushed off the ground and Revna resisted the urge to step back. He took one step then another, eyes flaring impossibly gold, flashing canines that grew longer with each advancing step. She held her ground until he was nearly pressed against her chest.

"Believe me, I wouldn't admit to being the most hated God in the realms unless it were true," he seethed through gritted teeth. "Now, how did you arrive here?"

She took the tip of her dagger and placed it under his chin. "You can't just tell me that you are a fucking God and act like it doesn't matter."

She'd return to the *where* of things later.

"Which part offends you exactly? That I am a God, or the God that I am?"

Red seeped into her vision, bitter anger flooded her tongue. "The part that *offends* me is that you lied to me."

He growled, knocking the blade away from under his chin as if it were a fly, crowding her space again until she could feel his hot breath on her face. But she refused to move, waiting for an answer.

"I had no choice. I was banished and bound to that realm. I couldn't tell you who I truly was—it was too big of a risk."

"And your master disguise was to change your name from *Fen-rir* to *Fen-rick*? How cunning you are!"

Fenrir growled again low in his chest. Revna, in all her fury and frustration, growled right back. They stared at each other, panting, when something inside of her cracked. She had lost so much in such a short time, and she was tired. She heaved out a sigh and closed her eyes briefly, regaining her composure.

"Why?" she whispered. "Why did you get on the boat in my place?"

Fenrir swallowed, his eyes scanning her face like he was searching for the answer there. "I owed you a debt. You unbound me and stayed with me when I was ..." he trailed off. "I owed you a debt."

Somehow that answer only made her more weary.

"Do you know how long I tortured myself? How long I *mourned you*?" She couldn't help the ache that crept into her voice.

"How long?" he asked flatly.

"I'll let you know when I stop," she whispered before she could stop herself, and she knew he heard by his flinch. Fenrir took one step back, then two, until the space between them felt as great as it had been between realms. Silence hung heavy in the air for a few moments before Revna lifted her chin and answered his first question.

"Since your sacrifice, the boat never returned. Until this year. It called me again and brought me here. Although, this time, it didn't take me down through the waters like it did with you. I came through a cave system—"

"You came through a cave system?" Fenrir interrupted. She nodded and his eyes turned distant, as if searching the air for explanation. "I'm unsure of what that means."

"Am I dead?" she asked, still not sure of her current standing.

"No, you are very much alive. Just in another realm."

"So, all the sacrifices that were made before you and I are still alive?" It seemed like an important question to ask, though she dreaded the answer.

He shook his head and shifted on his feet. "No, I don't think so."

Revna's head started to throb—a slow creeping pain that ran from her temples, through her jaw and neck. She wanted to lie down, she wanted to rage—everything within her was at odds, and for the first time in years, she didn't know what to do. Revna's main purpose, along with a piece of her heart, had been ripped from her. Fenrir opened his mouth as if to speak when a knock sounded on the door.

"Enter," he said instead.

Through the door strolled her original captor, carrying what looked like a bundle of fabrics. When he looked at Fenrir and his bloodied nose, he smirked knowingly.

"I thought to bring a change of clothes for you since yours are wet," he explained. "Perhaps I should have brought a rag for your face. What happened, Fen? Did you take a little tumble?"

"Yes, into my poor knee," Revna answered for him.

Fenrir gave her a sardonic smile as he reached up with both hands and cracked his nose back into place. He ripped a strip of fabric off the bottom of his tunic and wiped away the blood.

The other man rolled his eyes at Fenrir. "I would have healed you," he said. "After I gave you a hard time, of course."

Fenrir waved him off. "Have you properly introduced yourself yet?"

"I was waiting until you talked to her first." With that, he strode forward a few steps and offered Revna the bundle of clothes. "I'm Tyr."

Tyr. The God of Love and War, and a son of the Allfather, Odin.

Revna blinked once, twice.

"I'm Revna," she responded slowly, taking the clothes and depositing them on a nearby table.

"Pleased to meet you, Revna. Fenrir has told me a bit about you and what you did for him back in Myddheim."

Her eyes shifted to meet Fenrir's, whose face was a mask of stone. She didn't know him—not now. Or possibly she never had. But she could tell by his face that their conversation was over.

"I apologize for the slight roughness earlier," Tyr said, diluting the building tension. "But with Thor being here, things were uncertain."

Thor?

Revna felt it building in her stomach—a quick and sudden beast that couldn't be caged. She threw her head back, gave in, and laughed. It grew and fed off the bewildered looks the two men gave her, until she was doubled over, bracing her hands on her knees.

Gods, monsters, realms, life, death. She was unmoored and she didn't know how to find solid ground, so she let herself drift in the flood of uncertainty.

Tyr leaned a bit toward Fenrir and asked, "Did she hit her head? Does she need healing?"

Her laughter doubled, tears streaming down her face. She squatted even further until her ass hit the stone floor, peals of laughter finally giving way to sobs of sorrow and exhaustion. This wasn't like her, this outburst of raw emotion. Perhaps she should feel embarrassed, given who her audience was, but she didn't have the energy left to care.

These Gods could just witness and weather the storm flowing through her—she was only human, after all.

She wrapped her arms loosely around her knees and hung her head forward, trying to take deep, calming breaths. A new kind of fear had taken residence in her chest. But not for her—for all those she had left behind. Revna thought she was doing something kind and noble in sacrificing herself, a debt that was long overdue. But stomach-souring guilt seeped in thinking of the burden and danger she had placed on the Maidens.

Vaguely, she heard a murmur of voices, footsteps, and the quiet click of a door being closed. But she knew she wasn't alone. A shadow and sudden warmth bled into the air surrounding Revna as Fenrir took a seat next to her. Any slight movement had her shoulder bumping against him. He didn't say anything, didn't reach for her. Just sat with her as tears stained the stone floor. Revna searched for the anger and energy to push him away, to tell him to leave, but she couldn't find the will.

Suddenly, she was the young woman she'd been over nine years ago. She had just killed and escaped from her master and fled into the night. The storm that night had been a wicked combination of rain and ice—the sharp cold of it had stung her skin as it sliced through her thin dress. Her bare feet had torn open on exposed rocks, her hands had caught on every nettle and bramble. She couldn't tell what was blood or dirt as she picked herself up over and over again. And then the cave had appeared, as if Freyja had heard her cries. Inside was the man beside her. Bound and bloodied.

Lost in her own thoughts, Fenrir's voice startled her when he spoke. "It's been a trying day, and sitting in wet clothes and feeling sorry for yourself won't change anything."

Revna lifted her head and shot him an incredulous look, the embers of anger once again stoked.

"I'm going to send someone to take you to another room where a warm bath and food will be waiting. Then, you are going to get some rest, and we will talk again in the morning."

Revna stared at him as he rose to his full height, cold bleeding back into the space he'd occupied.

As he started to walk away, she found her voice. "Is there no way to go back?"

His retreating body froze at the question, and he took a long, deep breath before turning.

"No. There's no going back."

Her spine straightened. "And if I run?"

Something like a challenge flashed in his eyes as he gave her a mirthless smile. "You can't outrun a wolf."

Revna willed her face to remain impassive, even as the hairs on her arms rose. She glared at him even after he'd shut the door, leaving her alone and surrounded by the stains of her tears.

EIGHT

FENRIR

F ENRIR WENT IN SEARCH of Hel. While he trusted the residents within his territory, it was his sister he wanted to assist Revna for the evening.

His jaw clenched as he remembered how cruel he'd been—the look on her face as she'd met his stare with pure anger.

But he would rather have her anger than her sadness.

He knew anger, knew how to feed that fire and bank it to best serve his needs. She would need to learn how cruel the realms of the Gods were if she was going to survive them. More importantly, she was going to have to learn how to keep hidden. At least until he figured out what was going on.

But first, a bath and food.

His first stop was by the kitchens—assuming Tyr was there, perhaps he'd know the whereabouts of Hel.

As soon as he reached the stairs leading down into the warm space, his stomach gave a low growl at the smells that invaded his nose. Roasted meats spiced with black salt and herbs, the unmistakable warmth of fresh bread, and root vegetables tossed in honey and goat cheese. Cooks bustled around the kitchen, swatting away reaching hands. One youngling gave Fenrir a toothy smile as he darted for the stairs with his stolen sweet rolls, escaping an exasperated cook.

Somewhat unintentionally, his territory within Vanaheim had become a settlement for those who'd felt out of place within their realms. One by one they'd showed up looking for belonging, purpose, and respite from the growing disputes. Some were expelled from their clans for questioning the way of things. Others had dwelled here long since Freyja had abandoned the keep after the Aesir-Vanir war.

There were giants from Jotunheim, light elves from Alfheim, and dwarfs from Nidavellir. It wasn't uncommon for him to see two to three errant Gods on any given day. A clan of outcasts that somehow found home with Fenrir as their protector. He didn't take that honor lightly.

And now their outcast clan had a new, angry member. A human from Myddheim.

At a table in the corner of the warm kitchen, Fenrir spotted Tyr chugging a large mug of ale. Across from him, also chugging, was Fenrir's sister, Hel.

The God of Love and War and the Goddess of Death were engaged in a drinking game.

Fenrir sighed, hoping he'd caught them early on in their games so Hel would still be useful—and not loose-lipped to a certain guest.

"Hel, I need your help," he said by way of greeting as he reached the table. "Please."

She held up one finger, head tilted back as she drained the last of her cup. But just as she swallowed her last gulp, Tyr slammed his mug down on the table, the victor.

"Ha!" Tyr yelled, reaching his still intact hand across the table to wiggle a finger in front of her face. Hel grabbed that finger, bent it back, twisted his arm, and pinned him on the tabletop.

"What can I help you with, brother?" she asked, even as Tyr struggled beneath her grip.

"We have a new guest, and I would like for you to bring her some food and take her to a room with a bath."

"Should I bathe her, too?" she quipped, one dark eyebrow raised.

"Give the poor man a break, Hellie. It's *the* mortal woman," Tyr chided, cheek still pressed against the wood of the table.

At that, Hel's eyes whipped to Fenrir's, and she released her hold on Tyr. She pushed herself off the bench and rounded the table to stand in front of him. She barely came to his chin, but the deathly power that thrummed under her skin made her presence invading.

"The woman from Myddheim who unbound you?" Hel asked in slight awe.

Fenrir nodded. Several moments passed as she searched his eyes, the golden hue nearly the same as his—save for the black flecks and the roiling cloudiness when her draugr form paced just under the surface.

"Austri!" Hel called to the dwarf in charge of the kitchen. "May I please have a little bit of everything you made tonight. Oh! And a large pitcher of berry mead."

"Hel—" Fenrir started, but she was already moving through the kitchen, grabbing things as she moved.

"Maybe a tonic for a good night's sleep." She turned back to Fenrir. "Is she injured?"

"No, but Hel—" he tried again, but she was already sorting through the shelves for something else, saying something to Austri, who only encouraged her to load her arms.

"Hel!" Fenrir boomed and the whole room froze as the ground shook beneath their feet. "Listen to me."

His sister's eyes briefly clouded over in that smoky way that reminded everyone how close they were to death. "Do *not* take that tone with me, brother."

Fenrir sighed and took a step toward her, placing his hands lightly on her shoulders. "I apologize. I'm out of sorts today."

Between constantly being pulled to settle disputes in other realms, the Aesir showing up to remind him of his place, and now Revna—he was beyond tired. He was weary to his very bones. He glanced around the space; all the younglings had fled at his outburst, but the cooks pretended to carry on as though nothing had happened. Guilt churned in his stomach, knowing that the outbursts had become more frequent. So frequent that the residents of his territory didn't even react anymore. It was unacceptable. They'd fled their entire lives, giving up all they had known, hoping for a better life. The least he could do was make sure they felt safe and comfortable.

"I apologize," he said, addressing the entire room. "Forgive my outburst. As always, your work is appreciated."

He received a few small smiles from the cooks, just as Hel's fist reared back and hit him right on his shoulder. It was a punch of annoyance, not violence, and he barely moved from his stance.

"Don't apologize," she said exasperated. "I mean, yes, apologize, just …"

Fenrir quirked an eyebrow at her, waiting for her words to catch up with her thoughts.

"Everyone here knows who and what you are," she said slowly. "And they know what you sacrifice to keep the peace."

"She's right, you know," Tyr piped up from his spot at the table.

It didn't excuse frightening children, or creating an environment where his temper was viewed as normal. That's not who he wanted to be—the monster the Aesir had painted him to be.

Being monstrous and being an actual monster were two completely different things.

He refocused his attention on his sister. "That's what I wanted to discuss with you, Hel. I don't want Revna to know anything about my deal with Odin."

"Why?" she asked. "Is this a trust concern?"

Always, he wanted to say. Instead, he said, "Because it's my choice when and if I want to tell her."

Everything surrounding Revna was a knot that would take time to untangle. They had a history. Although it was brief, it was a kind of bond that endured for lifetimes. However, he didn't know who she was anymore. And she'd never truly known him—not the real him. Not the man or the monster.

"Fine." Hel agreed. "I won't tell her. But I will not lie about who and what I am. You can have your secrets, as they are yours. But I stopped hiding from the light long ago."

He knew she didn't mean it as an insult to him. Just as a reminder as to what she had endured and how she would never let herself feel that way again. She didn't often talk about it, but spending so much time in darkness, so much time with death, so much time with the shame of her existence ... it weighed on her.

He gave her an understanding nod and helped her load up a tray with food and drink. After she had enough to feed three adults, his sister disappeared up the small set of stairs in pursuit of Revna.

"Drink?" Tyr said from the table, already pouring ale into a spare cup.

Part of Fenrir wanted to refuse. He wanted to lurk outside of Revna's room and wait for her to do something. Scream, cry, fight, run.

If she screamed or cried, he would make her angry instead.

If she wanted to fight, he'd give her something to fight.

If she ran, he wouldn't let her get far.

Let me out. Let me run. Let me hunt, the wolf underneath begged and clawed at his mind. Fenrir shoved the temptation down until it made his stomach ache with want.

He absentmindedly rubbed at the inked bands around his forearms, a reminder of the deal he'd made.

Shaking off the urge, Fenrir crossed to Tyr and took the cup he offered, taking the seat Hel had vacated. Bringing the cup to his lips, he drained the whole thing in one go. Tyr gave him a tight-lipped smile and slid the jug across the table.

"So," Tyr said, eyeing him over the rim of his own cup, "where are we off to tomorrow?"

Leaving Revna so soon after she arrived felt wrong, but he'd made a deal. He had to keep doing his assigned duty, or the Aesir might come sniffing and find things that didn't belong.

"Jotunheim."

NINE

REVNA

REVNA WAS LOSING FEELING in her ass. She'd been sitting on the hard, cold stone floor for too long, not having moved since Fenrick—*Fenrir*—had walked out the door, leaving her to wallow in self-pity. Her thoughts were moving too fast to grab, and it left her unwilling to move, unwilling to acknowledge her new situation. When she tried to approach it with the logic and tactfulness she'd used as a commander for all those years, she felt nothing but exhaustion.

Perhaps she just needed sleep. And something to eat. To come up with a plan. Something to give her purpose and focus. She just couldn't bring herself to get up.

Fenrir had said there was no going back. For some reason, she believed him.

A sharp, rapid series of knocks sounded on the door, startling Revna. With a dagger still in her hand, she stood, sending a trickle of sharp tingles down her legs.

"Enter," she called, taking a defensive stance.

The door creaked open and in walked a woman balancing a tray on one hand.

Revna wasn't sure what she'd expected, but this terrifying beauty wasn't it.

She exuded strength in both spirit and body. Her rich brown skin was decorated by various patterns. Most inked with black, blue, or red, but this woman had inked herself in opalescent white. Revna had never seen anything like it—it was breathtaking. Dark hair was woven into dozens of tiny braids and hanging loosely.

When the other woman looked into her eyes, Revna started. They were the same unmistakable golden as Fenrir's. But where his were a pure golden, hers were threaded with little bits of black.

She eyed Revna's dagger and gave her a half smile.

"I don't think you'll be needing that. The meat is so tender it falls right off the bone," the woman said, her voice laced in mirth. She walked over to a table and set down the tray.

"And what about you? Will your meat fall right off the bones?" Revna had meant it as a warning, but it came out half-hearted at best.

The woman threw her head back and laughed. It was loud and so full of life that Revna had a hard time fighting back her own smile, despite her bleak mood.

"After you've finished eating, I'll take you to a proper room with a bed and a bath," she said, still chuckling.

Something about this woman felt familiar in a way that was somehow both calming and scary. She turned to face Revna, and they assessed one another for a long moment.

"And you are?" Revna asked finally, wanting to gather as much information as possible.

"I'm Hel."

Revna's hands slackened at her sides. The woman—Hel, the Goddess of Death—gave her a coy smile. As if she didn't just tilt the world, sending Revna gripping for anything that was familiar.

"You really should eat something. You look a bit pale," Hel said. She went about uncovering small pots and plates of food as if the Goddess didn't have anything better to do. As if she wasn't death incarnate and ruler of Helheim. Revna had the insane urge to bow. Instead, she walked to the table and sat.

Once she sank into the chair, her mind finally caught up. "You're Fenrir's sister."

"And Jormun's. Daughter of Loki and Angrboda. But who I am to other people is the least interesting thing about me." She put a plate in front of Revna, whose stomach gave an impressive growl as the scent wafted to her nose.

"And why are you here? In Vanaheim?" Revna asked.

Hel's place was in the realm of the dead. She was said to reside there with all manner of beasts and the unwanted deceased, hiding from the light of day. Those who fought and fell with valor took a place in the halls in Valhalla. They said that some were handpicked by Freyja herself to reside in her mountain hall. But Helheim was for the leftovers—the murderers, the sick, the old, those who didn't fight. In fact, all the stories about Hel said she was a grotesque, half-rotted corpse. The woman in front of Revna was none of those things.

Hel raised a questioning brow at her. "I could ask you the same thing."

What to reveal ... Revna knew nothing of the true ways of the Gods. After all, the legendary monstrous siblings were the product of a trickster god and a giantess witch—she wasn't sure how much trust to place in any of them. "I'm still trying to figure that out myself," she offered.

"Hmm." Hel regarded her. "Well, go on. Eat."

Revna considered refusing, wondering if they would poison her. But she found she was too tired and hungry to care. She tore off a hunk of meat and shoved it into her mouth, nearly moaning at the perfect melody of spice and tenderness. Forgoing any kind of manners, she hastily began shoving bread, root vegetables, and berries into her mouth. Hel grabbed for the pitcher, pouring them both a cup and then helped herself to a piece of bread with goat cheese and berries.

Revna swallowed a giant bite, suddenly worried. "I apologize, I didn't realize it was for both of us."

Hel waved her hand dismissively. "You were just eating with such enthusiasm, I had to see what the fuss what about. Austri will be very pleased to have such a passionate guest to feed."

Revna slowed, reaching for her cup and taking a gulp of the mead, once again stifling the urge to make inappropriate sounds of appreciation. Then she went back to eating while the Goddess of Death looked on.

"I realize this is all a lot to take in," Hel said, breaking the silence. "And I understand more than most that trust is earned. With that, I will offer some things about myself, but I will not tell you anything of Fenrir because his story is for him to share. Is this agreeable?"

Revna put down her food and nodded.

"To answer your question, I am here in Vanaheim because I like to divide my time between the realms in order to be closer to my brothers. No one who enters Helheim leaves it. Save for me, of course." So at least part of the myth was true, Revna thought. "My brothers and I were separated when we were younger. Now I'm trying to make up for lost time, and giving the Aesir pause should they think to take my brothers away from me again. Even for Gods, it is hard to look upon the face of death."

Hel's tone shifted to one of bitterness and anger. Revna wanted to ask dozens of questions—wanted to know how close to the truth the stories she'd heard her whole life were. But she didn't want Hel to stop talking, so she stayed quiet.

"I won't bore you of what happened before Fenrir's banishment. But, in a way, when you unbound Fenrir in Myddheim, you freed me as well," Hel said, meeting Revna's gaze. "So, thank you."

The look the Goddess of Death was giving her made Revna shift in her seat. It laid her bare, that assessing gaze. Accepting any kind of gratitude had always been hard for her, so instead, she did what the Goddess had. She offered a truth for a truth.

"I came here on a ship through a cave system. It showed up in Myddheim for the first time in nine years. The last was when Fen—your brother—sacrificed himself in my stead."

Hel looked down into cup of her mead, searching its contents as if she would find the answers within.

"It called for me," Revna continued, still slightly disbelieving that she was having this conversation with a Goddess.

"Called for you how?"

"I heard it whisper my name as if it snaked inside my ear. It told me to *come see*." Revna decided to leave out the, *"He waits and waits…"* part.

An oddly comfortable silence settled between them. When it became clear that Hel wouldn't push for more answers, Revna went back to her meal, eating until a comfortable warmth nestled between her ribs. Hel had been watching her, a thoughtful look on her beautiful face.

"You know, you never did introduce yourself to me. Quite rude, really. Here I am telling you of my horrible upbringing and I don't even know your name." Hel set her cup down and crossed her arms, the opalescent markings catching in the candlelight.

"Your brother didn't tell you?"

Hel shrugged. "Even if he had, I would prefer to hear it from you. It's your name to give."

Suddenly, Revna had a startling realization about her effortless connection with Hel. Because that's what it was, a connection—not unlike the ones she'd made with the Maidens.

There had been times as a slave that she was beaten so badly she hadn't known if she would survive the night. Sicknesses that had left her debilitated and delirious. And, after some time, she'd decided that death wasn't something to fear. What scared Revna far more than dying was living a life that was not her own. Being reduced so low that she questioned whether she was worth loving, or even knowing. Over those years, death had become a friend—a promise in a world of cruelty. Now she felt like she had known Hel her whole life, because part of her had.

"I'm Revna."

"Ah, the raven." Hel eyed her black hair. "It suits you."

Revna held the Goddess's gaze and felt a small smile lift her lips. "So, what happens next?"

Hel leaned back in her chair and picked up her cup of mead. "I'm going to take you to a bedroom where you can bathe and get some rest. As for the rest of it, we will deal with it tomorrow."

Revna didn't ask if she was a prisoner again. It didn't matter either way, really. She was stuck here, and a bed was a bed.

Everything within Revna wanted to rally, to figure out a way back to Myddheim and to her family. Guilt was heavy in her stomach for leaving them during such uncertain times. What if the crops didn't yield and they didn't have enough stores for winter? What if that caused an increase in raiding, then a resurrection of the slave trade? No longer hungry, she set down her cup and leaned back, dejected. She wanted to go back, needed it ... and knew she couldn't.

She wouldn't even know where to start.

"If you're finished, I can take you now."

Revna nodded, then followed Hel out of the room.

Earlier, when she was being pulled along by Tyr, she'd taken note of possible escape routes, things that could be used as weapons. She hadn't really appreciated how breathtaking the mountain keep was. It was in complete harmony with the nature surrounding it. Most halls were open to the elements, one passing behind a waterfall, the cool spray clinging to her face.

They went up a small set of natural stone steps, which led to more moss lit halls. Revna ran her hands along braided wood rails and smooth stone walls with bits of climbing vines. In more open areas that they passed through, great stalactites dripped from the ceilings. Everything felt comfortable without being closed-off from nature. And the smell ...

Revna inhaled, trying to place it. Woodsmoke and the trees, and something clean. It called to a part of her that she didn't want to look at too closely.

They turned down a hall that was wide and lined with lush, color-ful rugs. Several doors lined the walls, ending in a grand balcony. Hel stopped in front of a large walnut door.

"My room is right across the hall. Tyr is next to me, and Fenrir's is the closest to the balcony. And this one shall be yours." Hel opened the door, and Revna was surprised by the room within.

It wasn't gilded and stuffy, as she'd expect rooms of a God to be. Instead, it was normal, but richly furnished. A large bed was off to one side, covered in furs. A small table and chair sat next to a low burning fire. More rugs layered the space, and giant windows framed a small balcony overlooking the forest. In one corner there was small partition. Revna circled it and found a wooden tub waiting with billowing steam.

"There are a few sets of clothes for you on the bed. If you leave yours outside your door, they'll be washed and returned to you. We'll look at getting you some more options in the morning."

Revna turned and looked at Hel, unsure of what to say. She was being so kind, and it caused an unwanted ache.

"Thank you. I appreciate your help. And honesty."

Hel dipped her head in acceptance. "I'll see you in the morning and we will eat together again."

With that, the Goddess of Death left her standing alone in the room. *Alone.*

Revna could not remember the last time she was this alone. Not just physically, but because she could feel the distance between herself and her life, her purpose.

Trying to avoid being pulled under by the current of her thoughts, she stripped down, keeping her weapons within reach, and stepped into the tub. The heat was still intense, but she sank into it, sighing.

She sat in the water until her skin reddened and the pads of her fingers became wrinkled. Instead of letting her thoughts drift to everything that had happened and what she'd left behind, she focused on tomorrow and what she needed to discuss with the lying God—wolf—whatever he was.

Thinking of his deception had her chewing on the inside of her cheek to quell the growing rage. How had she not known? When she'd found him in that cave, he was a broken and bleeding thing. It had taken days for him to be able to move around without getting light-headed, but Revna couldn't leave him behind. She'd taken one look at him, at the scars and brands of cruelty marking his body and offered to be his ally. And for nearly two months, they were. Allies and companions. Until Krussa.

And now, she was here. There had to be a reason. Like their lives were threads of fate that were always meant to cross.

She thought of the way his shoulder had brushed hers, his warm body solid and real next to hers. The comfortable quiet that had pulled her back to nine years earlier. For a moment, it felt as though he had never left Myddheim. Then he spoke, ruining the small moment of comfort. She shook those thoughts off.

She grabbed the soft weave that was draped over a nearby chair and wrapped it around herself as she exited the tub. On the bed she found a sleeping gown, a pair of trousers, and a few tunics, as well as a pair of boots. The proud side of her revolted at just being given things, but she took them. Her other option was naked. And her display of emotion earlier was about as naked as she wanted to get.

As she pulled the night dress over her head, the wine and warm bath suddenly hit her. She was so *tired*, in mind and body. But that exhaustion was followed swiftly by wariness. The thought of sleeping across and down the hall from Fenrir ... from Gods.

It hadn't truly hit her until that moment. *She was in the land of Gods and monsters.*

The very Gods that could potentially rid Myddheim of the festering darkness.

Maybe she shouldn't be trying to find a way back. Instead, she could help Myddheim from the source.

Revna nearly cried at the relief she felt in her body at the thought. The slight unclenching of her jaw, the breath that pulled more easily from her lungs. The sense of purpose settled her. She could still fight for Myddheim, still fight for those who needed her.

And she knew exactly who she wanted to fight with first.

TEN

FENRIR

THE GIANTS OF JOTUNHEIM were restless.

The realm of Jotunheim was one of the first crafted into existence, and deep veins of primordial power ran strong through the lands. Fenrir, being half-Jotunn, felt its call in his blood the moment his feet touched the ground. It had been his home for many years, after all.

Fenrir and Tyr had spent most of the day lurking about villages. Their presence had been enough to deter any kind of violence, but Fenrir could smell a fear-coated anger on the air. Most emotions had a scent, and with his heightened senses, it was impossible to ignore.

Odin and most of the Aesir were convinced that Jotunheim was preparing for a war, but really, it was an excuse for control. To keep power within their hands.

Fenrir could not admit it to anyone, aside from Tyr and Hel, but he didn't blame the giants for their anger. They were kneeling to a power that cared nothing for their actual well-being or traditions. The Aesir claimed to provide protection, but they tended to start more wars than quell them. Anger was warranted.

As Fenrir walked back through the rune gate, the smells of Vanaheim hit him, settling his mind. Day and night fought for dominance in the sky, creating a dusky blue threaded with pinks. The trees rustled excitedly in his presence. As he and Tyr made their way back to the tunnel that led to the keep, Fenrir let his hands run over every tree that they passed, greeting them as old friends. Easy peace settled over him amongst the trees and earth, and even his wolf half hummed in contentment.

The feeling was short lived. He knew what was waiting—a woman who was just as likely to kick his ass as she was to make him wither in his seat from her glare alone. And that was just Revna. Hel wasn't too pleased with him either. Before he had left with Tyr for Jotunheim that morning, he'd told Hel to keep an eye on Revna all day. Before agreeing, she had called him a coward.

Which, he could admit, was fair.

He had run away. Fenrir had needed more time to clear his head, and his duty in Jotunheim, even with his perfectly valid reasoning, had also supplied a convenient excuse. They had so much to discuss, he and Revna, and he was at a loss at how to bridge the gap of years and distrust.

Not running the other direction would be a start, he chided himself.

Once in the tunnel, their pace quickened with the promise of a good meal. Most people would have already eaten dinner, so the dining hall would be fairly clear. He would eat and then go talk to Revna. He could feel Tyr looking at him out of the corner of his eye, no doubt sensing the growing tension radiating through Fenrir's body. As they rounded the corner leading into the cavernous dining space, Tyr spoke hesitantly.

"Perhaps we should invite Revna to ..." he trailed off, gaze landing on two women sitting at a table in the middle of the hall.

Hel and Revna were already present, chatting and laughing as if they were long lost friends, not strangers who had just met last night. Not human and Goddess. Just friends. Revna threw her head back and laughed at something Hel said, and Fenrir felt his face burn in a new kind of feeling. It wasn't quite anger, nor was it sorrow. It was an indistinguishable combination of the two.

Jealousy.

Fenrir made his way around the tables that dotted the hall, preparing to chide Hel for bringing Revna to such an exposed place and flaunting her obvious humanity, but he stopped short. He needed to trust his sister and the people who trusted him enough to stay within his territory. There were only a few others within the space, and none seemed to be paying any mind to the two women sitting in the middle of the room.

Hel glanced over as they approached. "Brother! Tyrie! Come join us."

Fenrir's eyes slid to Revna, but she occupied herself by taking a long drink out of her cup. Fenrir had two choices: he could take the seat right next to Revna, or he could take the seat next to Hel. Tossing both of those options aside, he chose the seat at the head of the table right between them. Tyr gave him a look of confusion as he took a seat next to Hel. Fenrir never sat at the head of the table, save for the times they had visitors from other realms.

"Revna," he said in greeting.

She turned to him then, giving a saccharine smile. "Hello, *wolf*."

His hope that a night's rest and a day of relaxation would cool her ire were quickly proved false.

She stared at him, and he at her, engaging in a juvenile game of who would look away first.

He couldn't get over how different she looked. It wasn't in physical appearance, but in the way she held herself. She still had the same black hair, though longer, and the same gray eyes. The years had been good to her, judging by the weight and muscle she had put on. Her hair was pulled back, and he could see a small bit of the marking that decorated the back of her neck where her slave brand used to be. He wondered how far down the markings went ...

"Good evening, Hel. How was your day Hel? Thank you for being a courteous host when I ran away this morning, Hel." His sister's voice mocked, drawing Fenrir's attention to where she was sitting, smirking

over the rim of her cup. He ignored her sly smile, grateful that she'd given him reason to look away. Tyr snorted and nudged her with his shoulder.

"How fortunate I am to have a sister such as you," he responded.

"And don't you forget it."

Fenrir looked between the two glossy-eyed women. "Have you two eaten anything or are you just drinking your dinner thus far?"

"I was eventually going to get us some food. Revna was just telling me some incredible stories about what she did in Myddheim."

Fenrir looked at Revna, who was currently leaning back in her chair, picking at her nails. He wanted to huff out a sigh of irritation. Or growl. Instead, he chose what he hoped would be an equalizer.

"I'll go get some food for the table."

"I'll give you a hand," Tyr said, standing with a wink at Revna and Hel.

Fenrir made his way over to the doorway leading down into the kitchen, Tyr quiet at his side—always giving Fenrir silent support and letting him work things through in his mind. Once their arms were brimming full of meats, soft cheese, bread, fruits, and ale, they made their way back to the women. Each step back to the table had Fenrir's mood shifting, but he couldn't quite figure out what it meant. His mind and body couldn't agree whether he desired to be near her or very far away. Frustration pulled taut in his chest.

They set the trays on the table, taking their respective seats. Hel reached for the food first, then Tyr, digging in as if they had never eaten before in their long lives.

Fenrir handed Revna a plate. "Go ahead."

She took it without so much as a thank you, reluctantly reaching for random bits and placing them on her plate. When she took her first bite, she made a little moan and nodded her head in pleasure, the noise making him shift a little in his chair. Fenrir was the only one who'd heard it, as

Tyr and Hel argued about something ridiculous and unimportant. He watched Revna eating with enthusiasm out of the corner of his eye as he tried to remember how to chew his own food.

A few days after she'd found him in the cave, when he was still too weak to do much but lay around and sip water, Revna went out hunting. He remembered how she'd walked into the cave with three rabbits slung over her shoulders, and a few wild onions in her hands. He'd watched her skin and cook them over an open fire but then hesitate when it was time to eat. When he'd asked her what was wrong, she had said she'd never been allowed to eat the first bite, let alone any of the good parts of the hunt. Her sadness had flared quickly to determination, and she'd taken a big bite right to the middle of the rabbit. From that moment on, no matter how weak he was, he made sure she ate first.

Watching her now, he wondered if she remembered.

Fenrir didn't realize he was staring until Revna turned her head toward him and narrowed her eyes, the gray shining bright in the candlelight.

"Shall I save the bones for you to chew on later?" she asked, waving her chicken leg around.

Fenrir leaned into her space enough that he saw interest spark in her eyes—a sight that delighted him far more than it should. "I prefer the bones of those who taunt me. The marrow is much sweeter."

Tyr choked on his ale and Hel muttered something under her breath as her hand swatted his shoulder. But Fenrir refused to look away from Revna. He wanted to see if she would flinch or cower at the monstrous side of him. Instead, she gave him a challenging tilt of her head and extended out her arm.

"Go on then," she said, pulling up the sleeve of her tunic, thrusting it toward him. His canines descended the tiniest bit as her scent invaded his nose. It wasn't fear he was smelling, but something else that blended with the slight tang of apprehension.

But then he eyed her arm and was reminded of another time and of the arm of his friend sitting at this very table. Fenrir leaned back and picked up his cup, letting Revna have this victory.

"So, Revna." Tyr started, undoubtedly attempting to diffuse the tension that thickened the air. "How are things faring on Myddheim?"

Fenrir held his breath as she took a great gulp of ale and then met Tyr's gaze.

"Well, we are at the mercy of mercurial Gods who've decided to abandon us, poison our soil, and instigate wars for their own amusement. How do you fare here in your gilded halls?"

The hall was silent as he, Tyr, and Hel looked at Revna in variations of surprise and confusion.

"Abandoned you?" Fenrir asked, finally finding his voice.

Revna shrugged and studied the contents of her cup. "After you took my place, the realm seemed to devolve into chaos. More fighting, more seasons of wasted crops, more people getting taken for slaves. The Maidens and I could barely keep up."

"Maidens?" Tyr asked.

"Revna started a group of elite warriors to take down slavers and rescue those taken. She even got a king to outlaw the practice," Hel said, giving Revna a soft smile that she rarely used.

"It wasn't just me, it was—"

"Did you really?" Fenrir cut her off.

"Yes." A simple and emotionless reply.

Something like pride sparked in his chest.

When Fenrir had started healing, and Revna became more trusting of him, she'd asked him if he knew how to fight. The situation in which she'd found him notwithstanding, he had said yes. She'd wanted to learn to *fight*—not just defend herself, but learn the skills to fight for others. They had a few lessons, but not enough before he had left for her to have become a warrior. She must have continued her training with someone else given how well she had matched his intensity during their squabble the previous evening.

"What makes you think it's the Gods playing with you and not just the work of fate?" Tyr asked sincerely, and Fenrir could see the warrior within calculating the possibilities.

Revna looked distant for a moment as she put together words in her head. "I can't say for sure. I do not pretend to know the whims of the Gods. What I do know is that every year the boat never returned, things grew worse, and people ..." she trailed off.

"Needed somewhere to place the blame?" Hel supplied.

Revna nodded and then glanced around at each of them. "So, are you?"

"Are we what?" Fenrir asked.

"Playing with us mortals for your own amusement? Punishing us?" She lifted her chin, the question both a request and demand.

Embodiments of destruction, death, love, and war all sat at the table with Revna, so Fenrir didn't blame her for asking. For wondering.

"I swear to you," Hel promised, "it's not us."

Revna nodded and took a sip out of her cup. Her cheeks were becoming flushed with drink, her eyes tired. Fenrir had questions he'd planned to ask, each one that would lead to more. But judging by the way her shoulders started to slump, he decided they could wait until tomorrow.

He needed to talk to Tyr and Hel about this new development in the human realm. There were too many coincidences of dissent throughout all nine realms, which meant the Aesir would undoubtedly be sending more representatives to remind him of his place. Fenrir didn't want to know what they would do if they found out a human was living in his realm. What Odin would do to further ensure his obedience.

But the boat had returned ...

Fenrir resisted the urge to rub at the twin inked bands encircling each forearm, their presence answer enough.

"Perhaps we should call it a night," he said. "Revna, may I walk you back to your room?"

She let her gaze lazily rove over him. "Escorting your prisoner back to her cage?"

"You are not a prisoner. What you do with your days and nights is completely up to you. You're welcome to roam as you wish." Within reason, but he didn't add that.

"Except the woods at night. Wouldn't want to encounter a draugr." She raised an eyebrow at Tyr who let out a loud bellow of laughter.

"You told her there were draugr here?" Fenrir couldn't keep the small smile out of his voice.

"I didn't lie—" Tyr started before Hel interrupted him with a whack on the back of his head.

"I am the only ghost that haunts these lands," Hel chided. "Maybe I should send my draugr form to watch over you while you sleep."

Tyr turned to face Hel, face paling. "You wouldn't dare." Hel only shrugged and popped a berry into her mouth.

Fenrir heard Revna chuckle at their ribbing and decided it was a good time to depart. He pushed his chair back and stood. Revna's small smile faded, but she stood and followed him without question.

The quiet seeped in from all sides as they made their way down the moss-lit hall. His teeth gnashed together as he tried to think about how to approach this. How to approach *her*. What could he possibly say to this woman who was more stranger than friend? This woman whose sharp edges threatened to cut right to the heart of him.

"Did you have something to say, or did you just want to brood in proximity to me?" Revna asked, shattering the silence.

Fenrir sighed. "I just wanted to make sure you're feeling comfortable here. And as I said, you're not a prisoner. But I do have some boundaries I would prefer that you respect."

"Such as?"

"Do not wander far from the keep without Hel, Tyr, or myself. And if you ever hear thunder or the crack of lightning, you hide."

Revna stiffened. "So, I'm not a prisoner, but I am confined."

They turned down the hall that held all their rooms, a night-kissed breeze coming from the open balcony at the end. They were running out of time for this talk. Tomorrow. He would fully explain things tomorrow.

"It's been a long couple of days. We'll talk more tomorrow when you're rested." And didn't have a jug of mead swimming through her veins, he decided not to add.

She rounded on him, causing him to stop abruptly, but not before he bumped into her, sending her back a step. Her face was still flushed, and wisps of her dark hair hung around her face. Her scent shifted to something spiced. *Anger.*

"Let me make something very clear," she seethed. "You do not get to tell me how I am feeling or what I can handle. You don't know me, *Fenrir*. You have no idea who I've become. I don't care that you're a God. No one gets to tell me my limits. Not anymore."

She was breathing heavily, but she didn't take her eyes off of his. They burned him ... and he wanted to see how long they could both withstand the heat. How long before they both caught fire. He closed the distance between them, making her head tilt back, exposing her neck.

"Fine," he said through his teeth. "But nor do you know me. This is my realm, and it has rules in place for a reason. To keep its residents safe.

And I won't have you fucking that up just to be a pain in the ass. Do I make myself clear?"

Between one heartbeat and the next, her face morphed into one of sweet-smiled innocence. "Of course, *Wolf God.*"

With that she turned and walked to her room. Once she was shut inside, Fenrir tipped his head back and released a low, long growl.

Pain in the ass, indeed.

ELEVEN

REVNA

S MUCH AS REVNA tried, she couldn't find one thing to dislike about the keep. Hel had given her a thorough tour the day before, and around every corner, in every crevice, there was beauty. From the open-aired halls to the creeping vines and arched doorways. From the smooth stone floors to the textured moss that lit up the dark halls, everything was both wild and purposeful, and full of warmth.

She wasn't sure how many, but easily dozens upon dozens of residents lived within the great keep's stone walls. People of every kind had passed her and Hel in the halls, and Revna had to hide her awe at their varying appearances.

She had awoken early and made her way to the kitchen in an effort to rid the throb behind her eyes from too much mead and ale. A dwarf named Austri had sat her down in front of a kitchen fire and stuffed her full of fresh bread, fruits, cheeses, and smoked meats. He didn't say much, just gave her gentle smiles. Every time she would hum in satisfaction biting into a piece of food, he would fill her plate once again.

Uncomfortably full, she walked about the keep, trying to memorize every turn and fork and out of place stone. But even with this self-appointed task, though, Revna could not keep her mind from slipping. A kind of darkness was starting to seep into the cracks of her strength, threatening to pull her under, and back to a place of despair she thought she'd defeated long ago. Revna's steps faltered as she fought the current of her mind. Reaching down to her belt, she gripped both daggers in hands and took a deep breath.

She'd felt a burst of purpose hoping to get to the bottom of the Gods misuse of her people, but she'd just had dinner with the only three Gods at her disposal, and it had been clear they had not a clue what she was talking about. That left her unmoored once again, unsure how to attack the problem.

When was the last time that she had just … existed? No Maidens to train with, no slavers to hunt, no impending reports to the king.

Revna froze and swallowed down the feeling of grief. She had begun again many times before this, she could do so again. Still, she hadn't realized how much she had to lose until it was gone, and it felt as though she would be forever unbalanced by the missing weight of her life in Myddheim. Ingrid's face flashed into her mind, followed by Asta, Hildi, Brynn, Haesten, and Torsten. And Ellika …

We do not break.

"I hope you aren't planning on using those on me," a deep voice said from behind her. Turning, she saw Tyr striding toward her with his ever-present grin.

"I'm still debating," she responded, which only made his smile broaden.

"Have you eaten?"

She nodded.

"So you met Austri?" he asked knowingly.

Revna huffed out a laugh. "I don't think I've ever eaten so much food."

At that, Tyr's brow furrowed, and his smile turned into a grimace. "Is there such little food on Myddheim?"

She turned to lean against the stone wall, crossing her arms. "For some, there's enough to waste. For others, you are lucky if you eat a few times a week."

Tyr nodded as if he understood, but Revna doubted he knew what it was like to feel truly hungry. To wonder if all the effort you put into your crops would be for nothing—completely dependent on the moods of the Gods.

"I was coming to find you. Wanted to see if you'd accompany me to the training yard to spar a bit."

Revna had the urge to laugh. The God of Love and War was asking to spar with a mortal.

"Would you like to train with me?" he asked.

Revna couldn't deny the longing to work out some of her frustration through blood and sweat. It had been days since she'd gone toe-to-toe with someone. But his request was slightly suspicious. What could he possibly think to get out of training with a mortal?

"Why?"

"It's good for my ego to beat someone every once in a while," he said, winking at her. "Fenrir and Hel put me on my ass more than I care to admit. It's time I had a win. What do you say?"

Revna loved when people underestimated her. "Lead the way."

⇥———⇤

The training yard was more of an arena than an actual yard. Revna had expected an open field with mud and weapons strewn about, but, like the rest of the keep, it held enough beauty to inspire admiration.

It was separate from the main living and eating areas of the mountain hall and tucked into an opening of the cliffside. There were stone steps that led to walkways and seating along the top rim. Little shadowy alcoves were nestled into the bottom, giving areas of respite from the glaring sun.

Various racks of weapons were placed along the edge of the arena, and several partners were engaged in brutal fights. Others were watching, goading and laughing. Most raised a quick hand in greeting when she and Tyr entered the space and went back to their fights or taunts.

Revna felt something ease within her at the familiar distraction. She looked sideways to Tyr and wondered if he knew what this would mean to her. Behind all his jests and easy smiles, she sensed he knew more than he let on—a master of observation and strategy. Which made sense, given who he was. Love and war were not without consideration and intent.

"Let's start with hand-to-hand and work our way up to weapons," he said, coming to a stop in a marked-out circle in the middle of the arena. Being on display should have made her uncomfortable, but it didn't. Revna welcomed the challenge.

Tyr gestured toward the belt strapped at Revna's hips. "You should probably rid yourself of the temptation to stab me."

She hesitated. Parting with weapons, let alone her favorite daggers, was not something she was willing to do. "I think it's better to practice having weapons and choosing not to use them, don't you?"

Tyr narrowed his eyes playfully at her and then her daggers. "As you wish. May I see one of them? On my honor, I promise to give it back."

She held out a hand. "Give me something of yours in exchange."

"You really don't trust anyone, do you?" His smile was still in place, but she was starting to see beneath it. Tyr's easy-going nature was a kind of mask—one to put people at ease, and get them vulnerable. Revna wouldn't fall for it.

"Trust is earned. And so far, only Hel has earned a portion of my trust."

Tyr rolled his eyes and murmured something along the lines of, *"Of course she has."* He took a couple steps toward her, reaching for a knife secured in his boot, and handed it to her. Biting her cheek, she reluctantly handed him a dagger.

His brows furrowed as he assessed the craftsmanship. "Where did you get these?"

"I had them made." That was all she was willing to offer. The secret of where the materials came from, what she had to face to obtain them, would remain hers.

Tyr's probing gaze traveled from the daggers back to her. A few moments passed, and he heaved a big sigh. "Trust is earned," he said, handing it back to her, handle first.

She sheathed the dagger back into her belt and handed his back. He grabbed it by the blade with his remaining hand and tossed it effortlessly to the border of circle.

"Let's warm our bodies with a game. First one to retrieve the dagger wins. Deal?" He offered his hand to shake.

Revna smiled and reached her hand toward his, angling her body in preparation. "Deal."

Shaking his hand, she swept her leg fast behind his, striking the backs of his knees and twisting his arm, until he had no choice but to land flat on his back.

Tyr coughed and laughed as Revna sauntered over to the knife and plucked it out of the dirt, winning the first round.

"Again," Revna panted.

After the first bout, Revna had lost several rounds in a row before they switched to weapons. She should have known better than to assume that just because Tyr was missing a hand, he would have a weak side. He had slid his arm through the leather straps of a shield and wielded a sword with the other hand, his movements unpredictable and honed. Tyr was a storm of power and grace, and he had Revna chasing after her breath as his stayed even.

And he'd said Hel and Fenrir often bested him. *By the Gods ...*

"Are you sure you don't want to take a break? Maybe I can ask one of the younglings to come over here and teach you a thing or two."

Revna swung, and Tyr parried. She was getting tired and careless. They'd been at it for hours, but every defeat only furthered her resolve to continue. Oddly, she wasn't angry or annoyed. Loath to say it aloud, she was having fun. There was so much to learn from the God of Love and War, and she felt hopeful at having something to look forward to.

"You're going on the offensive too quickly, fierce one." Tyr reminded her. Again. "You are quick and agile and strong. Let your opponent come to you, especially if they're bigger."

Her shield arm was starting to tremble, so she tossed it aside, gripping the sword he gave her in both hands. Tyr smiled and unstrapped his arm from the shield as well, tossing it next to hers. She took his advice and let him make the first move. For a while, they danced, the occasional clang of metal on metal ringing out, joining the other sounds of sparring. Sweat dripped down her temples, rolling onto her neck. Clouds of dirt wafted and clung to her sticky skin, but she felt *good*. Like herself.

"Better," Tyr encouraged, as she deflected another blow. He glanced over her head and gave a little nod. "I think that's enough for today."

"No," she protested. "I want to keep going."

Tyr gave her a look. She knew she probably looked dead on her feet, but she wasn't ready to quit.

"Don't say I didn't try to give you an out. Best of luck," he whispered, winking at her, then retreated toward the side of the circle. She was about to follow, confused, when a dark shadow moved onto the ground next to her. Revna swiftly ducked and rolled just as a sword came down in the spot she'd been standing. She pivoted, raising her blade just in time to make contact with her assailant's, the metal-on-metal reverberating through her bones.

Fenrir smirked down at her from between their crossed blades. "My turn."

TWELVE

FENRIR

WELL AFTER THE SUN crossed the highest point in the sky, Fenrir stood in a dark alcove of the training yard and watched Revna. Watching her move. Watching her fall into that single-minded tenacity. It was fucking entrancing.

Tyr challenged her to her limits, but he had centuries of experience. She was holding her own and learned through every mistake. Revna calculated Tyr's movements with a focus that could only come from years of walking that balanced knife-edge of being the hunter and the hunted.

Something about the way she moved, the way she fought, was worrisome. It was as if she would never stop, even at her own demise. And it tugged at something in Fenrir's chest.

He flinched when Tyr's sword came down hard atop her shield. She bore the weight of it, but he saw the way her arm trembled. Fenrir heaved a sigh and ran a hand down his face.

"Still keeping your distance, I see," Hel said from somewhere behind him in the shadows. Only years of witnessing her using the darkness as a cloak kept him from jumping as she appeared next to him. His sister walked through darkness as though every shadow was an extension of her being. Perhaps it was. Or perhaps it was because she'd spent years being buried and hidden, and chose to become allies with the darkness instead of its enemy.

"I'm letting her adjust. She's clearly angry with me." He gestured his chin toward her chaotic assault on Tyr. At Hel's pointed silence, he admitted, "I don't know where to begin. I don't know how to tell this new, yet familiar woman all that's happened. Does she need to know?"

"Only you can answer that. It depends on what she means to you. And what you want her to mean to you in the future." She nudged her shoulder against his arm. "But keeping her in the dark and expecting trust is like expecting a flame to survive without air."

Fenrir heaved another sigh, knowing, once again, that his sister was right.

"Cheer up, pup. It could be worse."

Fenrir ignored the taunt of a nickname, knowing she was trying to bait him as she had when they were younglings. "How so?"

"Hammer-head-thunder-nuts could have looked too closely and dragged her to Asgard. At least she's with us for now."

A small chuckle morphed into an irrepressible growl. *They could fucking try.* Frustration at the danger she was in, and all the answers he didn't have as to why and how Revna was there, made every muscle in his body taut. He was exhaling harshly through his nose when he felt a slight prick of his canines on his bottom lip.

"Easy, brother," Hel soothed, noticing the wolf coming to the surface. "We'll get to the bottom of this. If not, there's always binding."

Fenrir turned and shot Hel an incredulous look. She returned his look, her face totally serious.

He lifted his marked arms up. "I would never want this for Revna. For anyone."

"I know." Hel's face softened a bit as she reached out and squeezed his arm. "But there are other binds aside from the *Skyldu*."

"One is nothing more than a myth," he said, ignoring what she was implying.

Hel pushed a few braids over her shoulder and crossed her arms, facing the arena. "You know that was not the one I was referring to."

A Hjarta bind.

Fenrir didn't know what to say. He grunted dismissively and turned to watch Revna and Tyr. Dirt was a cloud around their feet, the clang of metal a song they danced in time to. Revna tossed aside her shield and Tyr followed suit. He rushed her again, but Revna spun, avoiding his reach. Tyr complimented her and Revna returned it with a nod and a smile.

Fenrir huffed out a sigh, forgetting Hel was standing right next to him.

Hel pinched his arm. "Go talk to her and quit brooding in dark corners—that's my specialty."

Fenrir frowned over at his irreverent sister. He sometimes had to remind himself that when they'd been separated, Hel was cast down among the unwanted dead. And she'd remained there, alone, until Fenrir had returned from Myddheim and made his deal with Odin. Those days after he was reunited with Hel and Jor were confusing and dark—until they realized that the people they had become while in captivity were not who they needed to be while together.

To most, Fenrir, Hel, and Jormun were monsters that should never have been created. A danger to the hierarchy of a robust and tainted pantheon. The Aesir feared their powers almost as much as they feared their shape-shifting abilities. When a whole group of people fear you, punish you, and degrade you for just existing—who is the real monster?

Hel reached for a sword hanging on the wall near her head, handing it to him, then gestured toward Revna and Tyr. "Go. It would do you both some good to take out some frustration on each other. Let weapons do the talking ... for now." She winked at him as she put special emphasis on *for now*.

"Don't you have better things to do than pester me? Like rule a realm?"

"This is far more interesting. *Go.*" Hel shoved him toward the middle of the training yard.

He nodded at a few others training, most too focused on their own fights to notice the wolf on a hunt. Tyr flicked his gaze toward Fenrir's pursuit and gave a small nod. Fenrir focused on the tail end of their conversation.

"... best of luck."

He was a few steps away from where Revna stood, her sword hanging loosely in one hand, shoulders slumping as Tyr started to walk away. He almost hesitated at the defeated sigh she released.

Almost.

He wouldn't allow her to pout.

Closing the short distant, he raised his sword up to catch the sunlight, and took a swing. Revna pivoted just in time, rolling away from where his sword carved through the air. Fenrir chased after her until she was on one knee, her blade connecting with his.

"My turn." He smirked down at her.

Revna, to his surprise, smirked back. His momentary confusion at her face contorting into an actual smile had his falling in disbelief. This awarded Revna with an opportunity to push up and then fall back to another roll, giving herself distance from Fenrir and his blade.

"The coward surfaces. Are you done avoiding me?" she asked as he circled her slowly.

Perhaps Fenrir should thank Tyr for expending some of Revna's energy, as she seemed quite content on standing in the middle of the training circle. She didn't move to attack him, just turned slowly as he made his way around, her eyes not leaving his.

"I'm not avoiding you." *Lie.* "I have other responsibilities than coddling a mortal woman. Like watching over this realm."

Revna rolled her eyes. "Forgive me, *mighty Wolf God*. I am but a poor mortal woman who doesn't understand the weight of having power beyond measure."

It was Fenrir's turn to roll his eyes at her obvious mockery. He took a quick lunge toward her, but she took a step back, leveling her sword at him.

Ah, so she was letting him come to her. That wouldn't do.

"Perhaps it's you who is avoiding me. You've been out here most of the day training with Tyr. You could have sought me out."

She smiled knowingly. "And how do you know where I've been today, wolf?"

Fuck. He'd backed himself into a corner while trying to goad her.

"A guess from how worn down you seem. Maybe I'm wrong. For all I know, you followed me here. I train daily with anyone who wants to." He lowered his voice, running the edge of his sword down hers until they were nearly sharing breath. "If you wanted to see me shirtless and sweating, you could have just asked."

Her scent flared, but he couldn't quite determine its meaning. Irritated, yes. But something else had her eyes dilating even as her gaze remained stony.

But then a wicked smile spread across her face.

"And panting like a good boy?"

Enough talking.

Fenrir charged, but instead of spinning away from him like he'd been watching her do, Revna lunged at him savagely. They were a storm of blades and counterattacks. He had come over here to talk, to maybe ease some of the tension and distrust between them. Instead, they'd dissolved into beasts aiming for each other's throats.

Everything else faded away. The only sounds he could hear were her heavy breathing and the clash of their blades. The only smell was the scent of her sweat and that sweet earthiness. With every push against each other, with every slight graze of their skin, Fenrir sank further in the heat of the fight.

He launched a rapid series of strikes that had her rolling below his blade. They were well out of the marked-out circle, but Fenrir didn't care. Didn't notice if others moved out of their way. Revna backed up to the wall of the arena, but just when Fenrir thought he had her cornered, she ducked, spun, and lunged until she was pushing him against the wall, their crossed blades between them.

"Well, look at that. You do pant *so* pretty." Revna purred, her breath mingling with his.

When the glint of victory shone in her eyes, Fenrir growled and shoved her away. No longer restraining himself, he attacked, backing her up until they were back in their designated circle.

Letting muscle memory take over, he leveled his blade with his shoulders, spun, and nicked Revna's upper arm. Blood welled immediately and ran down to the crook of her elbow. Fenrir's step faltered, heart dropping to his stomach at the realization of what he'd done. Revna seemed completely unfazed—not so much as glancing at the crimson trailing down her arm.

This wasn't what he'd wanted—this look of coldness, of anger. He'd thought he would rather have her anger than sadness, her contempt over her aloofness—but looking at her now, he realized he would rather suffer a blade in his gut than any of those things. Fenrir was looking at a woman who'd spent her entire life defending.

And he didn't want to be another monster for her to fight.

Movement from the corner of his eye had both him and Revna turning their heads. Hel had moved from her spot in the shadows to the edge of the marked-out circle. She flipped over a wooden bucket and sat on it.

"Just ensuring you two don't kill each other." She waved her hand in a gesture that said proceed.

Fenrir turned his eyes back to Revna. Her breath was still heavy, her body thrumming with energy. He could smell her sweat and blood—the former, he found, was not unappealing. She tilted her chin a bit in challenge, but Fenrir had already made his decision.

He tossed his sword on the ground at Revna's feet. "I yield."

He could tell she saw the concession for what it was—an apology.

"Don't you *dare*. Pick up your sword and fight me," she seethed.

"No, Revna."

Fenrir speaking her name had her advancing toward him, picking up his sword in her pursuit. She pointed her sword at his heart while offering his back, her hand gripping low on the hilt.

"Fight me." Her tone edged into something worse than anger.

Instead, he slowly went to his knees before her, watching her eyes flare in suspicion and then confusion. He lifted his hands and gently gripped her lower legs, pulling her closer. She took the swords and crossed them, placing both edges so that they pressed on either side of his neck, the coolness kissing his skin. Her breath came in erratic and harsh pants. Looking up at her like this, sweat dripping down her neck, pieces of hair falling from where it was pulled back, gray eyes burning—Fenrir would swear she was a Goddess in her own right. He was loath to remove his hands from her legs, but he let one drop, not wanting her to feel trapped. The other he kept so she wouldn't and couldn't pull away from this—from him.

"I'm sorry, Revna," he said, not taking his eyes off hers. He felt the blades press a little harder into his neck, still not enough to draw blood, but enough that he saw Hel stand from her perch on the bucket and take a couple steps toward them. Revna either didn't notice or didn't care.

"For?" she asked, barely above a whisper.

There were many things he could apologize for—*should* apologize for. He gripped her leg a little tighter.

"For not telling you who I was," he said, watching as her nostrils flared. "And for leaving without saying goodbye." *For leaving you*, he didn't add.

This time when the blade pressed firmer, he felt the sting of it breaking his skin. Her eyes went to the small drop of blood that rolled down his neck and she reared back as if she had been pulled by the hair, her scent souring. Fenrir let his hand drop from her leg, letting her put distance between them, but still didn't move from his knees.

Hel appeared to the left of Revna, lightly touching her arm, and said, "Why don't we go get that fixed up, and then I'll show you the cavern with the hot springs."

"What?" Revna asked, sounding far away.

"The cut on your arm. We wouldn't want it to fester."

Revna's eyes snapped to Hel's. Fenrir watched as they regarded each other, and wondered what memory his sister had unwittingly brought to the surface that had such a flash of surprise crossing Revna's face.

With a small nod, Revna tossed the swords down in front of Fenrir and turned, walking toward the path back to the main mountain hall. Hel reached a hand down to him and helped him stand, giving him a quick once over and a smile before chasing after Revna.

He watched as Revna's long black braid and graceful form disappeared around the corner on purposeful steps. His wolf half did not like her walking away from him. It made the muscles in his legs twitch, wanting to run, wanting to chase. He picked up the swords and used the bottom of his tunic to wipe the blades clean before returning them to the weapons rack.

Be patient.

Fenrir owed her that. In the mortal realm, never once had Revna shamed him for his initial anger and snarling threats. Instead, she'd given him gifts no one had ever given him before. Kindness and understanding. He didn't feel as if she owed him anything, even her forgiveness, but he also wouldn't stop trying to earn it.

Fenrir stood taller and felt a dangerous warmth flicker in his chest. Hope.

It was a start.

Thirteen

Revna

H EL LED REVNA TO a room well-stocked with healing supplies.
Cloth for bandages, tonics for pain and nerves, balms for soothing. Herbs and flowers hung from wooden racks in various stages of
drying. A low burning fire danced in the hearth, lighting and warming
the small space.

Ingrid would love this room. She would have loved to be in a place long
enough to establish such stores. But they'd kept busy on the road, and if
it wasn't necessary or couldn't fit in her healers traveling kit, she couldn't
take it. Thinking of her, of all the Maidens, chafed at the still raw wound
of losing them.

*Not lost—separated by Gods and realms and things beyond her con-
trol—but not lost.*

It was a strange kind of grief, and one she had felt before when Fenrir
took her place. Trying to find the strength to build a life, an existence,
with someone in your heart, but no longer at your side. A grief that felt
like teetering on the edge of darkness with one hand holding onto the
past, while the other is trying to let go. An ache had nested in her sternum
at the conjunction of so much feeling.

Revna shoved down the pain and focused on the things she *could* do.
She wanted to help the Maidens, help all of Myddheim. She believed Hel
when she said it wasn't them who played with her realm, but there were
many other Gods with the will and disposition to do so.

And there was the mystery of why she was here to begin with. Why had the boat brought her here and not to Asgard where all the previous sacrifices were said to have gone? Brought her right to …

"I'm sorry."

The words echoed in her mind over and over as Hel cleaned and bandaged her arm—the Goddess of Death taking gentle care of life.

In many ways, Revna had needed to hear those words, needed to know that there was some human emotion underneath the wolf. But when he'd finally said it, on his knee with blades at his throat, no less, she'd felt conflicted. Fenrir had said it with such sincerity that it made her stomach knot in confused gnarls. The grief she'd felt for him had morphed into something that resembled relief, but it still had the slight taste of deceit.

She understood that Fenrir's past and being were more complicated than her mortal mind could ever hope to understand. But she wasn't quite ready to let it go. Hanging on to the anger was easier than admitting the truth. That he had wounded her heart.

"Where are you right now?" Hel asked, calling Revna out of her darkening thoughts.

She looked down at the bandage on her arm and then over to the Goddess of Death. Ingrid would be impressed by Hel, Revna decided. Her arm was clean from dirt and blood and wrapped neatly in white cloth.

"May I ask you something?" she asked. Hel nodded. "Why are you being so kind to me? If it's because you feel like you owe me a debt for freeing your brother—"

Hel cut her off. "Not at all." She walked over to the table in the middle of the room and started putting away the leftover balm and bandages, tossing the bloody rag into the fire.

"Does it bother you? My *kindness*, as you put it."

Yes. The answer came easily to Revna, but she didn't say it aloud.

Hel nodded as if she could sense the unspoken response. "Is it because of who I am?"

"No, of course not." Revna jumped down off the table and went to the other side, facing the Goddess. "It's just ..." She sighed and looked up at the wooden beams on the ceiling. "In my world, kindness is rarely free. And after so many years of not accepting it because of what kind of repayment it would cost—it can be difficult for me."

She knew she wasn't explaining it very well. The feeling of suspicion and guilt that accompanied a kind gesture or favor. It had taken years of unlearning to trust the kindness that came from Ingrid, Gunnilda, Asta, and the rest of the Maidens.

"I understand," Hel said quietly. When sincere, those two words meant a great deal. Judging by the look on Hel's face, the way her eyes were bleeding into cloudiness as she stared down at the table, she was utterly sincere. "The Allfather said he was doing me a kindness when he sent me down to rule over all nine realms of the dead. It took me a very long time to realize that I didn't need to stay in that darkness—to realize that I could leave. I thought I would be forever buried, forever separated from life."

Revna nodded her head in encouragement. Of course she knew the legends and tales of the Gods. They were told and sang about by various skalds. But the only one who truly knew Hel's story was Hel, and Revna wanted to know her truth.

Revna leaned her hip on the table. "How did you figure it out?"

"In that darkness, I became a half-living thing. What they always thought me to be. I was angry, sad, and bitter. I reveled in punishing those who had done wrong to others." She gave a crooked smile. "I still do. But I realized I enjoyed it so much because I wasn't able to punish the people who'd wronged me."

"Odin."

"Yes." Hel shrugged, running her fingers along the wood grain on the table. "As well as my mother and father. I was even angry at my brothers for a time—all of my brothers."

Revna didn't miss the coldness in the Goddess's voice when she mentioned *all* of her brothers. Loki had two wives, after all.

"I hurt people because I was hurt. But I was able to leave Helheim because I finally *chose* to. Because I was tired of living with that darkness in my heart. I chose to finally accept those parts of me, while also choosing not to let it consume me."

Revna knew she was missing much of Hel's story, the hurts and the healing that compounded to create this version of the Goddess, the woman, standing in front of her. For now, she was grateful for the trust and vulnerability.

She gave Hel a small smile. "So, you just walked out the door, then?"

Hel laughed. "I kicked that fucking thing down."

Revna loosed an unrestrained laugh.

"And I created a bridge between the dead and living, the dark and light, for me to come and go as I please," Hel continued. "And I learned. Someone may cast you down, but they cannot keep you there."

A lump formed in the back of Revna's throat. Hadn't she said similar things to the Maidens and those they'd liberated over the years? Even when there were times when she'd barely believed it herself.

"Would you have done it?" At Revna's confused stare, Hel clarified. "Killed my brother?"

"No," she replied easily. "Like you said, I wanted to hurt because I'm hurt. It's complicated."

"For what it's worth, he is sorry. And he doesn't dole out apologies easily."

"And I don't forgive easily."

"Make him earn it." Hel gave Revna a wink, rounding the table and heading toward the door. "Come along, let me show you the hot springs."

⫶——⫶

When Hel had mentioned hot springs, Revna had imagined some murky reservoir of warm water in a small cave. Instead, she found herself in a cavernous space gently lit by that mesmerizing blue-green moss. Pools of various depths dotted the space, steam billowing off them in a gentle haze. Natural walls made of stone and stalagmites kept some pools more private than others, and she had found one in a back corner to give herself some solitude. After Hel showed her the space, she'd left, explaining she needed to return to her realm for a few days to assure all was well.

There was a family in the space when she and Hel had entered—a light elf with two rambunctious girls, whose constant laughter had Revna smiling. After a bit, Revna heard the man telling the girls it was time to go, and the cavern was quiet.

So quiet that thoughts came rushing back in with the absence of distraction. She sat with them for a bit, let the discomfort morph into a familiar pain. It was easier, sometimes, to sit in the pain rather than look for a way out of it. To know that no matter how sharp, she could withstand it, and it would pass in time.

The sound of boots slapping on wet stone had Revna sitting up a little straighter, reaching one arm toward where her daggers sat close by. She suddenly regretted getting fully naked and soaking for as long as she had. She wasn't ashamed of her nakedness, it just made defending herself a little more precarious with no protective layers.

She regretted her lack of clothing even more when Fenrir rounded the corner. Revna willed her face and body not to react—not to flinch or hide. Instead, she leaned back against the stone and let her gaze trail over him in a bored way. He was still wearing the leathers and dark tunic he'd worn in the training yard, but his bound hair now fell loosely to his shoulders. He carried no weapon, but that didn't surprise Revna with what lurked beneath his skin. She wondered when she would finally see the wolf. She found that the idea didn't scare her as much as it intrigued her.

Fenrir's nostrils flared and he cocked his head. She swirled her hands around in the milky-blue water, waiting for him to speak.

"May I join you so we can talk?" he asked, his voice quiet and deep.

"That depends. Will you make the place stink of wet dog?"

Fenrir laughed low in a way that had her stomach disobeying her orders to be bored and unaffected.

"Good to see you've retained your sharp wit and manners over the years." With that, he kicked off his boots and pulled his tunic overhead, exposing tanned skin, muscle, and ink. When he went to unlace his trousers, he looked up and cocked an eyebrow.

A blush crept up her neck. She hoped he would assume it was the heat of the pool. "It's nothing I haven't seen before, Fenrir. You included, in case you forgot."

He shrugged and pushed down his pants, stepping out of them one leg at a time. Revna tried her damnedest to keep her gaze locked on his face. She didn't want to give him the satisfaction, but her treacherous eyes couldn't ignore the intricate designs of inked vines that wrapped around his legs, disappeared behind his back, and peaked up around his shoulders. As he stepped into the water, she averted her gaze, pretending she needed to dip her head back and then ring out her hair.

Fenrir disappeared under the water for a moment and then resurfaced, pushing his hair out of his face. He leaned back against the stone edge, draping his arms out on either side as water ran down his chest in rivulets. The large pool suddenly seemed small with him in it. If she straightened out her legs, they would undoubtedly tangle with his.

"How's your arm?" he asked as he looked to the bandage around her bicep.

"Nothing more than a scratch." Revna started combing her fingers through her gnarled hair. Her bandaged arm was soaked, but Hel had assured her it would be alright, stating the waters contained some healing properties. Already she felt the deep ache in her tired muscles starting to alleviate.

"I'm sorry, Revna," he said again, getting right into the meat of it.

"You're saying that a lot today. I question whether it's sincere," she retorted.

He ran his fingers through the water, drawing her attention to the bands of ink on each of his lower forearms. "This is a separate apology from the one earlier. I apologize for the cut on your arm. That wasn't my intention."

Revna remained silent, baiting him. Steam from the heat of the pool billowed gently between them as Fenrir stared at her through the haze. Just when she was about to give in and accept his words, his impatience won out.

"Aren't you going to apologize for bleeding me?" Fenrir quirked an eyebrow.

"I would, but I feel no such remorse," she lied. Revna didn't like that she'd made him bleed at all. That she'd let emotion rise red within her until it had crumbled her control.

His answering chuckle sparked that red again. "I never thought a lie could smell so good."

"What?" she asked, confused.

"*Lies*, Revna." He inhaled deeply, his eyes flashing gold. "I can smell them. Among other things."

Fucking Wolf God.

She willed her emotions to remain tempered. "You would know all about lies, wouldn't you, *Fenrir*?"

He didn't so much as flinch. "I can't deny that I lied to you for my own benefit, for my own protection. But it was also for yours. Revealing myself to you would have only resulted in your running off because you thought I was mad. And we needed each other."

"In case you forgot, *wolf*, I freed you."

"And I taught you how to defend yourself. Based on what I saw today, you haven't forgotten our lessons."

"Don't flatter yourself. I trained with many warriors after you," Revna spat back.

He let out a low growl of frustration and tilted his head back. When he brought it back up, a few pieces of hair fell in front of his pulsing amber eyes.

Fenrir took his arms off the edges and leaned forward. "You drive me fucking mad. Why can't you just listen to what I have to say?"

Revna also leaned forward, until she could almost feel his breath on her face. "I'm listening, wolf. Please, continue with how you decided on what I could handle and what I deserved to know."

"Believe it or not, you were not my sole reason to get on that boat."

It took everything in her not to flinch. There was hurt, but there was also relief mingled in hearing that confession. She wondered what that smelled like.

"I needed to get back to my sister and brother, and to right many wrongs. The boat was an opportunity to return back to the realms of the Gods. And yes, it was also a way of saving you from your demise."

He cocked his head and gave a baiting smile, showing his teeth, which seemed longer. "Perhaps I shouldn't apologize. Perhaps you should be thanking me."

Revna stared at him for a long moment, trying to mentally work through all the answers she was finally being given, when his last words sank in. Thank him, should she? She looked into his haughty eyes—two could play that game.

She stood up languidly, a wicked smile playing at her lips. The water was to her waist leaving her top half completely exposed. To his credit, Fenrir's eyes didn't stray from hers. She saw his nostrils flare, though, inhaling her scent, and his corded throat swallowed.

"Would you like me to get on my knees and thank you, wolf?" She took one step toward him, then another, the water sloshing around her, until he had to tilt his head back to keep his eyes on her face. From this angle, she knew that he was likely seeing the curve of her breasts.

Fenrir rose slowly, water sliding down his chest and stomach, until it was Revna's turn to tilt her head back to look up at him. Her eyes flicked down to where she had nicked him earlier with the sword and found only the faintest of pink lines.

"There is no need to kneel," he said, leaning until his lips nearly grazed her ear. "I am not a God one bows to. I am one you run from."

She pulled back to regard him. There was a glint of challenge in his eyes, a tension in his jaw. As if he was testing her. To see if she feared him. A muscle flickered in his cheek as he stared her down.

Maybe the God of Destruction had his own monsters.

"I run from nothing," she said, trying to keep her tone and breath even, and only half-succeeding.

He gave a rueful smile. "We shall see."

Revna gave a small roll of her eyes and went to turn her face away when his hand snapped up and gripped her chin. She tried to pull away in surprise, but he held fast—not enough to hurt, but enough to let her know she wasn't going anywhere.

"You and I have a lot to work through, but mark my words, Revna, we are going to work through it." He released his grip on her chin, but Revna could still feel the rough heat of his skin on hers. She held his gaze, knowing her eyes were likely blazing. "Now why don't you go put on some clean clothes and meet me in the hall for dinner."

Before she could think, or worse, act, on the feelings rising in her body, she turned and stepped up out of the pool, her backside on full display. She took her time twisting and ringing her hair out, feeling his eyes burning on the ink that decorated her back. After bending over to pull her pants back on, arching as she pulled the tunic overhead, she turned to see him still standing in the water. This time, the Wolf God had his fists clenched at his side, his gaze staring off to the side.

Revna was strong and disciplined and patient, but by the Gods, she couldn't help when her gaze dipped to where the water met his lower abdomen. Her gaze caught on the muscle dips leading to what lurked below the waterline, just for a moment, before training them away. Before she could let what she'd assume would strongly resemble desire stain her scent, she picked up her boots and the belt with her daggers.

"Perhaps another time. I'm tired," she said in response to his almost forgotten request to join him for dinner.

Finally, he allowed his eyes to come back to her body, her face. He sat back into the spring, retaking his position with his arms draped over its natural edge.

He gave her a smile that was pure male arrogance. "Rest well, Revna."

She didn't say another word as she turned and made her way back through the cavernous space. It felt a lot like running.

FOURTEEN

FENRIR

ON NIGHTS WHEN HE couldn't sleep, Fenrir longed to be able to shift to his wolf form and run under the watchful moonlight. Nights where he wished he could get lost in the sensation of running on the loamy earth and breathe in the scent of the trees. After his evening with Revna, he was on the edge of doing just that—deal with Odin be damned.

His body felt coiled and restless as he lay in his bed, turning over every moment since Revna's arrival. His plan had been to find her and ask her to join him for dinner. To talk. To have it out and hopefully move on. He should have guessed she wouldn't make it easy.

But, oddly, a warm sense of pride flooded his chest every time she went toe-to-toe with him. And he found he was willing to cut himself on her sharp edges until she was ready.

Her back. The ink markings ...

The scars on her skin were not new to him, but the ink that went from her neck to the base of her spine were new. And he couldn't look away from them. As a slave, Revna's master had branded her by burning a mark on the back of her neck. The scar was barely visible now, covered with inked runes of protection, strength, and the symbol of Freyja, all dark and entwined on her pale neck. Not surprising that she'd chosen Freyja, given the Goddess's story.

Fenrir had looked his fill before she'd pulled her tunic back on. From the neck, roots of what looked like a tree branched out and then braided together down the line of her spine, strengthening her.

It was beautiful and heartbreaking to look at—knowing she had sat through days and days of breaking, bleeding, and healing. A woven tribute to her own past, present, and future.

Fenrir saw such strength in Revna. On every scar, every soft curve ...

He ran a hand down his face and rose from his bed, pulling on a pair of loose trousers and tunic, but left his feet bare and hair loose, wanting to feel as unrestricted as possible. Low torch light cast shadows on the stone as he walked down the hall. Tyr's snores echoed from outside the thick door, but no sound came from Revna's. Either she slept like the dead or she was lying in wait, scheming for her next attack. He inhaled the scent of her still lingering just outside her door. Who she had become over the last nine years was still veiled in stubbornness, but pieces were starting to shine through. He found himself wanting to know everything—wanting to know *her*. He raised his fist to her door, preparing to knock, but thought better of it and walked on.

Hel had returned to Helheim for a few days to ensure all was well with her realm and her appointed guardians. How his sister could slide back and forth between the living and dead never ceased to amaze him.

Thinking of Hel, Fenrir knew where his current wanderings were going to end up. He left the keep and made his way through the woods, feeling the dirt underfoot, and stopping to greet some trees along the way. They thrummed under his touch, awaiting command.

Growing up, shifting into his wolf form had been as natural as breathing. Sometimes he'd spent months in that form just to anger his mother. Far less easy it was once he'd fully stepped into his powers, possessing a kind of earth magic that allowed him to manipulate the trees, earth, and other things that grew. That magic was wild and willful, and demanded respect. After long years of struggling to control it, he had let go and allowed it to be a part of him, an extension of his soul, like his wolf. Something to work in partnership with.

Hel could split herself in two—a draugr form that was half-rotted and terrifying. She could cast it out from herself to kill with ease, or to guide someone to Helheim. Her power lay in darkness.

Aside from shifting in his serpent form, Jormun's power lay within the waters. Tides, waves, and whirlpools were his to manipulate, though Fenrir suspected that Jormun had never truly revealed the capacity of his powers.

Coming down the path of the cliffside, Fenrir looked toward the fjord where Tyr had found Revna—where Jor had dumped her. The waters were still, the moon reflecting off its surface. The rocks on the shore dug into his feet as he made his way to the water's edge.

Fenrir squatted and dipped his fingers in the water. "Jor."

For a moment, nothing happened. Everything was eerily still. The trees and the water holding their breath in anticipation. Slowly, large yellow eyes broke the surface and narrowed on Fenrir.

"I want to talk to you." Fenrir took a couple steps back and sat down, draping his arms over his bent knees.

Jormun huffed, sending a slight mist in his direction.

"Will you *please* join me, brother?" Fenrir pleaded mockingly, which earned him a further narrowing of Jormun's eyes.

His brother disappeared under the surface, and Fenrir thought perhaps he was not in the mood to talk tonight. Then, a quick splash and thrash of his serpent tail had water soaking Fenrir completely. When he wiped the water out of his face, Jormun stood naked up to his knees in the water, scowling at Fenrir.

"What do you want?" Jor asked, crossing his arms.

Fenrir scoffed. "Good to see you, too." His brother only raised a pale eyebrow. "Why don't you come sit with me and get that thing out of my face?" Fenrir said, gestured to his all-too-visible cock.

Jormun lifted one side of his mouth. "Jealous, brother?"

Fenrir feared the day that Revna and Jormun met. He wouldn't stand a chance against their combined verbal assault.

"I didn't come down here to have a pissing contest with you."

Jormun made his way to sit next to Fenrir on the rocky shore, the smell of fresh ocean air wafting off him in great waves. There was no other scent, no mixture of earth, and that concerned Fenrir.

"I'm curious, do you lift your leg while pissing in your human form as well?"

"Oh, *fuck* off." Fenrir shook his head, ridding his hair of excess water.

"Mongrel."

"Worm."

Jormun gave a low chuckle and they sat there for a few breaths, just enjoying the semi-easy moment between them. It wasn't always so.

They'd butted heads growing up, one beast of the earth, the other the sea. Fenrir sometimes had a hard time believing they came from the same womb. Hel's skin and hair were a rich brown paired with amber eyes like his own. Fenrir's skin wasn't as rich as Hel's, but Jormun had gotten all his features from their father, save for the hair.

Fenrir glanced over at his brother's profile, wondering at the stark contrast yet again. Jor had white hair and lightly tanned skin. White eyebrows sat above white lashes, framing yellow-slitted eyes that were as cunning as the God who'd fathered them.

Jormun looked nothing like his siblings, and Fenrir had always wondered if that was a sore spot.

After some time in tentative peace, Fenrir broke the silence. "Do you recall tossing a woman on the shore a few days ago?"

"Yes. Why?"

"Any idea where she came from? She mentioned something about arriving through a cave system."

Jormun looked over at him, slitted eyes unreadable. "She is mortal."

"And how do you know that?"

Jormun scoffed. "Please, you can smell it on them."

Fenrir repressed an unexpected growl at the thought of his brother smelling Revna. He reached for a rock next to him, gripping it firmly. "Did you follow her here from Myddheim?"

Deep waters flowed through all nine realms, and Jormun was able to pass through each in his serpent form. He couldn't enter Helheim or surface in Myddheim, though. As a youngling, he had tried, but some barrier had made him recoil and become sick for days—though their mother had kept encouraging him to try again, stating pain was necessary for greatness.

Jormun remained quiet, and likely devising a way to avoid the question. Which made Fenrir all the more suspicious. After a few moments of silence, Jormun spoke.

"Mother sends her regards."

Fenrir's whole body reacted to the mention of their mother—muscles tensing, jaw clenching, stomach twisting. The giantess witch still lived in a remote cave system in Jotunheim, but Fenrir never felt the need to see her. Why Jormun still did was as concerning as it was frightening. Her hold on his brother had his canines elongating.

"She wants to know why you haven't visited her in all your *travels* to Jotunheim."

Fenrir crushed the stone in his hands, crumbling it with the strength of his frustration. He wouldn't have this conversation with his brother again—especially when Hel wasn't here to mediate. He took a couple of deep breaths and felt his teeth slowly retract.

"You are always welcome here, brother." Fenrir tried. "You can have your own room, come and go as you please—"

"I have my own place." Jormun interrupted.

And no one knew where it was—neither he nor Hel could get Jormun to tell them where he dwelled. Fenrir had worried that his brother spent too much time in his other form, retreating to a dark deep-sea cave, isolating himself from everything. But worse yet was the idea that Jormun was staying with their mother when not traversing the seas.

"The woman that you tossed ashore was the woman from Myddheim who released me from my bonds," Fenrir said, navigating the conversation back to the problem at hand.

Jormun didn't so much as blink a reaction, not the way that Hel had when she'd found out.

"Odin will want her."

Another rock crumbled under Fenrir's grip. He spoke through gritted teeth. "What makes you say that?"

Jormun stood, walked back to the water, and started wading in. "She is a sacrifice from Myddheim. A loose thread of fate he will want to control—as he does with all things that threaten his carefully constructed existence." Once the water reached his hips, he turned back to Fenrir, the shock of white hair like a beacon on the dark water. "Maybe the question isn't *how* she got here, but *why*."

With that, Jormun dove back into the fjord, shifting and writhing in the waters before disappearing completely. Waves lapped the shore reaching Fenrir's feet, but he was frozen in place. His brother's words had struck a chord, and he was concocting a plan.

Fate.

Fenrir stared at the spot where Jormun had disappeared under the water. For all his cunning disposition, his brother's transparency was offensively obvious. It was clear he was not being entirely truthful. If

Odin knew Revna was here, he would have found her already. And if Odin had called forth a sacrifice from Myddheim, Fenrir would have known. He gripped his hands, making the muscles on his inked forearms flex.

Someone else called forth the boat. Sending Revna right to Fenrir.

The thought had cold dread prickling along his skin.

He was tempted to call his brother back and demand honesty, but nothing good ever came from pushing Jormun. Instead, Fenrir made his way back to the keep and went right to Tyr's room. His friend opened the door moments after he knocked softly, pants haphazardly pulled up.

"Everything alright?" Tyr asked sleepily.

"Get dressed and prepare for a journey," Fenrir said. "We're going to see the Sisters."

Fifteen

Revna

WITH HER BEDROOM DOOR open just enough to let a small thread of light in, Revna couldn't see Fenrir, but she could hear him. She'd been awake and pacing her room, since hearing steps she'd somehow known were his pause outside her door earlier. She cracked the door when she had heard the light knocking sound.

Fenrir spoke with Tyr in low tones about going to see *the sisters*. Revna searched her brain for who the sisters could be, but too many possibilities left her dizzy.

The sound of Tyr's door closing and Fenrir retreating down the hall spurred her into action. Revna thought about opening her door and calling after the Wolf God, demanding to know where he was going, but her scheming half won out. Her blood still hadn't cooled since their moment in the hot spring, and she needed something to pursue, to occupy her mind.

The clothes she'd been wearing when the boat arrived had been returned to her clean and dried, and putting them on felt comforting. The fire had long burned out, the ash and embers cooled. Revna dipped her fingers into the black soot and ran them down her face, the ceremony of it calling the warrior in her to the surface.

Prepared as she could be, Revna crept back to the crack in her door and waited. As the moments passed, she began to question whether this was a wise idea. Following two well equipped Gods into the unfamiliar with unknown obstacles and traps lying in wait. A voice that sounded like Ingrid scolded her in her mind for recklessness, giving her pause.

But she hadn't become commander of Myddheim's largest and fiercest group of shield maidens by hesitating. When she heard Tyr's door open and shut, she waited a few heartbeats before pursuing his retreating steps.

The halls were lit with low-burning torches that created moving shadows. Revna kept to the darkness, following sound as much as she could. A light breeze slithered through the stone halls, making the torches hiss. She kept her footsteps light as she trailed Tyr, hoping to remain unheard. He slowed, and a second pair of footsteps sounded from a hall to Revna's right. Blood pounded in her ears as she searched for a place to hide. There was an open window to her left that looked just big enough. She crawled up onto the ledge and looked down ... and down.

Fuck.

To each side of the window was a small ledge, just wide enough for her to stand on. Hopefully. With no other option, Revna climbed up on the windowsill and stepped out onto the narrow stone. Her fingers gripped painfully against the uneven rock, nails digging in the divots. She couldn't see what lay below, so she kept her breath steady and deep, her grip unrelenting.

The footsteps stopped. Low voices started speaking.

"Should we tell Revna we're leaving?" Tyr asked, and she decided that the God wasn't all that bad.

"I informed Austri and he will tell her in the morning," Fenrir's voice rumbled. "I would take her with us—in fact, we should. To see what the sisters would say ..."

"But?" Tyr pushed.

"I met with Jor earlier." Fenrir sighed and she could practically see the way his jaw likely twitched. "He got in my head about Odin and ..."

The rest of the conversation was carried away on the wind and with their retreating steps. Her arms trembled as she carefully moved herself back to the safety of the open sill. Seeing that the hall was clear, she lowered herself onto the floor and steadied her breath before hurrying down a set of stairs.

Revna followed them down halls and stairs until they came to a tunnel, and the draft of the wind became stronger. Vines crawled on the ceiling and moss lit the space, eating away the shadows and her hiding spots. She pressed herself to the wall and continued her pursuit. A cool breeze rushed over her skin, leaving a wake of bumps as the tunnel came to an end and dumped out into the woods. The moon shone bright, though only partially full, and she could see Fenrir and Tyr disappearing into the bracken.

Creeping through solid stone halls was one thing, but trampling through unknown woods where one misstep could have her snapping a twig and alerting them to her presence was risky. But she could not sit idly in the keep until the end of her days, hoping someone would give her the answers to aid the family she left behind.

Even in the ill-lit night, Revna could discern Fenrir from Tyr. Fenrir moved quietly and carefully, whereas Tyr moved without caution or restraint, making enough noise to easily follow.

Something about Fenrir's back, seeing him walking away from her, aggravated the scar of him leaving all those years ago. She hated that the memory—that *he*—still had such an effect on her. It would still sneak up in the most unwelcome ways, leaving her body unwilling to cooperate with her mind.

She wouldn't be left behind again.

The moon gave her just enough light to watch her step, but the extra caution was slowing her down, and she feared losing them. Her clothing snagged on branches and sliced her skin as she tried to stay in the thick cover of the underbrush. A strong breeze had Fenrir stopping in his tracks, and Revna ducked behind a large tree.

"What is it?" Tyr asked.

She heard the slight shuffling of feet but didn't dare look.

"I smelled ..." Fenrir trailed off. "It's nothing. Let's go."

Fucking Wolf God. He could smell her.

Revna redirected her path so she was no longer up wind. Hopefully.

Up ahead she could see a faint blue glow, unlike the moss, and more vibrant than the moon. A stone path led up to a sheer side of a cliff. Carved into said cliff was ...

By the Gods.

An arched gate faintly aglow was surrounded by various runes, none of which she knew the meaning of. They were not of her world.

Squatting behind a boulder, she watched as Fenrir and Tyr approached the arch. Reaching out a hand, Fenrir tapped nine runes in succession. Revna watched in awe as the stone faintly shifted and glimmered, the nine runes he touched shining brighter than all the rest. Then, they walked through the stone.

Revna stood quickly from her squat; mouth slightly ajar. Her feet started carrying her up the stone path before her mind could fully comprehend what had just happened. It was a kind of gate, not unlike the one she had come here through.

Maybe she could go back ...

The thought went from sweet to sour in her stomach. The thought of returning to her life in Myddheim had sent a surge of warmth through her body, but Fenrir had said there was no way back, and she trusted his word. She didn't know why—had every reason not to—but she did.

There were so many reasons she wanted to go back to Myddheim, so many people she wanted to return to. But fate had been pulling her down this path her entire life. She'd freed herself, found Fenrir, unbound him, lost him, and found him again. There were so many questions and she was tired of waiting for answers. Tired of waiting for the Gods, fate, whatever controlling power was playing with her, and not knowing why.

She reached up, tapping the nine runes in the same pattern Fenrir had, and held her breath as she walked through the stone.

⇥——⇤

Cold.

A cold that had all her muscles clinging to her bones.

The landscape was rocky, but bits of green peaked through the gentle layer of frost and snow. Harsher than what she'd observed back in Vanaheim.

Revna combed through her mind to figure out where she was, what she remembered about the other eight realms outside of Myddheim. She couldn't be in Asgard, as there were no gleams of gold and vast palaces in sight. It wasn't Myddheim, because everything was larger and more severe. Nothing was aflame, so Muspelheim, the land of fire beings, seemed unlikely. Tales of Helheim and the dark underground world did not match what she was currently seeing.

Unless...

Revna's blood froze at the possibility that she may be in Niflheim—a land of ice, fog, and mist, where lost souls dwelled. Perhaps her mortal form couldn't handle going through the gate, and now she would wander eternally.

But looking around, she didn't see any ice or fog. In fact, the landscape seemed vibrant and alive. Even the frost glistened in the rising warmth of the sun.

The only other options were Nidavellir—home of the dwarves, Alfheim—home of the light elves, or Jotunheim—home of the giants.

Quieting her breath, Revna listened for signs of Fenrir and Tyr. Birds were singing hello to the morning sun, disrupting her ability to listen. She looked to the ground and found two sets of footprints leading away from the stone wall with the gate. Revna turned to look back from where she'd come, and hesitated. In her compulsivity and eagerness to seek answers, she'd never thought about how she would get back.

Ingrid's voice sounded in her mind again with a smug, *"I told you so."*

Revna waved the thought away. Nothing she could do now but see it through. She withdrew her axe from its strap on her back and started a light jog, following the tracks out of the woods into a clearing. Straight ahead were the two Gods. Instead of taking the path right across the clearing, she kept to the wooded edges but moved quickly. She kept that pace for a bit, wondering where they were heading.

They passed no living beings, no villages. Just giant rocks, trees, and bits of snow. She could see black snow-capped mountains in the distance, and she hoped they wouldn't be traveling all the way there on foot.

BOOM.

Revna froze and crouched behind a tree as she felt the ground shake beneath her feet.

She looked ahead to where Fenrir and Tyr had also stopped, but they seemed unconcerned as they lifted their hands in surrender.

"Back so soon, mutt?" a loud, deep voice asked from somewhere she couldn't see.

"Just passing through, Jalmir," Fenrir responded.

"The Aesir are not welcome here," Jalmir, as Fenrir had called him, replied. "Nor do we appreciate others sneaking into our realm unin-vited."

Tree branches cracked and snapped overhead before another loud boom sounded from just behind Revna. She turned and saw a boulder land, sending chunks of dark earth in every direction.

The realization of what realm she'd followed the Gods into struck her, stalling her breath.

Jotunheim—land of the giants.

"Jalmir, you know that I'm not one of the Aesir. And you know Tyr left long ago. We mean you no harm—I swear to it."

"Lies," Jalmir spat, his voice sounding closer and louder. "You lie like your cunning father."

The ground shook again, leaving Revna slightly disoriented. She moved out from behind the tree and went to duck behind a boulder.

"You took my brother from me!" Jalmir yelled, becoming more enraged. "You sneak into our realm, and you strike us down where we sleep!"

"What—" Fenrir started before being cut off by another crash. "Enough!"

She peeked out from behind her giant rock just in time to see Fenrir climb atop one that had been tossed at him. But instead of facing forward, his body was angled back toward Revna.

Shit.

"Jalmir, I don't know what you speak of, but I would be happy to discuss it when you aren't trying to crush me. What happened to your brother? What happened to Spjut?"

"I want no more of your lies! We know you killed him! We know the whispers of Asgard." The tree branches snapped and groaned overhead, making Revna duck to protect her face from the shards. "I will have payment in blood. And I know just where to get it."

The cracking of branches and pounding footsteps sounded from near Revna. She gripped her axe in both hands and was preparing to fight when a giant—an actual giant—crashed through the trees, running right toward her. The Jotunns who resided in Vanaheim were large, yes, but most were not much taller than Fenrir. What Revna was preparing to fight, however, gave meaning to the name of giant.

Jalmir was a whole body-length taller than her, packed with muscle, and covered in blueish-gray skin. He snarled as he lunged for her, and on instinct, she swung her axe, striking his hand as it reached for her. The Jotunn made a sound of pain, backing up a bit, affording her the chance to raise her axe overhead and throw it, burying itself into where his shoulder met his chest, unbudging.

As she withdrew her twin daggers and prepared to strike again, an arrow pierced her side.

"NO!"

She heard a distant roar and felt the earth tremble. The edges of the world blurred, and her very blood was burned cold with a cracking ice.

She couldn't see, could barely hear, couldn't feel her feet underneath her body. And as she collapsed, she called out one name.

"*Fenrir ...*"

Sixteen

Fenrir

S HE THOUGHT SHE COULD stalk a wolf?

Her scent had invaded his nose the moment he'd met Tyr in the hall. Fenrir knew she was following them, and he'd wanted to see how far she was willing to go. He'd caught her scent again outside the keep, but had chosen, still, to let her have her freedom to follow if she so chose. He'd never thought she'd make it through the gate, but he should have known.

She was clever, persistent, and fucking maddening.

And now ...

"NO!" he roared, the ground shaking, his teeth elongating.

"Fenrir ..." she called lightly.

There were moments in the time since Odin had bound him that Fenrir had lost his temper and barely withheld shifting into his wolf form. But nothing compared to this. Nothing compared to seeing Revna get shot with an arrow and then collapsing.

Let me out, the wolf clawed at his throat as blistering rage coursed through his blood.

Fenrir called to the earth, called to the trees—roots and branches eager to do his bidding. He sprinted toward Revna, throwing up a barrier of root and bramble between her and the next arrow. Absently, he saw Tyr withdraw his sword and sprint toward Jalmir and the unknown archer.

But he wouldn't reach them in time. Not before Fenrir was through with them.

Hel would be receiving a new resident soon.

Roots shot out from the earth, wrapping the giant tightly, until Fenrir heard him gasp as the air was squeezed from his lungs. He held the Jotunn there, kept him on that edge as he reached where Revna collapsed.

Fenrir gently gathered her in his arms and looked to where the arrow had pierced her side. It was a clean shot, the arrowhead just poking through her back, but the smell of her blood was off. She was unconscious, skin pale and clammy. Carefully as he could, he tore her shirt in preparation to remove the arrow.

Blood drained from his face as he exposed her skin. There was blood, but it was crystallizing. As if it were freezing her body from the inside. Dark blue veins branched out from the wound, turning her skin to ice.

"Tyr!" Fenrir yelled. He could hear the panic in his own voice.

Moments later his friend knelt next to where he sat with Revna in his lap and hissed. "Fen …"

"I know." He tried to take calming breaths, but his body was shaking in anger and fear. So much fear.

Revna was shot with a poisoned arrow—a poison that was born to the land of Jotunheim. A mere scrap of a blade dipped in it would make the strongest God sick. And it had been shot inside of Revna. Through her.

"We need to remove the arrow. I'll hold her if you can break off the end and then pull it through," Fenrir said. He didn't want to let go of her.

"I don't know if that's—"

"The entire arrow is coated in the poison. If we leave it inside of her, it will only spread faster."

Tyr nodded. "Once it's out, I can heal her just enough to slow the poison, but I fear healing the wound fully with the poison still inside of her. It will live in there and continue to corrupt. We need the antidote."

A strangled cough had both their heads turning toward the source. Jalmir was still wrapped in roots and struggling for breath. "The other?"

"Disappeared." Tyr moved, getting ready to snap the longer end of the arrow. Fenrir gripped the base closest to her skin and gave Tyr a nod. Revna's eyes flew open as Tyr broke off the end and she gasped for breath.

"I've got you, Revna," he reassured her, thanking the runes that she was awake. "Tyr needs to pull it out now. It's going to hurt, but you are so fucking strong and stubborn. Be stubborn, my *máni*."

The name slipped from his tongue easily, pulled from a long-ignored alcove in his body.

Fenrir could tell she was disorientated. She kept giving her head little shakes as if she could rid herself of the feeling. Stubborn as ever, she tried to sit up and look at the wound.

He gently grabbed her face and tilted it to his. "No, look at me. Keep your eyes on mine."

She didn't fight him. Instead, she sharpened and focused her eyes on his. Fenrir met her intensity and didn't falter as Tyr began to pull, and Revna's eye filled with tears. He knew the pain she was feeling was begging her to let go, begging her to fade so she could drift from the present, but she held on.

Fenrir moved his hand so his fingers were on the back on her neck, his thumb caressing her jaw. He heard the squelch of blood as one of Revna's hands shot up and gripped his forearm. Tears were spilling over now in a steady flow, creating trails through the black soot on her face. Her breath came in short, restricted gasps.

"So fucking strong," he whispered to her.

"Hang on, fierce one," Tyr warned. "This last little bit is going to hurt. The poison is freezing you from the inside and holding fast to the arrow."

Revna gave a little nod, eyes never leaving Fenrir's. "Do it."

Tyr pulled as gently as he could. Fenrir tightened his grip on her neck as her nails dug into his forearm.

When she could no longer contain it, she screamed in agony.

And Fenrir knew in that moment that he would rather take every arrow meant for her than see her in this much pain again.

"It's out," Tyr confirmed.

Fenrir gazed down and saw the edges of the wound were a dark blue before Tyr covered it up with a bit of shredded cloak. With the arrow out, blood flowed effortlessly from the wound, the red darkening to near black.

Revna's eyes began to droop, her breath slowing.

"Don't you fucking dare," he warned her, deepening his voice. She made a noise of protest, shaking her head. Fenrir could see the fight happening in her eyes, could see the way she struggled to stay. The grip on his forearm loosened and tightened as she fought the painful poison.

With the flow of blood staunched, Tyr placed his hand gently atop the wound. Revna flinched as his powers sparked with lambent light. It knitted the wound nearly closed, though the veins remained dark blue and creeping. Tyr was right, they needed the antidote. They needed ...

Damn all the nine realms.

They needed Fenrir's mother.

The witch lived almost a day's journey from here in a remote cave system. But that wouldn't be a gentle or easy journey for Revna.

"Tyr, I need you to go find my mother and convince her to come to us." Fenrir said, knowing the cost would be worth it to save her.

Tyr, being who he was, didn't even question Fenrir. "Tell me where to go and what to say, and I won't rest until I reach her and bring her back."

The journey would be an arduous one, and Fenrir didn't know what kind of spells his mother still had in place to ward off unwanted visitors.

Not that they'd worked before. He gave careful instructions, warning Tyr to be wary. Convincing her to come would be the hardest part.

Fenrir looked away for something to give to Tyr to prove that Fenrir needed her. His eyes settled on the removed arrow. He gently shifted Revna so he could grab the arrow, and then he sliced his own forearm.

"Fucking runes, Fen!" Tyr chided him.

Fenrir handed Tyr the broken arrow, now with his blood on the tip and the poison in his veins. It was a small cut, and it would take hours for the poison to take root in his body. "She'll be able to sense my blood and the poison within." For all his mother's faults, she still loved her monstrous children and would do anything to protect them—just not from herself or their father.

"Help me get her into a cave with a fire, and then be swift." Fenrir stood, cradling a barely conscious Revna in his arms. She hissed when he shifted her, and he watched her eyelids flutter. Every sound, every movement she made had the fist on his heart twisting in both panic and relief.

He scanned the area. No sign of the Valkyrs, Hel, or Freyja's boar—no one to claim the dead or dying. They still had time.

"What about him?" Tyr gestured toward a now unconscious Jalmir.

Fenrir growled. "He stays."

The look on Fenrir's face must have said all Tyr needed, because he turned and made his way toward the small cluster of caves nearby.

Revna began shivering in Fenrir's arms.

"Hold on, Revna. I'll get you warm," he promised her.

After Tyr confirmed the caves were unoccupied, Fenrir entered the one most closed off from the elements and set Revna down as gently as he possibly could, leaning her against the stone wall. He quickly ripped off his cloak and laid it on the stone floor. Tyr shrugged his off as well and threw it to Fenrir.

"I'll go gather wood and get a fire started," Tyr said.

Fenrir nodded absently as he squatted in front of Revna and gently placed his hands on her knees. Her lips were tinged blue and her heart beat ravenously through the skin on her neck.

"We need to keep you warm. The poison in your blood"—*our* bloods, he didn't say—"will fill your veins with ice. We need to keep it thawed as much as possible."

Her gray eyes were blinking rapidly, but she gave a subtle nod, acknowledging his statement.

"I'm going to take my clothes off, and then yours, and keep you warm until help arrives. Is that alright?"

Please say it's alright.

She nodded again, more eagerly this time. The corner of his mouth tipped into a small smile. He knew her eagerness was the promise of getting warm and not that their naked bodies would be entangled, but he let himself enjoy the small moment of want. Even in this way.

He kicked off his boots, pulled his tunic overhead, unlaced his trousers, and then turned to Revna. Gently as he could, he undressed her. Boots, weapon straps, daggers. He had to tug her pants a bit, causing her to give a low whimper. He whispered apologies to her over and over with each slight movement of her body.

When only her tunic remained, he paused. He didn't want her to have to extend her arms overhead, so he grabbed one of his blades.

Her eyes were barely open, and her head rolled a bit from side to side. "I'm going to cut your tunic off and then we'll get you under a nice fur cloak next to a fire."

Another small nod.

The sleeves were removed first, the thread at the shoulder seams ripping easily. He pulled the bottom taut, running the blade right up the front, revealing a leather band with straps laced in the front covering her breasts.

"Fucking runes, woman." He ran the knife right through the leather laces and severed the straps. "Next time don't make it so difficult for me to get you warm."

"Th-there won't be a n-next time," she muttered, eyes closed.

Fenrir chuckled and lifted a hand to touch her forehead, then the skin at the base of her throat. The skin on her head was burning hot, but the rest of her body was cold as ice. He could still smell her under the poison and blood, but it was muted.

"This next part is going to be uncomfortable," he warned as he lifted her to move her over to the cloak. She sucked in a breath and gripped at his shoulder. He was setting her down gently when Tyr returned with a giant pile of wood. Fenrir set Revna down as gently as he could and got under the second cloak with her, pressing his body to hers.

She sighed as he wrapped his arms around her, nuzzling her face into his chest. Fenrir's body stiffened for a moment, overcome by the conflicting nature of the warm and cool parts of her body, but more overcome that he didn't mind it at all.

Tyr stacked the wood and used a flint and some brush to coax the flame. He moved a large pile of wood right above Fenrir's head for him to easily grab to keep the fire burning throughout the cold night.

When Tyr was finished preparing the cave, leaving the little supplies that they had, he looked over to where Fenrir held a shivering Revna.

"Don't die while I retrieve your mother. Hel would kill me, and then we'd just be two idiots being bossed around by her in Helheim," Tyr joked, but Fenrir could hear the underlying worry. "Do you need anything else?"

"No, thank you." Revna gave a larger tremble and a soft whimper. "*Go.*"

Tyr nodded and then ran out of the cave with nothing else said.

The cave became still. He could hear the crackle of the fire and the chattering of Revna's teeth—the sound filling him with dread. The poison wouldn't hit him for hours, possibly even a full day, but he worried he wouldn't be able to stay conscious to tend to Revna. He needed to keep her awake as long as possible.

"Revna?"

"H-hmm?"

He stroked a hand up and down her back, feeling the edges of raised skin at the base of her neck. "Tell me about your time on Myddheim? Tell me about the group of warriors you started?"

For a moment, he thought she'd fallen asleep. He pulled back a little so he could look down at her face and watched as several tears escaped the corners of her eyes, rolling over the bridge of her nose, and pooled on his bicep.

"I hate this," she whispered.

"What do you hate?"

"Fe-feeling weak. Vulnerable."

He removed his hand from her back and used his finger to wipe the moisture from her face. "Do you remember the state I was in when you found me in the cave?"

"This isn't th-the s-same." Her eyes squeezed shut as a large tremble wracked her body.

"Perhaps not. But accepting help is not a sign of weakness, Revna."

She didn't respond, but she opened her eyes again and stared at the dip at the base of his throat. No good would come from arguing with her right now. He knew he couldn't get her to see that she was so strong it terrified him almost as much as it amazed him.

"Tell me about your group of warriors," he prompted again.

"Not j-just me. Ingrid, too." She huffed a small laugh. "Sh-she was probably th-the only r-reason we were able t-to recruit."

Fenrir wasn't sure if the Ingrid she was referring to was the same one he'd approached for the sleeping tonic all those years ago, a sleeping tonic he had used on Revna while he took her place, but he was sure he would learn. He hoped he would.

"Tell me more. Tell me about Ingrid."

Tell me everything.

It was stilted and sometimes incoherent, but she told him. Told him about how she'd become friends with Ingrid, who was that same girl from the village, though reluctantly at first. How they'd started training seriously with the jarl and other warriors of the village. She told him that she'd known she wanted to liberate those from slavery when a raiding party came in the cover of darkness and tried stealing women and children from their beds. Revna, along with Ingrid and the jarl, killed them. And that was just the beginning.

Fenrir could hear the strength in her words as she spoke of the Maidens. He could only imagine how much she missed them. If he could send her back, he would. But some force around Myddheim made it impossible.

He should know. He had tried.

He realized she'd gone quiet, so he rubbed his hand up her back, gently squeezing the muscles on either side of her neck. She gave a soft sigh and nuzzled deeper into the crook of his neck.

"You know," he started, "this is the first time since your arrival that you aren't fighting with me."

"G-give me time," she muttered.

Fenrir smiled against the top of her head and decided that he liked both. The fighting and the ... whatever this was. But he grew solemn as he prepared to ask the question that had haunted him for nine years.

"Do you hate me, Revna?" he whispered.

The words seemed to echo into every corner of the cave, as they had in his mind since she arrived. Some kind of emotion caused her scent to flare, but it died out under the strength of the poison.

"I d-don't hate you, Fenrir," she responded, and warmth surged in his chest.

He let it be enough for now.

Occasionally she would doze off, and Fenrir would count her breaths, and then wake her again and coax her to talk. When her throat became raw with use, he would hold her head so that she could drink. When the fire burned too low, he would reach an arm to toss more pieces of wood. He checked her wound often, the skin hardening and turning bluer with each passing hour. Dark blue veins spread from it like poisonous lightning. Afternoon sky bled into inky night, and each hour felt longer than the last.

When the sun came up on the next morning, he started to feel the first effects of the poison in his blood. His wound was turning blue, and it felt like dozens of ice shards were stabbing his skin. He couldn't imagine the pain Revna was in.

"Brother."

Fenrir jolted, having accidentally fallen asleep. He reached quickly for his knife, before realizing that Hel was standing in front of him.

His head cleared quickly. Hel was here.

Which meant ...

"No." He warned his sister, pulling Revna closer to his chest.

She looked at him sadly, a pitying smile pulling at her lips.

"I'm not here for her."

Seventeen

Revna

THE WORLD CAME AND went with each sharp stab of the blight under her skin. Revna was so cold, so overwhelmed by sensation that she felt as if fire and ice were vying for her pain.

Time seemed to cease, then drag on endlessly. Delirium and consciousness tugged at her mind, making her cling to Fenrir as an anchor to this plane of existence. She was afraid if she let go, she would lose herself.

He talked to her, asked her questions. She answered the best she could, forgetting her responses almost as soon as the words crossed her lips. Her mind begged her to sleep. When she drifted, Fenrir would call her back—his voice rumbling against her face where it was pressed to his warm neck.

It could have been moments or lifetimes. All Revna knew was that she was trapped in endless agony.

"No," Fenrir snarled, startling her from a light sleep. She didn't recall saying anything, but perhaps she had.

Then another voice filled the air. "I'm not here for her."

It took Revna a moment to recognize the voice as Hel's. Gone was her usual confident and playful demeanor. In its place was something close to pity.

If Hel was here ...

I'm not here for her, she'd said.

Revna moved her hand slightly and clutched onto Fenrir's side as much as her remaining strength allowed.

"Not again," she whispered, the request reaped from a buried place. She felt him stiffen at her words, and then his hand dug into the skin of her back, pulling her tighter.

"I've sent for mother," he told Hel. "Please let me stay until I see her healed."

"It's not you either, brother. Although I can smell the beginnings of death in this cave, it's not you." Something Fenrir did that she missed must have prompted Hel to continue speaking. "The giant Jalmir lies dead not far from here, smothered in root and earth."

Revna felt Fenrir sigh. "I didn't mean to."

"What happened?" Hel asked.

"Jalmir was angry, and Revna was a convenient place to put that anger. He attacked her, but the one who shot her escaped."

Guilt, oily and nausea-inducing, curdled in Revna's stomach. She was no stranger to killing others, had done so with eagerness in the past. But something about a person being killed *because* of her—because of a situation she'd put herself in—had remorse tightening her chest.

"Why would you think I was here for you?" Hel asked.

Fenrir's deep voice rumbled against Revna's face as he told Hel all that had transpired, and how he'd poisoned himself to ensure that their mother would come.

"You d-did what?" Revna said with as much venom as she could infuse. She didn't remember him poisoning himself. She must have been adrift. "You f-fucking *fool*."

"I tend to agree with her," Hel seethed. "Why are you in Jotunheim? Was something happening?"

"I came to see the sisters. I have questions about Revna's arrival and what it means," Fenrir said, his voice a low rumble.

A ray of clarity shone through the fog of Revna's mind. The sisters he'd set out to see were *the* sisters. The Norns, the three Sisters of Fate.

Revna tried to push away from Fenrir, livid at him for putting himself in harm's way for her, at herself for causing all of it, but he held fast, and her strength gave out. The cave was silent for a few moments, save for the occasional sound of Revna's chattering teeth, the pop of the fire, and the wind howling outside. She tilted her head just enough to look at Fenrir's face, but he was staring to where Hel must have been glaring back.

"You think our mother will—"

"Your mother will what, my daughter?" a voice said from the opening of the cave, startling them all. "Ignore when my children call?"

The very air in the cave seemed to thicken in Angrboda's presence. No one spoke, no one took a breath. Revna heard the shuffle of boots and then the familiar tenor of Tyr's voice saying that he would *go after her*.

Icy fire erupted down Revna's spine and she hissed, arching into the pain. Her stomach roiled and she heaved. Fenrir helped roll her as black bile spewed from her mouth.

"Heal her," Fenrir said to his mother, urgency ringing in his voice.

"I came here for you, not some poor mortal girl."

"I refuse to be healed until she is. Heal her now."

Grit and the excruciating pull of the pain were the only things keeping Revna conscious. Spots sparked in her vision, and she felt as if the whole cave was tumbling around and around. Her blood was on fire—she wanted to claw her own skin off just to get it to cool.

"Why? Who is she to you?"

Revna could practically hear the hesitation is Fenrir's breathing even through her pounding agony. But she didn't blame him. What they were to each other—in the past or otherwise—was not easily defined.

In Myddheim, their allyship and tentative trust had budded into a kind of companionship. At the time, Revna hadn't known what having a friend meant—what it felt like. She hadn't realized the depth of her care for the man she'd come to trust until she'd watched him disappear. And now, beneath the hurt of deception, something else that had been growing between them was clawing its way to the surface. Something that had laid dormant but was now awake. And hungry.

"She freed me on Myddheim. I am here because of her, and only her." Fenrir's voice took on a sharp edge. "For that, I want you to save her. Please."

Quiet settled into the cave again.

"It will not be pleasant. Death would be a mercy at this point. The poison has taken root."

Fenrir growled. "She can handle it. She is strong."

From somewhere behind her, she heard the rustling of things moving, stone grinding on stone, the cracking of dry wood being added to the fire. An earthy, sour smell invaded Revna's nose making her want to purge again.

"Sit her up, she needs to drink this."

Fenrir moved her with care, but she couldn't stop a groan of discomfort from escaping. He pulled her gently between his legs, her back pressing to his front. Her eyes were having a hard time focusing, but they settled on the figure in front of her sitting by the fire.

Angrboda glared at her with icy blue eyes. She was a lean, tall woman with brown hair streaked with white. Her skin tone sat somewhere between Hel's and Fenrir's, but with an undertone of grayish blue. She was both beautiful and terrifying.

Angrboda moved forward and pressed a small clay pot to Revna's lips. "Drink, girl."

Her hesitation must have been all over her face. "My son will be drinking it right alongside of you. But your purge will be greater. You will be sick for many more hours."

Revna still hesitated, so Fenrir grabbed the pot from his mother's hands and took a drink. Then he brought it to Revna's lips. She didn't need to trust his mother, she just needed to trust Fenrir.

And in that moment, she realized she still did.

She took a long pull of the gritty liquid, the taste significantly worse than the smell. As she forced her throat to swallow, she could already feel her blood starting to boil, her stomach clenching in refusal of the new invasion. As soon as the liquid reached her stomach, it came back up. She leaned to the side and shook as black sludge poured from her mouth.

She couldn't stop, her vision blurred so much so that she could barely make out the dancing flames of the fire. At some point, she thought she felt Fenrir shift and lean to expel his own stomach, but with the roaring in her ears, it was hard to tell.

"Steel yourself, girl. That was the easy part," Angrboda warned.

"Give her another moment—"

But the giantess didn't listen, and Revna screamed as a hot knife was shoved into the wound where the arrow had pierced her side. Her legs spasmed, the room spun. She turned her head as more black bile ran from her mouth. She wanted it to end. Perhaps death would be a kindness.

From somewhere outside herself, she felt firm arms secure across her chest, and heard a voice in her ear. But sound was fading. Light was fading. Touch was fading.

And the world went dark.

A hot iron was being shoved through Revna's temples. Her limbs felt laden and sore. She could feel soft fur pressed against her cheek and hear the unmistakable sound of a whetstone sharpening a blade.

Hesitantly, she cracked opened her eyes, the small movement exhausting. Her vision was still blurry, and she could only make out the contrast of dancing flames. Blinking slowly, the fogginess dissipated.

"Welcome back, fierce one," Tyr said from the other side of the fire. "She's awake!"

Revna heard the shuffle of footsteps on the cave floor, then Hel was squatting in front of her, placing gentle fingers to her forehead.

"Fever is fading. Do you think you could sit up to drink some water?" she asked. Revna nodded. It was slow moving, but with Hel's help, she was able to sit enough to lean against the cave wall. The Goddess adjusted the fur cloak so it covered Revna's still naked body. When she raised a cup, Revna gave her a questioning look. "Don't worry, it's just water."

The cool liquid burned as it went down Revna's throat, but she ignored the pain, drinking deeply.

Fenrir came barreling into the already tight cave, his mother following close behind. His pants hung low on his hips and were not even fully laced. His top half was bare, and his hair was loose and dripping water, sending rivulets down his bare chest. Amber eyes pulsed from dark to light as he let out a harsh exhale. A fever-like warmth spread through her body, a very different ache deepening.

After holding that golden gaze through a few more sips of water, Revna leaned her head back against the wall and took a moment to assess her own body. She was too scared to look, so she started by wiggling her toes and tensing the muscles of her legs. She took as deep a breath as she could, sending the air as far into her belly as possible. It burned in her throat and encountered some resistance in her stomach, as if the muscle and tendon surrounding the wound were hardened and trying to protect it. She felt terrible, but she was alive.

"How are you feeling?" Fenrir asked.

Revna tried to answer but found that no sound could pass through the burning pain in her throat. She gingerly reached her hand to the column of her neck, probing the skin there—even the light touch hurt.

"She purged much poison. It will be a day or two before her voice returns," Angrboda said from behind Fenrir.

"I also purged. How am I able to speak?"

"Because you are a strong God, my son. Not a frail mortal woman."

Revna furrowed her brow at the barbed insult. Hel rose from her kneeling position slowly and faced her mother.

"Do *not* speak of her that way—as if she's not here." The air around Hel seemed to blur and pulse before settling again.

Angrboda sneered. "I only speak the truth, daughter."

Revna looked from Hel to Fenrir to their mother. Each body was fraught with tension—it made the air in the cave feel oppressive. She wondered if the stone walls could hold up to a fight between three Gods and a powerful witch.

Revna's chest tightened as another cost of her choice to follow Tyr and Fenrir through that gate became clear. Unintentionally, Revna had caused a family reunion that neither Fenrir nor Hel seemed to want. Hel had spoken about getting out of darkness, and Revna was terrified that she had just plunged the Goddess right back in.

And Fenrir ...

Revna searched his face, but his eyes were fixed on the space between Hel and Angrboda, as if at any slight movement, he would step in the middle and take the blow.

She never should have followed them—never should have left Vana-heim.

Tyr cleared his throat and stepped up to the very tense and powerful beings. "Hel, why don't you and I take Revna down to the lake to clean up and then try to get some food into her belly."

He didn't say it, but they all heard his real meaning. The sooner Revna was able to travel, the sooner they could leave this realm.

Fenrir walked to where Revna leaned against the wall. "I'll carry her down. Then Tyr and I will go hunt." He looked at his mother. "You stay here."

Fenrir bent down to pick her up, fur cloak and all. His brow furrowed when she cringed at the pain of moving her tender body, but he strode quickly out of the cave with her in his arms, Hel and Tyr close on their heels.

Revna looked around at the craggy landscape as they passed through the mouth of the cave. The sunlight was muted and dull, and it cast the already gray landscape darker still. Trees with moldering leaves bent in submission to the wind, bringing with it the smell of impending snow.

She shivered as the breeze and a droplet of water from Fenrir's wet hair hit her exposed shoulder. As if he felt her body tense with the cold, he squeezed her tighter, and she felt the pad of his thumb rub absentmindedly on her back.

"The lake is slightly warmer than the air, but I wouldn't linger long," Fenrir said. She nodded.

Even if she had the ability, Revna didn't think she'd have the energy to speak. The last few days were coming back to her in flashes, and with each moment of clarity, a conflicting torrent of emotions brewed in her mind. Fenrir kept glancing at her out of the corner of his eye, and she wondered what all those clashing emotions smelled like.

They rounded a cropping of boulders and came upon the lake. It was small and blue, with hazy air hanging just above the water. Fenrir set her down at the water's edge and she immediately grieved the loss of the heat of his body.

Hel approached her and Revna tried for an apologetic smile—a slight furrowing of her brow and a small tilt to her lips. But Hel's eyes still seemed distant, so Revna reached her hands out to grasp the Goddess's and their gazes finally met.

I'm so sorry—she tried to say with her eyes and the weak squeeze of her hands. *Please forgive me.*

Hel narrowed her eyes at Revna, but there was a small twitch on the corner of her lips. "We can discuss your foolishness when you're feeling better. For now, let's get you clean."

She helped Revna to her feet. Revna swayed a little. Fenrir reached out to steady her, but she shook them both off, wanting to stand on her own. Once steady, she turned to where Fenrir and Tyr lingered apprehensively and flicked her hand in a motion that said *go away.*

Tyr chuckled, Fenrir scowled, but they listened, disappearing into the woods to hunt.

Walking into the water was a slow and agonizing process. The lake was warmer than the air, but not comfortable like the hot springs back in Vanaheim. When the water reached Revna's waist, she slowly sank to her shoulders and then tipped her head back.

Splashing from beside her drew attention as Hel approached her in the water, also naked. "We didn't keep you alive just for you to drown."

Air huffed out of Revna's nose in an attempt at a laugh.

When she was sufficiently clean, ridding her body of the layer of fever, she wrapped herself back in the fur cloak just as Tyr and Fenrir appeared, four rabbits in hand. Instead of going back to the cave where Angrboda waited, they got to work skinning them, creating a fire, and roasting the rabbits. No one spoke, all lost in their own minds.

When Tyr handed Revna a whole rabbit, she gingerly pulled a piece of charred meat off and chewed slowly, ensuring her stomach wouldn't revolt. After the first few bites, she couldn't resist bringing the entire rabbit to her mouth and eating eagerly. When there was nothing left but bones and eyeballs, she leaned back against a boulder and sighed, exhausted.

"If you're up to it," Fenrir started, "we'll make the journey back to the gate and return to Vanaheim. It may take a while, but I think it would be best—"

Revna held up a hand to stop him. Fenrir's mouth snapped closed, jaw clenching.

While bathing, Revna had thought about this. She wanted to continue on Fenrir and Tyr's original journey to see the sisters. Fenrir was right, her arrival in Vanaheim was strange, if not unsettling. Fate was playing a game, and she was not content to sit by while it strung her up in its web, waiting to be feasted on. She wanted to do what she did best. Fight. But she needed to know *what* she was fighting ...

She chewed the inside of her cheek for a moment and thought about how to explain. One of her Maidens, Gyda, had been a slave, too, and she'd had her throat slit. Though she hadn't died, she was never able to speak again. Revna and the other Maidens communicated with her by using hand signals.

Revna caught Fenrir's gaze. She walked two fingers across the palm of her other hand, then held up three fingers, and pointed to Hel.

Journey. Three. Sister.

Tyr understood first. "Journey to the three sisters?"

"You want to go see them?" Hel asked.

But Revna was staring at Fenrir and he at her. His jaw was clenched as the wolf battled for dominance in his eyes. Revna tilted her chin, issuing a challenge.

"The risk—" he started, but Revna shook her head and waved her hand in dismissal.

The risk was worth it. To know her purpose, to aid Myddheim in whatever way she was still able. To figure out why she'd been brought there—and not by slinking behind the Gods, but with them. To understand why, when she looked at Fenrir, she felt a taut thread that begged her to grab on and pull him closer.

Whatever Fenrir saw in her face had him softening, then sighing in resignation.

"Fine. We journey at dawn to see the Norns."

EIGHTEEN

FENRIR

FENRIR SAT AT THE mouth of the cave and watched the sun rise. Jotunheim was a harshly beautiful realm with giant rocks, trees, and an earthly magic that called to his very blood. Whether it was because this was where he was born or because it was one of first realms crafted into existence by Ymir, he couldn't say. The earth and trees called to him, begging his wolf to come out to play, to run, but he ignored the temptation.

He had killed Jalmir.

It wasn't intentional, but intentions meant nothing to the dead. Or the living that may seek retribution. As far as Fenrir knew, Jalmir's only family was Spjut, his brother. And if Jalmir was to be believed, he was also dead. Fenrir made a note to ask Hel if he had entered her realm.

Behind him, Revna, Tyr, and Hel still slept. Where his mother had disappeared to, he wasn't sure. He surmised she'd gone to a cave of her own. When they all woke, Fenrir would need to relay his plan. He and Revna would be the only ones to journey to see the sisters—Tyr and Hel would return to Vanaheim.

Unfortunately, he had one last favor to ask of his mother. He ground his teeth together thinking about what she would ask for in return—nothing came without reciprocation with Angrboda.

After Revna's gruesome healing, she'd healed him with a gentle care she hadn't extended to Revna. He'd fallen asleep for a bit, letting the healing potion take root in his body, and when he awoke, she and Hel were spewing venom at each other—Tyr trying his best to make sure they didn't tear each other's throats out.

It was a long night. Fenrir had kept Revna tucked in close, one hand always placed lightly on her pulse. She had purged many times, until Fenrir was covered in the black bile of the poison leaving her body. When the sun rose, and she hadn't been sick in a few hours, Hel and Tyr had convinced him to go wash off. When he'd returned, Revna was awake, and he could breathe again.

The intensity surrounding her well-being concerned him. There was danger for those he cared for. She had just come back into his life, and yet he couldn't help the feelings she had awoken in him—something that tasted a lot like longing.

The sweet smell of a winter-bitten flower tickled his nose, followed by the sound of light steps from behind him. Hel sat next to him for a moment, eyes fixed on the colors that came awake with the rising sun, the opalescent ink on her arms catching the light.

"You want to go without us, don't you?"

Fenrir smiled and let out a quiet, disbelieving chuckle. His sister could always see right through him.

"It's for the best. This is something that Revna and I need to do together. And I'm going to ask Mother to open a door and take us as far as she can. I find it safest to limit your interaction with her." Fenrir nudged Hel's shoulder with his own.

She nodded but kept quiet.

"With Revna still not fully recovered, I don't want to have her make the journey on foot. It would take us days. By the time we reach the sisters, she'd have nothing to give them." Fenrir shuddered, thinking of what was to come.

He had seen the sisters once in his life—when his mother had taken him and his siblings as younglings. He'd seen things that still haunted him. Learning the many possibilities of your fate was like living with a storm cloud overhead, waiting for it to break.

He and Revna wouldn't be the same after this, and he was still tormenting himself on whether it was a good idea. Something had thawed between them over the last few days. He wasn't sure it would last. He hoped it would. And he didn't want to ruin it with visions of an uncertain future.

Fenrir looked over to find his sister smiling knowingly at him. "What?"

"You care for her," she whispered.

The intensity of that statement made his heart pound uncomfortably in his chest. He did care for Revna. He always had. Not just because she'd freed him, but because she made him feel safe in a world where being himself was met with fear and hatred. When he'd shared his true identity, she'd recovered quickly. There was no scent of unease—just a low-simmering anger that he'd lied to her.

He cared for her more than he could afford to. Seeing that arrow go through her had only made those feelings undeniable. And now that Hel had spoken it aloud, bringing it out into the open for him to face ...

He glanced over his shoulder to where Revna still slept, his stomach fluttering with both yearning and guilt. He still hadn't told her the full truth. Of everything that had transpired when he'd left Myddheim, the things he had done. He knew now just how much she'd tortured herself because of his sacrifice, and he didn't want to add to that burden.

Still, she deserved to know. After their journey to the sisters, he would tell her. Everything.

"What if I lose her?" he asked quietly, finally responding to his sister's statement. Whether by the truth or by fate, there were many ways Revna could be lost to him.

Hel threaded her arm through his and leaned her head on his shoulder, the low hum of her power soothing his nerves. "Then you find her again."

It was a statement both simple and profound, one that rooted into his heart with its truth.

But for now, he needed to prepare for what lay ahead. Whatever that may be.

⁂

Fenrir's mother was being too agreeable, and it was making his hackles rise in suspicion.

He couldn't discern her scent.

When he proposed his plan, she agreed, only requesting that they stay with her for one evening before continuing their journey so she might ensure their wounds were fully healed.

He didn't see what choice he had. His mother's home was less than a half-day's walk from the sisters. They would need to return so she could send them back to the gate to return to Vanaheim anyway. It was a risky magic, but his mother loved risky magic. Loved pushing the bounds of what she was told she wouldn't be able to do.

After saying farewell to Tyr and Hel, he and Revna joined his mother in the cave she had scouted out the previous evening. Revna still hadn't regained her voice, and Fenrir found he missed the sound of it—even if it was usually sharp retorts that she directed at him. He offered her a hand to step down from a large boulder, wanting an excuse to touch her. She ignored the hand, sitting instead and sliding down until her feet struck on the ground, causing her to sway.

Damn iron-willed woman.

His mother stared at the roughly hewn cave wall, muttering to herself. She knelt and drew a circle of runes around her. He recognized some symbols of protection and journey, but others were chaotic combinations of unknown. Revna watched her apprehensively, crossing her arms over her chest. She was wearing a cobbled together outfit of her own bloody pants and Hel's top and cloak, with Hel heading back to Vanaheim half-naked. Daggers were strapped to Revna's hips, but she'd lost her axe. It was likely still embedded in Jalmir's decaying body.

She looked a little more like herself, and Fenrir was glad for it. The scowl on her face was oddly comforting.

"I need your blood," his mother said over her shoulder. Fenrir approached her. "Not you, my son. The mortal one."

"Why?" he growled.

"The portal needs payment, and since you and I share blood, I've already taken care of that price."

Revna uncrossed her arms and walked over to where his mother knelt, stepping carefully over the marked-out runes. She presented her hand in tribute. Swift and severe, his mother's blade swept across the tip of Revna's finger, though she didn't flinch. Instinct begged Fenrir to step forward and take Revna's finger into his mouth, to make the pain go away, to taste her heartbeat in the wound. He gave his head a little shake, ridding himself of the urge as his mother waved him forward.

The cave wall blurred and melted, looking as if the stone had turned to liquid. The runes pulsed around them and the air turned bone-chilling cold. Fenrir stiffened as a familiar smell wafted through the door—bitter and earthy, with a hint of brine.

He'd been so focused on Revna, it hadn't dawned on him that he would have to return home.

He hadn't been home—or what was supposed to be home—since he was taken by the Aesir. When he'd returned from Myddheim, he had met with his mother a few times, but always on the outskirts of her land. He hadn't stepped foot inside the cave that was supposed to have shielded him, his sister, and his brother, since the morning of their abduction. He swallowed emotion in his throat that threatened to boil over.

"You first, my son." She smiled and gestured toward the door.

So she could be alone with Revna? *Not a fucking chance.*

"I insist you go first, and then Revna and I will follow. Together." He said it in such a way that left no room for argument.

His mother's mouth thinned, but she didn't say another word as she stepped through the swirling door.

Fenrir didn't stop to overthink it. Instead, he grabbed Revna's hand and pulled her to him, until her chest was pressed against his upper abdomen. He took her hand and draped it up around his neck, doing the same to the other one. He looked down and met her gray eyes, so bright they shone like the moon, and saw such conflicting emotion. His brows dipped in question, but she just shook her head and focused her gaze on a spot in the middle of his chest.

He leaned down to whisper in her ear. "Hang onto me, my *máni*."

She whipped her face up to his, but he didn't give her time to react, instead tilting their bodies until they fell through the door.

⌖

Home.

Revna swayed in his arms as they landed in one of the lower parts of the cave system that his mother claimed as her own. Much as he selfishly wanted to touch her, he'd had other reasons for holding onto Revna while traveling through one of his mother's doors. Much like the woman herself, her doorways were chaotic and disorienting.

Revna's arms dropped from his neck, one going to cover her mouth, the other to her stomach. She shot him a glare and then turned to vomit all over the cave floor.

He reached out to rub her back, but she swatted it away. He chuckled softly.

His mother was standing near a tunnel entrance not far off, sneering at Revna. Unbidden, a growl climbed up his throat. She only cocked her head at him, then turned to continue to the main cavern.

Once Revna was done, Fenrir gestured her to follow. Each step, each curve of the tunnel, each familiar carving in the cave walls had his stomach knotting and shoulders tensing. Every corner was filled with the ghost of possibilities, of a childhood that could have been so full of love and laughter, but instead was wounded and infected.

The smell threatened to reopen those wounds—an odd blend of his mother's power and a hint of earth, sea, and deadly flowers. A subtle memory of who else once dwelled in the caves.

Inside the main living space, everything looked the same. In one corner was a large wooden bench littered with various pots, mortar and pestles. Flowers, herbs, branches, and vines were drying on twine that hung between stalactites. The center of the room was a large dug out fire-pit. A large cauldron sat above the always burning flames. His mother's loom sat near the fire, a weave in progress. Large pelts of fur covered bits of floor and led to a pile in a corner where his mother slept—where they'd all used to sleep.

Revna's shoulder brushed his arm. He turned to meet her gaze, but she was looking to the side where three large weaves were hung. Fenrir's breath halted in his chest.

There on the wall was a woven image of him in his wolf form, standing with his siblings. Hel was in middle, her two forms as terrifying as in real life. Jormun's serpent form coiled in wait on her other side. The three of them—the monstrous children of Angrboda and Loki.

Fenrir had never truly seen himself as the wolf, save for the occasional reflection off still waters. And he'd never lingered to look. But he looked at the woven image of himself now—the black fur, the molten gold eyes, the sharp fangs in a perpetual snarl, his hulking form almost as tall as the tree-tops—and found he was more concerned with Revna's reaction than his own judgments. Now that she'd seen the monster lurking beneath, would she fear him? Hate him?

Revna slowly approached the weave, eyes wide and mouth slightly ajar. She reached up as if to touch the fur but pulled back, looking almost guilty. Her eyes scanned over Hel and she gave a small smile. When her eyes landed on Jormun, she pointed wildly and then looked at Fenrir.

"Jormun." Fenrir nodded at her wide eyes. "My brother from the fjord. Sorry about that. He doesn't do well with ... well, people."

Revna huffed air out of her nose in agreement and regarded his weave again. As she took a slow, measured breath, he came to stand next to her.

"Does this scare you?" he asked, gesturing to the visage of his other form. *Do you fear me?*

She turned to him and placed a hand on his arm, gray eyes warm and earnest as she shook her head in a clear and resounding *no*. Something eased within his chest. Too quickly, she seemed to realize she was grabbing his arm and pulled her hand away.

"I need to check your wounds," his mother's raspy voice called from behind them, startling them both.

She led them to her work bench and quickly looked at the scratch on his arm, already forming a blue-gray scar, and then moved on to Revna's sizable one, which was newly scabbed over but healing.

"Thank you," he said to his mother. "If we could trouble you for some provisions, I'd like to make our way to the sisters immediately."

She scowled at him. "I told you that I should observe you for the night."

"We should be back this evening," he told her, resolute in this change of plans. Something was telling him to get out of this cave. Probably his past.

His mother swiped a gray-brown lock of hair out of her face and began looking around her table. "Fine, but she'll need more healing salve. It will take me the night to make it, so you must return, unless you do not want her to heal properly."

Fenrir narrowed his eyes at his mother, but remained silent as she filled a small canvas bag with apples, cheese, and a hunk of bread. Begrudgingly, she also gave Revna a warm fur cloak after he requested it. Revna seemed a bit hesitant about taking anything from his mother, but she'd need it for their journey. They said their temporary farewells, but before Fenrir could follow Revna out the cave, his mother grabbed his arm—her strength still halting and commanding.

"Be careful of what vision you receive from the Norns, my son," she warned. "The truth can haunt you more than any ghost."

Her blue eyes were dimmed and distant, and Fenrir gave her hand a squeeze before gently removing it from his arm. He looked to Revna, who was scowling in their direction at the mouth of the cave—her ire was directed at his mother. He made his way to her but she kept her eyes on his mother as if she was trying to solve a riddle. He placed a hand at the small of her back and directed her out of the cave.

"Let's go get some answers."

Nineteen

Revna

Angrboda was hiding something. With the loss of her voice, Revna felt like her other senses were heightened. Or maybe it was just her intuition yanking on her gut, screaming that Fenrir's mother was withholding.

It itched at her mind during the first part of their trek. Fenrir would occasionally say something, but she was so deep in thought that she could only respond in small nods.

Seeing his other form on the weave had allowed something inside of Revna to, oddly, settle. He was huge and terrifying, and magnificent and beautiful—and she finally understood. Perhaps not everything, but she understood why he'd lied. He'd expected that side of himself to scare her. She could see it in the set of his shoulders as he looked upon himself and his siblings—the fear and shame that had followed him for all these years. So much disappointment, so much broken.

And she didn't want to be another of those things.

After walking for several hours, with several breaks, the craggy and harsh landscape of Jotunheim was softening into lush trees and thick underbrush. Gnarled roots broke free from the earth, large enough to duck under. A gentle layer of fog settled just above the ground, devouring the sound of their careful steps. As she ducked under another root, she placed a steadying hand on its rough surface and the root trembled with the contact. Revna whipped her hand away, brow furrowed. She was about to point it out to Fenrir, but he spoke first.

"We should be there soon, but I need to prepare you." He turned and faced her fully and her breath caught in her chest.

Now that the fog of anger toward him had started to dissipate, Revna's mind and body were lingering on the other things she'd taken notice of since they'd been reunited. Like the set of his shoulders, the veins in his forearms, the small dip in his chin, his lips ...

But the attraction, that pull she felt toward him, left her feeling conflicted. They were from different worlds, and she felt like a fly in his mead, sure he had to view her as such. She had already cost him, Hel, and Tyr more than enough. She didn't need feelings and desire to get involved and cause more complications for them all.

And, with all that had happened in such a short time, she wasn't sure how she felt. A shiver ran up her spine, though, remembering his words before he'd pulled her through the door. My *máni* ...

"Are you with me, Revna?" Fenrir asked, reclaiming her attention. She nodded. "The sisters dwell at the base of one of the three main roots of Yggdrasil where Urd's well resides."

That much Revna knew. There they watered and tended to the root of Yggdrasil to keep it from corruption as they wove the web of fate.

"When we arrive, they will demand a price. No past, present, or potential future comes without a cost. It may be blood, a truth, or a memory."

Revna swallowed at that. Blood she would easily give. But a truth? A memory? The vulnerability of those possibilities made sweat break out on the back of her neck.

"Then you will submerge into the well, and all your senses will be taken from you. You will exist as a possibility, and nothing more. The things you see and hear while submerged are all parts of a whole—a unique web that is woven for you. There may be clarity or more confusion. The sisters weave, but fates can change depending on what string of the web you decide to follow."

Revna sat on a wide root to give her feet a rest. She looked at Fenrir and started gesturing. *Will you go into the well?*

"Yes," he said with an unreadable expression.

Nerves tingled around the edges of her body, but the benefit had to outweigh the cost. Didn't it? She needed to know why she was here—why she was called forth from Myddheim, but taken to Vanaheim, to Fenrir.

Revna sat a while longer, stretching out her sore limbs, then stood and waved her hand. *Let's go.*

Fenrir pushed on, and with each step, Revna watched his shoulders climb toward his ears. The thickening air clung to her skin. Pulling breath into her lungs felt as though she was inhaling water. Fenrir reached back to secure her hand on the back of his weapons strap. Normally, she'd have argued about being led around, but the fog hung in the air like a storm cloud dropped from the sky, and she knew enough to understand that she'd be lost for days if she didn't have him guiding her. They walked on until, between one blink and the next, they entered a clearing completely free of the condensed air.

Revna's face slackened at the sight before her. Ahead, in the center of the clearing, the Yggdrasil root stood as wide as three large trees. The root split in three as it reached the ground, a heavily flowing waterfall threading through each opening. The waters met in a large crystalline pool—Urd's well. As they moved closer, Revna could see faint markings of runes and the Web of Wyrd climbing up the life tree's root. It climbed and reached until it disappeared into a bruised sky.

The threat of tears burned at the back of her eyes—seeing the connection of all nine realms in this dazzling display of nature made unnamed emotions rise to the surface.

In Myddheim, there were several kingdoms that claimed that they held a root of Yggdrasil. That the fates had bestowed them the great honor of having a direct line to the realms. But seeing it here, witnessing the overwhelming nature of the great root—it wasn't possible something like this resided in Myddheim.

"Where there are wolves, there are ravens," an ethereal voice whispered from behind them. Revna whirled and came face to face with an old woman. Deep wrinkles carved her face, and all color was leeched from her hair. But her dark blue eyes held a wisdom and warmth that had Revna relaxing.

Fenrir inclined his head in a respectful motion. "Urdu."

"Sisters!" she yelled with more gusto than Revna would have thought her capable. "We have seekers."

Revna hid her smile, as the old woman—Urdu—hobbled around them to go stand at the edge of the well. From behind one fork of the fall a young woman with deep red hair emerged. She was dressed in fighting gear and Revna could see the top of some kind of mark on her chest beneath her tunic. She looked fierce, but her brown eyes held a dimness that looked out of place. She joined the elderly women in front of the well just as the third sister rose from the water itself. She slowly climbed out, eyeing them in a knowing way. Long dark hair with a large white streak clung to her soaked form. She was an odd combination of hard and soft angles, with one eye completely clouded over. Grabbing the bottom of her dress, she rang out the excess water then folded her hands in front of her, waiting.

"Urdu," Fenrir said, nodding to acknowledge the older woman again. "Verdhandi." He looked at the woman who crawled out of the well. "Skuld," he said, finally to the young warrior.

The Norns, the weavers of fate— past, present, and future.

Like her first meeting with Hel, Revna had the sudden urge to drop to her knees in reverence. Instead, she bowed her head.

"What do you seek, Fenrir, God of Destruction?" Skuld asked, and Revna was surprised by the soft but commanding voice she possessed.

Fenrir didn't show whether the title burned him, instead speaking slowly and with respect. "My companion and I seek answers to her arrival in Vanaheim. She is—"

"Obviously mortal." Urdu waved her hand in annoyance before he could say it.

"Can she not speak for herself?" Skuld asked.

Frustrated, Revna shifted a little on her feet, letting the softness of the earth ground her. Fenrir quickly explained her arrival to Vanaheim and everything that had happened while in Jotunheim—including why she currently could not speak. But as Revna listened, she noted something missing from the beginning of his story when he detailed his sacrifice on Myddheim and his return to Asgard. She couldn't quite figure it out, but there was something he wasn't relaying. If the Norns knew, they didn't call him on it.

Revna's senses were tingling as she felt a gaze on her. She lifted her eyes slowly and met Skuld's. Concern and confusion were etched onto the Norn's face—her gaze searching up and down Revna's body as if looking for an answer. Revna's gaze reluctantly left that of the future weaving Norn and took in all three sisters together. They looked strained, but who wouldn't when you constantly held the balance of past, present and future of all nine realms on your shoulders. It was a burden she didn't envy.

"Choose your sacrifice, wolf," Verhandi said. "A truth or a memory."

Revna looked to Fenrir's tense form and watched as his jaw clenched under his layer of scruff. "A memory."

He didn't want to speak a truth. *Interesting*.

"You will also live a memory, child," Urdu said, her voice not without pity. "If you cannot speak a truth, then it is not one that is given in sincerity."

The clearing began to dim as the sisters stood aside and gestured to the pool. Revna looked from the sisters to Fenrir, then back to the pool. Fenrir started shedding his weapons. She crossed her arms over her chest, relieved she wasn't going first.

"You will go together," Skuld said, making Revna's blood go cold. Fenrir froze and glanced to where the sister spoke.

"I sense it, too, sister," Verhandi concurred. "There is a knot that needs unraveling. A thread that needs to be pulled free."

Urdu nodded in agreement. "To be weaved anew."

What would he witness from her past? She swallowed back the rising bile in her throat—a feeling of foreboding as a dozen bad memories fought to the surface of her mind.

"We will see each other's memory?" Fenrir asked, his voice an echo of her own strain.

"You will see exactly what Yggdrasil needs you to see," Urdu explained. "There is something that looms behind you both that needs revisiting. That needs releasing."

Sudden fear slipped its way past her carefully mortared heart. Fenrir's attention snapped to Revna, and he strode back over to her with purposeful steps. "We don't have to do this. I would never ask of you anything you aren't willing to give."

She stared into his amber eyes, thinking on his words, then nodded. He would see what he was meant to see, she told herself. Tilting her head, she lifted a hand and gently tapped it on the center of his chest. *What about you?*

Fenrir looked down to where her hand still hovered over his heart. She blushed, preparing to pull it away, when he flattened his hand atop hers, keeping it there. She could feel his deep breaths and the strong thud of his heart.

"I would be honored to share this with you," he whispered, his voice so deep that it sent a trail of shivers down her spine. Or maybe it was the words themselves. He was willing to let her see *him*. Even the darkest parts.

Not long ago, she'd told him that she ran from nothing. Maybe she needed to prove those words true and stop running from herself.

She lifted her chin and gave Fenrir an indisputable nod. They would do this. Together.

"Thank you." He gave her hand a long squeeze before turning away from her, heading straight for the pool, stripping his clothes as he went.

Only the distraction of wondering which memory she was about to see kept her from looking Fenrir up and down as he waited for her at the water's edge. The sisters looked at her expectantly, so she began to undress. A small intake of breath broke past her lips as she extended her arms overhead to remove her shirt—the movement pulled at her healing wound. Fenrir's head whipped to the side, eyes casting down to the ground, but he didn't utter a word.

Naked, vulnerable, and shivering, Revna approached the pool and stood next to Fenrir. Once again, she found herself naked with him. Once again, it wasn't the nakedness that bothered her.

She took a deep breath and exhaled slowly through her nose. Living people she could fight, but her own ghosts? Her own past? Her own hurts? Those caverns within herself where she'd shoved every horrific thing that had happened to her and then blocked them in with stone—that, she didn't know if she was prepared for someone to witness.

A small brush against her hand caused her body to lock up. Looking out the corner of her eye, she noticed Fenrir had moved closer, until any small shift caused them to touch. She turned her gaze to him, his eyes already searching her face. Apparently finding whatever reassurance he'd been looking for, he gave her a small nod and then stepped into the pool, submerging all the way until his head was no longer visible.

"By these threads, let the past, present, and future be known," the three sisters said in eerie unison.

Steeling herself, she stepped into the well behind him ... and felt nothing. The water was so soft and light that she couldn't feel anything, including herself. When she was up to her shoulders, she gave the sisters one last look before dunking her head under the water. She felt it envelop her, hold her, until she had no beginning or ending. She was suspended in possibility.

Then a bright light pulled her under.

TWENTY

FENRIR

REVNA WAS TIED TO a tree. Her neck bent so far forward that her chin nearly rested on her chest, the curtain of her hair blocking her face.

It took Fenrir a moment to realize what his mind had been summoned into. But he recognized this version of Revna, this tree, the knots that bound her to its trunk.

He was seeing the day that he'd taken her place.

Somewhere in his body, through the haze of the memory, Fenrir felt sick.

A raven's raspy call startled her awake, and Fenrir watched as she tried to make sense of where she was. Watched as her breath came in panicked pants, struggling against the ropes' hold. She shifted from side to side, trying to get free, but only chafed the exposed skin near her collarbone in the process, creating small trails of viscous blood.

Fenrir watched as she grew more furious, her nails digging in the earth, face reddening. And then she screamed. Not for help, not in fear, but in such bone-chilling anger that he had a hard time witnessing it.

This is the price, he thought.

When the loud snap of a branch echoed through the woods behind her, she froze. Listening.

They had never talked about what happened that day, and as the sound grew louder, Fenrir wondered what manner of beast was about to find Revna tied up as an offering.

But then an out of breath redhead slid to a stop upon seeing Revna, sighing in relief.

Ingrid.

The healer in training that Fenrir had procured a sleeping draught from. The young woman who, by Revna's recounts in the cave, had become her second in command.

"He told me you were out here, but he didn't mention how far away from the village he'd tied you up," Ingrid said, getting to work on unknotting the ropes. Revna's brow furrowed in confusion, and Ingrid clarified, "Fenrick."

Guilt thickened in his gut as angry words gritted through her teeth. "Where is he?"

"When he came to me last night asking for a tonic for sleep, I never expected he'd do this," Ingrid said sympathetically, her small knife fraying through each rope.

"Answer me!" Revna shouted. To her credit, Ingrid didn't so much as flinch.

"He's taking your place."

Through whatever power the Norns possessed to share this memory, Fenrir felt a tremor of innumerable emotions wrack through him, overwhelming him. Revna's face blanched white and her head was shaking from side to side.

"No." The word was barely more than a whisper. "He can't—"

The smell of her fear hit him strongly, even through the memory.

The final rope was cut free and Revna pushed up to unsteady feet, wobbling and limping her first few steps. Then she was running.

Fenrir's mind followed her around trees and down ravines, watching as branches and bramble ripped her skin. Heard as her labored breath became tinged with a desperate rattle.

All this, trying to reach me in time.

Her steps faltered, and she barely caught herself as her footing slipped. On hands and knees, she started to crawl, then reached for a sharp rock, slicing into the meat of her palm as she pushed to standing position. He'd seen the scar on her hand before, had never known …

She let her blood drip over the earth as she started to run again.

"Freyja," she panted, calling to the Goddess. "Give me the wind. Give me speed. Give me the strength."

From somewhere close by, Fenrir heard what must have been Ingrid chasing after Revna, heading back toward the village, but Revna didn't stop to wait.

"Please, Freyja. Don't let him be taken from me."

She was bleeding for him. Begging for him.

If able to do so, Fenrir would have dropped to his knees at the intense flood of emotions. Whether they were coming off Revna or himself, he couldn't tell. He was so with her in this moment that they were inextricable. Where he began and she ended had no bearing.

Legs shaking and blood still dripping, she finally made it to the edge of the village. Fenrir knew what she would see next. Remembered the resolve he'd felt when climbing up onto the boat's deck.

She barreled around one last corner to the path that was a straightway to the docks and the people gathered there. It was strange seeing himself through the murky haze of a memory, but over the heads of the gathered village, he watched himself climb aboard the boat.

"Fenrick!" Revna screamed, so loud that most heads turned to look at her. Many of the faces were mixed with sadness and fury. She tried pushing past them, but most seemed intent on stalling her. If Fenrir had the ability, he would have shoved them aside. Even in this memory, he was irrationally angry at these villagers trying to keep her from one last look at him, and him at her. Even though with each passing moment the pain in his chest burned and twisted, knowing what came next.

Unable to push through the people on the small stretch of beach, Revna ran toward the dock. Fenrir remembered this moment in startling clarity, because it was the moment when he'd faltered in his resolve. Revna hadn't known how to swim, yet she'd launched herself off the end of the dock toward the boat's retreating wake. Toward the hungry, gulping chasm that had opened in the middle of the fjord.

Fenrir watched as she struggled to keep her head above the water's surface. Heard as she screamed his name between coughing fits, arms and legs fighting against the water's desire to consume. He was there with her in the water, feeling its icy sting and breath-stealing pull. Or perhaps it was his own breath that felt painful in his lungs. Witnessing, feeling, this shared moment from her perspective.

"*Please*," she choked out.

His attention turned from her in the water to his form standing on the boat. He saw the shudder that went through his shoulders at her call, and watched when finally, he turned.

He remembered attempting to craft his face into something neutral, but seeing himself now, he had failed. Anger, fear, desperation, sorrow—so much existing in one moment that it beat against his ribs begging to be released.

The memory of him stared at her from the deck of the boat, and she at him. His eyes never left Revna until the moment the hungry mouth of the whirlpool swallowed him whole.

The waters went still.

Revna screamed.

She stopped kicking and let the weight of the water pull her under. But instead of fighting for the surface, she reached down, down, down. As if still trying reach him. Trying to follow him. Fighting to get him back.

Fenrir felt sick and helpless. So helpless. All he wanted to do was reach her through memory and time and pull her from the waters. To give her all the breath from his lungs. He wanted to warm her, comfort her, make the pain go away.

Pockets of air broke free from her lips as her breath billowed out from between her lips and nose. But still, she attempted to swim down.

The wolf under his skin raked its claws across his heart and he felt a howl build in frustration.

He had done this to save her—to protect her home in Myddheim. To free Hel and Jormun. But in his haste and eagerness to shield Revna, he hadn't considered the pain it would cause. The repercussions it would have. He hadn't stopped to consider how old wounds from the past would tear open the moment someone he cared about was in danger.

Just when he was sure he was about to watch Revna drown, the water disrupted on both sides of her and then two sets of arms were tugging her up to the early morning sunlight. Ingrid and an older woman with whitening hair lifted Revna until they were grabbing the edges of a small boat, panting.

The older woman had one arm banded around Revna's waist as she gasped for air. Revna's gaze turned back to where Fenrir had disappeared. It was quiet for a moment, save for the gentle lapping of the water against the side of the small craft.

As a choking sob finally broke through her throat and tears mixed with the water of the fjord, Fenrir tried to lunge for her, even in his formless existence. But the water started swirling and pulling again. Revna and the other two women remained unflinching, as if the water wasn't churning around them. He reached for Revna again just as something grabbed a hold of his ankles and yanked.

No. He wouldn't be taken from her again.

Fenrir wanted to stay in this moment, in this hurt with her, until he could find a way to reach her. But the pull on his legs grew stronger, until his gaze was pulled completely under the water, and he was dragged down to its rocky depths.

And then, it swallowed him whole.

⇒⫶———⫶⇐

A golden thread appeared in front of him, and he followed it as its sinuous form guided him. He was no longer a memory, but fully clothed, weapons strapped, and running through the woods.

Something was wrong.

The branches and roots were silent, not answering any of his calls. The trees looked as though they had been scorched by fire, and the smell—the smell of rot, decay, and sulfur stung his sensitive nostrils. But he didn't stop running to inspect—he couldn't stop, but he did not yet know why.

He ran and ran, until the trees suddenly dissolved into a long, gilded hall. He stopped abruptly, blood turning icy. He'd been in this hall before. And as he looked toward the end, he saw it.

The cage.

This time inside the cage sat Hel and Jormun. They stood and cried out, and then he was running again. He would free them this time—this time, he wouldn't—

The hall dissolved again into a barren and burning landscape. As he roared in fury at not being able to reach his brother and sister again, he noticed his height. He felt the earth under foot, the taste of the air. He was in his wolf form, tall and imposing and ... alone. All around him was scorched earth. There was no sun, no moon. Just little fires burning everywhere and the smell of ash and destruction.

Fenrir felt himself whine and then he was running again. There had to be someone else here, some other path.

He ran and howled; ears pricked for an answering cry.

Alone.

Alone.

Alone.

He ran until he reached what looked like a root of Yggdrasil, and there, nestled in its crook, was a woman with dark, raven hair. She was lying on her side, knees pulled up to her chest, and crying. Fenrir padded over to her, slow, frantic whines coming out in rapid succession. As gently as his enormous form allowed, he gave her a little nudge with his nose.

She dissolved—her body turned to ash under his gentle touch.

Fenrir roared and raged, digging and growling at the earth—anguish roiled through his body until he, too, wanted to completely dissolve.

But no one could hear him.

He was alone.

His hind legs collapsed first, then his front. He slid to the ground, his high whines giving way to low whimpers. As he lay his head down, he didn't think he would ever get back up.

Everything was gone, and he wanted to be gone, too.

⊰—————⊱

Fenrir's head broke the surface of the well with a harsh intake. His hand shot up and grabbed his chest, as if he could slow his heartbeat by ripping it from his body. He still felt the prickle of being in his wolf form. It had been so long and for those moments, even through the fear and desperation, he felt whole.

He didn't think the water running down his face was from the well alone.

This was the cost for seeking your fate. For many days and nights, Fenrir would be thinking about all that he had seen and what it could mean. Everything was a possibility—half-truth, half-lie.

Fenrir shook himself from fate's grip and looked for Revna.

The sisters still surrounded the well, a golden thread pulsing and leading down to Revna, who was still submerged. He dropped his hand from his chest and waited for her to resurface. Her dark hair floated around her, distorting the golden light, leeching it of its color.

Fenrir's heartbeat chased the dread that headed for his stomach.

"Why isn't she resurfacing?" he asked the sisters.

The thread pulsed and the carved runes and fates engraved on the tree sparked with a muted glow. The light pulsed as if ...

Thump-thump.

It was a heartbeat.

"*The tree speaks to her,*" the Norns said, their voices coming from somewhere beyond.

Fenrir exhaled sharply, seeing his own breath curl in front of him. The edges of the well started to freeze, the heartbeat of the tree increasing as the ice crept to the well's center. To where Revna remained submerged.

A gasp from all three sisters redirected his gaze. They were staring at the thread in their hands, its golden glow bleeding to black and heading straight for Revna.

Ice cracked and groaned as it thickened. "Revna!" Fenrir yelled.

"Do *not* pull her out, wolf," Skuld commanded. "It will make her go mad."

He may not be able to pull her out, but that didn't mean he couldn't join her.

Fenrir plunged back under the freezing water.

TWENTY-ONE

REVNA

R EVNA SQUINTED AGAINST THE hot kiss of the sun, her eyes finally focusing to find Fenrir laying upon the shore of a river. Younger, and with skin unmarked by scars or ink, he was stretched back with one arm behind his head, water droplets on his bare chest, face submitting to the sun. A loud thump sounded, and more water rained down on his body.

Revna looked toward the source and saw Jormun in his serpent form, writhing about in the waters. Fenrir didn't say anything to his brother's attempt at goading, just gave a small smile while shaking his head. Nearby, Hel was kneeling near a bush collecting some kind of berries.

Happy. Content.

Sunshine and warmth. No darkness or hiding.

These were the feelings permeating Revna's body as she looked upon this moment in Fenrir's memory.

Like the sharp inhalation of the air before a storm, Revna's body became attuned to the taste of the air around her. Everything was loud and bright and textured. Impossible to ignore and so, so real. She wanted to join Fenrir on that riverbank. To bask in the sun and get lost in meaningless conversations. But something like the soft whisper of nails on the back of her neck had Revna tensing.

Fenrir jumped to his feet.

"Jor," he murmured just loud enough for his brother to pause and turn a giant serpent head toward him. "Come here."

"Hel—" he called to his sister, but she was already at his side. Trusting in whatever instinct had her brother's teeth elongating and a rumble building in his chest. Jormun shifted and climbed the riverbank to grab his trousers. Revna had only seen him in his serpent form, but she couldn't take the time to study him closely in this moment, though the surprising shock of white hair nearly compelled her to. Jormun finished putting on his bottoms as a man stepped out from a thicket of bushes on the other side of the river.

He was tall and lanky, with shoulder-length white-blond hair and eyes that seemed to shift colors depending on the angle of his head. He was clothed in fine garments, rich blues, woven with silver threads. A mischievous smile pulled on his mouth.

"What are you doing here, Father?" Fenrir asked.

"My children." Loki smiled. "How wonderfully you have grown."

Even through the veil of memory, a warning that felt like teeth sinking into her skin had Revna's body preparing to fight.

"Shouldn't you be back in Asgard with your *real* wife and children?" Hel sneered.

Loki looked unaffected by his children's apparent anger. "I told you I would return, so here I am. In fact, I am here to collect you."

Revna knew then. Knew what memory she was being shown, and already she felt a sorrowful ache pull at her bones. She watched as Fenrir's whole body became taut, and she had the desire to reach out and grab his hand.

"I've told all of Asgard about you, and they are very eager to meet you. In fact, they want to hold a banquet in your honor. Where all can witness your strength, cunning, and abilities!" Loki continued, raising his hands in a surrendering motion. "I know you are apprehensive, and I do not blame you. So, I have brought two friends to meet you—to assure you there is nothing to fear."

Fenrir growled, Jormun hissed, and Hel's draugr separated from her body and stood slightly in front of the three of them, as two men stepped out from behind Loki. One was large, with hair and beard as red as fire. Thor. Revna recognized him from her first day in Vanaheim. Much like then, she had the desire to snarl at him.

The other was ...

Tyr. Younger, with both hands intact, and dark eyes wide and staring at the three siblings.

"You weren't lying Loki, they are quite monst—impressive," Thor said, stumbling on his words.

Monstrous was what he'd meant to say, and Revna saw the way the word struck all three siblings differently. Fenrir's nose wrinkled in a snarl. Jormun's eyes narrowed, and Hel flinched and cast her eyes over to her brothers.

"Children, this is Thor, and this is Tyr, a son of the Allfather." Loki clapped his hands together. "Now, come. We can't be late for your own feast, can we?"

"What about Mother?" Jormun asked.

Loki's smile became brittle. "Do not worry about your mother. She will understand."

"And if we don't come with you?" Hel asked.

"Odin will be very disappointed. In fact, he will take great offense and may send others to *speak* with your mother," Thor replied.

Revna watched as both Jormun and Hel looked to Fenrir for guidance in how to proceed. But Fenrir was looking across the river to where Tyr stood. There was still wariness there, but Revna could sense of undercurrent of curiosity.

"We will be back before the morning?" Fenrir asked his father. Loki dipped his head in agreement. "Then we will come with you. But only if you go tell our mother right now."

"Go on ahead with Thor and Tyr, and I will be along shortly." Before Fenrir could say another word, his father shifted into a bird and flew in the direction of their caves.

Revna's eyes felt blurry as images and movement raced across her vision. Things tilted and shifted until they became solid again. Her senses were overloaded by flowers, intricate stonework, and lush greenery. Not the deep, rich green of a quiet forest, but a loud and vibrant array that demanded notice.

Fenrir, Hel, and Jormun stood before a dais, surrounded by warriors. Sitting on the throne, spear in hand, was Odin, the Allfather.

He had ash-colored hair that was brushed back from his face, making his missing eye all the more stark. It was covered with a rough brown eye-patch, a rune of wisdom at its center. Though he was lounging at ease, with one leg outstretched, Revna could tell he likely came only to Fenrir's chest. He wasn't overly muscled, nor was he thin or lithe. Altogether he seemed ordinary.

Revna had thought she'd feel a sense of reverence and awe upon seeing the mighty Allfather. It seemed the young Fenrir felt the same, because he stood taller, lifted his chin, and glared. Odin only snorted in derision.

"I do not rise to provocation, young one." Odin's rich voice echoed off the ornately carved domed ceiling.

"And I do not bow to liars," Fenrir said, his voice coming out a half-growl. "We were promised a feast and safe return to our home. So far this feels more like an ambush." He eyed the warriors and their varying weapons with disdain.

Revna watched as Odin's grip tightened on his spear, but his eye remained unflinching.

"Tell me, what do you know of the nine realms?" Odin looked between Fenrir, Hel, and Jormun.

"Why are we here?" Fenrir demanded, ignoring Odin's question. He took a slight step in front of his sister and brother. It was in these little moments, these little movements that Revna recognized parts of herself in Fenrir. The need to protect, the need to bear the weight. Core-deep impulses they shared, and a sense of responsibility she hadn't realized she'd learned from him. A jagged piece of her heart softened.

Odin pushed off his throne and walked down the steps to where they stood. He stopped three steps above them and looked down his nose. "The balance of the nine realms is crucial to its survival. Chaos and harmony, light and dark, love and war. All need to remain in balance for life to survive. To thrive. And I am burdened with its protection. You three"—he pointed his spear in their direction—"are also under my protection. And I do not think you are thriving within a remote cave system in Jotunheim. That is why I am setting you free."

The hall was so quiet, so still, that Revna could feel a storm gathering strength.

"I don't understand," Hel whispered.

Odin looked upon her pityingly and sighed. "I know. But in time you will understand this kindness."

"Then explain," Jormun seethed.

"In due time. For now, you've had an arduous journey and need rest. At daybreak, we will gather for a meal and discuss things further. Attendants will show you to your rooms." Odin raised his hand and three attendants appeared and gestured to follow. In three separate directions.

Hel shrugged out of her attendant's grip, her draugr form sliding from her body, causing everyone to shuffle with unease. "I will *not* be parted from my brothers."

Odin, however, did not react. He stared, unseeing, at Hel, having a silent conversation within his own mind.

Loki, who'd entered the grand room while Odin spoke, grasped the opportunity. "My children, if I am not mistaken, the Allfather has prepared you each your own dwelling in relation to your *uniqueness*."

Revna could smell the lie on the air. She wanted to scream out to Fenrir to flee.

"Hel," Fenrir called to his sister. She turned, but her draugr form's eyes remained locked on Odin. "We will see each other at the meal. All is well."

Hel eyed him warily and then looked at Jormun. She gave a nod and pieced her two halves back together. Revna felt a weight land heavy in her stomach as she watched Hel and Jormun being led away. Fenrir's eyes didn't stray from their retreating forms. Didn't hear Thor and a handful of warriors' approach in time. Didn't hear when Revna tried to scream out in warning as a collar was snapped around his neck and a cage slammed down, surrounding him.

Revna watched as Fenrir struggled not to shift. Or maybe there was an enchantment within the collar and cage that prevented him. But there was nothing withholding the waves of anger and despair coming from him, and wracking her body with the emotions.

"Listen closely," Odin said as Fenrir pulled on the bars. "Because your capitulation will be the only thing that protects your siblings."

Fenrir paused, but his hands remained wrapped tightly around the metal of the cage. His chest was moving up and down in heavy pants and his eyes burned holes right through Odin's skull.

"Hel and Jormun are safe for this night, but if you do not agree to my terms, then drastic action must be taken to ensure the realms may never fear their abominable existence." He adjusted his spear to his other hand, still standing on a step above. "Should you agree, they will be given homes in their rightful place. Hel will thrive amongst her kind, and Jormun can swim free."

And for Fenrir?

"What do you want from me?" Fenrir's voice was so deep and full of warning that several warriors shuffled on their feet.

Odin finally took that last step down and came to stand right in front of the cage. He took a moment to look Fenrir up and down with his one eye, but revealed nothing of fear, though Revna could smell a hint of it. Or maybe Fenrir could. It was hard to tell what she was feeling apart from him.

"You will *obey*," Odin stated calmly. "You will reside here in Asgard, and do as you are told, when you are told. You will be mine to—"

With barely a grunt of force, Fenrir's hands pulled the bars apart, and faster than anyone could react, he grabbed Odin by the collar and pulled his face against the bars.

Revna's momentary pride dissolved into dread when Odin spoke next.

"Go *kill* them."

Warriors moved in the direction of where Hel and Jormun had retreated.

No. Fenrir's hand dropped from Odin's tunic, the blood draining from his face.

"No! Wait! I'll do it. I will." He swallowed as if a bitter taste filled his mouth, "I will obey."

Odin gave a sneer-like smile. "I thought so."

The edges of the memory were starting to blur as the cage lifted from around Fenrir and long poles were attached to his collar. Guards began shuffling him away from the main hall. Fenrir's neck twisted uselessly in the collar, trying desperately to look over his shoulder to where he knew

Hel and Jormun had been taken. Odin was lazily walking behind Fenrir's form, still speaking, but Revna could hear none of it.

She could only feel Fenrir. Feel every thought and emotion coursing through his mind and body as if they were her own. Could feel the prickling heat of his need to shift. The anger-shrouded fear that coated his tongue. The immense strength it took to not fight back—to not resist.

Revna felt how a part of him fractured, and it broke her heart just the same. But something within her sternum loosened. A tightness unraveled as she finally understood another piece of what had made him into the man she knew. As she saw him as not a man, monster, or God, but as a reflection of her own self. Her fears, her hopes, her hurts.

She compelled herself to chase after him through the doorway the guards had pulled him through. Somewhere in her muscles, a memory strained to the surface of another place, another time, another chase. But as she approached the door, a wall black as pitch met her, and Fenrir was nowhere in sight.

Revna didn't hesitate to walk into the awaiting dark.

⇥—————⇤

All around her was endless white. Heavy, wet snow clung to Revna's clothes and hair as it fell in eager and unrelenting heaps.

She could see her hot breath mingling with the cold, could feel the way her lungs burned on an inhale. Could hear a whisper in the biting winter winds. The whisper grew louder, as if trying to get her attention without disturbing the surrounding air.

She turned, searching for its source and took a step back as she looked up at the boundless height of Yggdrasil. Its gnarled roots and twisted branches occupied everywhere she looked. It was shadowed in the fiery setting sun—black against crimsons and orange.

No, not a sunset. Fire.

Revna ducked as the wind picked up, blowing flame and snow around in conflicting torrents. The snow started to melt under the fire's continuous assault, flooding the area until a current was sweeping Revna under. She fought for the surface but was thrown against something hard.

Whether it was root or branch, she didn't care. She clung to it, nails digging into the bark. Calluses ripped open, and blood black as night coated her hands.

The nine began with fire and ice
What happened once, shall now be twice

An ancient voice spoke, calming the current enough for Revna to pull herself up on the tree, her fingers finding purchase in a smooth divot. Heaving her sodden body up, she came face to face with a skull—her fingers punctured where eyes were once inlaid. Everywhere she looked, bones jutted from the tree, floated in the water surrounding her. An eerie hollow song rose as they clashed together in the current.

A moon-kissed raven, shadows in wake
With unbound chains, the darkness break
A sharpened wing, strong bleeding heart
To softened shadows where sorrows start
Sky rends, earth roars, full winters mourn,
From rise, things found again be torn

The voice had wormed into Revna's ear, its echo vibrating through her entire being. It came from everywhere and nowhere. It was ancient and new and full of power. But something within the words was strained and pleading. She rested her head against the bone-encrusted root and closed her eyes to the circling storm of fire, snow, and water. Listening …

These roots and wings, fates intertwined
A cov'nant sealed, both power and bind
Slumb'ring beasts rise from lore and from flame
Bringing both ruin and a new world's name

The voice faded into the wind, and the fire was suffocated by snow. Ice triumphing over the flame. Revna lifted her head and looked upon a new and terrifying landscape, watched as the water she hovered above froze with thunderous cracks.

She tried pulling herself up higher on the tree's curved limb, but her fingers slipped on the ice-glazed surface. And then she was falling and plunging into frigid depths. She opened her eyes, but only darkness greeted her. There was no up or down, no here or there. Only cold, seductive darkness. It held her, whispered to her. Tempted her to let go—to let it in.

And for a moment, she wanted to.

Just as her lungs started to burn with near surrender, a warmth trailed up her arms and cupped the back of her neck. It traced her jaw, parted her lips, and filled her lungs. Revna leaned into that heat. Let it pull her from whatever attempted to keep her frozen in place.

Light filtered in. Then sound.

"Revna!" She broke the surface with a gasp, her face pressed against the solid warmth of Fenrir's chest, his arms wrapped around her waist.

With trembling hands, she pushed herself back a little and gazed up at him. Chunks of ice clumped together in his hair and coated his lashes, but his eyes were bright and full of worry. His hands left her waist and started making long strokes up and down her arm.

Her head felt so heavy, as if something wanted to pull her back under. Images and heart-squeezing feelings battled in her body.

Fenrir's memory.

The prophecy.

She needed to move, needed to do something, but when she tried to take a step, her knees buckled. Fenrir was there in an instant, scooping her up in his arms, pushing his body through the chunks of floating ice to the edge of the well.

The moment she was set on its edge, Verhandi was there draping a weave around her shaking body, the fabric soft and warm, as though it had been kept by the fire. Fenrir pulled himself out and took the weave that was handed to him, then sat next to Revna, putting his arm around her and pulling her close.

Revna had so much she wanted to say, but she couldn't. Even with the use of her voice, she didn't know if she would be able to find the words. Didn't know how to describe the ache and understanding.

So she sat with him, and he with her, sharing warmth and letting their skin and bones thaw. And as her heart beat loud and strong, she thought maybe that had thawed a little, too.

Twenty-Two

Fenrir

FENRIR WAS STARTING TO warm up under the heat of the weave, but he refused to move. Revna had stopped trembling, but something still had its teeth in her. She stared at the waters of the well, unseeing, her scent shifting too fast for him to read. He wouldn't let her go until she was ready.

It was maddening—watching what *was* become what *could* be. Fenrir had no idea what she had seen or experienced, but if it was anything like his ...

His skin prickled at the memory of being in his wolf form, surrounded by ash and destruction. Watching Revna crumble to nothing under his touch. True fear nested in his sternum, breeding terrible, monstrous thoughts.

Maybe he was her ruin. Her destruction.

His arm tightened around her shoulders to give her a warning before he spoke. "I'm sorry, Revna."

She turned her head to him with brows furrowed in a question. Though he'd already apologized for leaving her in Myddheim, for lying to her, he knew it wasn't enough. He hadn't fully comprehended the depth of her hurt until he'd witnessed it for himself. Had *felt it* for himself.

"We don't have to talk about it, and you don't need to tell me what you saw, but ..." He paused, clenching his jaw. "The day I left you, the day of the sacrifice, I didn't realize how it would hurt you. For that, I am truly sorry."

She gave a slight bob of her chin and opened her mouth as if to speak, but then gave a frustrated sigh through her nose.

"When you found me in that cave in Myddheim," he continued, "I was broken, defeated, and hopeless. I'd had a long time to let things fester inside of me. I'd become so full of anger that it poisoned me. Then, you came into the cave seeking shelter from a storm, covered in blood, with nearly the same look in your eyes."

He glanced over at her, but her eyes were distant, as if she was recalling the night. "Ignoring all my snarling and threats, you sat with me. You saw through it and freed me. In more ways than one, Revna."

She turned her face back to him then, eyes brighter and color returning to her lips and cheeks. He knew words couldn't pass the pain in her throat, but for the first time since her arrival, she was letting him see her. No looking away. No hiding behind clever words.

There was so much strength in her vulnerability in this moment, and he wouldn't let her do it alone. He returned her stare, letting God, man, and wolf come to the surface. Letting her see.

For the first time in a long time, Fenrir felt hopeful.

He knew there was still a long way to go, and he still had so much to tell her, but for now, he accepted the moment of peace. She broke the stare first and glanced over to the other side of the well. Fenrir followed her gaze to where the sisters stood close together talking in low tones. Beyond the scents of the tree and well, Fenrir smelled a tangled knot of emotion coming from the sisters.

"We should leave," he whispered to Revna. They untangled themselves, Fenrir already missing her body pressed to the side of his. They were almost fully dressed, securing their weapons, when Skuld approached.

"There is no going back now. No way to unsee, no way to unravel your threads. Things in motion cannot be stopped." She glanced over at Revna, her face blank. "In time you will understand what is, what can be, and what needs to be."

Fenrir tried to refrain from scowling at the future-weaving Norn, but then his brows dipped as he noticed the illuminated mark peeking from beneath her tunic. She noticed his gaze, and lifted her chin, a gust of sorrow hitting his nose.

"I'm sorry," she said under her breath.

Without another word, she turned and left them staring at her back. Urdu and Verhandi had their hands on Yggdrasil's root, eyes closed, brows furrowed in concentration. Revna gripped his arm, pulling his attention.

She made a gesture toward him. *Let's leave.*

They made their way back to the fog, but before he could breach the barrier, Fenrir turned back for one last look at the sisters. He frowned at what he saw.

Skuld, tears running down her face, was staring at Revna.

TWENTY-THREE

REVNA

*S*OMETHING WAS COMING.

Revna wasn't sure what to make of the barbed words of the prophecy, or how they snagged her thoughts anytime she tried thinking of something else. The things she'd seen ... if she dwelled on them for more than a moment, she felt as if it would swallow her whole.

Ice and flame and darkness.

So much darkness.

Revna felt her heart beat faster, her breath change, so she resorted to old tactics. Distracting herself.

Fenrir was a few strides ahead, so she reached under her tunic and lightly pressed on the still healing wound. She bit her lip to keep from making noise. The pain anchored her, let her refocus and halt the thoughts currently unraveling in her mind. She took a couple deep breaths in and out, and slowly removed her touch.

Branches moved aside as Fenrir approached them, holding open long enough for Revna to move around or under. She stared at the broad expanse of his back, but he showed no physical signs of using his power. After what she'd witnessed in his memory, she wondered that she'd never seen him shift to his wolf form. Was it because of what he'd suffered? What Hel and Jormun had suffered?

How many times had he been collared? Chained? Called a monster?

Perhaps when her voice returned, they would talk about it. But for now, she decided to let her own old wounds scab over and begin to heal.

The blanket of fog lessened as they drew closer to Angrboda's cave system. All the trees this deep into Jotunheim seemed to be in a suspended state of moldering, half-bare and varying in browns and dull reds. From somewhere above, a raven called and took flight.

A moon-kissed raven, shadows in wake

With unbound chains, the darkness break

The words tumbled in Revna's head round and round. She tried to parse through them, but couldn't even seem to wrap her mind around the first line. Raven ... was that meant to be her? Some instinct within her knew it was, but what did it mean? She'd thought by going to see the sisters she would find answers, but all she'd found was more questions.

Sky rends, earths roar, full winters mourn

From rise, things found again be torn

Skuld had said she would understand when the time was right. Until then, Revna would have to live with the confusion. But that didn't mean she had to live with it alone.

Ahead of her, Fenrir reached up and rubbed the back of his neck, the inked bands on his forearms catching the light. She had to make a choice. When her voice returned, would she tell Fenrir of the prophecy? Did he already know?

Revna gently rubbed at her throbbing temples. She was exhausted. She wanted to eat some of Austri's food and then sleep until her body no longer felt like she took every step through unforgiving mud. But she knew she had to push through a little bit longer. Angrboda had said she wanted to check their poisoned wounds one more time before they could head back to Vanaheim. Fenrir's scratch was fully healed, save for a faint blue scar. Revna's wound ached deeply but was manageable. She had the sinking suspicion the giantess witch just wanted to see her son one more time.

Fenrir slowed to a stop and retrieved the leather pouch of water from his side. He took a sip and then handed it to Revna. She gulped down the cool water, then noticed him watching her. She cocked an eyebrow at him in question.

"We don't have much further, but if you're too tired or in pain, we can stay with my mother tonight," he said, the chords of his neck tightening. She shook her head and tucked the canteen into the crook of her arm, making the gesture for home. A twitch of a smile pulled at the corner of his mouth. "If you're in too much pain, I don't want to push—"

He stopped mid-sentence as she shoved the water pouch back at him with an irrefutable look of dissent and started trekking ahead. Right now, the pain was the only thing keeping her upright and moving forward. Without it, she was afraid the weight of everything would cause her to crumble.

Angrboda's caves came into view a short while later and Revna nearly sighed in relief. So far, she didn't care for Fenrir's mother, but the giantess was skilled in the ways of doors and could get them back to the gate quicker than walking.

She turned to face Fenrir, wanting to ask him if he minded seeing his mother again. If not, they could walk. Even if it took them a few days. When she looked at him, she could see the heaviness in his eyes, the exhaustion in his body, and she felt something inside of her clench with worry. From his look of sudden concern when his gaze swept over her, he must have seen the same thing on her face. She had to shove down the fear that rose with her shield falling, with letting anyone see her pain.

His face softened. "Revna, I—"

Fenrir's head snapped up and a low growl sounded from the back of his throat. She grabbed both blades from her hip and whirled, preparing to take on whatever intruder had caused Fenrir to react. He immediately stepped past so that he was next to her, but slightly in front.

"Come out, you fucking coward," Fenrir snarled.

Revna readied herself to fight. She was sore and stiff but knew her body would respond. She would not fail to protect herself, and Fenrir, too.

What she didn't expect was a gray dappled mare to lazily walk out from between the trees, grazing on the wild grass as if it didn't have a care in the world. She sheathed her daggers just as Fenrir whipped out a knife and threw it at the horse. Revna sucked in a breath and grabbed at Fenrir before he could throw another blade, but before the knife struck true, the horse disappeared.

In its place was a smiling man. One she recognized, though they'd never met.

"It's wonderful to see you, too. Son."

Loki.

Revna's momentary shock quickly abated as Fenrir stalked toward his father. She stepped in front of him and placed her hands on his chest. His whole body was vibrating, gold eyes flashing, teeth elongating, lips pulled back into a snarl. Revna hadn't been with Fenrir long, but he'd never shifted into his wolf form, even when they'd faced danger. She wondered if it was going to happen now.

She knew he already felt guilt for killing the giant who'd attacked her. She'd felt in his body in the cave, heard it in his tone as he'd told Hel. She wasn't about to let him attack his father and add to it.

Revna dug her nails through the thin fabric of his tunic and gave it a little tug, demanding his attention. His breath was coming in heavy pants, but slowly his gaze found hers. She took a deep breath, indicating he should do the same. Another low growl was building in his chest underneath her hand, so she dug her nails deeper and furrowed her brows at him. His nostrils flared and his eyes lazily roved from her hands, to her chest, her neck, her lips, and finally her eyes.

Without breaking eye contact with her, he said to his father, "Leave."

"I'm afraid I can't do that. You see, Odin demands your presence."

Fenrir's eyes left hers and snapped up to Loki. Revna slowly removed her hands and turned to stand next to Fenrir but kept him within reaching distance. What she could do if two Gods decided to fight, she didn't know, but she would have to try anyway.

"What?" Fenrir demanded through clenched teeth.

"Rumor has it that you killed a giant and he wants to know why. I am expected to return with you to Asgard presently."

If possible, Fenrir's body coiled tighter, freezing at Loki's request. Asgard was the seat of the nine realms, and home to the powerful Aesir Gods. From the little she'd pieced together from Fenrir, Hel, and Tyr, it was not a place they were keen on returning.

"I will bring myself to Asgard as soon as I attend to something in Vanaheim," Fenrir said, and Revna's stomach dropped.

"Ah, yes. Are you what he needs to attend to?" Loki asked Revna, finally acknowledging her presence.

"She is none of your concern and you would do well to remember that," Fenrir snapped.

Loki only smiled and kept his eyes on Revna. "Perhaps. But I'm certain Odin would be *very* interested in hearing about a mortal woman being kept as your pet."

Fenrir growled and took two quick steps toward Loki. Revna stepped in front of him again, pushing against his large, solid body. Her wound gave a painful twinge, and she hissed in a breath. Fenrir froze and lifted the edge of her tunic to inspect her wound. Seeing that she was not bleeding, he sighed and looked at his father again.

"I will go with you, as long as I can send her back through the gate to Vanaheim. She needs to heal," Fenrir said, and she saw what it cost him. Revna narrowed her eyes at him acquiescing because of her, and considered punching him.

"Wonderful. I will go retrieve your mother to open a door for us. She was wondering whether you would return." Loki sauntered away.

Revna looked at Fenrir, reared back a fist, and punched him in his arm—it probably caused her more pain than him.

"Please don't argue with me on this, Revna." He sighed, then stepped into her personal space again, eyes flashing gold, and lifted her chin in his hand. To both their surprise, she let him. "Trust me. For your safety and mine."

She did trust him.

Trusting *him* wasn't the problem. It was him going to Asgard alone when she did not trust those who resided there. For a moment, she considered demanding to go with him. Looking up at him, his exhaustion, the tension, and the burning in his gaze—she decided she might be more distraction than help.

Reluctantly, Revna nodded and watched as some of the tension released from his jaw as he dropped her chin.

Angrboda and Loki came back into view, the witch and the trickster.

"Is this why you asked us to return?" Fenrir growled at his mother. "To lure me back to see him?"

Angrboda only lifted her slightly pointed chin and narrowed her eyes at her son. "One day, you will understand." She glanced at Revna then, and Revna had the urge to bare her teeth at the giantess.

Quicker than she'd expected, though, Revna found herself stepping through Angrboda's door to arrive at the gate. She braced her hands on her knees, barely holding down the urge to retch. She felt Fenrir's hand on the back of her neck, but this time she didn't push him away. Once the world stopped spinning, they walked the short distance to the gate embedded in stone.

"Will you be able to find your way back to the keep?" Fenrir asked quietly, his back to his scheming parents. Revna glared at them. Loki smirked, Angrboda looked as if she was considering turning her into a worm. Fenrir gently gripped her chin again, redirecting her attention. "*Revna.*"

She relented with a slight nod.

"When you return, will you please tell Hel and Tyr where I am? And that I'll be back as soon as I can."

What was soon? What did time mean for a God?

Panic crested in Revna's throat, the knot in her chest tightening. How long would he be gone? What if Odin decided to cage him again, and this time Revna wouldn't be able to free him?

This was all her fault.

She would inform Hel and Tyr—and hopefully they could conspire a way to ensure his return to Vanaheim. He would not be sacrificing himself again. Not for her—not for her sneaking and carelessness.

He dropped her chin to reach up and tap the nine runic symbols of the realms, the gate sparking awake under his touch. Before looking at Fenrir to say farewell, she stepped slightly around him and made sure she met the stare of his mother and father one last time, conveying all the disgust she could in one cold look. She knew only a small portion of what they'd put their children through, and she hoped she would never have to see either of them again.

As they glared at back, Fenrir gently grabbed her by the shoulders and positioned her back in front of the gate.

His body was a solid wall behind her, shielding her from the eyes of his parents. The hair near her ear stirred as his hands skimmed from her shoulders down to her hands. She let herself give in and leaned back, feeling the heat of him permeate through her layers. His thumb stroked the sensitive skin of her inner wrist.

"Does this mean you've forgiven me?" he whispered in her ear, a chill cascading down her spine. She felt warm lips graze her neck, just for a moment, her body arching into the warm sensation. Revna felt his hands tighten on her wrists, and a low growl radiate into her back. "See you soon, my *máni*."

Before she could respond, he pushed her through the gate and back to Vanaheim.

⇥━━━⇤

The lush forest was cooling under a dusky sky as she stepped through the gate. She found it was a relief to be amongst the green of Vanaheim. As quickly as her body allowed her, she followed the well-worn path back to the tunnel that led to the keep. As she approached the entrance on the side of the mountain, Revna startled.

Standing in the mouth of the tunnel like a sentry was Hel, but not Hel.

The draugr version of her—rotting and sharp—was waiting for her and Fenrir. Revna tamped down the fear of looking death directly in the eye. She dipped her chin in greeting when Death noticed her. The draugr turned and Revna followed quickly, uncaring of the pain in her side.

Soon, she heard the echo of boots slapping against stone, hurrying toward her.

When Tyr and Hel came into view, Hel wove herself back together and then searched the space behind Revna. Shame and guilt nearly pulled her to her knees, wanting to beg for their forgiveness. She had returned without Hel's brother and Tyr's best friend.

"Where is he, Revna?" Tyr asked first as Hel continued to look behind Revna as if her brother would walk out of the forest at any moment.

She wished she had her voice back so that she could quickly explain what happened and then apologize until his safe return.

She didn't know how to sign for Asgard, and the sign for Valhalla would surely alarm them, so she drew the rune for Odin in the air between them.

"*Asgard*? He's—" Tyr hissed in anger. She had never seen him anything other than jovial and calm, until now. "*Fuck.*"

Hel was looking at her, and Revna felt like crumbling under the Goddess's scrutiny.

"Tyr, can you—" Hel started.

"Leaving now," he said before she could finish, taking off down the tunnel where Revna had come from only moments before. Revna turned to follow, but Hel gripped her arm.

"*No*," she spat. "You've already done enough."

The statement hit Revna square in her stomach. Hel was right, of course. Even if she could speak right now, nothing Revna could say would cool the burn of concern that Hel was feeling for her brother.

In appearance, Hel looked to be around the same age as Revna. But she knew hundreds of years and lifetimes of sorrows rested under the Goddess's skin, and Revna suddenly felt very small and young in comparison.

She nodded and followed Hel, the air of the tunnel becoming oppressive and cold.

They stopped by the kitchen to grab a plate of food—Austri piled hers high and sent her looks of concern. She didn't deserve any of it.

Hel then took Revna back to her room and left her alone without another word.

The fire was burning low, as if someone kept it constantly revived until she'd returned. She stood in the middle of the room, plate of food in hand. Only the low crackling of the fire kept the silence from engulfing her.

Calmly, she walked over to the table and the twin chairs and set her plate down, and then stood in front of the fire.

Clenching her fists at her sides, she opened her mouth to scream. But nothing came out. And no one would hear.

Twenty-Four

Fenrir

T HE NAUSEATING UNDERTONES OF overly ripe apples burned Fenrir's nose as he stood in the middle of a half-circle of the Aesir. The scent brought forth memories that set his teeth on edge. One chair sat slightly above the rest at the center. And one, as always, remained empty—the Goddess Freyja having not left her mountain hall since she'd escaped a seedy marriage bind and was burned for it.

Thor, Baldur, Loki, Heimdall, and Frey all sat in torch-lit chairs surrounding Fenrir. Frigg and Idunn, the only two Goddesses present, stood behind Odin at the center. Fenrir tried to ignore the other two that stood behind his father. Loki's sons from his marriage to Signyn. His brothers, he supposed, but would never call them as such. They'd never spoken a word to each other.

Fenrir kept his arms clasped loosely behind his back in an effort to look relaxed.

After he saw Revna safely back to Vanaheim, he gave his mother a terse goodbye before stepping through the gate with his father—neither of them saying a word to one another as they made their way to the twilight lit courtyard.

Behind Odin, a root of the Yggdrasil towered and stretched to the sky. The sight of it caused his thoughts to drift to another root and another realm. No matter his circumstance, his thoughts always seemed to drift to Revna. Surrounded by all these Gods, that was dangerous.

"What do you have to say for yourself, dog?" Thor asked.

Fenrir ignored the taunt. "You will need to be more specific."

Baldur gave a soft snort and Thor glared toward the young God as he placed a fist over his mouth, clearing his throat. Fenrir's lips twitched. Baldur, like his brother Tyr, never quite fit in with the other Gods. He was peaceful and kind and warm. For Tyr's sake, Fenrir wished Baldur would get out from under their father's thumb.

Odin stamped his spear on the marble floor, redirecting attention. "You killed the giant Jalmir."

It was a statement, and one he wasn't planning on denying. But he would withhold a few of the details. "I did."

"Why?"

For a moment, Fenrir wanted to ask how they'd found out, but one glance over to where his father sat had him answering his own question.

"He attacked first and wouldn't listen to reason." Fenrir swallowed down the bitter guilt he felt. He should have tried harder to talk sense into the giant, but when Revna was bleeding in his arms, every ugly part of his being had roared to the surface.

"And why would he attack you?" Odin's voice remained level and low.

Fenrir chose his next words carefully. "He claimed the Aesir had killed his brother, Spjut. He wanted revenge."

Confirming silence met Fenrir's ears.

"He's not dead—he is currently being questioned in our dungeons," Heimdall said, waving a hand in dismissal. "He and a few other Jotunns tried sneaking into Asgard. We detained them."

Fenrir remained silent, willing his face to remain neutral.

"It seems you have not done your duty to quell the rising insurrection currently festering in Jotunheim," Odin stated, refusing to ask a question directly.

In truth, Fenrir's trips to Jotunheim had been uneventful and mild, save for a few squabbles. But unrest was slowly unfurling, and this would not help matters. The work he'd done to appease the residents of Jotunheim—listening, settling conflicts, fostering compromises and good will—would now be for nothing. Fenrir couldn't even fully blame the Aesir—his hands were just as dirty. Here was the monster they all thought him to be. The giants were a wary and suspicious bunch, and they presumed two of their own dead. It could lead to war. They had fought over less.

"In a way, you could argue that Fenrir has done his duty. The brothers were very vocal in their distaste for Asgard, and now one voice is silenced while the other sits in our dungeons," Frey's unexpected voice reasoned. Fenrir looked to the God, who gave him a subtle nod, his sunlit hair catching in the torch light. Fenrir wondered how much Frey and Freyja resembled each other—wondered how much he grieved her absence.

He also wondered how Frey could sit so at ease among the Gods who were responsible for his sister's torture and isolation.

Thor scoffed loudly, but Odin spoke over him. "You pull at your leash. Perhaps some time back in your cage here in Asgard—"

"No," a familiar voice said from behind him. He didn't need to turn to know it was Tyr. A knot behind his shoulder blades lessened in relief—Revna had made it back.

"And why should we listen to you, my errant son?"

Fenrir glanced just beyond Odin to where Frigg was standing, her face softening and brightening as she took in her son. Fenrir had never spoken much to the Goddess, but he did hear stories from Tyr about her once-sweet nature—one that his father had morphed into bitterness in Tyr's absence.

Tyr came to stand next to Fenrir. He looked at his friend, but Tyr's eyes were fixed behind where his father sat. First to his mother, then to

Idunn, the second look lingering too long. Fenrir could smell the slight change in Tyr's scent. Shifting to stand closer to Tyr, he subtly bumped his shoulder into his friend, disrupting his gaze.

"I accompanied him to Jotunheim. If not for him, I could be dead." Lie. Tyr was trying to appeal to what little affection his father still had for him. Fenrir wondered if his old friend would ever tire of sticking his neck—or hand, as the case was—out for him. He'd never be able to repay Tyr for his friendship and kindness. He only hoped that, in turn, he was the friend Tyr deserved.

"Your life would not be in any danger if you would just make your apologies and come home," Odin said, followed by grunts of agreement from Thor and Heimdall.

Fenrir took a step forward, reclaiming Odin's attention before Tyr had to respond. "I will be more cautious. Any whisper of insurrection will be brought directly to you."

Another lie. One that Fenrir wondered if Odin could see.

"As is in your best interest. We made a deal, after all." Odin glanced down to the twin inked bands on Fenrir's forearms.

"And does this deal still hold?" Fenrir asked, keeping his voice level. The Allfather's expression remained the same. Nothing to give away whether he'd sent the boat to Myddheim.

"Why wouldn't it, wolf?" Odin tilted his head, his remaining eye all too observant.

With so much at risk, Fenrir didn't dare respond with the question he really wanted to ask. Even with Tyr here, it was careless to goad the Aesir to their limits. Unending life did not give unending patience, and these Gods had very little. One wrong word, one sudden movement, was all they would need to punish him again. Even though a part of him feared that kind of torture, it would be those he left behind who would suffer the most.

Hel. Jormun. Tyr. The residents of Vanaheim.

And Revna.

The pull he felt to get back to her, to ensure she was well, was a constant ache in his bones. He would need to sort through those feelings later, but first he needed get out of Asgard and out from under the watchful eye of the Aesir.

"We will take our leave of you." Fenrir dipped his chin and turned to leave.

Odin's spear slammed once again onto the marble dais, the sound provoking the wolf underneath Fenrir's skin, and he turned back.

"Any further missteps and I will recall you to Asgard," Odin said, his voice placid. "It is a privilege that I allow you to reside in Vanaheim. But I will take that privilege away should you need reminding of your place."

No.

To be taken away from Vanaheim, to be taken away from …

His fists tried to clench at his side, but he stopped them, swallowing back the defensive snarl that burned in his throat as well. Beside him, Tyr's anger flooded his senses. Fenrir couldn't speak, so he dipped his head in acquiescence. As he turned his back once more to leave, Odin spoke again.

"You have one more duty to perform before you may leave."

⇥———⇤

Giants bled blue.

It stained Fenrir's hands as a reminder of what he'd done. A reminder of what little power he possessed. It would take hot water and a skin-tearing scrub to rid it completely from his skin.

He'd have to burn the clothes.

Tyr was waiting for him in the hall that led down to the dungeons. He eyed the sack in Fenrir's hand, the one containing Spjut's head, and let out a harsh breath.

"I'm so sorry Fen—"

"Do not apologize," Fenrir said, cutting his friend off. "This is not your fault."

Tyr remained quiet but fell into step beside him as they made their way through the halls of Asgard, the blood-soaked sack and his boots leaving a morbid trail through the pristine halls. They could clean up the fucking mess.

Odin had demanded that Fenrir torture information out of Spjut before cutting his head off and delivering it back to Jotunheim with a message.

The Aesir will not tolerate disobedience.

Fenrir realized he was still holding the dull knife they'd given him and tossed it on the floor. He couldn't remember the last time he'd slept, and he felt it down to his very marrow. But it would be some time before he could collapse into his bed.

The last time he had dozed was with Revna in his arms, fever coursing through their bodies. He wondered how it would feel to hold her in sleep without the threat of death. He wasn't sure it was likely, but he held onto the thought, held it close in his mind, to keep the darkness from closing in.

As they rounded the corner that would lead them to the gate, Tyr's steps slowed. Glancing up, he saw Tyr's mother, Frigg, waiting for them. Her posture was stiff, and her gaze skittered around in constant vigilance. Her complexion was almost identical to Tyr's richly tanned skin, but where Tyr and Baldur had dark hair, Frigg possessed a unique golden-berry shade. As they approached the Goddess, her eyes seemed in complete contrast to her stiff and alert body. She looked depleted.

She eyed the sack and closed her eyes briefly—as much of an apology as she'd allow.

"Mother?" Tyr's voice was full of unnamed emotion, his scent muddled.

She sighed and placed a careful smile on her face. "I just wanted to look upon you one more time before you left. You look well—*strong*."

"I am well," Tyr said, as she took a step forward, reaching for his arm without a hand. Fenrir still couldn't look upon it without feeling immense shame. Never once had Tyr used it against him. "And you, Mother? Are you well?"

"I am fine. Don't you dwell on me." She looked up at her son and Fenrir felt the love in that gaze. So different from what his own mother looked at him with. No, Angrboda didn't gaze with love. Hers was one of assessment and plotting.

He watched Tyr's jaw clench as she placed his hand atop of hers on his arm. Fenrir wondered if he should look away, take a few steps back, to give them privacy for this intimate moment, but then Frigg turned her eyes to him.

"Be cautious in the coming days. Any small excuse is enough to push them into the war they crave." Frigg looked between him and Tyr. "Last time, so much was lost with such little purpose."

The Aesir and the Vanir had gone to war before. When Freyja and Frey had once lived among the Vanir, the Aesir sought Freyja's powers. The Goddess was powerful and could divine much that Odin couldn't even begin to understand. Her powers ranged from divination and healing to control over the natural world. Freyja could see past lies to the truth. She could see a person's fate almost as well as the Norns. When Odin had recalled her to Asgard, asking her to share the skill of her powers among the Aesir—to teach them—she obliged. But the power decayed in their greedy hands, as she warned it may. Furious, the Aesir conspired to marry and bind her to another, tricking her to stay within Asgard with false love so they could use her powers always, so they could twist and bend her to their will.

When Freyja found out, she killed her husband, freeing herself. The Aesir gave her a choice: remain in Asgard or be burned. Freyja begged for the flames. They burned her three times, and three times she rose from the ash, remade into a Goddess with fire in her heart.

She and her brother, Frey, returned to Vanaheim, and thus the Aesir declared war. It waged on for nearly three years, death and destruction taking its toll on both sides. Eventually, the fighting ceased, neither side able to gain ground or victory. They exchanged hostages in order to en-sure the fragile peace remained. Frey volunteered himself, and the Aesir sent the god Hoenir. With Frey gone, Freyja retreated to a mountain hall. She had not been seen since. Hoenir lived deep within Vanaheim, perfectly content to live out his days in a shack in the woods with all manner of creatures.

Fenrir was only a child when the war had waged, but he'd learned the intricacies of it from Tyr.

"Do they talk of waging war on the Vanir again? Or just the Jotunns?" Tyr asked his mother.

"On whoever challenges their power or place." Frigg's voice dropped to a whisper. She looked at Fenrir again. "You, most of all need to—"

Frigg swallowed her words at the sound of footsteps echoing off the polished stone. Thor appeared, face reddening as he took in the sight of the three of them standing close together. Fenrir's hand gripped the sack in his hands even harder, and he had the urge to swing and knock Thor out with the giant's head.

But that wouldn't be fair to the dead giant.

"Frigg, your husband calls. You should attend him," Thor admonished.

She pushed up on her toes and placed a kiss on Tyr's cheek and then turned and fled.

Tyr frowned after his mother and then glared at Thor.

"You two should be on your way to Jotunheim by now." Thor crossed his arms over his barreled chest. "I do hope the giants don't retaliate against you. It would be a shame if we lost our well-trained mutt."

Tyr, surprisingly, started advancing on Thor, but Fenrir held out his arm, stopping him. "It's not worth it."

Thor smiled and flicked his hand. "Run along then."

Fenrir's arm was still firm across Tyr's chest. He gave him a little push. They needed to leave before things escalated, before he or Tyr were pushed to do something that kept them locked away in Asgard. Tyr finally relented, spinning on his heels, walking purposefully to the gate.

Fenrir glanced at Thor one last time before stepping through—the loathsome brute already staring at him with a half-snarl, half-smile on his face, thunder rumbling overhead.

"See you soon, *dog*."

Twenty-Five

Revna

R EVNA WOKE UP NEXT to the long burned-out fire. After her silent screaming, she'd collapsed, staring into the fire until her eyes grew heavy with exhaustion, and sleep pulled her under.

Now standing, she gently stretched her arms over head, testing the limits of her wound. Sleeping on the hard floor had done nothing to alleviate the stiffness in her body, though she felt as if she deserved the discomfort. Ingrid's voice woke inside her head trying to convince her that punishing herself would not change anything or help anyone.

Revna hated it when she was right, though she deeply longed to hear her friend's chiding voice.

Massaging the vocal cords on her neck, she tentatively made a noise. To her surprise, a raspy, strained sound came out. She took a sip of water, and tried speaking into the silence the first word that came to mind.

"Fenrir." The name cracked quietly into the empty room, but it was there.

Revna strode to the door of her room and pulled it open, crossing the space to reach his door. Hesitantly, she lifted a hand and knocked, hoping he'd come back sometime in the night. As she waited, she looked down at herself. She hadn't changed out of her clothes from Jotunheim, or bathed for that matter, but she couldn't be bothered. Silence met her second knock, and her shoulders drooped in disappointment. She repeated her inquiry at Tyr's door and was again met with still silence.

When she came to Hel's door, she thought better of it, not wanting to see the anger and disappointment in the Goddess's eyes. Revna turned and looked at her own door, as well, but decided against retreating back into her chambers.

She passed a few residents on her way to the kitchens, already used to the slight otherworldliness of the elves, giants, and dwarves. Their namesakes did nothing to describe them, which had taken her by surprise. They came in all shapes and sizes; giants who were short, dwarves who were tall. Elves who looked completely ordinary. Skin with undertones of gray, blue, and gold. They sometimes nodded in greeting, but mainly let her be. Their refined senses probably could smell her coming, and a slight self-conscious blush stole across her cheeks.

Austri, solid and bushy-haired, was busy in the kitchens, as always. The warmth and the smell wrapped around her. She found the kitchens soothing. Revna watched as he carved sections out of a wild boar, twisting and wrenching a leg until it popped out of its socket. When he noticed her, he dropped the leg and strode to grab her a plate.

"Please don't trouble yourself, Austri," she said, her voice coming out on a croak. Revna rounded his workstation and attempted to take the plate from his hands. "I can serve myself."

The plate remained gripped between both of their hands as he surveyed her. He gave a small grunt and let his side go. "You look wan. You need to eat more. Fix yourself a plate and then come sit across from me so I can watch you."

Revna huffed out a small laugh and did as the dwarf bade. When she returned to his worktable, Austri leaned over to inspect her plate, giving her a small nod of approval at the meat, mushrooms, and berries. He placed a cup of warm tea in front of her, the smell of honey and herbs hitting her nose.

"It's pungent, but it will soothe your throat," he explained.

Some of the sullenness drained from her body with each bite of food and sip of tea. Austri remained quiet, but the silence was a companionable sort. He was giving her space and time while keeping her company. When the plate was clean, she leaned back in her chair and released a long breath, the warm food expanding to the spaces between her ribs.

Revna wanted to know more about this dwarf, who she'd taken to liking despite herself even before her journey to Jotunheim. "How long have you been here, Austri? In Vanaheim?"

He looked thoughtful for a moment before answering. "Not long after the war ended. However long that's been."

"Do you ever miss Nidavellir?"

The blunt question had Austri pausing his movements, but he regained his composure and started dicing meat in even cuts. For a moment, she didn't think he would answer her. The sounds of the kitchen surrounded them. She listened to the low bubbling from an iron pot over the fire and the occasional hiss of whatever was inside boiling over to strike the flames below. Austri's knife slid against the wooden table in a comforting rhythm. Just when she was about to apologize for being too forward, he cleared his throat.

"When war rages between Gods," he said, his resonant voice quieting the kitchen, "it's the little folk that bear the cost. In the time the Aesir and Vanir were at war, many lifetimes ago, Nidavellir was caught between them. The Aesir demanded we use our skill as crafters to forge great weapons, and it divided us. Some wanted the renown and gold it would bring, others wanted to be left out of it, stating it wasn't our war. Some sided with the Vanir, disgusted at what the Aesir did to Freyja." Austri let out a deep sigh, staring down at his scarred hands, now slicing vegetables. "It created an unbridgeable divide among all of Nidavellir. Our home was never the same." Revna watched as he struggled to choose his next words, the knife coming to a halt on the table. "I had a husband and a wife—Ymar and Vesprie."

Had. Revna's stomach sank to her feet.

"They loved the Goddess Freyja—were devoted to her in a way that sometimes had me exasperated, but I couldn't help but admire the way they'd felt her injustices so deeply as their own. So much so, that when the time came, they went to war. They fought for the Vanir, Freyja's side, and lost their lives. I begged them not to go—I was not permitted to battle because of my forging skills. I was a smith back then, able to forge and imbue weapons with power and protection, but it wasn't enough. It wasn't enough to protect them. Especially when they fought against weapons of our own making."

Austri took a deep breath, putting down the knife and placing the ingredients into a bowl. "I put out my forge and left Nidavellir. Came to Vanaheim to be closer to where they'd fallen—to see if I could feel them here. Sometimes I think I can. Hel tells me they are not in her realm, so I can only hope they reside in Freyja's mountain hall. Together." He looked at her then, and she looked back, standing witness to his story.

"So, yes. I do miss Nidavellir. But it's because I miss the things that *were* in Nidavellir—the people I loved, the person I was before my life was torn from me. I do not think I would ever go back. Fenrir, Tyr, and even Hel, have created something here that feels like comfort and safety. And I will do all I can to help protect that."

Revna could feel the wetness in her eyes, but refused to let it spill over. She got up and rounded the table. Austri went rigid for a moment as she threw her arms around him in a tight hug, then his shock melted away, and he gently placed one arm around her while the other patted the back of her head. They were nearly the same height, and the dwarf's thick, frizzy braid tickled her nose so much that she had to pull away, but not before his arm gave her one last squeeze.

She wanted to ask more questions, to fill in every gap in the story of his life, but she refrained. What he had given her was enough. And she felt honored that he'd shared it with her.

"Thank you," she said.

He looked at her in confusion. "For what?"

"Sharing your story. It was important."

"All stories are, in their own way." He assessed her, his light brown eyes searching hers. They softened as he seemed to come to some sort of conclusion. "Whatever it is that you are holding on to, young one, don't let it blind you from the things that truly matter. The good things that bring you joy and peace."

Too much discernment had Revna taking a step back. She placed a hand on his shoulder and gave it one more squeeze before going back to the other side of the table. At the urge to leave Austri alone with his thoughts, she decided it was a good time to hit the training arena. She'd try to slowly stretch her muscles, put herself to use by sharpening some blades. When she thanked Austri and bid him farewell, he pointed a knife at her.

"You come back for a second meal later today, or I'll send someone to come find you. Oh, and I will have hot water delivered to your chamber when darkness falls. You need a bath."

Revna couldn't repress the guttural laugh that slipped out through her tender throat.

⁂

Hours later, Revna was covered in more sweat and grime, hands blistered and aching from her time spent training with a wooden staff until she trembled. She sat on a bucket in a shaded alcove of the arena, whetting blade after blade, trying and failing to keep her thoughts from drifting to Fenrir and Tyr. To what had happened with the Norns.

Every now and then, she would glance up, hoping to see one or both striding into the arena with irksome smiles on their faces. Throughout the day, several residents came and went, training and laughing—a few offers were extended to her for sparring, but she politely declined. She knew she needed rest, though it was hard to sit still. In the past, she would have pushed it. Distracted herself with the pain. But she found herself wanting to heed the words of those who cared. Ingrid, Asta, and all the Maidens whom she, herself, would have encouraged to rest and heal in her place. Hel, Tyr, Austri, and ...

Fenrir.

Revna tried to focus on the sound of the whetstone gliding across the blade of a throwing knife, counting each pass, each moment—keeping her thoughts carefully focused only on the task at hand. One slight pause in her movements, and her mind would cycle through all that had happened. The boat, her goodbyes, finding Fenrir, Jotunheim, the arrow piercing her, Fenrir, the sisters, Fenrir—it all threatened to drown her, but she would continue to fight for the surface.

One.

Ingrid weeping.

Two.

Fenrir, alive and well.

Three.

Fenrir holding her through fever.

Four

With unbound chains, the darkness break

Revna stood abruptly and threw the knife into a nearby practice post, her wound screaming in pain at the movement. She checked to ensure it hadn't broken open, glad to find nothing but hardened, blue-stained skin.

"And what did that accomplish, you fool?" she mumbled to herself. She would rather face battle than her own thoughts. Pathetic. Grabbing an axe, she sat back on the bucket, the wood digging uncomfortably into her ass.

"Talking to yourself?" Hel stepped out from the shadows next to Revna, startling her enough that she almost tipped over. The Goddess grasped Revna's shirt and righted her. "Glad to see your voice has returned."

"Yes." Revna recovered quickly, though her heart felt as though it would escape her chest. "Who else would give me such sage counsel?"

Hel made a noise of agreement and pulled a bucket over to sit across from Revna's. She picked up a knife and twirled it deftly over her fingers.

"Revna ..."

"Hmm?" Revna kept her focus on the blade, still too ashamed to meet Hel's gaze.

"I'm sorry."

Revna paused her movements and finally looked up. There was sincerity in the Goddess's eyes—the fire from the day before had cooled. "What—why are you sorry, Hel? You have nothing to be sorry for. This is all my fault."

"I could blame you, but I could also blame many others. Years of events leading up to this. If you hadn't, if Fenrir hadn't, if Odin hadn't—"

"If Fenrir hadn't what?" Revna interrupted.

Hel pursed her lips, ignoring her. "The point is, I'm sorry for lashing out at you. I get protective over my brothers, especially when it comes to Asgard. That is a fraught history, as you're learning."

The knife in Hel's hand whipped out and struck the ground nearby. She picked up another, doing the same, striking the same spot.

"I have much to apologize for, Hel. And not just to you." Revna set the small axe and whetstone aside, leaning forward to brace her elbows on both of her knees. "I shouldn't have put Fenrir, Tyr, or you in a situation so dire. One that made you rely on someone who's hurt you." She placed a hand over her heart. "I am truly sorry."

Revna didn't beg for forgiveness. It wasn't something she could ask for. Forgiveness, like trust, was earned. She hoped that Hel would forgive her, and Tyr.

Fenrir, on the other hand, would be more complicated. Their relationship was firmly planted in a place that held both hurt and longing. Whether the longing was desire-filled or violence-filled, of course, depended on the moment.

"Seeing my mother always brings up things I strive to keep buried. But every once in a while, it's good to see how far I've come. If you can believe it, that was one of our better interactions." Revna gave a disbelieving chuckle. "When we were younglings, I cowered from my mother. I wouldn't speak up for myself or my brothers. It's progress that I fight back now, that I no longer tolerate her venom."

Revna hummed thoughtfully. Though she'd never had a mother to speak of, she understood the shift that took place when you decided to no longer tolerate that kind of abuse. It's slow at first, then all at once, like waking by being doused in icy water. Revna's shift had happened not long before she'd killed her former master. It had come to head the night he'd murdered Helga, another slave girl, for Revna's mistake. He'd learned early on that Revna could and would take beatings, but watching others be harmed for her defiance is what broke her, and he'd used it against her.

"Your father also seems pretty rotten," Revna said.

Hel looked up. "Loki? You met him?"

Fuck. There was a lot left out of their journey to the sisters and what had transpired after. Revna quickly recounted everything from their arrival to their mother's cave, to the journey to the sisters, and how Loki was waiting for them upon returning. Revna did not divulge what the sisters had shown or told her, and the Goddess didn't ask.

Hel was silent for a while, eyes turning cloudy as she thought on what had happened. Revna resumed her task, filling the silence with blade and stone.

"It's getting late," Hel finally said. "I was told by Austri that I was to make sure you came to him for another meal today. He also mentioned something about how badly you needed a bath."

Revna snorted and put away the axe and whetstone, standing to follow Hel to the kitchens, hoping that they may find two vexing Gods waiting for them.

TWENTY-SIX

FENRIR

DARKNESS HAD COMPLETELY SETTLED when Fenrir and Tyr stepped back through the gate in Vanaheim.

And not a moment too soon.

Fenrir felt as though he was going to collapse—his body and mind barely hanging on to consciousness.

As predicted, the Jotunns weren't pleased with the Aesir's declaration, nor his delivery of it. He and Tyr had prepared for a fight, but what happened was worse. They'd stayed silent, eyes never leaving the proffered head of Spjut. Not one giant cried or yelled out—and their lack of reactivity was more concerning than outright violence. He saw the small trust he'd built with them bleed from their very eyes and, for the first time in all his years, he feared retaliation. Which put him in a precarious position, given Odin's threats to keep him in Asgard.

Fenrir took a deep inhale, letting the smell of earth and crisp night ease the ache of turmoil in his body.

If only he could shift and run ...

The ache grew teeth.

Hel's other half was waiting for them as they approached the tunnel, an odd spectral sentry among the glowing moss. No expression crossed her draugr's face, but the solid white eyes flared brighter for a moment before turning to make her way down the dimly lit tunnel. A few moments later, Hel appeared and threw her arms around Fenrir's neck, then Tyr's.

"Are you alright?" she asked, looking between them.

"Starving and ready for sleep, I think," Tyr said, gesturing his head toward where Fenrir stood.

Hel approached and looped her opalescent inked arm through his, leading him down the rest of the tunnel.

"How is Revna?" Fenrir's voice sounded as exhausted as he felt.

"She is well, brother. Don't worry. Austri stuffed her full of warm food and she is now enjoying a much-needed bath in her room."

His stomach tightened at the thought of her bathing, momentarily chasing away the weariness. Perhaps he should go check on her ...

Hel read his mind. "She will want to know you've returned. I can go tell her while you get some food and rest."

Fenrir glanced down at himself. He was filthy, with giants' blood still staining his hands. Perhaps he should want to hide this part of himself from her, but a strange pull at his center compelled him to go to her. To let her *see* him.

"I can hold out a little longer. I'd like to speak with her." *I need to see for myself that she is well*, he didn't add.

As they entered the main halls of the keep, Hel and Tyr split off to go to the kitchens to gather some food, Hel promising that she would have some delivered to his room, as well as some warm water for a bath. Normally, he would just step under the small section of waterfall off the balcony in his rooms to bathe, but a warm soak was hard to refuse. And he was too tired to venture down to the cavern with the hot springs.

His steps were slow and measured as he turned down the hall leading to their rooms. His heartbeat became hungry with each step to where Revna waited. She had made it back. He had made it back. And now he wanted to ensure that the trust they'd built in Jotunheim could grow, with the hope of becoming solid enough to stand on without fear of wavering.

But he still had so much to tell her.

He lifted his blood-stained hand to the heavy wood and knocked.

"Revna," he called softly to announce himself.

No response, no sound. But her scent called to him through the wood like the full moon called to his wolf.

He knocked again, calling her name a little louder this time. Still no response.

Panic that she'd fallen asleep and slipped under the water had him opening the door and rushing in. As he rounded the small divider that blocked the tub from the rest of the room, he stopped in his tracks. She *was* asleep in the tub, but in no danger. Head tilted back on the edge, dark, wet hair dripping onto the floor, body submerged in hazy water. Her face relaxed in fragile peace. One hand was rested on the side of the tub. It held a dagger. The sight gutted him—proof she felt the need to always be on guard. He could smell the oils that had been poured into the tub, ones meant for soothing muscles and relaxing the mind. They'd worked well.

Unable to help himself, he rounded the tub and knelt next to where she held the knife. Gently, he gripped his hand around her wrist, stroking his thumb along the soft skin. "Revna."

She startled awake, trashing in his grip. He placed his other hand to span across her shoulder and collar bone, willing her to calm. He told himself it was to keep her as still as possible so she wouldn't irritate her wound, but in truth, he couldn't resist the urge to touch her—to feel something warm and real.

Her panicked eyes found his, emotions flitting across her face. He watched each feeling hit her until she finally settled on one.

Relief.

Loathe to do so, he removed his touch from her warm, damp skin. Surprisingly, she let him remove the dagger from her hold, as well, the worn leather of the hilt still warm from her grip. It looked like a normal blade, well taken care of and sharpened like a fatal promise, but it was heavy—burdensome. Fenrir wondered how Revna could stand to carry two of them at her hips. Reverently, he set the blade down on a stool near the tub.

"You're back." Her voice came out low and raspy, but to his relief, it had returned. He'd hated not hearing it.

"So is your voice."

Revna narrowed her eyes playfully. "Yes. Now I can fight with you properly."

"Good." A stirring smell flared from her that had him gripping the edge of the tub. Clearing his throat, he continued, "Apologies for barging in. I knocked and called your name, but you didn't answer. Fearing you may have slipped under the water—"

"And drowned?" She rasped a chuckle. "I'm much too stubborn for that."

She chewed on the corner of her bottom lip. Suddenly food wasn't the only thing he was starving for.

By the fucking runes.

Fenrir wanted to kiss her. Madly. He wanted to take her bottom lip between his teeth and taste her, to pull desperate sounds from her throat. Wanted to score the soft skin of her neck with his fangs and then soothe the indentations with his tongue. He wanted to lift her from the tub, sit her astride his lap, and devour her until they were both panting and grinding and begging for more. He wanted—

Fenrir stood abruptly, shaking his head, fighting against the urge. Though his wolf rumbled in encouragement.

He swayed, and Revna pushed herself up out of the tub and stepped out to grab onto him before he could fall over. Water dripped from her naked body and, just for a moment, his decency failed. He let his hungry gaze skim over her curves, her scars, the water droplets rolling from her collarbones to her breasts.

Fenrir closed his eyes and reached up to pinch the bridge of his nose.

He heard the rustle of cloth being draped around her body, then her hand grabbing onto his elbow, and he removed his fingers from his nose and glanced down at her.

"You need rest," she whispered. "I'll walk you to your room."

Fenrir could refuse her nothing as she tugged at his arm, guiding him to leave her room and go to his. They entered the torch-lit hall to find Hel walking toward them with a tray of food, and several others leaving his room with empty buckets.

His sister frowned as she approached them. "Are you alright? You look flushed."

"He wavered on his feet a bit," Revna responded in her scratchy voice before he could say he was fine.

Hel came to stand on his other side. "Let's get him to his room."

These women were herding him as if he were a lost lamb. "I am perfectly capable of making it to my own room," Fenrir grumbled.

Neither paid him any mind as they guided him through the door. Hel went to the table near the fire and set down the food. As she uncovered it, the smells hit his nose, and his stomach gave a hungry growl.

Revna chuckled softly as his side. "Bath first, I think. The hunger will keep you awake a bit longer."

Heeding Revna's directions without complaint, he walked across the expanse of his rooms toward where the tub waited behind a half-folded divider. He pulled off all of his weapons, tossing them in a large trunk. Somewhere behind him, Hel was telling Revna she was going to check on Tyr. He stood, waiting, until she left them alone with a soft click of his door.

He pulled his tunic overhead and kicked off his boots. When he reached for the laces on his trousers, he turned his head, finding Revna staring at his back, a flush of her own creeping up her neck. That intoxicating scent floated from her that went straight to the base of his spine.

Interesting.

As he yanked at the laces, she quickly moved to the tray of food, keeping busy by rearranging the tray and pouring him some drink.

Fenrir sank into the tub and released an audible sigh as the heat allayed his mind and muscles. He released the tie from his hair, dunking his head down, digging his fingers through the gnarls and grime. When he resurfaced, Revna was sitting near the tub, holding a mug of what smelled like tea.

"Drink," she instructed, handing him the mug. He pushed his wet hair back out of his face, then reached for the mug—and her eyes landed on the giant's blood still marring his hands. Fenrir felt a bitter mixture of fear and shame curdling in his stomach.

Monster.

"Fenrir." Revna's eyes were on his now, and her voice had softened. "I've met men with duller teeth who are more monster than you."

The proclamation challenged the loudness in his mind. He didn't think he'd spoken aloud, or maybe she'd read it on his face, but when her words sank in, a warmth like he'd never known spread through his entire body.

Revna grabbed a cloth and handed it to him. He didn't know what to say, didn't know if he could mold the words to thank her, to tell her everything. Instead, he scrubbed at his skin.

"You don't need to stay. You need your rest as well," Fenrir told her.

She shrugged. "You stayed and took care of me."

He sighed, her words sending a chill over that warmth. "I don't want that, Revna."

"Want what?"

"This game where we exchange debts and owe favors. I have no expectations when it comes to you. I do things because I want to, not because I want you to feel beholden to me."

He watched as Revna's face grew wary, and then settled into understanding.

"No more favors. No more debts," she whispered.

"No more favors, no more debts," he affirmed.

They said nothing else as he got out of the tub, dried off, and ate the food on his tray. When he was done and his eyelids grew impossibly heavy, she guided him to his bed, where he collapsed face down. Through the haze of being half asleep, he heard her retreat and reached his hand out, his body wanting to touch her one last time. His thumb ran along the smooth skin of her wrist and settled on her pulse, feeling its comforting beat. Then it fell out of his hand, and he heard the small click of the door, and fell into a dreamless sleep.

Twenty-Seven

Revna

A young Jotunn named Havvar watched Revna with rapt seriousness. He lifted his shield higher, narrowing his blue eyes on her, and lunged with his spear. She stepped back easily as he stumbled forward, slightly off balance.

Revna raised an eyebrow, silently urging him to understand his mistake.

"I know," he sighed. "I'm forgetting my footwork."

"And?" Hel called from her perch on a wooden crate.

"The weight of the shield," he muttered.

Revna set down her own shield and used her spear to stretch out her shoulders, being mindful of her still-healing side. Training turned out to be more wincing than actual movement, but it felt good to push through the discomfort.

"Knowing what you're doing right and wrong is part of training. You're doing well, Havvar."

The giant gave her a bashful smile and toed at the dirt, his long braid falling over his shoulder. Above them, clouds parted, and beams of sunlight streamed down into the arena. Revna turned her face to its warmth and took a deep breath. For the first time in many days, she had woken feeling lighter, less weighed down by anger and grief. She felt relieved that Fenrir and Tyr had made it back. That Hel had forgiven her. Though the prophecy still taunted her ...

Revna didn't know how to make sense of it, the words and images that created sticky webs that caught her and left her feeling trapped within her own mind. It felt too dangerous a game to unbraid the threads of a prophecy. Obsessing about it could drive her mad. And bearing it alone felt heavy, but she had yet to decide as to whether she would tell Fenrir and force him to bear it with her.

She couldn't stop thinking about him.

How it had felt when she realized he'd come back safely. The way he'd touched her gently. The way she'd let him. Revna had felt safe. Seen.

And on fire.

A fire that continued to thaw through the coldness she'd felt for him when she'd first arrived and added flame to the warmth of their regained trust. She was shedding the anger, the hurt, like a snake shedding its skin, but she still felt apprehensive about who she would be without it.

Revna had spent so long letting anger and fear lead her. But after what she'd witnessed with the sisters, she'd had enough. She didn't understand the prophecy she'd heard entirely, but it was clear there would be darkness in her future. And she wasn't sure how long she'd have until that time came.

So, it was time to lead with her heart.

And that meant truly forgiving Fenrir. And herself.

Hearing Fenrir call himself a monster while looking at the blood on his hands after witnessing his memory … she wouldn't be another person in his life to punish him for what he was. For what he did to survive, and to save the people he cared for.

Was she so different?

As if reading her mind, Havvar spoke. "Do you think that Fenrir will be here soon? I'd love to get a chance to learn from him, too."

Revna tore her gaze from the sky and turned to Hel, who sat watching them. She regripped her staff and gave her friend a nod. The Goddess smiled conspiratorially and stood, grabbing a staff of her own. "Oh, are we boring you, young giant?"

His blue eyes widened as he noticed the two women started slowly circling him. "No! Of course not. I just—well, I mean, I just thought ... by the runes, this is terrifying."

Revna and Hel erupted into laughter at his unfiltered honesty.

"I should go attend to my duties in the stables," Havvar stammered. He rested his spear on the rack and hung his shield before turning to them one last time with an excited smile on his face. "This isn't over. See you tomorrow!"

Then, with a final wave, he took off running, leaving Revna and Hel shaking their heads. As Havvar exited the mouth of the training yard, she found herself watching it for a moment longer, hoping that a certain Wolf God might make an appearance after all. But she knew Fenrir was still sleeping and may do so for most of the day. Revna wasn't surprised; he'd carried on for days with little rest.

She found herself wondering how he looked when he slept. Did he sleep on his stomach, exposing the small dips at the base of his spine? Did he lay on his back with his arms stretched overhead? Revna, though delirious and consumed by pain at the time, hadn't been able to stop her mind from drifting back in quiet moments to how he'd held her through her fever. How his body had felt, entangled with hers. How he'd talked to her and kept her anchored to herself.

Something shifted in Revna's chest as a realization stuck her.

She wanted Fenrir.

And yet, she couldn't. Could she?

He was a God, she was mortal, and she felt more a burden than an equal.

Revna tried to shake away that feeling of being less. She was the commander of the largest group of shield maidens in Myddheim, she reminded herself. She had escaped slavery, traveled realms, and survived. Perhaps they were more alike than—

Revna jolted at the feeling of a wooden staff swatting her backside.

"Well, hello. Welcome back to our sparring session," Hel joked, leaning on the staff. "You were deep in thought. Care to share what you were thinking about that had you making that face?"

Did she want to tell Hel she was thinking about how her brother slept, and the revelation that she desperately wanted to see for herself? No, she did not.

"Sorry, I'm still a little out of sorts." Revna shook out her shoulders and bounced on her feet a couple of times. She gripped the wooden staff in her hands and gestured for Hel to begin. "One more round."

They moved slowly, letting Revna's body stretch, reach, and twist to her current limits. It was slow and methodical, but Hel was patient and met her wooden staff with just enough effort to challenge the burning pain in Revna's side. It felt a little more like a dance than actual sparring, but she wouldn't do anyone any good if she prolonged her healing. Ingrid would be proud of her for using such forethought and caution. Revna felt her lips pull into a sad smile.

In that moment, her heart ached with the absence of the Maidens.

Revna had thought going to see the sisters would somehow show a clear path in aiding Myddheim. To keep them as safe as she could. But what she'd seen instead ...

"What is it?" Hel asked.

Revna struck Hel's staff with her own. "I was just thinking about my second, Ingrid. She's a fierce warrior, but also a healer. She used to scold me for not heeding her instructions."

"Was she your lover?" Hel asked.

Revna chuckled. "No, it wasn't like that. We were friends." It seemed such a small word for what Ingrid was to her, but it would have to do. "What about you, Goddess of Death? Any lovers?"

"I've had my share," Hel said with a wry smile. "But it's been some time. Unlike that one over there."

Revna looked to where Hel pointed with her staff. Tyr was flirting with an elven warrior—the two men had their heads bent close together, smiling and laughing. Revna watched as Tyr grabbed the male by the collar and pulled him into a dark alcove, disappearing into the shadows.

"By the runes, he doesn't rest." Hel rolled her eyes. "Let's go get something to drink and check on my brother."

They left the training yard and stopped by the kitchens to grab food for Fenrir, Austri fussing over what to bring the Wolf God as if he was a young boy to be taken care of. Both women carried trays laden with food and drink, the smells making even Revna's mouth water. As they approached his door, Hel forwent all manners and walked right in.

Revna hesitantly followed and swallowed at what she saw.

She no longer had to imagine what Fenrir looked like in sleep. He was on his stomach, one knee hitched up, head buried into his folded arms above him. Inked vines wrapped around his legs and crawled up the muscled expanse of his back. She couldn't see his face under the mess of dark hair covering it, but she could see the steady rise and fall of his breath.

The position was so vulnerable, so endearing, that Revna's step faltered, jostling the tray in her arms, and causing Fenrir to bolt upright—his nakedness on full display. His eyes immediately found Revna.

Breath halted in her chest, and she tried to think of anything that wouldn't alert him to the shift in her scent. Her hands gripped the tray as his eyes darkened, and she knew that look. A wolf marking his hunt.

Fuck.

Hel set her tray down and walked over to a trunk, pulling out a pair of trousers. "Put these on, brother. Then come sit and refill your stomach. You've been asleep long enough."

Hel tossed the bundled-up pants and Fenrir snatched them out of the air, eyes never leaving Revna's. To hide the burn creeping up her neck, she turned and placed the second tray where Hel had set hers, busying herself with uncovering pots. Warmth bled into the air behind her as she felt him approach.

"Thank you," he said, his voice still rough from sleep. Behind them, Hel cleared her throat. "Both of you. Thank you."

Revna looked up at him. His normally bound hair was falling into his eyes, and she had to repress the urge to push it away. Her gaze ran over the places where the dark strands covered his brow, his warm eyes. As if reading her mind, he reached over to a small table and grabbed a leather strap, placing it between his teeth as he gathered the hair back and secured it.

Fenrir sank into a chair near the food. "Hel, would you mind giving Revna and I a moment to talk?"

"Of course." Hel winked as she passed, leaving Revna alone with Fenrir and the growing temptation in her body.

Unsure what else to do, she sat in a chair across from him and waited for him to speak first.

"How are you feeling?"

"Shouldn't I be asking you that?" she countered.

"*I* didn't get shot with a poison arrow." Fenrir stood and crossed to her. "May I see?"

Somewhere in her mind, Revna thought she should show more hesitation, but she found herself standing and lifting her shirt. He knelt at her feet and inspected the healing wound, still hardened and blue, but getting less tender by the day.

Though she didn't care for Fenrir's mother, she had to admit that the giantess witch knew how to heal. If she had suffered that kind of wound on Myddheim, she doubted she would have survived, let alone be up and moving a couple of days later.

Revna's skin broke out in shivering bumps as Fenrir's knuckles gently traced the skin around the wound, then rubbed the pad of his thumb along its rough edges.

"It's healing well, but I'm afraid a scar is unavoidable. It will probably remain blue in color, as well." He lifted his arm to show where he'd cut himself with the arrowhead. A faint blue line spanned from the backside of his wrist to his mid-forearm, stopping short of three inked bands.

Revna, unable to stop herself, traced the scar on his arm with her fingers. At his shudder, she quickly withdrew her hand and sat back down in her chair, lowering her shirt.

"I have many scars. What's one more?" Revna waved her hand in an effort to look relaxed and unaffected.

Fenrir stood from his kneeling position and regarded what food was on the trays before grabbing a plate and filling it with meat, roasted vegetables, and a chunk of bread. He turned, handing her the plate he'd just made.

"Eat with me."

Revna took the plate and watched as he sat back in his chair and reached for a piece of meat. He gestured for her to take a bite. And, because he'd had a long few days, she indulged him. The chicken was perfectly roasted and tender, full of spice and warmth. Fenrir gave her a small smile and dug into his own food, picking everything right off the tray.

They ate in silence for a while, but Revna tasted the food less and less. She knew a conversation was coming and it was causing her stomach to clench with worry. Plans, actions, strategy—those things she could talk about. Feelings were more difficult. A vulnerability she was still learning to be comfortable with.

Being in Vanaheim, and getting to know Hel, Tyr, Austri, and Fenrir, was starting to wear her down. These Gods, these otherworldly beings, were so open with their experiences and feelings. It was a different kind of bravery than that of her and her Maidens waging battle. She found she wanted to be brave like them.

Revna set her plate back on the table and waited.

"I won't ask you to tell me what you saw with the sisters," Fenrir began, "but I wanted to see if you needed to talk about it. I know from experience that the possibilities can make you feel alone."

Revna took a deep breath and looked at the fire. "I'm still trying to understand without dwelling on it. It feels like if I think on it too much, it will swallow me. But if I don't think about it, it'll dissolve like a dream. I'm not really sure what it means or where to begin. There was ice and fire and a voice ..."

Revna's tongue felt heavy in her mouth. Speaking the prophecy aloud felt ruinous to anyone who heard it. But the sisters had sent them into the well together. Maybe it was something they needed to face together. Through realms and time, fate had brought them together again and again. Fighting it felt futile.

Being truthful with herself, she didn't want to fight it.

"Go on," Fenrir encouraged her softly.

She tore her gaze away from the flames and looked to where he sat. He was leaning forward, his forearms braced on his knees, his face open and encouraging. Revna rubbed her thumb along the scar on her palm, reminding herself of all she had to fight for.

So, she told him. Every twisted and snagging word. Revna felt it carve into her bones, become a part of her, of them.

It was relief and pain. Relief to share, painful to burden.

They sat in the heaviness of it for a few moments, Fenrir's eyes searching the stone floor in front of him. "So, you're the raven."

Revna gave a half-hearted laugh. "It seems fate has a sense of humor. Did you hear anything?"

Fenrir shook his head. "No, I just saw images. The tree didn't speak to me like it did with you."

Odd, she thought. Considering his nature.

"What does it mean?" Revna asked, not expecting any kind of answer.

He sighed and ran a hand over his jaw. "That's the maddening thing about prophecies. It doesn't make sense until it does, until the moment you need to understand."

"I don't know if I can be that patient," she mumbled.

Fenrir laughed, and Revna decided that he should do it more. He was beautiful in his joy. His smile faded into something more serious under her gaze.

"When I was a youngling, my mother took us to see the sisters. And the fate I saw was a temptation more than a taunt. I saw myself amongst the Aesir and walking through the forest here in Vanaheim. I thought I was seeing freedom. A freedom like I had never known in the dark caves on Jotunheim ..."

He trailed off, and Revna gave him the space and quiet encouragement to continue even though she knew what was coming next.

"When my father showed up to take us to Asgard, I had thought my fate had finally come to collect me. That I could free myself, Hel, and Jor." His jaw twitched, and his eyes flashed gold. "The guilt of it eats at me still. That by following my fate, I doomed them to theirs. So be cautious, Revna. Not all is as it seems."

He sounded so defeated, and Revna didn't want him to travel down that dark path alone. "I saw you, on that day." His eyes found hers, and she swallowed past the nervous knot in her throat. "And I see you now, Fenrir."

His gaze burned into her, holding her captive. "And I, you, Revna."

She nodded and it felt like something settled between them. The tension lessened, and she picked at the remaining food on her plate. "I still don't know why I'm here. What's the purpose?" *What is my purpose?*

"I don't know. But we will figure it out. Together."

He reclined in his chair and leaned his head on his raised fist. Firelight dancing off his shirtless body. Want flared, followed by a sudden urge to flee—to put distance between them and let her desires cool.

"I'll let you get some more rest. I think I need a soak in the hot springs."

Revna strode quickly toward the door, but he called her name just as she reached for the handle.

"I don't know why you're here." Fenrir stood and walked slowly toward her, stopping bare breaths from her. "But I'm glad you are."

Twenty-Eight

Fenrir

"**I** NEED YOUR HELP."

Fenrir stood with his hands braced on the table of the meeting room, looking down at the carved rendition of Yggdrasil and the nine realms. The tree's many roots and branches created a delicate web that cradled the nine realms in its hold. Asgard sat watchful and foreboding at the top of the tree, among its highest branches. Vanaheim sat just below, always in Asgard's shadow. The lower branches held both Alfheim and Muspelheim. In opposition, spread out among the great roots, were Jotunheim and Nidavellir. Lower still, Niflheim and Helheim.

And at the tree's heart, Myddheim.

Tyr came to stand next to Fenrir. "What do you need?"

"I would like to ensure our defenses are ready. Assign leaders to legions and maintain a rotation of guards. I don't want to be caught unprepared if a fight should come."

Tyr grunted, turning to lean against the table, arms crossed.

"Do you not agree?" Fenrir asked.

"Of course I do. But you know we're always prepared. Everyone here knows how to fight and withstand an attack."

Fenrir stood and stretched his neck from side to side, blowing out a breath of frustration.

"What's this really about?" Tyr asked.

"The quiet is grating my nerves," Fenrir said over his shoulder as he walked toward the large window—the very window he'd stood next to when Revna was first brought here.

It had been nearly half a moon's course since their trip to Jotunheim. Fenrir hadn't heard a whisper from the Jotunns or from Asgard. He should be thankful, he supposed. But it was the calm before the storm—he was sure of it. The Aesir and the giants were never idle for long.

"I'm considering sending Jormun to Myddheim, if I can convince him." Since his conversation with Revna, he hadn't been able to stop thinking about Myddheim, of her concerns and accusations from when she first arrived. With Revna's permission, Fenrir had also discussed the prophecy given to her by the sisters with both Hel and Tyr. Though confoundingly clouded, they agreed that the prophecy warned two sure things.

Revna was the moon kissed raven. And something was coming.

Fenrir and Tyr had made trips to both Alfheim and Nidavellir, and what they'd found had only fed their suspicions. The two realms that were once full of vibrancy were completely devoid of color in places—a perpetual grayness shrouded the lands. Hel's realm hadn't faced much change, but Fenrir wanted to check on Myddheim. For Revna's sake.

He still hadn't told her about his deal with Odin—he was sure that wasn't the reason for Myddheim's misfortune. Why else would all the other realms be suffering as well?

"You still haven't told her, have you?" Tyr asked quietly, as if reading his thoughts.

"I want to."

He didn't know how to explain it, but he knew that Revna would be furious and continue to blame herself. From his time with her, and the stories she had honored him with during their time spent together, Fenrir knew she didn't take kindly to anyone making choices for her—especially in order to protect her.

But she deserved better. She deserved to know.

Fenrir knew that Tyr's silence was intentional—letting him come to his own conclusions. He would withstand anything Revna aimed at him. What he couldn't stand was her retreating within and blaming herself, as she too often did.

But they had started to bridge the gap between them, and continuing to withhold information from her was not how he wanted them to move forward. What he wanted with her, it was a desirous ache that grew every time he looked at her, every time he talked to her. Found an excuse to touch her.

"I'm going to tell her right now." He left the meeting room without a glance at Tyr.

This time of day, she could usually be found at the training yard. Her strength had almost fully returned, and she trained relentlessly. If not with himself, Tyr, or Hel, she would convince anyone who was in the training arena. Some days she would remain so late that Austri would stomp out of the kitchens to go collect her, always demanding to stuff her full of food. The dwarf looked after her as though she was his own blood.

The sun was just past its peak as he entered the yard, his senses immediately finding her amongst the swirl of dust and the metallic song of swords. Sure enough, she was in the middle of the arena—her opponent a young Jotunn by the name of Havvar. Though he was as tall as Revna, he was in that awkward age where his movements were aggressive and clumsy. Revna side-stepped and dodged all his swings with ease. They paused and she called out a command. He corrected his stance, and the young giant flushed as Revna complimented him, smiling in encouragement.

He loved her smile.

Her gaze swung to where he approached, her smile softening. She was covered in a sheen of sweat, and still, he didn't think anything could smell more maddening.

"You're improving, Havvar." Fenrir said by way of greeting. "It must be your teacher."

The young giant blushed more at his compliment.

"I can't take the credit. It's his hard work that has him improving." Revna tugged on the giant's long braid and then nudged his shoulder with hers.

"If you have time," Havvar said, his voice cracking, "I would love to spar a little with you, too."

"I would be happy to, Havvar," Fenrir replied. "But perhaps maybe tomorrow? I'd like to steal Revna for a bit if I may." He turned his attention back to her even gray gaze. "Would you mind taking a walk with me?"

She nodded, her brow furrowed, then tossed her staff at Havvar, leaving him with instructions for the rest of his training session. Fenrir waved goodbye and strode to the mouth of the training yard.

They walked in silence for a bit, Fenrir's mind unwilling to form the words he needed to say. The leaves rustled in the breeze, or maybe it was his own nerves making them dance, as he pulled them deeper into the forest. Without thought, he realized he'd steered them to the rune gate. Perhaps it would help him explain.

Or you can escape her wrath through it, he thought wryly.

Revna sighed. "Out with it." He stopped to look at her, and she cocked her head knowingly. "I can practically feel you battling with yourself inside your head. Why don't you bring it out into the open so we both can fight it?"

Fenrir swallowed. She'd said it in a tone of jest, but he could see the growing worry in her eyes and smell the truth in her statement. She would help battle whatever was plaguing his mind—just as he would for hers.

He took a deep breath. "When I left Myddheim—"

Fenrir stopped as a burning smell invaded his nostrils, acrid and unfamiliar to this realm. He whipped around, searching the woods, and felt Revna tense beside him. At first, he could see nothing, hear nothing, but the smell grew stronger, and the trees fell still.

Revna sensed it too. "What is that smell?"

A gust of wind from the direction of the gate had them both reaching up to cover their noses. Fenrir took a step to approach the gate, but halted as a giant reptilian arm punctured through, smoke rising from its ember-mottled skin.

Fenrir grabbed onto Revna's arm as a great lumbering fire beast crawled through the gate. A massively long snout with rows of teeth, slitted eyes, thick legs that ended in dagger-sharp claws, and a barbed tail. Its skin was black as coal, but red-hot cracks emitted the acrid smoke that he'd first smelled. It was massive. From tail to snout, it had to be three times Fenrir's height.

Slitted eyes landed on Revna, and a deep hissing sound emitted from its throat.

Fenrir watched in horror as it opened its mouth, spitting a flaming orb. Without hesitation, he dove in front of Revna, grabbing her and turning to take the hit. He moved just fast enough that the fire only grazed his upper arm, but he hissed anyway as his entire skin became filled with a burning sensation.

"Run!" He turned Revna and pushed in her the direction of the tunnel entrance. "Run to the tunnel!"

Fenrir rolled the earth, trying to give them speed as he pulled his sword out. Balls of fire struck the ground behind, beside, and in front of them, scorching earth and tree. Trees were burning, smoke was growing heavy. Revna's balance faltered a bit as the earth churned under her foot, but he grabbed onto her tunic to keep her upright.

There was no way Fenrir could let this thing get anywhere near the keep.

The tunnel came into view and Fenrir placed his hand on Revna's upper back, pushing her faster. His teeth began elongating, his body begging to shift, his wolf enraged at his denial. Fenrir summoned the earth, the roots, the suffering trees.

"I'm sorry," he said as he pushed Revna through the mouth of the tunnel, blocking the entrance with roots, branch, and vine.

"No! Fenrir!" Revna screamed over and over as he turned to face the fire beast alone.

He growled as the creature spit another mouthful of flame at him, grazing his exposed forearm. The skin instantly bubbled and charred.

Sword strong in his hands, and Fenrir began to move, drawing its attention away from the tunnel, where Revna was still screaming. He could hear the sound of her trying to hack away at the blockade but knew she would never make it through.

The fire beast rushed him, turning swiftly to swing its barbed tail right at his face. Fenrir ducked and rolled, swinging his sword to strike the tail. A hiss of pain sounded, but his sword left barely a scratch. He briefly lamented that he couldn't shift into his wolf form—this would be over in a heartbeat.

They circled each other, the beast's great claws churning the earth. It bared its teeth, and this time Fenrir was prepared for the spit of fire. He moved quickly, observing the way the beast's chest and throat glowed red before releasing. In the glow, he spotted its beating heart.

The absence of Revna's screams made him pause a moment, and that pause cost him a burn to his legs, the fire burning right through his leather trousers. He felt his body strain against the on-coming shift, the wolf begging for him to let go. *No.* He stalked toward the fire beast. As if sensing what lay beneath Fenrir's skin, the beast ducked its head and backed-up. It scaled a tree, rising above Fenrir's head.

Fenrir took a step back, as if in submission, laying the trap. The beast, confident in the higher ground, launched itself. At the last moment, Fenrir pivoted, reaching his sword arm out, letting the beast impale itself through the heart. It shrieked and fell dead on the ground, but not before its falling body burned one last brand into the skin of Fenrir's forearm.

He groaned and gripped his arm just as Hel's draugr walked through the blocked tunnel, rushing toward him and the beast. A loud boom sounded as Tyr's power blew through the roots. Tyr, Hel, and Revna all rushed out, panting and searching the smoke-filled air.

As they took in the scene, Hel's draugr approached the beast and sent out pulses of power, ensuring it was truly dead.

Tyr slowly approached. "By the runes, are you alright, Fen?" Fenrir knew what they were seeing. He was on that edge—teeth long, eyes burning, body swelling with the potential of shifting into his wolf form.

He ignored Tyr's question and looked at Revna. For some inexplicable reason her furious gaze calmed him. The wolf within receded, the pain from the burns taking its place.

"You should go tend to those, brother," Hel said, nodding toward the scorch marks on his skin.

"I can—" Tyr started, but Revna interrupted.

"No, I'll take him," she said, her voice and face at odds with each other. He couldn't tell if she was concerned or pissed. Undoubtedly both.

Hel nodded. "We'll clean up here, scout the area, and then come find you."

Fenrir wanted to object, but he found himself stalking toward the entrance of the tunnel when Revna pointed to it, throwing him a look.

They walked to the healing room in silence. Fenrir could feel tremors of emotion coming off her in waves, the smell too chaotic and jumbled to discern. But she held her tongue. As they entered the warm space, Revna went directly to the fire, dipping a cloth into the water kept near the coals. She turned and stomped toward him, whipping out a dagger in the process.

"I need to cut this off." She gestured to his shirt with various holes burned through. Not waiting for his permission, she pushed him into a chair and started cutting his tunic from the bottom, then ripping it the rest of the way with her hands.

Arousal slammed through him, distracting him from the pain.

Her touch gentled as she made quick work of his tattered sleeves. With the fabric removed, he could smell the slight tinge of burning skin on his arms. Revna's eyes were roving over him, her brow furrowed, nostrils flaring as she gently traced the burns with her eyes.

She turned from him abruptly and started rummaging through the various pots and herbs, slamming things as she went.

"You may as well say what's on your mind, Revna," Fenrir said, his voice tired. "Before you take your temper out on the rest of the room."

She slammed down a hand full of herbs and whirled on him.

"What were you thinking?" she yelled. "You could have gotten yourself *killed*."

He ran a hand down his face. "It could have been a lot worse."

"Really? How so?" Revna's voice continued to rise as she gestured to his burned skin. "Honestly, what were you—"

"It could have been you!" He stood, his voice rising to meet hers. "It could have been *you* and I can't stand to see you in pain, Revna. I have never in my long life felt fear like I did when I watched that arrow go through you. And I won't do it again."

Fenrir watched as the words hit her, the fury slowly melting from her features. He took a deep breath, leaning back against one of the worktables and watched as she worked through his confession. He gripped the side of the table, feeling the wood give under his fingers.

He hadn't meant for it to come out like that, hadn't meant to shout, but he no longer cared.

He couldn't hide his feelings for her any longer.

Her gray eyes were searching his, no doubt looking for some kind of half-truth she wouldn't find. He stared back, nothing to hide. She took a step toward him, then another, her face morphing into one of pure determination as she closed the distance between them.

Before Fenrir could take another breath, her mouth was on his, firm and commanding. His momentary shock passed as she went to pull away, leaving only triumph and want.

He growled and pulled her back, threading his hand through the hair at the nape of her neck, taking her mouth with a consuming fierceness. Her nails scratched at his chest, digging into his skin. He wanted her closer, wanted to *devour* her.

He hooked his other arm around her waist, lifted her up, turned, and brought them both down so he was sitting back on the chair, and she was astride his lap.

A soft moan escaped her throat as he gripped her hips and ground her against his lap and the hardness that was growing there. The lightly spiced smell of her arousal only drove him into further madness. They were teeth and tongues, devouring, biting, panting. She dug her nails in the hair at the nape of his neck, sensations shooting straight down his spine.

"Revna," he growled her name, squeezing her hips, feeling their movement as she ground herself on him.

But hearing her name seemed to wake her from her desire-fueled haze. She froze, reared back, then stood.

"Don't ever do that again."

"Do what, my *máni*? Kiss you?" *By the runes, he hoped not.* Now that he had tasted her, heard her sounds, he didn't think he could live without it.

Still panting, she slapped him across the face and then pointed a finger at him.

"Don't you ever fucking shut me out again. Do you understand?"

With that, she turned and strode from the room, leaving him to tend to his wounds alone.

Despite the pain, Fenrir rubbed the side of his face and smiled bigger than he had in a long time.

Twenty-Nine

Revna

D AYS LATER, REVNA STILL felt flushed.

She didn't understand what had come over her, but in that moment, she'd given in to her impulse. She'd kissed him, and it now consumed every moment—sleeping and awake.

In sleep, she dreamed of no barrier of clothes between them, the weight of his body atop hers, and she would wake up feeling scorching and unsatisfied. In her waking moments, her mind drifted constantly to his lips, his tongue, his hard length, the way he'd groaned her name …

She felt no shame or regret. But she didn't know how to move forward, either. It was clear that they cared for one another. He'd quite literally stepped into fire for her. Which was something she would not tolerate. If he constantly tried to save her, and she him, they would suffer worse for it. She couldn't be with him if he didn't trust her to stand beside him, God or not.

But by the all the fucking Gods and the nine realms, she wanted him with an ache that would not dull.

Having already trained for several hours at dawn, Revna found herself wandering around the keep, giving herself some time and space to let her mind breathe. She'd gone to the gardens, the stables. Walked dark, moss-lit halls and sat in beams of sunlight in quiet corners.

Now she walked down a hall and found the door to the meeting room she'd first been brought to was open. She stepped inside, taking in the space. In the center of the room was an oblong table with a beautiful, ornate carving of Yggdrasil and the nine realms. Revna leaned forward, placing her hand over the runic symbol and familiar landscape of Myddheim, a longing spreading through her chest.

She so terribly wanted to know that all the Maidens were alright. After talking with Fenrir about the unrest throughout the nine realms, she worried that they were unprepared to deal with the reverberations of the realms of Gods, monsters, and apparently, fire beasts.

Somehow a fire beast from the realm of Muspelheim had crossed through the gate—though they did not know how, according to Tyr and Hel.

Revna rounded the table to stand at the end, nearest to Helheim, and looked at the carving of the realms in its entirety. So much connected, and yet, so much separation. The lifeblood of Yggdrasil flowed through all the lands, and yet, the thing that connecting them most was war, bloodshed, and greed—a sickness that infected the hearts of man and God alike.

Revna traced the roots of Yggdrasil, feeling its worn grooves, when the echo of what she'd heard in Urd's well hummed in her ears.

These roots and wings, fates intertwined

A cov'nant sealed, both power and bind

Revna pulled her hand away, her heart pounding in her ears. She had that feeling of *knowing*. A sense that the answer was right there, like a word stuck on the tongue, but unable to form. She felt so close to that edge—the one that Skuld had claimed she would understand when the moment of the prophecy was to be. But it remained trapped in her mind, unbudging.

Revna crossed her arms over her chest, tilted her head back, and took a deep breath.

The sound of a knock had her lifting her eyes to the door. Tyr leaned against the frame. "How is your wound feeling?"

"Good, thanks to you." She cocked her head, considering. "How *did* you heal me anyway? I didn't realize you possessed that kind of power."

Tyr took a few steps into the room, smiling. "You can't be the God of Love and War without knowing how to repair wounds of both. No war has been without love, and no love has been without war—even the twisted sort."

It was easy to forget he was an ancient God of anything. That he had been around for dozens of lifetimes. Looking back at the table, she recalled her conversation with Austri not long ago. "Were you around for the war between the Aesir and Vanir?"

The easy smile faltered on Tyr's face, and Revna suddenly felt like she was prying. But he took a deep breath and nodded. "I was, but I was young and untried in my powers. Perhaps if I hadn't been, things may have ended differently. When I look back and think upon Freyja, I feel only guilt and shame. I should have done more."

"You were young—" Revna tried.

"Even so. I still did unspeakable things in the name of my father for his war. I can't take it back, but I can do better moving forward."

Tyr came to stand by her side, and they lapsed into a reflective silence.

War in their past ... would there be war in their future? Is that what she'd seen? How much should she tell Fenrir, Hel, and Tyr about her visions in Urd's well? About the kind of rot and darkness that she could nearly taste.

Over the past several years, Myddheim had become plagued with ever-growing maladies. Crops and people corrupting alike. Revna had always thought it to be a symptom of the Gods punishing them. They did revel in challenging mortals and watching them fight. How else would one earn a place in Valhalla? But learning about the war between the Aesir and Vanir, and the seemingly constant tension between the other realms, perhaps Myddheim was not suffering for the Gods but *because* of them.

Myddheim could do nothing but brace themselves. But Revna was still here, and she hadn't given up. Her fight was just beginning.

Tyr bumped his shoulder against hers, severing the thread of her thoughts. "So, are you still mad at the old wolf?"

Surprisingly, his face was not his usual teasing one—but rather a mixture of concern and pity.

"It's complicated." Revna sighed, rubbing at the bridge of her nose. Complicated was a pretty word for it. She couldn't decide whether she wanted to lose herself with Fenrir's naked body atop hers or hit him again. It varied from moment to moment.

Tyr glanced down at the table with an unreadable look on his face. His eyes stuck on Asgard as he absentmindedly massaged his arm with his missing hand.

"You know, when he made the deal with Odin, I was raging mad that he would bind himself to my father in such a way." Revna froze, wondering at his words, but he didn't notice. He'd turned away from the map and perched on the table's edge, looking to the windowed opening. "After all he'd been through, to throw himself right back into a position of abuse, I couldn't understand what had happened to him on Myddheim that he'd make such a choice."

She stared, the words ringing in her ears, the blood seeming to still in her body. *No ...*

"Then he told me about you, and how you had helped him—saved him, taken care of him. This mortal stranger who owed him nothing. He said he'd witnessed the true heart of Myddheim, the true heart of the nine realms. Something fierce and loyal and resilient. And now that I've met you, I can see it."

Tyr paused and gave her a soft smile, unable to see the effect of his words chilling her blood as she stood frozen in place. "I see *you* are the heart he was talking about. And I don't think he's been the same since. In fact, I know he hasn't. He was angry and broken when he was banished. When he returned, he seemed alive. And determined."

Revna forced herself to breathe. Not to interrupt. Not to stop the axe she felt slicing through her with his words.

"So, binding himself to my father, to do Asgard's bidding? In exchange for no sacrifices from Myddheim—for saving you? I think he would pay that cost over and over again, for you."

Revna stopped breathing entirely, her lungs and eyes burning. The room grew smaller as the air pressed in around her.

"*What* did he do?" she managed to grit out.

Tyr tilted his head at her in question. He must have finally read the tension thrumming through her body because his arms and jaw went slack.

"*Fuck*, he hasn't told you yet? He said he was going to. On your walk—"

"We were conveniently interrupted," Revna spat out, barely recognizing her voice.

It felt like her mind was trapped in a whirlwind, the thoughts slamming her from every side. She'd never felt such a maelstrom of emotional power in her life—like she didn't know where her mind and body existed with how much her world had just shifted. But she knew where to aim it.

Fenrir.

"Tell me where he is. Right now."

He winced. "I don't …"

"*Now*," Revna seethed.

Whatever look was on her face had him relenting, hand raised in submission. "I last saw him in the training yard."

She strode for the door with such anger she was amazed the entire keep didn't tremble under her purposeful and heavy steps.

For nine years, Revna had wondered why no sacrifices were being demanded from Myddheim. For nine years, she'd worried that it was her fault—that because Fenrir had taken her place, the Gods were punishing them for being thwarted their prize.

For nine years, she had fought and fought, trying to be worthy of his sacrifice.

For nine years, she had wanted the boat to return so she could finally let it take her and take away the guilt that ate her alive.

Fenrir.

That fucking wolf—he had made a deal with Odin to protect her and Myddheim.

And he hadn't fucking told her.

Even after their promise. *No more debts, no more favors ...*

She'd decided to approach things with her heart—to lead with it. But that was the thing about hearts. They were wild and unpredictable things. And now the ravenous, angry beat of hers felt as though it was going to eat right through her ribs.

She started running, her body needing to keep up with her raging heart. It pounded loudly in her ears, whispering such tortured things. With each step, each thump, things became clearer. The way he'd carefully worded why he'd gotten on the boat in her place. The gaps he'd left in his recount to the Norns. The anger at her arriving here—his sacrifice for nothing.

She very well may kill him herself.

As she walked into the training yard, a few noticed her and nodded hello, but she ignored them, her eyes glued to the God off to the right side of the yard. His back was to her, and he stood casually with a sword hanging loosely in his hand, talking to a few other warriors—laughing.

He had the audacity to fucking laugh.

Not for long.

Revna stalked toward him, grabbing a bow and arrow from the hand of an unsuspecting light elf as she went. She ignored the exclaims of protest, eyes completely focused on her prey. The other warriors Fenrir was talking with took notice of her, their smiles fading as they read her body language. Revna nocked the arrow and let it loose, almost impaling Fenrir's foot.

His head whipped around, seeking an attacker, but his face softened when his eyes found hers. She grabbed a sword out of another warrior's hand as she passed by and watched as Fenrir's face morphed into confusion. As she reached him, she swung, uncaring if he lifted his blade in time. With the clang of the metal, the other warriors scattered. Revna moved, lunging again.

"What's wrong?" he asked as he continued to meet her blow for blow.

She didn't know if she could form words right then, so she ignored his question and pressed her attack. Sweat was dripping down the small of her back, her breath coming in heavy pants—she felt like she was drowning in too much feeling. She needed to stop, but she couldn't.

"Revna!" Fenrir yelled as she swung again.

"You didn't fucking tell me." Her blade struck his, and he took a step back. "You didn't tell me about your deal with Odin."

He paused, nostrils flaring. He at least had the decency to look remorseful.

"So you're just going to fight me? Until what? You maim the truth out of me?"

She swung, striking his blade again. "*Yes.*"

Fenrir advanced on her this time, sliding and hooking his blade until it brought her close to his body, to where they could share breath.

"Then let's go, my *máni*. Take what you need from me." Their gaze held for a moment longer than she could bear, and he shoved her away again, readying for her next attack.

This wasn't the first time he'd called her that.

My *máni*—my moon.

At Revna's momentary shock at his closeness, his words abated, and she attacked again, and again, and again. Fenrir met her in every strike. The whole training yard fell away. She didn't hear anyone, couldn't see anyone but him.

When the blades weren't getting the effect she desired, she stuck hers in the ground and sprinted, launching herself at him. At the last moment, he sent his weapon flying, and then they were on the ground, rolling and fighting for dominance.

Revna fought dirty, and he fought back. They tumbled over the ground until she shook with exhaustion, painstakingly holding back tears.

With one last move, Fenrir had her underneath him—knees digging into her inner thighs, hands pinned above her head. As they caught their breath, he stared down at her, a few strands of his hair falling forward, his scent of earth and sweat surrounding her, and she felt breathless for a whole different reason, adding lust to her emotional maelstrom.

"I'm sorry. I know it doesn't make up for withholding the truth, but I am so sorry, my *máni*."

That damn name again. She held his gaze, her body still under his, waiting for answers, waiting for *something*.

"I should have told you everything the moment you arrived here. I shouldn't have kept anything from you. I meant to. If you're done fighting me, I will tell you everything now."

In that moment, through the haze of betrayal, Revna needed the answer to one question—one truth to ease her mind. "Why do you call me that?"

She saw in his face that he understood what she meant. My *máni*.

His eyes briefly flicked down to her lips and then back to her eyes, the amber turning molten, sending a warmth through her body that she willfully ignored. And then he spoke, and her world tilted again.

"Because you are. When I was lost to the darkness of my own mind, you were the light that guided me back—you *are* my light in the darkness. Even after we were separated, you guided me. You comforted me and, yes, sometimes you drive me to *fucking* madness. I call you my *máni* because you are. Does that answer your question?"

Revna didn't know what to say. All the boiling anger she had felt only moments ago was reduced to a simmer, her throat burning with the threat of tears. He must have smelled the shift, because he leaned forward, pressing his forehead to hers, eyes closing, and sighed.

Her body relaxed beneath him, but he didn't release his hold. She was still beyond pissed, and she needed to hear the entire truth from him before she decided how she felt, but she was willing to listen.

Just as she was about to demand the whole story from the beginning, ice cold water doused them from above. Both her and Fenrir's heads whipped up to see Hel standing over them, a look of annoyance on her face.

"If you two are quite finished, we have a guest waiting in the meeting room." Hel tossed the bucket down and pivoted to make her way back to the keep.

Fenrir's grip loosened on her wrists. A hint of reluctance slowed his movements as he raised himself off her body, offering her a hand to stand. Ignoring it, she stood and tried to dust herself off, but the dirt had turned to mud thanks to Hel.

"I suppose you want me to stay here or hide?" Revna challenged, recovering the commandeered sword from the ground.

There was a beat of silence before she heard Fenrir sigh. "No. You're coming with me. No more hiding—for either of us."

Revna eyed him skeptically as he offered her his hand again. She didn't know what to do with it—so she swatted at it, knocking it aside.

Fenrir's mouth tugging into a crooked smile. "The sword, my *máni.*"

"Stop calling me that," she said half-heartedly, handing him the sword to return it to the weapons area.

"Never." He placed the weapon and turned back to her. "Come, let us go greet our guest."

⤞⎯⎯⎯⎯⎯⤝

Entering the meeting room, Revna immediately looked to Hel and Tyr. They seemed relaxed, talking cordially to a younger man who leaned against the table, the stranger giving her a small nod and smile as his eyes landed on her.

Fenrir came in close behind Revna and stood at her back, greeting the guest. "Baldur? What are you doing here?"

At some point she would have to stop being surprised by meeting the Gods, but today was not that day. Baldur was Tyr's brother, and a son of Odin. Looking at him more closely, she could see a slight resemblance to Tyr—mainly in the way his eyes crinkled when he smiled. Same dark skin, same warm brown eyes. But where Tyr was built like a boulder, Baldur possessed a leaner frame.

Revna couldn't place it exactly, but she felt at ease with Baldur. She could see why he was one of the more beloved Gods.

"I wanted to see my brother, of course," he said, clapping Tyr on the shoulder. Then his expression changed to a more serious one. "And to warn you."

Unease flooded Revna's body, hands itching to palm her daggers, but she withheld, waiting for him to explain. Instead, he turned to her, smile back in place.

"Forgive me, I have not introduced myself—"

"Yes, Baldur. I gathered," she said, crossing her arms.

"Don't worry, she's not as hard as she appears to be," Tyr told his brother.

Revna cocked her head. "Is that what you tell your lovers, *Tyrie*?"

Baldur threw his head back and laughed. "It looks like you've found the younger sister you always wanted."

Revna's lips twitched, but she didn't let the smile form.

"You came to warn us?" Fenrir gritted out from behind her. She turned to look at him, his body taut with an impending threat.

"Ah, yes. It's *you*, actually," Baldur said, gesturing to Revna, who froze again, her pulse rising.

All eyes in the room went to her now tense face, and Fenrir pressed in close behind, his fingers grazing hers as if he thought to grab her hand, but then decided against it. Anger and adrenaline still thinned her blood, but she didn't step away from him as she felt the heat of his body on her back.

"What about her?" Hel asked from her perch on the table.

"The Aesir know that you're here. They know that you came from Myddheim on the longboat, and think that all sacrifices belong in Asgard. They wanted to send Thor to come collect her, but I volunteered."

Between one blink and the next, Fenrir moved in front of Revna, and both Hel and Tyr moved to stand between them and Baldur, Hel's draugr form separating from her body. Unable to see past Fenrir's massive body, she stepped to the side to speak, but his hand shot out, and he threw her a pleading look. She clenched her jaw, but relented a nod.

"That will not be happening, Baldur. I will see you safely from my realm, but you won't be taking her." Fenrir's voice came out as a growl, his body thrumming with tension. "I made a deal with Odin that no more sacrifices would be taken from Myddheim in exchange for my submission—in exchange for not unleashing what lies under my skin. Has your father broken this deal? If so, perhaps I should pay Asgard a little visit."

Fenrir's body started to grow larger. Revna came around his side and grabbed his hand, lacing his fingers with hers. Slowly, he turned his head, his eyes on fire with molten gold, his teeth growing longer and sharper. She squeezed his hand, willing him to calm. She wasn't afraid of him—in any form that he may take—but she was certain a giant wolf wouldn't fit in the room.

"Forgive me, I should have made that clear from the beginning," Baldur said, hands raised in placation. "I'm just here to warn you. And, perhaps, help you."

"How?" Tyr asked.

Baldur shrugged. "To remind you of the old laws of the Gods—the laws of binding and marriage. Should she marry and bind herself to one of you, she can't be touched."

Revna went still again as she felt her heart drop into her stomach, her eyes still on Fenrir's.

The whole room fell silent.

Tyr sighed. "Well, fuck."

THIRTY

FENRIR

FENRIR WASN'T ENTIRELY SURE he was breathing. He was certain Revna wasn't, having heard her sharp intake of breath, with no following release.

Binding. Marriage.

Hel had jested about it in the beginning, though Fenrir had never truly considered it.

But Baldur spoke true. The Gods, for all their severity, violence, and scheming, held few laws with great reverence, a *Hjarta* bind being one of them.

When Fenrir had bound himself to Odin, it had created a shield of protection. Though the *Skyldu* wasn't as cherished as a *Hjarta* bind, it represented a bargain between the two Gods. Should either of them break the terms of the bind, they became vulnerable to the other. And the delicate peace that was fostered between them, and the realms, would dissolve, as would the inked bands on his forearms.

Fenrir couldn't do this to Revna—even if it was for her protection. It would be no better than what the Aesir had done to Freyja—trying to force her into a marriage to remain in Asgard, where they could use her powers as their own. He would not take away Revna's choice.

"Can someone please explain," Revna said, her voice oddly flat. Glancing back down at her, he saw she was strung tight, the hand not holding his curled into a tight fist, shoulders drawn up to her ears.

"It doesn't matter," Fenrir stated. "It won't happen."

"And is it not important that I understand my choices?" Revna dropped his hand and turned to him, a challenge in her eyes. "I want the *truth*. All of it."

He released a breath, reading the undertone of that statement. Looking to the other Gods, he gave a subtle nod to Hel to explain. Perhaps coming from her it would sting less.

"Long ago, the Gods agreed to certain laws among them in order to maintain civility and balance. Three binds were born out of this agreement: the *Skyldu*, the *Hjarta*, and the *Galdrloka*." Hel looked to Fenrir in question, and he nodded again, understanding what she was asking. "The *Skyldu*, like the one Fenrir has with Odin, is a bind of service, of obligation. Usually a bargain of compromises."

Fenrir smelled the shift in Revna's scent and resisted the urge to pull her close and comfort her.

"The *Hjarta*," Hel continued, "is deeper. Reverent. A bind of the heart and soul. Partners cannot be unwillingly separated. And should someone hurt their other half, justice would be severe and swift—death."

"And the third bind?" Revna asked, crossing her arms back over her chest.

This time, Baldur spoke. "It has never been successfully done, to our knowledge. No one truly knows its true power or purpose. The *Galdrloka* is a power sharing bind. Two of the Old Gods attempted it. They went mad and killed each other. It has not been tried since."

Revna turned and studied Fenrir. "So, if I were to bind myself to you, that would also grant you a certain protection from Odin?"

That Fenrir knew of, no God had ever bound themself to a mortal. He didn't see how it would make a difference—the binding was the same. But as he took in what she was saying, he took a step back, shaking his head. She had somehow turned this from guaranteeing her safety, to adding to his.

He gestured to the ink bands on his arms. "I have my protection. I won't do this to you."

"Marrying me is that abhorrent to you, then?" Revna retorted, eyes icing over, but not before he saw the hurt there.

"Everyone out," Fenrir growled.

Tyr, Hel, and Baldur hesitantly left the room, leaving him and Revna staring at each other in challenge. Fenrir broke his stare first, making his way to the table and pulling out two chairs to face one another. He gestured for Revna to take a seat as he sat in the other. Lifting her chin, she came to stand behind the chair, placing her hands on its tall back.

So fucking stubborn.

He didn't blame her. In a very short time, she had taken in a lot of information and was no doubt processing and assessing every angle.

"Tell me about your bind with Odin," she demanded before he could speak.

He did.

He told her everything. About his return from Myddheim and his proposal to Odin. That he would bind himself, do his bidding, be his enforcer, dirty his hands. In exchange, Odin wouldn't take anymore sacrifices from Myddheim, and he would allow his siblings to roam free, should they choose to. But the price, the sacrifice, was that he could not ever shift into his wolf form again. Never fully be whole.

"Your wolf is repressed by the bind?" Revna asked, her tone gentling.

Fenrir forced a dark laugh. "That's the torture of it. My body is a cage, but I also hold the key. I can let myself out at any moment, effectively breaking the bind." He didn't tell her how painful it would be.

"So why don't you?"

"And put everyone I care about at risk?" Fenrir shook his head. "Even with a *Hjarta* bind, even with you protected, Myddheim and Vanaheim would both be left vulnerable should I purposefully break my bind with Odin."

Revna started pacing, running her thumb along the scar on her palm. "Explain the *Hjarta* to me. The marriage part I understand well enough." She paused, looking over. "Unless that also means something different to the Gods?"

"It's usually one and the same. But a marriage with a bind is ... more. It's a choice not made lightly. When you choose to bind with someone, you are tying yourself to that person so inextricably that being apart from them is excruciating. Fate will always call us back to one another. Choosing to bind with someone is more than an exchange of vows—you are choosing and claiming that person as your life."

"Can it be broken?" she asked.

He nodded. "Only if both are willing. Or in death."

Revna hoped it would never come to that, but she wanted to understand as much as possible.

"How is the binding done?"

Fenrir leaned forward so that his forearms were braced on his knees. "A certain kind of runic magic— *seiðr* magic—is performed by a practitioner. It involves a ceremony, a hunt, a claim. Few can perform the ceremony. Tyr being one, ironically."

Revna snorted, but it held little humor. She gestured her chin toward his inked bands. "Are they part of it? If you bound yourself to me, would we both get markings?"

"I'm not sure." He furrowed his brow. "The mark of a bind manifests differently for everyone." She nodded but stayed quiet. "This is a terrible situation," he started, watching as hurt flashed momentarily across her face again. "I wouldn't want you to marry me out of need for protection—no person should have to."

She ran her hands along the back of the chair. "It doesn't have to be you. Tyr or Hel—"

"Absolutely not." His voice came out louder and more aggressive than he'd intended. They remained quiet for a moment, while Fenrir studied Revna's face, took in her scent. It wasn't disgusted or fearful, but curious. "You are truly considering this?"

She shook her head slowly. "No. I couldn't—I already feel ..." Revna looked away for a moment, and Fenrir let her find the words she searched for. "I feel like a burden. Ever since I arrived. Nearly getting myself killed, putting you all in harm's way. I would not add to that burden by forcing one of you to bind yourselves to me."

Fenrir's heart clenched. *A burden?*

He would gladly spend the rest of his days proving to her how wrong she was, if she'd let him. If she wanted it. But he didn't know if she would accept the truth; that he wanted her, and would gladly, *eagerly*, marry and bind with her.

It was a slow realization at first, but he knew now. Had for quite a while. He had loved her for nine years. Fenrir still didn't know why she was here, but he wondered if all those nights spent dreaming about her, all those nights staring up at the moon and dancing green lights wishing she were lying next to him, had somehow conjured her to his side.

He swallowed all the words he didn't think she was ready for him to say. "You are not a burden, Revna."

You are everything.

She took a deep breath and started pacing again. "If we did this, perhaps it could be as allies. We could—"

"*Allies?*" Fenrir stood out of his chair, his control snapping as her gaze met his. "I don't want to be your *ally*, Revna."

She threw her hands up in exasperation. "Then what do you want?"

"You! By the runes, Revna, I want *you*."

He stalked toward where she'd frozen in place, her eyes wide. "For nine years, there has not been a day or night I haven't thought of you. For nine years, I have ached to see you again. For nine years, I have—"

He stopped himself before he could say the words. Before he admitted that he loved her. He wasn't afraid of it, but a small voice told him it would overwhelm her. Fenrir came to stand before her, sliding his hand over her throat to grip the back of her neck gently, her smell heating to something tempting and dangerous.

"I would bind myself to you a thousand times—in every realm, every existence—without the looming threat." He gently stroked his thumb across her jaw. "But I would never want you to make that choice out of necessity, fear, or obligation. Do I want to protect you in every way possible? Yes. But only if you wanted *me*. Not because you felt forced. Not because you had no other choice."

He moved his thumb to her pulse, feeling the harried beat of it. And because he couldn't help himself, because he wasn't ready to hear her answer, he leaned his forehead against hers. When their lips were nearly touching, he paused, waiting for her to close the distance. With a slowness that lit his blood on fire, her mouth met his—soft and tender.

It unraveled him.

Fenrir had never been kissed with this kind of vulnerability and softness.

He tentatively nipped at her mouth, tasting the softness of her bottom lip. She opened immediately, hesitance seeping away, reaching her arms up and wrapping them around his neck. As the kiss deepened, and soft moans started to escape Revna's throat, Fenrir moved his hands to her ass, then her upper thighs, hoisting her up until her legs were wrapped around his middle. He sat her on the edge of the table, nestling himself between her thighs, and losing himself in her embrace.

Fenrir had never felt anything more perfect, and they hadn't done anything more than kiss. Given the chance, he would spend days in bed with her, learning all the ways to make her come apart. Feeling her, tasting her, devouring all that she would give him. His cock grew uncomfortably hard at the thought of her calling out his name if—*when*—he would finally bury his face between her thighs.

Hooking his hands under her knees, he pulled her closer. Slowly, he ran his hands up her thighs until he was palming her ass, grinding himself against her center. Revna gasped into his mouth, and he felt her hips start to undulate, her fingers dig into his hair. He growled into her mouth, and she bit gently at his bottom lip, then soothed it with a sweep of her tongue.

Desire burned in his veins, searing, ravenous. He wanted nothing more than to rip off her leather trousers and seat himself so deep inside of her that when she screamed, all the Gods would know who he belonged to. He was hers, and nine years, realms, and Gods, hadn't changed a fucking thing.

Revna reached down and palmed at his painfully hard cock, and Fenrir's whole body began to tremble.

"Revna," he ground out, somewhere between a plea and devotion.

With a control he didn't know he possessed, he removed her hand from his cock. He placed a kiss to the palm of the scarred hand and leaned his forehead against hers again, trying to slow his heartbeat.

When he'd regained a modicum of control he lifted his head, taking in her swollen lips, flushed cheeks and neck, the way her gray eyes were bright with lust. And the smell of her ...

Fuck.

She was so beautiful—so fucking strong, and smart, and brave, and full of heart. He ran a thumb along her bottom lip, resisting the urge to claim another kiss.

"Do you not ..." Revna started.

Fenrir chuckled darkly. "By the runes, Revna, I have never wanted anything more." He indulged himself by giving her one more slow kiss, then kept his mouth hovering over hers. "But if I have a taste of you, if I feel you come apart on my fingers, on my tongue, around my cock, I won't be able to let you out of my bed for days. And, unfortunately, there is a decision that needs to be made—and it's yours, my *máni*."

Fenrir placed one last kiss on her forehead and then stepped away from her, feeling the loss of her body keenly. He met her gaze and spoke his truth. "You have me if you want me."

Dazed and flushed, she slid off the table, straightening her mud-covered clothing. Just a short while ago, they had been fighting. He hoped that eventually she would use her words more than her actions, but he'd do whatever she needed.

"I need to think. Alone," she clarified.

Fenrir nodded in understanding. "Whatever you need."

With that, she pivoted and strode for the door. Before pulling it open, she paused and turned as if she was going to say something else, but then decided against it. She walked out.

Fenrir braced his hands back on the table, taking a deep breath, and settled in to wait as long she needed.

Thirty-One

Revna

SOFT RIDGES FORMED AT the tip of Revna's fingers as she sat in the hot spring. Her skin was flushed, her muscles soothed. But her mind

...

Her mind was a tempest.

Thinking over everything she had learned—the choice she had to make—had it spinning with no end in sight.

"For nine years, there has not been a day or night I haven't thought of you. For nine years, I have ached to see you again."

Hearing the words that were her own heart's reflection had mended something inside of her. That through time and realms, he too hadn't stopped thinking of her. And then ...

"I would marry and bind myself to you a thousand times—in every realm, every existence—without the looming threat."

He had laid his soul so completely at her feet—a raw offering that bore a new craving. But there was still a poisoned part of her mind whispering reminders of her deepest fears. That she was nothing more than a mortal woman, a former slave, a sacrifice for the Gods. No match for him, and he knew it. No match for anyone.

"You have me if you want me ..."

No. He didn't think of her that way, and neither should she. Revna took a deep breath, shoving the thoughts back into the corner of her mind, sealing them with stone.

She was more than her fear and anger.

Revna ran her hands along the surface of the water, steam billowing in a lazy haze, letting her mind spiral. Fenrir had withheld a big truth from her—a truth that had contributed to her suffering. All those years she'd blamed herself for the plight of Myddheim. But, try as she might, she couldn't find it in herself to be angry at him anymore. Though displeasure still itched under her skin, she understood why he'd done what he did. Would she not do something similar for the Maidens? Would she not sacrifice herself to lessen the suffering of those she cared about?

Without question.

Revna wanted him out of his deal with Odin. But to break that bind would leave Myddheim susceptible to sacrifices again. It could bring attention to Vanaheim and all the residents who dwelled there, effectively endangering everyone they cared about.

Perhaps if Revna made a deal with Odin herself, she could get Fenrir out of his, and help Myddheim. Just thinking about the reactions of Fenrir, Hel, and Tyr had her ducking her head under the water one last time, letting out her frustration until her lungs burned.

She emerged and leaned back, closing her eyes in defeat. She likely had nothing the Allfather would want to exchange for, anyway.

There was no right answer. It just felt too easy to marry and bind herself to Fenrir and think that all their problems would go away.

She wanted to. By the runes, she did.

The Gods may hold that kind of law with great reverence, but it didn't mean they also couldn't use it to manipulate them. Binding to each other would only show that part of their heart lay within each other, and that was a vulnerability that hardened her stomach in fear.

As much as she had fought it, she knew that part of her heart had always been with him. Fenrir had seen Revna in many facets—a nearly broken slave, a timid warrior, an angry woman. He had seen her cry, scream, rage, laugh, hurt, happy— and never once did he falter.

Revna had never thought she would marry, that kind of permanence and settling not boding well with her work in Myddheim. No one had ever made that desire come alive. But with Fenrir, it felt as though it was two pieces finding their way back to each other—a rightness she'd been missing for a long time.

Exiting the spring, she ran a dry weave over her body and dressed. She couldn't be bothered to put boots back on her damp feet, so she carried them and made her way back to her room. The moon was high enough in the sky that it perfectly aligned with the windowed openings in the hall. Nearly full and shining with brilliant light. Revna felt a blush creep up her neck as she thought of Fenrir's affectionate name for her.

She ran into no one on her way back, the keep quiet, perfect for her loud thoughts to echo. Once in her room, she changed into a sleeveless night dress, the material soft and comforting. She took a comb and sat in front of the fire and worked through the gnarls in her hair, trying to focus her mind on the task, when her decision struck her so violently, she knocked over her chair as she stood, staring into the crackling flames.

She wanted Fenrir.

She'd been trying to balance all the reasons and excuses, the repercussions and the worries, but in a life where she'd done all she could for others—because she wanted to help, because she was wracked with guilt, because she'd been forced—only one thing mattered in that moment.

Revna *wanted* to marry him, to bind with him—wanted him with a fierceness that made her shake with the intensity of it.

She threw the comb down and strode to the door, her feet bare, her hair damp. She pulled the door open, and there he stood, hand raised as if he were about to knock.

Fenrir, too, had cleaned up and changed. His muscled thighs strained against fresh leathers, his brown tunic tight across his chest and shoulders. His nostrils flared as he lowered his hand, unbridled desire flaring in his eyes.

"I was going to come find you," Revna said, her voice coming out breathy. She didn't care. "Do you want to come in?"

Fenrir nodded and walked past her as she stepped aside. "I wanted to come check on you. To see if you had any further questions or ..."

"If I had made a decision?"

He swallowed and nodded.

Revna walked over to the fire but couldn't bring herself to sit. The buzzing in her body was a living thing that made her want to keep moving. Fenrir followed her movements with his eyes, but kept his distance.

"If there was no threat, if there was no such thing as this binding, would you still want this?" she asked.

He gave her a soft smile. "I would have liked more time to pursue you. To let you adjust to this new life you find yourself in, but yes. I want you, Revna."

She swallowed and reached down to fiddle with the fabric of her dress as she let his words digest. "And you are willing to relinquish another part of yourself to someone else? To give up more freedom? To tie yourself to someone with a damning prophecy hanging overhead?"

He had already given up so much in his bind with Odin. And not knowing what darkness her prophecy would bring sat heavy on her shoulders. She needed to make sure.

Fenrir cocked his head at her, looking at her thoughtfully. "Do you remember when we got snowed into that cave after I had healed enough, and we began traveling?"

Of course she remembered. An unexpected spring snowsquall had them hunkering down for days. They'd had very little food, and the bitter cold forced them to sleep next to each other for warmth. It was the first time she had lain next a man and felt safe enough to sleep.

"Yes."

"It was the first time I saw you smile—the first time I heard you laugh. We'd been in the cave for nearly three days and were going a little stir crazy. We played that game—slap hands—and every time you were able to hit mine, your laughter became louder and more confident. As if you had never allowed yourself to make those sounds before. I recall a few snorts as well," he chuckled.

"I did *not* snort."

"Oh, yes, you did." Fenrir laughed, a rich and deep rumble that made Revna's stomach flutter. "And it was one of the most glorious sounds I had ever heard. But the thing I remember most about being in that cave with you was that I felt content and safe. Obviously, you didn't know who I really was, and that gave me permission to be something new. Something I was never able to think of myself as—an actual person. With thoughts, feelings, fears, vulnerabilities. I wasn't Fenrir—God of Destruction. I was Fenrick, man and friend of Revna."

He took one step toward her, then another. Reaching up to brush her hair over her shoulder, he gently grasped the back of her neck—a claiming gesture Revna was beginning to crave the more he did it. "You make me feel free to be myself."

Her whole body came alive with his words. The backs of her eyes burned, her limbs trembled, her chest flooded with warmth. He rubbed a hand up and down one of her arms, the firelight making his amber eyes glow.

"I know this is a lot to take in. I know I'll need to apologize several more times for the truths I've withheld and the mistakes I've made." He leaned down so that his mouth was on her ear. "I will get on my knees every night for my wife and beg for her forgiveness if she'll let me."

Revna's hands reached up to dig into his tunic, steadying herself. Whether it was the seductive timbre of his voice at her ear, or hearing him call her his wife, she couldn't say, but her body caught fire at his words. "Presumptuous of you to already call me wife."

He laughed and leaned back so that she could see his face again, his eyes searching hers. "In all seriousness, do you have any questions?"

She bit her lip, his eyes tracking the movement. "What happens when I die?"

Fenrir threaded his remaining hand on the other side of her neck, the touch possessive and firm. "That's not going to happen, my *máni*. I won't allow it."

Revna rolled her eyes to the ceiling, trying to take a playful tone to what was a serious question. "I am mortal. I don't possess the gift of endless life like a God. And I need to know that, when the time comes, it won't hurt you."

Fenrir growled in a way that she'd come to understand as frustration. "I wouldn't die with you, if that's what you're asking. But it would leave me fractured—like losing a part of my being that I could never get back. I'm not sure what that would make me."

"Promise me that you will continue on and try to find contentment."

Fenrir froze, and she watched as the realization dawned on his devastatingly handsome face. "Are you ..."

"Saying yes?" She reached up and gripped the collar of his tunic and jerked it down so that his face was level with hers. His fingers squeezed lightly on the back of her neck, his eyes flashing with such hope. "*Yes.* But don't ever keep me in the dark again. We join together as equals, as partners, and I won't have it any other way. Agreed?"

His answer was a deep and searing kiss, full of a joy she'd never known, and she kissed him back with all she had. She knew she hadn't said everything she wanted, all he should know about how she felt. But she could show him.

He broke the kiss too quickly, leaving Revna panting—wanting. Fenrir removed his hands from their place on her neck, placed them firmly on her waist. He pivoted her body and started backing her up toward the bed.

"We will inevitably fight," she sighed out as he dipped his head and his teeth scored her neck.

"Good," he groaned. "Fight with me."

"I'm not always good at using my words," she said on a half moan as he gripped her tighter, bringing her firmly against his hard body.

"Then I will find ways to encourage you to use them."

When the backs of her legs hit the bed, she dug her hands into his hair and met his gaze, letting him see the unabashed hunger. Letting him see that he was about to be devoured. He lay her down, and she pulled up her dress, and parted her legs to accommodate his hips. With a hand braced on one side of her head and his other sliding up her thigh, he dipped his head to kiss the base of her throat.

By the Gods, she felt like she would burst into flame.

His rough fingers came to the crease at the top of her thigh. She rolled her hips, wanting him to move his hand, needing him not to stop. His teeth found a sensitive spot on her collarbone, and she let out a breathy moan.

"*Fuck*, Revna."

Hearing her name growled had her whole body flooding with desire, then bereft with need, as, abruptly, Fenrir pushed away from her and stood.

He gave a strained groan as he looked down her body, running a hand down his face. "I'm sorry, my *máni*."

"Are you alright?" she asked, her voice shaking slightly.

"Barely." His laugh was strained, his body shaking. "If I touch you anymore, I'm not going to be able to stop. And there's much to do to prepare for tomorrow." His eyes raked down her body again. "You'll need to be rested."

It was Revna's turn to growl in frustration, at least until his words sank in.

"The ceremony will take place tomorrow?"

Fenrir nodded, taking a deep breath. He leaned back down to where she lay, picking her up and righting her on the bed, then tucking her in. She immediately threw off the fur. Her skin was too hot, too sensitive.

"Yes, I think the sooner the better. Just in case Asgard sends someone else. Baldur remains to witness and bring back the news to Asgard, but I think it wise not to waste any time." His hand moved up her throat, the curve of her jaw, until he ran his thumb along her bottom lip. "Besides, I can't wait any longer."

Looking utterly torn, he stood and walked away, leaving her aching. She pushed herself up so that she rested back on her elbows, the shoulder on her night dress sliding off. Fenrir turned when he reached the door and took his fill of the view. For a moment, she thought he might change his mind and come give her the ravaging she so desired. But instead, he dipped his head.

"Sleep well, my bride. You are going to need it."

And with that, he left.

THIRTY-TWO

T HE WHOLE KEEP WAS abuzz with the impending wedding festivities. Most of the residents didn't know the exact reason for the rushed ceremony, but neither did they question it, nor his choice of bride. They'd spent weeks watching the God and the human woman circling each other, after all. Austri and a handful of other cooks were preparing and transporting an enormous feast out to the ceremonial space in the forest. Tyr and Baldur were directing tent set-up and the digging of the fire pits. Hel was with Revna, keeping her company and explaining how the ceremony would work.

And Fenrir was trying to contain himself. The closer the ceremony got, the more he wanted it. The binding, the hunt, the claiming—he wanted it all. But most of all, he wanted Revna.

The little sleep he'd managed to get the previous night was full of dreams—some spine-tinglingly good and some terrifyingly foreboding. Revna at the center of them all. In some dreams she was running to him, and in others she was running away, disappearing into a fog so dense he coughed himself awake.

When rest was no longer an option, he made his way down to the fjord to tell Jormun and invite him to the ceremony. His brother had refused to shift into his human form, and had disappeared under the surface without so much as a huff of acknowledgment. Fenrir had left the water's edge feeling nettled. He wanted his brother there but wouldn't push him. The invitation was extended, and that was all he could do.

He made his way through the woods to the site of the ceremony, the trees rustling with pleasure, the smells of spiced food guiding him.

Upon stepping out from beneath the branches he stopped short, eyebrows raised. The residents of the keep had outdone themselves.

A long fire pit bisected the clearing, two tents on one end, and a slightly raised platform at the other. Benches and tables dotted the space—bits of greenery draped along their wooden surfaces. Lanterns hung from posts that would be lit with the setting sun. And two Jotunns were currently practicing the ceremonial hunting song on the drums next to the platform.

Fenrir's blood heated at the sound, and at the thought of what was to come in these woods.

Two warriors entered from the other side of the clearing, gave a wave, and crossed to him. Fenrir had sent several parties out to scout the area to ensure nothing seemed amiss—no lurking fire beasts or curious Gods. He'd also asked for rotating groups of volunteers to be stationed at the gate in case any visitors decided to drop by.

"We saw nothing on our scouting. We'll make our rounds again before the ceremony, but it looks like all is well, Fenrir," a light elf by the name of Kaneff said in greeting. Kaneff and Tyr were lovers on occasion, with or without other partners. As far as Fenrir knew, they kept things purely physical and uncomplicated.

"Thank you, Kaneff. And you, Alfa," Fenrir said, nodding to the two warriors.

"Well wishes to both of you," Alfa said, her smile reaching her dark eyes. "Everyone is looking forward to the celebration. It's been some time since we celebrated anything."

It had, indeed. With Fenrir constantly in other realms and focused on keeping Asgard away from Vanaheim, he'd let things like festivity and joy slips through the cracks. Looking at the excitement on the faces of his people now, he felt like he'd been a terrible guardian of the realm—because as sure as their safety and protection were part of his responsibility, so was their happiness.

He sighed and clasped Alfa's shoulder. "We will do better in that regard. Perhaps monthly full moon feasts." Tonight was a full moon, and he liked the idea of celebrating every full moon he would spend married and bound to Revna.

Both warriors took their leave smiling at his words, which felt like progress. Fenrir walked to one of the tents, peeking in, ensuring that Revna had everything she could need to get ready for the ceremony. As he exited the tent, Tyr was waiting for him, a knowing smirk plastered on the bastard's face.

He laughed, striding to Fenrir, grabbing him in a hug, slapping his back hard. "I'm relieved you two finally came to your senses."

"I can't say I'm not happy, but I worry I've backed her into a corner. She had to choose her safety or her freedom."

Tyr shook his head, placing his hand on Fenrir's shoulder. "The only thing she had to choose was *you*, Fen. We would have figured out a way to keep her safe from Asgard. This"—he gestured around and then at Fenrir—"you two were inevitable. By the runes and fates, I know that to be true down to my very bones."

Tyr wasn't wrong. Something about he and Revna had always felt ineluctable. Even time and realms were not enough to stop them from coming together again. Whether it was fate, or something else, he didn't care. All he knew was that he would endure it all and more to have this time with her.

Fenrir grinned and clapped Tyr on his shoulder. "Thank you for performing the ceremony. I wouldn't want anyone else."

Tyr slung his arm around Fenrir's neck. "Come along. Let's go have a soak in the springs and get you nice and cleaned up for your bride."

The sun was moments from setting as Fenrir paced around his tent, his wolf begging to run, to hunt. Through the thin canvas he could hear sounds of merriment as people gathered and waited for the ceremony to begin. More than once that day, Fenrir wondered if he and Revna should have done this privately, but a wicked and possessive part of him wanted everyone to witness, to see, to understand what they were to each other.

He hadn't seen Revna since he'd left her in her bed with her night dress sliding off her shoulder. Even in his wolf form, he'd never felt more powerful than he did in that moment when all he wanted to do was barricade the door and completely consume her, but he'd resisted—wanting to give her more time to make sure this was what she wanted.

Not seeing her all day had made his skin itch. How he'd survived nine years was nothing short of astounding.

A pulsing, rhythmic thump had Fenrir's pace halting. The resonant call awakened something primal, and he felt the wolf inside him sit up and take notice.

The flap to the tent opened and Tyr stepped inside. "It's time."

Fenrir nodded and looked down at himself one last time. He wore only loose trousers and a fur around his shoulders. Everything else was bare down to his very feet. He carried no weapons, aside from the power writhing in his blood. With eager strides, he made his way to the opening in the tent and stepped outside. He was greeted by a wall of fire, the tall flames instantly warming his already heated skin. The fire pit separated the space between his and Revna's tents, and he immediately hated the flames keeping him from her.

Fenrir waited, pacing, the sound of the drums increasing in rhythm. Voices sang out—calling, wailing, begging for the bride to come out.

And then the entrance to her tent opened and Hel stepped out, holding back the fabric.

Fenrir took an uncontrollable step forward as Revna emerged, the warmth coursing through his body nothing to do with the fire he was standing precariously close to.

His breath stopped as he took her in through the dancing flames.

She, too, was wearing very little. A dark gray dress with thin straps and a deep plunging front. High slits in the skirt showed her legs with every step she took. Her dark hair was down in loose waves, with small silver cuffs placed throughout catching the light.

She was a vision, but the most beautiful part was the smile that spread across her face. He smiled back, and happiness lit her eyes. She turned her body to the platform but kept her eyes on his as she walked. The predator beneath his skin perked at the sight of the glint in her eyes. He stepped with her, their smiles fading into something more reverent as they made their way past the crackling flames.

The drums grew louder still, the vocalizations more frantic as they reached where the fire encircled the platform. Without hesitation, Fenrir stepped through the fire and prowled to Revna. The flames were lower here, and Revna gathered the end of her dress in her hands and leapt over them, landing at his side. He reached a hand to hers, her scarred palm pressing against his rough one, and together they ascended the dais.

Now that the fire no longer separated them, Fenrir barely resisted the urge to crush his mouth to hers, dying to taste her, dying to be close.

When they reached Tyr, he raised his hand, and the drumming abruptly ceased.

"Friends, welcome and bear witness to the binding of Fenrir and Revna—" he started, addressing the gathered crowd, explaining that he would obtain their consent, perform the binding ritual, and then, finally, the hunt and claiming.

But as Tyr talked, Fenrir could focus only on Revna, drowning out the rest of the surrounding world. She returned the intensity of his gaze in a look that was part serenity and part anticipation. She quirked an eyebrow and then gave his hand a squeeze.

"I am," she said, her scent flaring sweet and true.

Fenrir furrowed his brows in slight confusion until he heard Tyr ask, "And, are you, Fenrir, here and ready to accept this bind willingly and without reservations?"

He didn't hesitate. "I am."

Fenrir turned slightly to see Tyr lift a rope from around his neck. He handed one end to Fenrir and then started circling him and Revna, each wrap bringing them close and closer until they were pressed together, their hearts beating against each other's skin. Tyr grabbed Fenrir's end and tied the rope together.

Before Tyr could start the invocation, Fenrir whispered to Revna one last time, "You are sure?"

She tilted her face to his, her expression unequivocal. "Yes." And this time he believed her.

The drums restarted a low and steady beat as Tyr laid his hands upon the rope, speaking low and quick.

He spoke in an ancient and imbuing language. An old language. Spoken when the realms had been but fire and ice and beasts and unknown Gods. He spoke of the power of love that gave strength to the bind. He spoke of the soul, and having it live within another. And with the words, he wove their two halves together.

Unlike the icy, painful binding Fenrir had made with Odin, this one filled him with warmth. It started at his feet, and he saw the moment it struck Revna. Her eyes widened and she tried to look between their bodies to the platform, no doubt wondering if the wood had caught fire.

The warmth unfurled through every corner of his body, coursing through his blood like liquid sunlight. As it crawled through his ribs to his heart, he felt it stutter briefly, as if trying to match its beat with Revna's. When it reached her eyes they flashed impossibly silver, almost as if they were the moon's very surface. When it swirled in Fenrir's head, he leaned forward as far as he could, touching his forehead to the top of hers. His body was on fire, and by the way she started to tremble against him, she was feeling the same.

He was burning—*burning for her.*

His nostrils flared as he took in her scent, an intoxicating melody of her sweet earthiness and heady desire. He imprinted it into his mind. There was nowhere, no corner of the farthest realms, that she could go that he would not find her, that he would not follow her.

Tyr started undoing the rope, and as soon as he was able, Fenrir plunged both hands into Revna's hair, grasping the base of her neck.

He needed to claim her. *Now.*

With great restraint at resisting the burning look in Revna's gaze, he released her and took a step back, watching as two others took the rope and tied it to posts above the fire.

"It's time for the hunt and the claiming!" Tyr shouted, followed by whoops and howls of excitement. He turned to Revna, his voice lower and a wicked glint in his gaze. "Revna, you have until the rope burns through to run as far away as possible. Once you hear the drums start again, Fenrir will be on the hunt."

Fenrir watched as she nodded, and with one last fevered look his way, she jumped off the back side of the platform and made her way into the thick copse of trees. An animal-like growl built in his throat at her walking away from him. When she reached the tree line, she turned one last time, catching his gaze.

He felt a slow smile light his lips and saw its effect on her, then mouthed one word. *Run.*

Her mouth parted briefly before she took off into the night.

Fenrir turned and watched the rope above the fire. As soon as it frayed, he would hunt and claim his wife.

Thirty-Three

THE FULL MOON LIT Revna's way as she ran through the forest, anticipation and pure need coursing molten through her blood. Trees swayed lazily, creaking and groaning under the caress of the breeze—a breeze that was doing nothing to cool her. She was burning with a ferocity and fever like never before. For a moment, she questioned why she was running from what she wanted. But something primal had her feet pounding against the soft earth.

She wanted to run.

She wanted to get caught.

Earlier, while getting ready, Hel had explained the elements of the binding ceremony. Walking through the fire, the consent, the binding invocation—calling forth the beginning of the bind—to be fully solidified in these woods.

Fenrir was going to hunt her and then claim her—body, mind, and soul.

But she wouldn't make it easy for him. If the wolf wanted to hunt, she would make him hunt.

Running without the weight of her daggers as her hip felt odd but liberating. She had wanted to present herself free of the burden of her weapons—her armor—in more ways than one. Hel had sensed her slight hesitation and promised to keep them in her tent just in case she wanted to put them on after.

Thick moss cushioned her steps to a whisper, but the steady pulse of her heartbeat called out to the silent wood. Called out to him.

No drums yet. She still had time until the wolf was released.

Pulling her dress over her head, she tossed it over a branch and then took off in the other direction. Perhaps that would confuse him for a bit—knowing that he would track her scent, as a wolf is want to do.

She circled a few trees, creating loops and confusing tracks. The moonlight dimmed as a cloud passed over, created deeper and darker shadows. Revna slowed her steps, catching her breath, calming her loud heartbeat—

No, not heartbeat. Drums.

The drums began their resonant pulse. The earth trembled.

Fenrir was free to hunt.

Revna took off, relying on years of training and good balance to make her way through the woods in the dark, and to ignore the small pains caused by errant branches and spiky plants in the underbrush. On she ran until the incessant beat of the drums grew distant. Her breath came in heavy pants, their loud, desperate call likely leading him right to her. She slowed for a moment, trying to steady herself and listen.

The snap of a twig to her left had her dashing right.

An out of place shadow paused her steps as she noticed something draped on a low branch. With ears perked, she slowly approached. Her stomach fluttered as she realized what she was looking at.

Fenrir's pants.

The hairs on the back of her neck stood on end, bumps raised across her skin.

He was close. Perhaps he always had been. She should have known better than trying to fool a god—a wolf god, at that, and one with nature at his call.

Revna turned in slow circle, gazing out into the umbral-dusted trees. She almost expected to see two golden eyes glinting from somewhere in the pitch but saw nothing. Heard nothing. No creature, no wind rustling the trees, nothing.

A tingling sensation trailed up her spine, igniting her urge to run. Not run from, but *to*—she no longer wanted to be the hunted, she wanted to be the hunter.

Revna wanted to find Fenrir and put her claim on him.

She entered a small clearing. The glowing moss that adorned so many spaces around the keep lit the area in a hazy like dreamscape. A small breeze twisted through the clearing, and Revna closed her eyes, letting it cool the sticky fever on her skin. Pulling air into her lungs, she felt surrounded by a familiar peace. The smell of the trees and earth and a first snow had always been her comfort, and now she knew why.

It was him.

She opened her eyes and froze.

Fenrir leaned against a tree across from her, inked arms crossing his chest, intense amber glowing eyes on her. Unquenchable thirst climbed down her throat. They had never taken in each other's nakedness like this. They had seen one another exposed for bathing or life-threatening purposes. They had teased and looked away. But they'd never truly looked freely, not like this, not flushed with desire.

Revna's knees felt weak as she looked at him—looked at her husband. The broadness of his shoulders, the light dusting of hair on his chest, leading down across a muscled stomach. Down farther to his hard length, his solid legs. The inked vines curled and wrapped around his legs and behind his back.

Revna swallowed and dragged her gaze back up his body meeting his eyes, letting him see her. Letting him see how on edge she was, how starving.

"Revna," he growled, clearly trying to restrain himself. "It's not too late. We don't have to do this tonight. We can walk back to the feast and complete the binding when you are ready."

Studying him, she realized he was completely sincere.

But so was she.

Her legs tingled as she took a step back, then another, a small smile pulling on the corner of her mouth. Fenrir unfolded his arms and pushed off his post on the tree, his eyes flashing molten—a predator ready to give chase.

"I want you," she said. "I want this. Come and get me, wolf—"

Revna sucked in a sharp breath as vines burst forth and pinned her to a tree, securing her wrists above her head. Vines snaked around her middle, around each ankle, and gently tugged, spreading them.

"Nine years, my *máni*." Fenrir prowled toward her, showing no external sign that he'd just used his powers on her body. "Nine years I have thought about all the things I wanted to do with you. Did you think this would just be some quick rut in the woods?"

Another vine snaked out and wrapped snugly around her throat— not enough to restrict air—just firm enough that she couldn't turn away from him. Heady desire pooled so heavily in her core that she whimpered. He looked so beautiful and wild, and utterly *hers*.

Desperate to touch him, she uttered a word she rarely used. "Please."

Fenrir reached out one finger and traced his knuckle across her jaw, down her neck. Revna arched, straining against the vines as he dragged his knuckle across one nipple, then the other. Down to her belly, down farther, until he gently slid his finger through her wetness. A growl sounded deep in his throat as a needy whimper came from hers. He stepped closer, one hand still sliding lazily through her folds. The other grabbing at her neck, pushing the vines harder against her skin.

"I told you to get some rest last night. Did you listen to me?"

Nodding wasn't an option, so she gritted out, "*Yes.*"

Fenrir leaned forward and hovered his mouth just above hers as his thumb pushed firmly against her the most sensitive spot at the apex of her thighs. "First, you are going to come apart on my hand, then on my tongue. And then, when you beg me, I will give you cock. Let me hear you say yes."

"Yes," she moaned as her hips tried to grind against his hand, her eyes becoming heavy-lidded.

"Look at me, Revna." She did, unable to defy his command. His eyes blazed, his canines slightly elongated. "If you want to stop, we stop. Just say the word."

She wouldn't, but affection swelled inside of her. In a life where she held tight to control like a lifeline, she longed, in this moment, to give it to him. Revna trusted him wholly, and wanted him with a sharpness that made her dizzy.

"Please kiss me," she begged. "Please touch me. Make me yours."

His thumb started moving in slow circles. "You've always been mine, Revna. Just as I have always been yours."

Then his mouth was on hers. Claiming and hungry. His thumb continued its lazy rhythm, but Revna wanted—*needed* more. Her hips started to undulate, desperate to create more friction against his hand. She bit gently on his lip in demand.

"Need more, my *máni?*" The vines at her ankles yanked, spreading her farther. Fenrir removed his thumb, and she gave a whimper of protest until one long finger slid deep inside of her. Then a second. She gripped the vine pinning her wrist and tried to arch into him—needing more, needing him. All of him. "So fucking beautiful."

With his fingers still buried deep inside, pumping and curling in delicious torment, he pressed the heel of his hand onto her most sensitive spot, grinding against it. Revna moaned as a deep ache built and built inside of her.

Eyes heavy-lidded, she focused on Fenrir's face and nearly came from the look in his eyes. His gaze traveled between her face and the apex of her thighs, hungry and burning. As his eyes met hers again, the pace of his hand quickened, and then slowed. Quickened, then slowed. Revna wanted to cry, wanted to scream—his touch brutal and gentle and unraveling her completely. She was close, so close. She just needed ...

Fenrir leaned in for another kiss, deep and slow in time with his hand. When he broke away, his motions increased their pace and Revna felt the heat coil inside of her, ready to strike.

"Come apart, Revna. I want to see you." He met her gaze, pressing the heel of his hand even harder. "*Now*."

She broke, her body coiled and tense, then melting and full of sensation.

"*Fenrir*," she moaned. He kept his steady rhythm until she was trembling with overwhelming sensation, but desire built and reached a new height, one she didn't know if she would ever come down from. Fenrir didn't relent, kept stroking and rubbing, until she was screaming again, another release barreling through her on the heels of the first.

She sagged, legs unable to bear her weight, Fenrir's vines holding her steady. With great effort, Revna kept her eyes open and watched as Fenrir took the fingers that were coated in her and rubbed them all over his cock, giving it a few hard pumps. She tugged against the vines, wanting to touch him so badly that she may weep.

"Fenrir," she said, her voice coming out as a command. "Release me. *Now*."

He took a few steps back, his hand stroking over his hard length. "Do you like seeing me like this? Hard and aching so badly for you that I can't help but touch myself."

She nodded, biting her lip, feeling more wetness run down her inner thighs.

"Fuck, Revna. I could come just from you looking at me like that." He released his cock, closing the space between them again. Just as he reached her, she felt the vines give, and then he was hoisting her legs around his middle, her hands going to his shoulders. She reached one hand down between their bodies to grip him and he let out a hiss as she gave his cock a firm stroke.

He dropped to his knees, taking her with him, and Revna used the movement to stroke his length again, feeling the heavy heat of it. But he laid her on her back and removed her touch. He hovered over her for a moment before sitting back on his heels. Revna let her knees fall open—opening herself to him. He ran his hand down his face, eyes roving up and down her naked body.

He started shaking his head slightly, a look of awe on his face. "So many nights and days I spent dreaming of you. Even now, when I can touch you, see you, smell you, I can hardly believe that you are here—that you are real."

Tears pricked at the corner of Revna's eyes as she stared up at him, bare to him on the mossy ground. "There wasn't a day that went by that I didn't think of you, Fenrir. You were the first thing that I chose for myself. I still choose you."

He swallowed and then leaned forward, placing his elbows on either side of her head, dropping his mouth to hers. There was no rush, just languid lips and tongues and teeth, until Revna was lifting her hips, trying to grind against anything she could make contact with. He kissed his way down, nipping at her neck and collar bone, dragging his fangs down to land above her heart, biting gently, then soothing the mark with his tongue. As if he would devour all of her, he took his time licking and biting his way down her body—stopping to pay lingering attention to each nipple, causing intense shocks of pleasure to course through her. When he reached where the arrow had pierced her, he placed a tender kiss to the rough scar.

Revna was bowing off the moss-covered ground, needy sounds coming out as he nipped at her hips, then her inner thighs. She could feel his breath *there*, right where she needed him, but then he went to her other hip and inner thigh.

"Fenrir," she warned. She reached down, threading her fingers through his thick hair, and tilted his head just enough so that his eyes met hers from between her legs. Her breath caught in her chest as he slowly licked her in one long stroke, moaning as he tasted her, and her admonishment slipped away on a wave of sensation. His tongue circled her already overly sensitive bundle of nerves, his eyes still on hers, the sensation nearly making her come undone from the first sweep. At her moaning his name, his control slipped, and he feasted as a starving man does, her head falling back to the branch-covered sky.

Revna was nearly sobbing, hands digging into his hair, grinding against his face, when he slid two fingers inside of her and she jolted, sensation rising to a new precipice. She was shaking with impending release when he sealed his lips over her most sensitive part and sucked hard. A scream burst forth from her throat, raw and primal, echoing off the surrounding trees.

She fell over that edge and tears leaked from the corner of her eyes, streaming down her temples as she gazed at the canopy above, her breath burning her lungs with each deep pull.

Revna felt undone and remade. She didn't know how she had lived without this—lived without him. He was still licking her slowly, savoring every bit of her, when she gently called his name. Something he heard in her voice had him lifting his head and crawling back over her.

"My *máni*," he said, his voice filled with fear. "Did I hurt you?"

She shook her head, and he placed a gentle kiss on her forehead, his eyes shuttering in relief.

Revna thought about how to explain, how to find the words to say that if she didn't have him now, if she didn't seal the bind immediately, she was afraid she would lose him. It clawed at her skin, simmered in her veins. "I need you. Desperately."

Revna had never needed anything desperately before, and something in the back of her mind tickled at a memory, as if she was trying to remember something important, but she pushed it aside for the moment as she ran her hands up and down the muscled panes of his back.

He nodded as if he understood, and she saw a near identical desperation in his gaze. He shifted and she spread her legs wide around his waist, feeling the thick head of him positioned at her entrance.

He hovered his mouth above hers. "You have me."

Thirty-Four

FENRIR

Something inside Fenrir's chest fractured and restructured itself to accommodate the swelling of his heart—of his entire being. The completion of the bind waited restlessly in his body. The wolf under his skin clawed at him to drive himself deep inside of Revna so that they would never be parted.

But he had waited nine years—would have waited until the end—for her. He wanted to touch and taste every inch of her. Watching her come apart on his hand and then on his tongue nearly made him spill prematurely.

Her taste, her smell, the sounds she made ... Fenrir had never been more certain that he was completely hers. He had spent most of his life without ever belonging. Now he knew, this whole time, he'd belonged with Revna.

The smell of tears and the call of his name had him pausing his tongue, stopping from the intense pleasure of licking her clean. He pushed himself to hover over her, and the tears streaming down the sides of her temples made his blood run cold.

"My *máni.*" Agony sliced through him. "Did I hurt you?"

Revna shook her head vigorously, and relief overwhelmed him. He pressed his lips to her forehead in comfort

"I need you. *Desperately.*"

Fenrir took in her eyes, her flushed cheeks, her swollen lips, understanding what she was telling him. She felt it too. The need to fulfill the bind. To tie it in unbudging knots. His head felt full of pressure, tilting into madness. But it wasn't just the binding incantation weaving its magic making him dizzy with desperation. It was her.

He adjusted himself, feeling her spreading for him, and took his cock in hand and guided it to her entrance. He leaned down so his mouth was nearly touching hers. "You have me."

He gave her a scorching kiss while he ran the head of his cock through the wetness of her, feeling her body twitch when he hit the apex. With great reluctance, he broke the kiss, wanting to watch her as he slid inside of her for the first time.

Sliding the tip in, he hissed at the sensation. Revna's mouth fell open and her breath seemed to catch. Fenrir grabbed behind one of her knees, hoisting it up to frame his hips. He braced himself on the opposite elbow, snaking his hand under the back of her neck and gripping it firmly. Then, so slowly, he pressed his hips forward, sinking into her delicious heat. Revna's breath exhaled on a moan. With one final thrust, he was seated fully inside of her.

The earth shook under them, and the trees danced.

He felt it then—a warmth that spread from his chest outwards, finding every part of him that ached, every part that had spent years in hiding, every part that had begged to see her again. It soothed him, invigorated him, completed him.

"Revna," he whispered her named in ecstasy that bordered on agony. Her gray eyes shined with new, unshed tears. He moved, slowly thrusting into her, over and over. "Hear these vows and know my heart. If hunger claims you, I will feed you. If you cannot walk, I will carry you. If you need strength, I give you my mind and body. If darkness stalks you, I will enter any shadow to find you. If love is what you need ... it is already yours. My *heart* is yours."

Revna threaded her hands into his hair, pulling his head down for a kiss. When his tongue met hers, he drove into her harder until he felt the telling tightening that his fingers knew. Just as he was about to haul her up, she pushed at his chest until he slid out of her. She rolled him until he was on his back, and she was straddling him.

Slowly she sank onto his length and they both let out long moans. Fenrir had never seen anything more beautiful, her hair mussed, naked body shining in the moon and faint glow of the moss. She placed her hands on his chest and began to rock.

"Hear these vows and know my heart, Fenrir. Should you feel adrift, I will help you find your way. If you need a hand to hold, mine will be ever yours. If weariness takes you, I will guard you while you rest. If you need love, if you need my heart" she said, as she leaned forward so that her face was hovering above his, "they are already yours."

Her pace quickened and Fenrir gripped at her hips, clenching his teeth. "You are mine, wolf. And I am yours."

Unable to help himself, he lurched up, wrapping his arms around her waist. He brought his knees underneath of him and sat back on his heels. He needed her closer, needed to feel every breath, every tremble. He thrust up into her and then pulled her hips down to grind against him. He kept that rhythm, Revna meeting every pulse with the intensity of a hunt.

Every movement, every breath he inhaled had the warmth in his chest flaring.

"*Revna*," he ground out as the warmth started barreling down his middle.

"I feel it." She unwound an arm from his shoulders and placed a hand at the center of his chest, her eyes meeting his.

Fenrir slowed their pace, wanting to savor every clench and sound. Freeing one arm from her waist, he reached a hand between them to gently stroke that bundle of nerves that he knew would send her falling over the edge. She tightened around him with each swipe, her movements becoming more desperate. Her fingers dug into him and Fenrir growled at the feel of her nails marking him.

"*Fuck*, Revna." She was squeezing him so tight, he was losing all sense as his release neared.

"Come for me," she panted, licking at his mouth. "Come for your *wife*."

Undone by her words, Fenrir came with a roar. He pounded into her, needing her to follow him. He pushed her down onto her back and pinned her hands above her head, fucking her in brutal thrusts. She screamed her own release, her inner walls clenching so impossibly tight, prolonging his own.

Fenrir felt it then—the bind settling into place. Whereas his *Skyldu* bind to Odin felt heavy and cold, this felt fortifying. The markings of that bind felt like shackles around his forearms, and this felt like the home he'd always been searching for. He lifted up, his breathing still heavy, his body still moving with the aftershocks, and searched his and Revna's bodies. There, nestled between her breasts, gleamed the *Hjarta* bind mark, golden and radiant. It mirrored the mark on his own chest, and in that binding symbol, he felt her presence. It wasn't overwhelming or painful, but soothing and completing.

Fenrir's lazy thrusts stilled as he leaned down to kiss her, then nuzzled his head into the crook of Revna's neck. "Wife."

He felt her chuckle and then stroke her hand down his back. "Husband."

Finding where they'd discarded their clothes took a while, but Fenrir kept them busy as they searched. He licked her again moments after they found his pants, and then took her against a tree when they found her dress, loving the way her moans sounded in the cool, dark forest.

Hand in hand, they made their way back to the celebration feast. He could smell the smoke of the fires, the roasting meat, and hear the boisterous laughter and revelry of those awaiting their return.

Revna had a soft smile on her face and a blush that wouldn't abate, the sight making him so deliriously happy that it scared him. When she looked over and directed that smile at him, he couldn't help stopping and wrapping his arms around her, lifting her off the ground in a tight embrace. He kissed her just as her stomach gave a loud growl.

"Is my wife hungry?" he asked, laughing against her lips. He was never going to tire of calling her his wife.

"Famished." She bit at his lips and then let out a squeal of protest as he tossed her over his shoulder and slapped her ass. Revna reached down and swatted at his backside. "I will be entering that feast on my own two feet, wolf."

Fenrir stopped immediately and set her down. "As my wife commands."

He offered her his hand once more, and together they ventured toward the beckoning smell of food. Just as they neared, a cloaked figure stepped out from between the trees, the scent hitting Fenrir moments before she lifted the hood of her cloak.

"I see well wishes are in order for my son and his new wife," his mother said, stepping into the pale moonlight.

Revna's hand tightened on his.

"What are you doing here, Mother?"

Rarely did his mother leave the comfort of her caves on Jotunheim, but for her to be here and to know what Revna was to him now flooded his veins with icy dread. He tugged Revna a little closer, and his mother's eyes tracked the movement, a smile blooming on her face.

"I'm not staying. I wanted to see the fruits of my labor, and oh my, did it yield."

"Don't speak in riddles. Say your piece and then leave."

Gathering her skirt, his mother took several steps toward them before stopping within reaching distance. She was a severe-looking woman with her icy eyes and angular features, but where Fenrir wished he could only see his mother, he saw just another tormentor. A potential threat to his wife. He gave a warning growl at her proximity. His mother rolled her eyes and folded her hands at her front.

"Do you know how you came to be here, girl?" Fenrir stiffened and smelled Revna's apprehension. "You are here because of me."

"What?" Revna asked, but Fenrir already understood.

"I called you forth from Myddheim. I sent the boat; I opened a doorway. I brought you here to be with my son." She smiled wider, her lips twisting into something unsettling, even crazed. "I even shot you with that arrow on Jotunheim."

Fenrir snarled, and the earth gave a slight shake in sympathy. "You *what?*"

She held up a hand to silence him. "I needed to be sure she was who I thought she was to you. Needed you to realize it, too."

Fenrir had known for years that he'd loved Revna, but he couldn't articulate the words because he was having a hard time concentrating on anything but wanting to rip out his mother's throat.

"Why? Why did you do this?" The demand and firmness in Revna's voice bolstered him.

"Because he needed to be reminded of who he is—*what* he is. For too long he has bowed to Asgard, forgetting where he came from. What he is capable of. And he needed something to fight for again—to protect. That's where you come in." She glanced at Revna. "I've known for quite some time of the mortal he'd left in Myddheim that he cared so much for. The girl he held such great affection for that he was willing to crawl back and make deals with Odin. The sisters aren't the only ones who see things, girl. You have a part to play, yet, in the things to come, and I grew impatient waiting for you two to find each other again. I did not give birth to the realms' greatest monsters for them to be fettered."

A torrent of anger and questions flooded Fenrir's mind, threatening to send him over into rage, calling to his wolf, when a sense of calm in the storm gave them both the strength to step back. He took a measured breath, focusing on the warmth at his center. The warmth holding his hand. He glanced down at Revna in concern.

Would his mother's truth change anything between them? Would she regret what they'd just done? Her hand was so tight in his, and the warmth in his chest flared briefly before she started to speak.

"Do not *ever* use my husband's affections for me against him. If any of your meddling results in him being hurt—or Hel, Tyr, Jormun, or anyone in Vanaheim—you won't like the enemy you've made in me. I have little tolerance for those who use people for personal gain. There are *many* in Helheim who can attest to that."

Fenrir's chest puffed up in awe and pride. That her protectiveness spread even to his brother—whom she hadn't formally met ...

That's my fucking wife.

"Careful, girl," his mother said, smiling almost as if in triumph. "That kind of love can burn the realms."

Fenrir wanted whatever this was to be done. If his mother lingered any longer, he wasn't sure what he—or Hel, if she found out—would do. Let alone Revna. She was cutting off all blood flow to his hand, and he guessed that the redness on her face was no longer that of happiness.

"Leave, Mother. You have played with your children like pawns and are not welcome, nor wanted here."

Her smile fell and was replaced by a sneer. "I will leave you with one last thing—a gift, if you will." Her eyes turned cloudy, and her voice came out as many woven together. *The moon kissed raven is soaring and searches for a branch to rest on through winter's misery, through the coming twilight.*

The moon kissed raven.

The prophecy.

A chill ran down his spine as his mother turned and disappeared into the shadowed night. He looked to Revna, no longer flushed but pale. He turned to her and cupped her face in his hands.

"I swear, I didn't know, my *máni.*" The last thing he wanted was for Revna to believe that he was withholding something from her again.

Revna's eyes softened as she looked at him, color returning slowly to her cheeks. "I know."

"Are you alright?"

"How do you think she knew? About me? About us?"

Fenrir didn't want to taint her to his brother before she'd even met him, but he had a sinking feeling that Jormun had told his mother a great many things over the years. Things he'd thought he was safe confiding to his siblings about. Fury beyond comprehension shot through his head as he contemplated whether his mother—and perhaps father—were responsible for Asgard finding out about Revna's presence in Vanaheim. He inhaled sharply, feeling his fangs prick his lower lip, his eyes sharpen, and his body swell.

Revna slowly peeled his hands away from her face and placed them on her chest, just above the *Hjarta* mark. "Do you feel me? Because I feel you here." She reached and placed a hand on his chest. "I need you to know that this changes nothing. I don't care how I got here, or why—I would do it again. I choose you, Fenrir."

He leaned his forehead against hers, feeling the change recede once more under her calming touch. "And I, you."

Revna pushed up until her mouth met his in a slow and settling kiss.

"Now, there was mention of feeding your wife. I may waste away before your eyes if I don't eat something soon."

Fenrir chuckled, tucking her into his side. "We can't have that. You need to replenish your strength. I'm not even close to being done with you tonight."

THIRTY-FIVE

REVNA

"**W**HAT DOES IT FEEL like?"

Revna raised her brow in question at Hel.

"The binding," the Goddess clarified.

It had been nearly half a moon cycle since the wedding and binding ceremony, and in many ways, Revna felt like she was still recovering. The celebration feast went well into the morning hours, most residents sleeping where they collapsed on the rich earth. Fenrir had carried her back to his room—their room now—and kept her awake even longer. They'd spent two days barely getting out of bed and getting very little sleep. But that's not what Hel wanted to know.

"It feels like getting a piece of myself back that I lost long ago. It's not consuming or overwhelming. It's warmth and comfort and acknowledgment."

Hel rolled her sword around in her hand and adjusted her shield. "Can you feel each other?"

"Oh, we *feel* each other plenty," Revna jested, for which Hel rewarded her with a push of her shield.

"We all know that," she teased, sounding half disgusted. "We can all *hear* that."

Revna laughed and pushed off Hel. On the stone ledge above the training yard, Fenrir was talking to a few warriors. Over the last week, he had been organizing more and more with the people of Vanaheim. Preparing, he always said. Just in case. There were so many uncertainties, so many reasons to stay sharp, but Revna still couldn't let it dilute the happiness she felt with Fenrir. With her place in Vanaheim.

She only wished the Maidens were here to share it with her. They were ever on her mind, and she often talked to Fenrir, Tyr, and Hel about how they could help them, and help Myddheim. If they could appeal to Frey to restore their fields. If Tyr could find a way to spread love and not war. But something surrounding Myddheim restricted them.

She agonized over the prophecy, as well, constantly turning it over in her mind. Looking in its corners and in its hidden alcoves. Until Fenrir had to distract her.

Her husband sensed her gaze and looked down at her, giving her a lopsided grin and wink. Hel whacked her in the ass with a sword before she could return the smile.

"Apologies." Revna focused back on the question. "It is a feeling, but more so a *knowing*. It's like having a heightened gut sense."

Revna swung her sword, striking Hel's shield in a resounding clang. A fine layer of dust clung to the sticky sweat of her neck. Revna had thought she was a decent fighter before, but the strength she had uncovered since training with these Gods had tapped into a latent reservoir of skill.

Hel considered her for a moment, then looked up at her brother and back to Revna. "Would you know if something happened to him?"

When Revna and Fenrir told Hel and Tyr about Angrboda's surprise visit, and her role in Revna's arrival, Hel nearly lost her mind. Ever since, it was plain to see the growing worry for her brother. It was maddening, knowing that Angrboda was trying to meddle Fenrir out of the bind with Odin, allowing Asgard to take action, but not how she planned to strike next.

"Yes, I think I would know." Revna lowered her shield a bit. "Hel, I will do whatever I can to keep your brother safe, you know that, right?"

"And yourself, Revna. You're my sister now." Hel gave her a rare soft, sincere smile. Then she tossed down her weapons and set about brushing some dust off her tunic. "Speaking of siblings, I need to go try to find Jormun. *Again.*"

Both Hel and Fenrir had tried several times to coax Jormun out of the waters, but he'd avoided them. Revna suspected it was because he may have had something to do with Angrboda's plans. Instead of feeling angry toward him, Revna just felt pity. From what she'd learned from Fenrir and Hel, Jormun was always the most susceptible to their mother and her machinations, and Revna felt sorry that she had him so tightly wrapped around her fingers.

Revna's stomach gave a slight lurch thinking on Angrboda's parting wedding gift.

The moon kissed raven is soaring ...

So like what she had learned at Urd's well. But she hadn't the faintest idea as to what it could mean, other than her acceptance that she, herself, was the raven in question. Revna had asked Fenrir one night while they were bathing if any of his mother's tellings had come true. He had said it was complicated, as all prophecies are, but yes. One way or another, they usually did. And now she felt as though she was bracing herself. Maddeningly, she didn't know what for—she just knew she had to be ready.

Bidding Hel good luck in her pursuit of Jormun, Revna hung up her shield and put away the sword she used for practice. She didn't mind the sword, but she still missed her axe. Greeting a few warriors as she crossed the yard, she made her way up the stone steps to where Fenrir was standing. His back was to her, giving his full attention to his conversation, but he reached back his arm as she approached. She let her fingers graze his as she stepped up beside him. His hand went immediately to her lower back and started gently rubbing up and down.

As she'd learned over the last couple of weeks, Fenrir felt soothed by touch. If she was within reaching distance, he had a hand on her. In sleep, he wrapped tightly around her. In passing moments, he would come in for quick kisses and caresses—always leaving Revna wanting more. She was coming to need it, too, that physical anchor of feeling him close.

"How's your wound fairing, Revna?" the warrior, a Jotunn named Dagmar, asked.

"Fully healed." She smiled. "Though I believe I will be able to predict when it's going to rain."

Dagmar gave a small chuckle, then lifted his shirt to reveal a deep scar running across his stomach. "This is the best predictor of weather I have. And the best story for seduction." He winked at her, and it was Revna's turn to laugh.

"What's the story?"

He puffed up. "That I went to Freyja's Hall and challenged her boar."

"And the real story?" Fenrir asked, amused.

Dagmar smiled conspiratorially and leaned in. "An enhanced mead that made me feel invincible. Turns out, I was not invincible to the sharp edge of the blade."

They all laughed, the feeling welcome and real.

"Well, I'll take my leave of you. I will go assign new rotations and let you know if anything seems amiss." Dagmar clasped both their arms and made his way down the stairs.

Revna turned to Fenrir. "New rotation?"

He wrapped his arms around her. "Mmhm. Just precautionary."

Ever since the fire beast had entered the realm, and with Asgard looming overhead more than ever, Fenrir had a steady rotation of warriors and guards walking the grounds of the keep, standing watch near the gate, monitoring the surrounding land. Fenrir took rotations himself, sometimes disappearing for hours during the day. But Revna didn't mind. She kept busy with training in the yard with all the other warriors. Austri had even convinced her to help in the gardens and kitchen. She suspected it was because he wanted to make sure she was eating and resting, but she was happy to oblige—happy to be of service.

Revna leaned her head back to look up at Fenrir and saw the worry creasing his brow. She reached up a thumb to smooth it out, but he grabbed her hand and placed a nip and a kiss to her scarred palm.

Revna knew he liked to switch up the rotations of the guards and scouts so that no one pattern could be established. Everything had been quiet, and sometimes the quiet was worse. She could see the worry and divided focus in his eyes. He needed a distraction; one she was happy to provide.

"Go for a walk with me?" she asked. He nodded without hesitation.

They made their way out of the training yard and into the surrounding lush forest. Revna would never tire of being surrounded by the trees. The rich verdant canopy and the smell of earth and pine—so close to that of Fenrir's scent. It settled her. Once far enough away from the keep, Revna turned to face Fenrir, taking a few steps back to create distance between them. Fenrir's brow furrowed at the absence of her from his side.

"You look preoccupied, wolf." Revna slowly took another step back. Then another. "Perhaps I could help you with that."

Understanding dawned in his eyes and his nostrils flared.

"Revna," he warned.

But before he could object, she took off running.

Weaving around trees and through thick underbrush, she chanced a glance behind her, but saw no sign of pursuit. She ran on, slowing to jog after time had passed enough to make her breath short. The sound of raindrops hitting the canopy above sounded before she felt the coolness hit her skin. Low thunder rumbled off in the distance, raising the hairs on the back of her neck. Ducking behind a tree, she waited and listened.

Smiling as a crashing noise came from her left, she ducked under a branch to the right and started a light jog. But straight ahead, across a small clearing, stood Fenrir.

Just as his eyes flashed and he bared his fangs, Revna felt two massive arms band around her—one at her chest, the other at her middle.

"Well, if it isn't the dog's new little wife." A memory from when she'd first arrived pulled her captor's name from her mind.

Thor.

Revna looked at Fenrir. His body stood so very still and his eyes blazed in barely restrained rage.

"Does this bother you, dog?" Thor goaded Fenrir. Revna moved slightly in his grip, testing the strength. Thor chuckled, no doubt thinking her movement was one of fear. "Aren't you going to tell me to remove my hands from your pathetic mortal wife?"

A small, feral smile pulled at the corner of Fenrir's mouth, his eyes finding Revna's through the haze of fury, and his unwavering belief in her pulsing in the center of her chest. "Wife, please remove his hands from you."

With a wicked grin in return, Revna slammed her head back and stomped her foot on his instep. Not satisfied with only the crack of his nose, she bared her teeth and bit down on his arm until she tasted blood. Thor released her with a hiss of pain.

Fenrir lunged toward Revna, meeting her half-way, pulling her body behind his. Then he was rushing Thor, pushing the God of Thunder until he was pinned to a tree.

Thunder cracked so loudly that Revna had to cover her ears. The earth beneath her feet trembled, roots and vines creeping to where Fenrir had Thor pinned to the tree. Revna palmed her daggers, but cold dread settled in her stomach. How could she possibly hold her own between these two Gods?

Thor spat blood on Fenrir's face. "Looks like the monster found someone equally beastly. You both should be put down." He reached for his hammer, but Fenrir's roots got to his wrists first. Thor thrashed against its hold, face turning a shade of red that rivaled that of his beard, but they held firm. Fenrir's body was shaking, enlarging, and terror went through Revna.

He was close to shifting.

Revna quickly closed the distance between herself and the two Gods and placed her hand on Fenrir's arm, trying to gently draw his attention. "Fenrir, don't. It's not worth it—*he* isn't worth it."

"He threatened you—touched you," Fenrir growled, his voice impossibly deep, the sound echoing in the air surrounding them. All the trees leaned in earnest, waiting for the call of their wolf.

"Do it, dog. Break your bind. I *dare* you."

Revna reached both her hands up to Fenrir's face, risking the snarl and bite of the wolf. Tilting his head to her, she dropped the mask on her face—the one she so carefully placed every day, pretending to be brave, pretending to not be afraid. The truth was that she was always afraid. Those fears lived so close to her heart that she was afraid at any moment it would pierce her, her mask would fall, and she would lose everything.

But for him—for her friend, her wolf, her husband, she let her fear shine through. Fear *for* him—fear of losing him. She let everything show on her face, giving him, and only him, this moment of vulnerability.

Rain started falling in earnest, and slowly he came back to her, back to himself. The storm cleared from his face. He released his forearm from Thor's throat and stepped away, tugging her to his body. Revna unsheathed a dagger as Fenrir unraveled the vines from Thor's enraged form.

"Leave now," Fenrir threatened. "Before I remember who I am, and you find out what this *dog* is truly capable of."

Because he needed to be reminded of who he is—what he is. For years he has bowed to Asgard, forgetting where he came from and what he was capable of.

Angrboda's words reverberated through Revna's body, and she stiffened.

It's happening.

Thor spoke. "You are summoned to Asgard. Your actions have consequences, and you will pay for them."

"And what actions might those be?"

Thor spit at the ground between them. "*Her.*"

"My wife," Fenrir growled, "is of no concern to Asgard."

Thor smiled, the view a terrifying one. "We'll see."

With that he spun and fled into the forest, thunder echoing in his wake. Revna's shoulders slumped, suddenly exhausted. She wanted nothing more than to retreat to the keep and lock Fenrir and herself into their room. She looked to Fenrir, but he was staring to where Thor had disappeared, face unreadable and distant.

"Fenrir—"

He swiped his thumb over her lips, still stained with Thor's blood, then grabbed her hand and placed a kiss to her palm. Pulling her in step with him, he headed in the direction of the keep. "I need to call a meeting."

Thirty-Six

Fenrir

GATHERED IN THE MEETING room, Fenrir recounted all that had happened with Thor to several of Vanaheim's residents, Tyr and Hel included. Fighting against the anger and fear in his body, he asked them to prepare for retaliation. He hated asking this of his people—because they were his people, just as he was theirs.

Asgard was coming—he felt it in his bones.

As predicted, Tyr and Hel were outraged, and equally determined that this be one order he not accede to. But he couldn't avoid going to Asgard forever—the power of the bind would compel him otherwise. They sprang into action, organizing everything from guard posts to contingency battle plans. Fenrir hardly heard any of it. Though he didn't want to endanger the people of Vanaheim, he could selfishly admit that the more people he had protecting Revna, the better. He wasn't so insecure as to not admit that he would take all the help he could. Protecting the people of Vanaheim was a priority, but Asgard didn't want Vanaheim.

They wanted Revna.

He looked back to where she leaned against the wall, staring out the open window. The same spot he was standing when Tyr had brought her here. Arms crossed, shoulders tight, and head tilted enough that he could see the ink on the back of her neck. The smell of her frustration and anger fed into his concern. She hadn't spoken a word since they'd left the woods, and he recognized that look on her face. She was retreating within herself.

Hel and Tyr were trying to talk over each other, in two different conversations. Fenrir spoke above them, loud enough for everyone to jump.

"Everyone out. Please."

Everyone paused their conversation and eyed him warily. With reassurance that they would meet later, they obliged. Revna pushed off her post on the wall and started to follow everyone out.

"Not you, Revna."

Fenrir waited until the last person was out and the door was shut before approaching her. "You've been quiet, my *máni*. Are you alright?"

She nodded and then walked to where he was standing at the head of the table and leaned against it.

"I can't stand not hearing you. Do I need to help you find your words?" Fenrir moved to stand in front of her and grabbed her chin so that she could see his intent.

The distance he had seen in her gray eyes started to fade as she understood his meaning, nodding more eagerly this time. Fenrir knelt, keeping his eyes on hers. He took off her boots, then undid her weapons belt. As he started unlacing her trousers, he paused.

"Is this alright?"

"Yes." The word breathy and edging into needy. She needed this, needed him.

Fenrir smiled, then placed a kiss to her exposed skin. "Hmm. I think we can do better than one word."

With a yank, he pulled down her trousers, exposing her beautiful sex to him. He inhaled the heady smell, a possessive growl building in the back of his throat. With both legs free, he tossed the trousers behind him and grabbed her ass in both of his hands, licking at the apex of her thighs.

Revna inhaled sharply and dug a hand into his hair. With one more lick, he stood and lifted her so she was perched on the table. He pushed her thighs open farther and stepped between them, giving her a devouring kiss, letting her taste herself on his tongue.

They needed to talk; he knew that. But if there was one thing he was coming to understand about his wife, it was that she wouldn't talk until she was ready. And when she was so far retreated within herself, she needed to be brought back. Right now, she needed this anchor, needed to find her voice again. Needed to regain control.

"Tell me. Tell me what you need, Revna." He pulled back to look at her face, flushed cheeks, kiss-swollen lips. He waited for her to find the words—wanting her to have complete control. He watched as she swallowed and then bit her lower lip.

"I want you on your knees. I want you to lick me." Fenrir growled in approval. "I want you to fuck me with your fingers and tongue until I am desperate and crazed for release."

"And then? Shall I hold you on that edge? Make you beg for it?"

She didn't respond, but the color was back in her cheeks, the distant look receding, as she leisurely moved her hand down and down until her fingers came to her center. She moved her fingers in small circles, then slid them down until one dipped inside of her. Fenrir dropped back to his knees, placing his hands on her inner knees, spreading her wider. His eyes couldn't settle on whether they wanted to watch her hands or her face. Gripping her thighs was the only thing preventing him from reaching down to touch himself. He was so painfully hard, but this wasn't about him.

"Revna," he warned. "Tell me to lick you."

A throaty chuckle escaped her throat. "Sounds like you're the one begging me, wolf."

Fucking runes, he was. He needed to taste her, needed to hear her, needed to feel her legs tremble. Patience wearing thin, he stopped her hand from its ministrations and brought her two fingers to his lips, sucking them into his mouth. The taste of her on her own fingers pulled him taut.

"Tell me. *Now.*"

"Taste me, Fenrir."

He lunged, pinning her thighs even wider, licking her in one long slow stroke. Bringing his tongue to her entrance, he pushed it inside, making her moan. Fenrir pulled away, causing Revna to make noise of protest. He smiled and kissed her inner thigh before grabbing her ass and pulling her closer to the edge, draping both her legs over his shoulders. With her ass fully in his hands, he looked up at her.

"Say it again, my *máni.*"

With one hand braced behind her, she reached down and parted herself to him. "Lick me. Taste me."

This fucking woman. Unable to resist any longer, Fenrir feasted in earnest, delving his tongue between her spread fingers. As he flattened his tongue on her most sensitive spot, her hand shot up and threaded into his hair. Per her demand, he slid a finger inside of her, curling and hitting that spot deep inside. Revna mewled and Fenrir could feel her upper legs starting to tremble on his shoulders.

He withdrew his finger and his mouth and placed open-mouthed kisses everywhere but where she wanted him. Revna dug harder into his hair, so he returned to her center, licking, sucking, thrusting and curling two fingers inside of her. When her legs resumed their shaking and he could feel her tightening, he stopped.

"Fenrir," she snarled. "Please don't stop."

"There's the begging I've been waiting for. What do you want, Revna?"

"Push me over the edge—make your wife come apart on your tongue."

Fenrir felt his cock twitch painfully in his trousers at hearing her command. At hearing her call herself his wife. At the smell of her arousal. This time he didn't hold back. He brought his mouth back to her center and gave her everything she demanded. Feeling her other hand thread into his hair, he lifted his eyes to see her laying down across the table, back bowing in pleasure. Her hands pulled him in tighter as she ground herself against his face. Fenrir growled, not taking his eyes off her as he slid both fingers back inside of her—her inner walls instantly clamping down on them. This time he didn't stop. This time he demanded her release as her breathing and moans became higher and fevered.

Screaming his name, Fenrir felt Revna's body lock up and a new wetness hit his tongue. Legs twitching with each pass of his tongue, she yanked hard on his hair until he lifted his head.

"Need more," she panted. "Need you inside of me."

Lurching up from his knees, Fenrir yanked at the laces of his trousers and shoved them down until his cock was out. He grabbed Revna's knees and in one fluid movement rolled her onto her stomach, her ass presented to him like a fucking feast. He guided his cock to her entrance and in one brutally slow thrust, seated himself inside of her, both groaning at the feel. Tugging the tunic she still wore up as far as he could, he leaned forward and kissed down her spine, over the ink there as he thrust into her. He reached forward and gripped a hand around her throat, pulling her up so she was braced on her hands.

Fenrir fucked her in slow deep thrusts. With one hand on her throat, he reached the other one around, pushing his fingers against her sensitive bundle, letting her grind against it with each of her meeting thrusts.

Never had anything felt more right in all the realms—in his life. Every time they came together, he felt more centered and surer than ever before. He found peace in that, for a little while, they trusted to let go and get lost within each other.

When he felt her starting to clench again, he hissed between his teeth—his own release so close. "Don't wait for me, Revna."

No sooner did he speak the words than she cried out, Fenrir following moments later with a loud bellow, his vision bursting bright at the feel of her. Both panting, Fenrir removed his hands from her sex and throat and wrapped them around her chest and middle. He dipped his head and nuzzled into her neck, feeling her rapid heartbeat in time with his.

"Well said. Beautifully spoken words," he grumbled into her ear. Revna laughed, the sound making affection course through him. She leaned her head back on his shoulder and they stayed that way for a few long moments. After he withdrew from her, they dressed in sated silence.

Revna resumed to lean on table, a flush still high on her cheeks. Before she could cross her arms over her chest, Fenrir grabbed her hands in his. "Talk to me."

Sighing long and deep, Fenrir braced himself for whatever dark thought was about come out of his wife's mouth.

"I think I should give myself to Asgard."

Thirty-Seven

Fenrir was so still, Revna worried for a moment that he wasn't breathing.

"What?" he finally grounded out.

She didn't repeat her statement. Hearing her wasn't the problem. She had been adrift in her own thoughts since the encounter with Thor. When Fenrir had called the meeting and started organizing, planning for war—she was devastated. Old habits quickly resurfaced, constricting her throat with their relentless demand. To protect, to sacrifice.

Asgard wanted *her*. Vanaheim was preparing to defend her. And every dark thought Revna battled rose to the surface in a great wave.

She wasn't worth it—wasn't worth anyone going to war for.

The last time the Aesir and Vanir went to war, it was over Freyja, and Revna was not Freyja. She was not some powerfully important Goddess. She was just a mortal woman who was at the mercy of Gods, fate, and her own heart.

Hating that her emotions were so close to the surface, she looked at Fenrir, the anger in his eyes quickly replaced by concern. The room suddenly felt too small, the stone walls too confining, the fire too warm. Revna steeled herself, swallowing back angry tears.

"I'm not worth it, Fenrir. I am not worth an entire realm preparing for war. I refuse to be an excuse for Asgard to finally have reason to cage you again. If I go to them alone, perhaps it will satisfy their hunger for—"

"If you think for one moment that I will allow you—"

"*Allow* me?" Revna dropped his hands and pushed at his chest "You don't *allow* me anything."

"Allow you to believe that you aren't worth it, Revna." Fenrir shook his head. "You are worth it—you are *everything*."

Overwhelm struck her in the center of her chest, tightening the muscles there. She reached up to massage the familiar knot that resided there. Only now, there was a warmth around its edges, gently soothing and coaxing it into a more bearable pain. She knew this new feeling came from her bind with Fenrir, but at the moment, it made her feel angry. Angry because now she was no longer alone in her burdens, she had placed them upon Fenrir—and she couldn't bear to live with herself if anything were to happen to him, Hel, Tyr, the people of Vanaheim.

Or Myddheim.

Cold dread pushed against the warmth, the sensation causing her to turn and find a seat in the nearest chair. What if the Aesir decided to retaliate against Myddheim? And she couldn't warn them, couldn't protect them.

Revna's breath caught in her throat and Fenrir quickly moved and knelt in front of her, placing a firm grip on both of her knees, leaning his forehead against hers. He whispered something to her, but she couldn't hear it past the curling and seductive darkness rattling in her mind. She became so still, like the wind and trees right before a devastating storm.

"I'm not—" she tried to speak past the block in her throat, to find her voice like he asked. "I can't be the reason others suffer. I wouldn't be able to live with myself."

As much as she wanted to, she couldn't meet Fenrir's gaze. Didn't want to see what she might find. The grip on her knees tightened for a moment, but then his hands started squeezing gently. His soft lips pushed against her temple, her cheek. His hands moved to her neck, and he tilted her face until she was meeting his amber stare.

"I would like to show you something. Will you go for a walk with me?"

Confused but curious, she nodded, taking his hand as he offered it to her.

Moss and low-burning torches were slowly coming to life in the halls with the setting sun. Walking down the stone steps that led to the kitchen, Fenrir stopped just before they could enter and leaned against the wall, holding his arm out to stop Revna from going any further. She looked at him in question, but his only response was a jerk of his chin toward the happenings of the kitchen. Austri was tending to the meat rotating over the fire, while a few others were laughing as they chopped vegetables and kneaded bread. A couple of residents were perched on top of the table in the corner, clinking mugs of ale together. It was warm and loud and full of life.

Fenrir grabbed her hand and led her back up the stairs. They walked until they came to the entrance of the dining hall. Again, Fenrir didn't enter, just leaned against the door frame, and they observed. People sharing their evening meal—some enthusiastically eating in quiet company, others talking loudly, laughing, arguing, challenging each other in games of chance. Tyr and Hel were sitting near the middle and noticed them, waving in greeting, but didn't beckon them or approach them.

Fenrir guided her to the gardens next, full of residents basking in the beauty, then continued around the entire keep—the training yard, the gathering spaces, the caverns with the hot springs.

So many people to protect. So much life.

Revna's stomach roiled like a storm-tossed sea, churning and unrelenting.

Finally, Fenrir led her outside to the comfort and coolness of the trees. His cautious steps relaxed as he surveyed the area, pulling deep inhales through his nose, finding nothing amiss. Revna's heart ached at his guardedness.

Inky blue darkness had completely settled as they came to the middle of a small clearing. Fenrir stopped and came to stand behind her, then tilted her chin up until she was looking at vibrant dancing green lights, framed by an opening of shadowy trees.

For several months a year, these dancing lights also appeared in Myddheim. Seeing their beauty soothed her fraying nerves. In the cool hush of the night, Revna leaned back into Fenrir, watching the hues of emerald and violet unfurl and swirl among a sea of stars. His arms banded around her front, pulling her tight.

"Growing up in the caves," Fenrir rumbled close to her ear, "I didn't see the sky much. For the first several years of my life, all I could do was sneak out at night to watch the night sky and all its beauty. I was led to believe that darkness was where monsters dwell—they hid in the dark because that's where they belonged. My sister, brother, and I were monsters. But every night that I watched the dancing lights, the stars, the moon, I started to understand that the darkness could be a source of such beauty. That it let you see parts of the light that can't be seen under the harshness of the day."

Fenrir was a wall of warmth behind her, his heart beating a steadying rhythm against her back. Just as an ache weighed down her shoulders at his story, he squeezed her tighter and continued.

"Do you remember the first time we left the cave you found me in on Myddheim?" Revna nodded. "You wanted to wait until night fell—fearing that someone would see us. But then we stepped outside, and the sky was alive with green. And I saw you in that moment—saw you in both dark and light—and the balance of both had a new meaning for me. I no longer wanted to hide from the light or be resentful of the dark. I wanted to embrace both."

They stood in silence for a moment, and Revna felt as though she was both back in that first night under the sky, and right where she was now. "When I left Myddheim, I came out here almost every night and watched for these lights. Knowing that you had them in your realm made me feel like there was still a path back to you, and it brought me comfort."

Fenrir turned her around so that she was facing him.

"I know what you're thinking, Revna. And it breaks my heart to hear that you think that you aren't worth fighting for." He cupped her face. "But whether it was me, you, Tyr, or any other small pebble that caused a ripple, Asgard would come eventually. By hurting and going after you, they go after everyone. The hurt of a single person can hurt the whole." He placed a hand over the center of her chest. "You are Vanaheim. And Myddheim. So, while my priority is protecting you, it's bigger than that. Protecting you is also protecting everyone."

Revna let the words crack her shield. As commander of the Myddheim Maidens, hadn't she lived by nearly the same principle? Only now instead of slavers, it was Gods.

She twined her hands on the back of his neck, pulling him down for a kiss. Letting the echo of his words and the warmth of his mouth chase away her misgivings.

Revna looked down at his arms, at the mark of Odin's binding. "Do you miss being able to shift?"

Fenrir smiled sadly, his whole face morphing into longing. "Very much."

She had known the answer before she asked the question but wanted to give him the opportunity to speak the truth of it out loud. She could only imagine how it felt, missing a piece of himself—one that he had to keep locked away for fear of retribution. Just for simply being who he was.

"I need you to know," she started, "that your wolf doesn't scare me. In the woods, with Thor, I didn't want you to shift because I was scared *of* you. I am scared *for* you. One day, when we figure a way out of this." She ran her thumbs over the markings. "I can't wait to see all of you—fangs, claws. Even the tail." She gave his ass a little pat.

Fenrir chuckled and leaned in to kiss her forehead. "I want you to see all of me, too."

"Does it ever bother you that Hel and Jormun are free to be themselves?"

He shook his head. "Not at all. I wouldn't wish this on them. Our existence was troubling enough—I made this deal to protect the people that I love and care for. I would do it again."

Good. He was so good that Revna felt honored to know him. To be with him. Honored that he chose her.

"Promise me that whatever may come, we will face it together," Revna whispered.

"I promise, my *máni.*"

⇥——⇤

Revna walked through a too-quiet forest. Not a creature or rustle of leaves in the wind could be heard. The stale air was thick with fog, and the overwhelming smell of decay burned in her nostrils. There were no green lights, no stars, no moon—just a muted grayness that blanketed the land—as if light itself was being eaten.

Careful of her step, she made her way forward. She didn't know why, but she knew that she had to keep moving. With each passing moment, with each step, the air became heavier. Her breath came in shallow pulls from her chest until it forced her to stop, to submit.

The hairs on the back of her neck rose in warning.

Slowly, she turned and watched as a creeping, inky darkness devoured everything in its path. Though it was not aflame, everything it touched looked as though it was scorched by an unforgiving heat. Trees bowed in submission to the darkness, their trunks and branches turning to black rot. Underbrush crumbled as if it was never there.

Revna felt frozen as the darkness paused, as if regarding her. A curling wisp reached out and circled her. It took her measure, and Revna felt a moment of familiarity. The more it circled her, the more she recognized it. But she didn't know why.

A smoky tendril came to her front and inched slowly closer, as if not to scare off a frightened animal. Revna was frightened but also curious. Raising her hand slowly, she reached out her fingers to the darkness.

The moment it touched her, she screamed.

In pain, in despair, in longing, in grief. In emotion so consuming and paralyzing, she wanted to lean into it and let it take her. Let it have her.

A sob tore from her throat as she yanked her hand back, holding it to her chest. Turning, she started to run. But everywhere she turned, the darkness closed in from all sides. She wanted to scream, and the only thing that came to mind was a name.

"Fenrir!"

Turning in a circle she searched for him, but she was alone. As she watched the darkness close in from all sides, she realized that she was glad that she was alone. She didn't want anyone else to suffer this fate. There was nowhere to run. Nowhere to go that the darkness hadn't devoured. She sat on the forest floor, pulled her knees to her chest, and bowed her head—waiting for it to take her.

Revna.

That name ...

Revna.

It was hers, she thought, but she was having a hard time remembering. She only knew one name, and she chanted it over and over.

Fenrir. Fenrir. Fenrir. Fenrir.

It was becoming harder to breathe. Harder to call out the name that kept her tethered to herself.

As the darkness touched her, thick tears rolled down her face, and she watched as they hit the ground in dark drops. Tentatively, she reached up to wipe them from her cheeks, only for her fingers to come away black as pitch.

Strangely, she no longer felt like crying, but relenting. But still, she held onto to the name ...

Fenrir. Fenrir. Fen ...

She fell sideways into the darkness.

"Revna!" A deep voice called. "Please, my *máni*. Wake up."

She jerked awake, eyes trying to focus. It was still dark, and for a moment she panicked. But strong, familiar hands were touching her, bringing her back to herself.

"Fenrir?" she croaked, reaching out to touch him. To feel his realness and warmth.

A sigh of relief. "I'm here, my *máni*."

Revna rolled into his embrace, shaking.

THIRTY-EIGHT

FENRIR

H E STOOD IN FRONT of the gate with Tyr, trying and failing to suppress a yawn.

Another full moon rose and fell, and Revna's nightmares still had her calling out his name into the dark. She would scream, thrash, then go eerily still, body growing cold as if marked by an icy grip. Her scent would become something unknown to him. In those terrifying moments, Revna would whisper his name like she was searching for him—trying to remember him.

He would hold her and call to her until she shook herself free of the nightmare's grip. When she woke, she would cling to him, but would remember nothing of the nightmare.

"Everything was dark," was all she could say.

As he'd held her night after night, Fenrir felt so helpless. He didn't know how to protect her from her own mind and the things that chased her in her sleep. When her trembling would subside and her body no longer felt cold, they would rise and head down to the training yard to greet the sun and move their bodies. She trained with an unbridled ferocity, as if trying to fight the things that haunted her in the night. Most days he had to force her to take a break for fear of her completely exhausting herself—though he suspected that was her intention. In that endeavor, he had enlisted Austri to request her presence in the kitchens for a few hours each day, and Hel to take her on patrol once a day.

He was due for a visit to check on the realms, but he feared leaving Vanaheim. Though he trusted the residents to stand and fight, he didn't want them to have to, should Asgard come knocking. Fenrir was afraid the moment he left, the Aesir would take that opportunity to draw Revna out to them. When she had proposed that she turn herself over to them, cold dread had iced his veins—knowing her, and that she would do it if she thought it would save him, save any of them, given the opportunity.

Ever since his mother's telling, Fenrir's mind had been consumed by the prophecy. Though he'd been pulling it apart daily, Thor's visit had ignited a smoldering ember of obsession, threatening to erupt into fire.

"You look tired, my friend," Tyr said. "And I can tell it's not just from your nocturnal activities."

Fenrir tried to chuckle, but it came out half-hearted. "You think they're only limited to the night?"

"Are the nightmares still happening?" Tyr asked, ignoring the attempt at redirection, concern bleeding into his voice.

"Yes." Fenrir scrubbed a hand down his face. "But she can barely remember anything when she wakes."

"Do you think it could be Asgard?" Tyr asked.

Fenrir froze. He hadn't considered that Asgard could be plaguing her with these terrors. He didn't think even they would be powerful enough to reach out between the realms. Even Odin—and the power he'd coerced from Freyja— wasn't that strong.

He didn't think it was the case, but he also couldn't rule it out.

"Who would have that power?" Tyr answered his question with a defeated shrug of his shoulders.

Fenrir's thoughts snagged back on his mother and her twisted meddling. He honestly didn't believe she had the power or reason to tamper with Revna's mind. Freyja, hidden away in her mountain, had no basis.

The only others with that penchant for power were the sisters, who were so deeply entwined with Yggdrasil—the source of light and dark, chaos and balance.

Fenrir didn't understand why Asgard was so desperate for Revna. They hadn't taken a sacrifice from Myddheim for years, shouldn't be taking one based on his deal with Odin. Did they just want her because Fenrir had her? It had to be more than that.

Because he trusted Tyr, he said, "I don't know what to do. But we can't live in constant fear, waiting for Asgard, Jotunheim, or some unnamed threat to attack at any given moment. I don't want anyone to live that way."

"Nor do I," Tyr said, nodding in agreement—the God of Love and War siding more often with love, as usual. "Perhaps ..."

"What?"

"It may be time for us to start seeking alliances. If war is inevitable, we can't go it alone."

Fenrir nodded in agreement, chewing on his cheek. Vanaheim had become a place for new beginnings, but it still bore the reputation of the place of outcast Gods—a place that Odin and the rest of the Aesir looked down upon as lesser. Though Fenrir and the rest of Vanaheim just wanted to be left in peace and build a life, the Aesir were not content to let any power of the Vanir go unchecked. They always wanted to control it—use it for their own twisted purpose. Just like with—

"Freyja?" He looked to Tyr, flabbergasted. "You want us to try to coax Freyja out of hiding? She hasn't been seen since the war."

Tyr rubbed at his forearm with the missing hand. "It's not something I suggest lightly. To try—to ask this of her ..." He shook his head. "But across all the realms, people love Freyja. Fought and died for her injustices—injustices that still are left unchecked. The war didn't stop because one side won—the war stopped because it was so evenly matched. There was no end in sight."

Fenrir had heard most of the stories of the Aesir-Vanir war from Tyr. The bloody and terrible truth of it. But like most stories, he knew there was another side. Freyja's side in all of this. And if so many had fought and died for her, Fenrir thought it unlikely that she'd hid away in a mountain hall all these years to prepare for war again.

She wanted to be left alone.

He knew the feeling. Fenrir let out a growl of frustration and crouched down toward the earth, taking in a big inhale of the rich scent. Tyr walked over to him and clasped a hand on his shoulder.

"Come on," he said, offering his arm to Fenrir. "I'm hungry and I think you need to see your wife. It's been almost a half-day since you've seen her, you love-besotted fool."

Fenrir grabbed at his arm and let him haul him back to a standing position. As they made their way back to the keep, Tyr told him to think about what he said— as if he wouldn't spend his time tonight lying awake to prepare for Revna's nightmare to obsess over every possibility.

With the sun close to setting, Fenrir knew Revna would be in the kitchen, getting pulled into whatever chopping or sharpening Austri had assigned her. He could smell the spiced aromas of dinner being prepared from the staircase. Missing, though, was the usual accompanying sounds of a loud and vivacious kitchen. Dread thickened in his stomach and Fenrir started taking two steps at a time, Tyr close behind him on high alert.

As he stepped into the kitchen, several eyes flew to him. Austri was in the middle of the kitchen, carving meat. He raised a finger to his lips in a quiet gesture and then pointed to the corner near the fire.

And there, with her back in the corner and head lolled against the wall, was his wife. Sound asleep.

His heart gave a squeeze at the sight of her. She looked so tired and vulnerable. Her arms were crossed over her chest, with one slightly lower and resting on the hilt of a dagger.

The kitchen workers moved and cooked quietly, their soft sounds becoming a kind of gentle music. Austri no doubt had seen her start to doze and ordered everyone to be quiet. Fenrir gave the dwarf a grateful smile.

"How long has she been asleep?" he whispered, approaching Austri.

"Long enough for the potatoes to boil." Austri looked over to her, a small affectionate smile on his face. "Why don't I send dinner to your room so you can take her to rest?"

Fenrir clapped the dwarf on the shoulder, thanking him, and made to approach his wife. Like when she'd fallen asleep in the tub, he gently wrapped his fingers around her wrist so she wouldn't go straight to stabbing him when startled awake.

"Revna," he called and stroked a thumb on her wrist. Slowly, her eyes peeled opened, and then widened in embarrassment. "Come on, my *máni*. Let's go to our room."

She nodded, stepping into his open arms. Before approaching the staircase, Fenrir turned and found Tyr. Not long ago, he had told Revna that asking for help wasn't a sign of weakness, and he needed to honor that. To lead by that. Even if that meant trying for an impossibility at the advice of a trusted friend.

"Tomorrow."

Tyr nodded in understanding. "Tomorrow."

Thirty-Nine

"YOU DON'T WANT ME to go with you?"

Revna watched as Fenrir warred with how to respond. They sat on their bed, picking at the remaining food between them, a fire warming the night-chilled room. She was still slightly mortified that she'd fallen asleep in the kitchen. She had only meant to rest her eyes for a moment to rid herself of an incessant and skull-tightening headache. The next thing she'd known, Fenrir was waking her.

Nightmares persisted, haunting her—weaving her mind with shadowy threads that left her bone-achingly weary. Only fragments remained when she awoke. Of darkness, of cold desperation. Its remnants clung to her like a fever long after she greeted the dawn.

As the food warmed their bellies, Fenrir talked of his and Tyr's plan to go see Freyja. To see if the Goddess would show herself after all this time and be receptive to a possible alliance, should the need come. But he wanted her to stay here. After the last time Revna had followed them, she didn't blame his caution. Still, it didn't lessen the sting of being left behind. Especially when she was a significant reason why they were going.

"I don't want to go anywhere you are not," he finally responded. "But Freyja has been reclusive for *many* years. I don't know what we'll be

"

walking into. All we know is that she has created her own sanctuary for the dead, and dwells within it, much like Hel."

Revna pondered for a moment. "How is it that Freyja came to collect the dead?"

As far as Revna understood, when someone died in battle, the Valkyrs had always appeared and decided which warriors were worthy of residing in Valhalla—Odin's Hall. In days before the war the rest, deemed unworthy, were sent to Helheim. But since the war she knew that Freyja's boar collected the dead from the battlefield, too.

"After the Aesir-Vanir war, in an effort to reach an agreement of peace, Odin gave Freyja first rights to choose from the slain. Likely also to pull her from her halls and out into the open, but she got around that, sending her battle-boar, Otta, in her stead."

For most of her life, Revna had heard the tales of the Gods spun by the Skalds in each village. But confronting the realness of it was strange and often unsettling. She had been taught that one should strive to earn a spot in Odin's or Freyja's hall by dying in glorious battle. It never occurred to her to question this belief. Why was there no honor in dying from old age surrounded by loved ones? And yet, both Odin and Freyja picked from those fallen in battle as one might pick a flower from the weeds.

Revna thought it was horseshit.

"To what end?" Revna asked, popping a berry into her mouth.

"What do you mean?"

"Why do they collect warriors?"

The fire cracked and hissed as Fenrir's body tensed and his gaze went distant. "My mother used to speak of a prophecy—one that was divined by Freyja herself..." Fenrir swallowed and looked at Revna. "There will be one final war—the battle of the end. A war between the Gods, a war of nine realms."

Revna's blood ran cold. "When?"

Her mind flooded with questions and possibilities, creating new knots and worries between her ribs.

Fenrir moved the food tray from between them, setting it on the table near the bed. Readjusting himself to lay flat, he opened his arm in invitation to Revna. Without hesitation, she burrowed herself into the crook of his arm, head resting on his shoulder, legs tangled with his.

"No one knows. Let's try to only worry about one thing at a time right now." He kissed her forehead.

Revna tried to push the thoughts away, to focus on the feel of his body touching hers. The solidness of him, the rightness. She placed her hand over the *Hjarta* bind rune on his chest, feeling the strong beat of his heart.

"How long will you be gone?" Revna tried not to let too much worry seep into her voice. She didn't like the thought of them being separated for too long. Though Tyr accompanying him offered some reassurance, Revna's protective instincts were hard to belay.

"Hopefully only the day. Any longer and I will cut my losses." He rolled so that she was underneath him, her blood heating instantly. "I don't think I could sleep without you, my *máni*. And your soft snoring."

He burrowed his head into her neck and mimicked a loud snore, causing laughter to erupt from deep in her belly. He growled and nibbled at her neck until tears were streaming down her face and laughter tightened her chest. When she was barely breathing, only then did he lift his head, an amused smirk on his face. Placing a quick kiss to her mouth, he rolled again until she was on top of him.

Seeing the dark bags under his eyes had her sobering. "I think you are barely sleeping now." She reached up and traced the area beneath his eyes. "I'm sorry."

"Don't apologize. It's not something you can help. I only wish there was something that I could do—a way I could enter your dreams with you and fight off whatever's chasing you."

She scoffed, trying to keep the mood light. "If you could enter my dreams, I think we'd get even less rest."

Reaching, he pulled her legs so that she was straddling him, her center pushing against his hardening length. Rocking her hips a little had him groaning. He sat up and hooked her legs around his waist and she slid her arms around his shoulders. He stood, carrying them toward the opening that led to the waterfall off their room. She furrowed her brow in question at him.

"I am still covered in the day's grime. When I leave tomorrow morning, I only want it to be you that I am covered in."

They didn't leave the cooling waters of the waterfall for a very long time.

⊱────⊰

It was only mid-morning and Revna was already exhausted with worry. Another nightmare had chased her from sleep, and then she'd had to say goodbye to Fenrir and Tyr in the waking sunlight. Hel was tending to things in her own realm but said she would be back by midday.

She spent most of the morning training with various warriors—all of whom were eager to learn and to bestow any fighting tactics. The young Jotunn, Havvar, was always ready and willing to go toe-to-toe with her. But the more that she trained him, the more skilled he became, Revna found herself hating that he was such a skilled fighter. Hating that anyone had to learn how to defend themselves. Knowing that if an attack

333

may come, Havvar would run out to meet it, and may suffer because of it. The thought made her stomach knot, so she retreated to the kitchens and the comforting presence of Austri.

As soon as she entered, Austri set down a bowl of apples that needed peeling and told her to get to work. She gave the dwarf a pat on the arm and retreated to a spot in the corner. When she was done with the apples, she got to work on some potatoes, then sharpened all the knives.

With each pause of movement, with each drift of her mind, the pit in her stomach grew heavy and sour.

At the very least, she was glad that Fenrir and Tyr were still within the bounds of Vanaheim—albeit to its very outer edges, but still within the realm. If Freyja's Hall was in Asgard, Revna didn't think she would have been too keen on being left behind. As it was, Fenrir and Tyr didn't know what to expect by trying to reach out to Freyja. There could be traps.

With a heavy sigh, Revna stood and reached for the salt and an iron skillet to season. Then Austri called her name.

"Come with me." He waved her to follow, heading up the steps.

She'd expected Austri to lead her to the gardens to gather more food, but instead, he veered down a different corridor, descending to the lower levels. She had only ventured down here a few times before, the most recent when she'd brought a few swords to be refitted by the blacksmith for the training yard.

To her surprise, Austri walked straight into the smithy's room. The air was warm and heavy with the smell of smoke, molten metal, and robust oils. The forge roared with a steady and flickering heat, reflecting off the meticulously organized tools. Not a single anvil, hammer, form, or chisel out of place. It was one of the cleanest shops she had ever seen.

Another dwarf occupied the space, giving Austri and Revna a small nod before continuing his work. Revna followed Austri to a wall where several swords hung, and he reached for the double-headed axe that sat in the middle.

"I wanted to give you a wedding gift. I noticed, upon your return from Jotunheim, that you no longer carried the axe you arrived with. I figured you wouldn't mind a replacement." Austri lifted his hands, handing her the axe.

Revna gapped at him. "You made this?"

Austri nodded and crossed his arms as she took it from his hands.

"But you said you put out your forge when you left Nidavellir."

A shrug. "I found a reason to light it again."

Emotion hit Revna in her chest. She turned to set the axe down on the nearest surface, pulling Austri into a tight hug. It was a near thing, but she bid the wetness in her eyes not to fall as she pulled away. Austri gave her a knowing smile and patted her twice on her cheek with his rough hand.

Turning, she grabbed the axe and took it in. No piece of weaponry had ever been so beautifully crafted, so carefully constructed. It was perfectly balanced, light enough to swing, but heavy enough to strike true. The handle was braided with good leather and worn enough that the grip didn't slip.

The head ...

Revna looked up at Austri in awe. A raven was stamped onto both sides with intricate whorls around it. Under each raven were the runes of protection and strength—just like the ones inked on her back. Among them, there were a few that she was unfamiliar with—no doubt some runes special to Nidavellir. As she tilted the axe to inspect the sharp edges, she noticed a light blue sheen that caught in the light.

"It's imbued. I wanted you to have all the protection you could get. Here." He grabbed her hand and ran her finger along the sharp blade, but to her surprise, it didn't cut her. Then, he did the same to his finger, and blood welled instantly. "No one will be able to hurt you with your own blade. And it will strike true. I know you prefer your daggers, but—"

"Austri, I don't have the words for how much this means to me. Thank you." She pulled free one of her daggers. "These pale in comparison."

Austri's head cocked as he looked at her dagger. "May I see that?"

Revna handed it over to him without hesitation.

"Where did you get this? How were they forged?" he asked warily.

Revna swallowed. She had kept the truth of her dagger's origin for so long. No one, not even Ingrid or any of the Maidens, knew where their metal came from. But she had grown and changed since she was on Myddheim, and had learned to trust. Perhaps it was time to let this truth go.

"They're crafted from the chains that bound Fenrir." Revna swore the air surrounding them paused to listen, but she continued even as a shiver rolled down her spine. "When I found him in Myddheim, he was bound up in restraints. They weren't heavy, but they were *strong*." She looked to the metal in Austri's hand, feeling the weight of the truth slide free of her shoulders. "Fenrir insisted on leaving them there. But after the boat took him, I made my way back to the cave, fetched the chains, and took them to a smithy to be forged into blades. I wanted a piece of him, a reminder of what he'd done for me."

Austri's brown eyes softened. "These are dwarven made."

"What?"

He gestured for the other blade and Revna handed it to him. He held them close to the fire, inspecting them. "Forgive me, the smithy was not a dwarf, but this metal, it is a rare metal from Nidavellir. Per Odin's request, Nidavellir crafted the chains that bound Fenrir—imbued with great power. I believe the enchantment still holds."

Revna didn't know what to say. Never did she think that she carried with her enchanted weapons imbued with the power from dwarven ore.

"What are they imbued with?"

Austri looked uneasy, his robust beard twitching with his mouth. "It is a powerful binding magic. Not like the one you share with Fenrir, nor the one he shares with Odin, but one that is only known to dwarven crafters."

He handed the blade back to her. "Keep those with you. *Always*. They—"

But Austri's words were cut off by three sudden blasts of a horn.

They were being attacked.

FORTY

FENRIR

FENRIR AND TYR RODE their horses hard to reach the mountain pass leading to Freyja's fortress by midday. As they went, the mountains grew sharper and more imposing, their peaks cutting into the sky like a jagged spine. The lush verdant lowlands gave way to snow-blanketed ground punctured with spots of dark rock.

Coming to the narrow pass, an instinctive chill of warning sent Fenrir's hairs rising. He glanced to Tyr, who nodded, acknowledging the same uneasy feeling. They dismounted their horses and continued on foot, the cliff casting longer shadows with each step.

All through the night when he couldn't sleep, and through the day's ride, he'd thought about what he would say to Freyja—should she even see them. She was a Goddess of Love, Sex, Beauty, and Life. But she also was a Goddess of War, Tyr's female counterpart, and the most powerful holder of *seiðr* magic. More powerful than Odin, and some even said more powerful than the Norns, when it came to divining fate. But possessing so much power had caused the Aesir to try to bind her, use her.

Much like Fenrir.

He hoped to find common ground with the Goddess—appeal to her sense of justice and understanding. They had both suffered at the hands of the Aesir simply for existing. She was in hiding because of them.

Maybe, were she not alone, she would find it was time for her to step back into the light.

The air became oppressive as the passage narrowed, rocks snagging his clothes like teeth. Turning his body sideways, he had to shuffle through the compressing gap. Fenrir glanced back at Tyr to find that his friend looked a little gray around the edges. He had tried to encourage Tyr that he should stay behind, to let him talk to Freyja alone, but Tyr had argued that he was Freyja's other half in the ways of Love and War, and she may feel a sense of kinship toward him. Fenrir knew better to than argue.

Just as Fenrir began to doubt that they could fit through the narrow pass, it abruptly widened into a perfectly circular gap. Ice blanketed the entire area and Fenrir nearly slipped as he stepped on it, head looking up to the towering crystalline ice formations. He scanned the vast, icy clearing searching for any way forward, but found none. No cave mouth, no stairs, no indication of life. No smell could be detected outside his own and Tyr's. The silence of the space hung heavy, only broken by the crunch of ice under their boots.

Fenrir turned to Tyr. "What—"

But his question was cut off by a loud huff. Turning, he caught sight of a large boar standing on the other side of the gap. It was nearly as tall as Fenrir, and had skin so deeply golden it looked gilded. Large tusks jutted out from its mouth and pure black eyes ate away the light as they watched and assessed him and Tyr.

You should not be here, son of Loki. And you, son of Odin.

A voice, deep and guttural spoke, directly into his mind.

Fenrir lifted his hands slowly in a surrendering motion. "We wish to have an audience with Freyja. We mean no ill will—we have much in common."

Lies fall from your tongue like poison. We know that you are bound to Odin.

"Not because I want to be. Because I felt I had no other choice to protect those I love. To free those I love."

There is always a choice.

Fenrir bit down on his cheek to repress the growl slowly building in his chest. He looked at Tyr, whose mouth was pressed in a firm line. They couldn't leave empty-handed. He turned back to the boar, stepped forward, and spoke.

"What can we do to prove our intentions are without malice?"

Leave.

Fenrir tried again. "And if we say that we won't leave without speaking to Freyja?"

Then my tusks will be stained in the blood of a wolf god—the blood of a trickster and witch.

"We are not our blood. We are not our fathers."

The boar remained silent, but his fathomless gaze remained steady. With each huff from his snout, wisps of hot breath rose in the air, but Fenrir could smell nothing of emotion from the beast.

He had to convince this boar to let them see Freyja. For Vanaheim. For Revna.

"Please." For them, he would beg. "We just wish the chance to talk to her—to seek her guidance in preparing for war against the Aesir."

The boar's head cocked in interest.

I'll make you a deal. Three times I shall charge, and three times you have a chance. Should blood not stain my tusks, I will let Freyja know you seek an audience.

"Deal."

The boar charged, its hooves steady and sure on the icy surface. Fenrir pushed Tyr to the side, then turned just in time for his hands to stretch out and brace against the boar's tusks. Its deep grunt echoed off the walls as he pushed against Fenrir, thrashing his head. Once close enough to the wall, Fenrir gave a little push, then rolled as the boar ran into the wall.

One.

Growling, the beast turned and watched with narrowed eyes as Fenrir backed up, preparing for the second charge. But instead of coming straight at him, where Fenrir had placed another wall at his back, the boar ran in an arc, coming at his side. The boar dipped his head, catching Fenrir by his legs, throwing him against the wall. Barely landing on his feet, he whipped his head up, canines elongating, eyes burning in anger.

A throaty chuckle sounded in his head.

There you are, wolf.

This time, Fenrir charged at the boar, both cracking the ice under their thunderous steps, when a firm, feminine voice called out.

"Enough!"

Fenrir slid to a halt, as did the boar, both looking up to where the voice called from.

Standing on a ledge, as if she'd walked out from the stone itself, was Freyja.

Hair like ice and a face with beautiful angular features, she glared down at him. Eyes of the brightest blue and full of the hottest fire assessed him. She was dressed in leather armor, and held a staff in one hand, the other resting casually on a short sword at her hip. Flanking her were two excessively large cats with giant tusks descending from their upper jaws—a throaty growl pulling back the skin of their noses as they bared their teeth. Fenrir clenched his hands into fists to prevent doing the same. Instead, he dipped his head in deference before looking back up, meeting her gaze.

"Forgive the intrusion," Tyr said coming up from behind Fenrir. "I am Tyr, and this is Fenrir—"

"I know who you are." Freyja's gaze remained unflinching.

Fenrir cleared his throat. "We are here—"

"And I know why you are here."

Of course she did. Fenrir guessed that her *seiðr* magic had told her they'd be coming—perhaps even before Fenrir had agreed to. But even a powerful Goddess such as Freyja couldn't see everything that lay inside his heart.

"Why do you think we're here?"

She slammed her spear once against the ground, the commanding sound echoing in the cold air. Her two cats, sleek and watchful, settled beside her, licking their chops. A sad smile disrupted her beautiful features. "For Revna."

Hearing his wife's name come out of the Goddess's mouth had the blood draining from his face, his stomach seizing with worry. Of all the things he'd expected Freyja to say, that wasn't it.

"I know all about your wife—I have watched her for many years. Heard her call. Taken in those she was too late to save on Myddheim." She gave her head a small shake, sighing. "I cannot protect her from what's to come."

"What is to come?" Fenrir asked, trying to calm his heart. When Freyja didn't respond, he took a few more steps until she stood just a body's length above him. The boar gave a warning snort. "It is said that you care about the mortals of Myddheim. Perhaps more than any God. That you don't use them as subservient sacrifices but treat them with kindness and respect."

As if she couldn't resist, her gaze flicked down to where Otta stood. Fenrir looked to the boar and saw that it, too, looked at Freyja. And for a fleeting moment, Fenrir smelled the unmistakable comfort of affection and something else that he couldn't decipher under whatever protective enchantments Freyja had placed.

He continued, "You may think that we have come to ask for your protection of Revna, but it's more than that. Odin and the Aesir are looking for any excuse to go to war again—to vanquish anything that challenges them. To muzzle anything that may bite back."

Freyja glanced pointedly at the markings on his forearms. "Are you not one of those things?"

Fenrir nodded. "I am. But so were you."

"That was many lifetimes ago, and that war is long past." The fire in her eyes became a living thing, but Fenrir couldn't heed the warning.

He raised his hands, gesturing to the icy tomb around them. "Is it? Because you hide away while the Aesir carry on as if they won. And maybe they have."

Careful, wolf, the boar seethed into his mind.

"I am where I am needed." She cocked her head, pale hair catching the light. "Perhaps instead of trying to goad me, you should be looking within, Fenrir, God of Destruction. Do you not have everything you need just under your skin?"

"I am bound—"

"Then break it," she said, as if it were that simple. "Until you are free, you cannot truly oppose him."

Frustration simmered hot in his veins. He turned, pacing away from her and looked to Tyr, pleading. Perhaps the balance of her counter-half could reach her.

"Freyja." Tyr's rich voice was soft and reasoning as he stepped forward. "We are not too proud to admit that we fear what repercussions may come to pass should Fenrir break his bind. The people of Myddheim, *your* people of Vanaheim, would be at risk."

Freyja reached up and pinched the bridge of her nose, squeezing her eyes shut. "I have protected Myddheim for as long as I could—have protected *her* for as long as I could."

The hairs on the back of Fenrir's neck rose in warning as the frigid air plunged to an even deeper cold. The ice around them came alive, cracking, popping, and groaning, the sound ricocheting off the solid walls. Each breath he took felt as though he inhaled shards of frost, the sharp bite of it stinging his lungs.

Freyja's hand dropped from the bridge of her nose, her eyes flying open, white as the snow on the ground.

"When this darkness breaks, when the moon kissed raven finds her wings ..."

Fenrir's heart plunged to his stomach "What—"

"When the night burns and the day bleeds ..."

Freyja's body shook as if an invisible force held her, and she fought to break free of its grip. Both cats stood as they sensed their mistress's distress. He and Tyr took a step forward just as the boar ran straight through the wall of ice, disappearing. A moment later, a fully dressed man appeared from behind Freyja, wrapping his arms around her, murmuring in her ear.

On a deep inhale, Fenrir smelled something unexpected.

Human and something else.

The man was perhaps a head taller than Freyja and solidly built. Light brown hair, dark eyes, and golden arms that held the Goddess as if he was holding her together. Touching her as Fenrir would touch Revna. With love and devotion.

"When beasts of old rise from root and rage, when winds blow ever cold ..."

"What's going on?" Fenrir called to the man and Freyja.

"Does she need healing?" Tyr asked.

Neither the man nor Freyja answered. Her words were half-coherent, her head thrashing around as if trying to search for something, frantic.

"Under black sunbeams, a teeth age, a tide age, a death age, a twi-light—"

Freyja gasped, the veil of white clouds clearing from her eyes. Still, the man continued to hold her, humming a soothing song to the quiet air. She rested her head against his for a moment, breathing. It was so intimate, so tender that Fenrir felt as if he was being intrusive by witnessing it.

"It's too much. There are too many threads, too many knots," Freyja said, her voice returning to its normal tenor, but tired. The man stopped his humming and removed his arms, but placed them gently on her shoulders, kissing the back of her head.

"Are you—"

Fenrir's question was silenced by an icy pang that radiated from the center of his chest, where he usually felt the reassuring warmth of Revna. He glanced to Freyja, the Goddess's eyes staring unseeing above Fenrir's head, her knuckles turning white on her staff.

"Otta, *go*. Now," she commanded, her voice sharp and urgent. With a final squeeze to her shoulders, the man turned and walked through the wall once more, the boar reappearing moments later, running at full speed past Fenrir and Tyr.

"What—" Tyr began to protest.

"You must leave now," Freyja nearly yelled.

Fenrir felt his body go cold with a knowing so intense, he felt like he would spill the contents of his stomach. He knew before the Goddess spoke her next words.

"Your keep was attacked. Revna is calling for me."

Forty-One

Revna

THE HORNS CONTINUED THEIR rapid call as Revna sheathed both of her daggers, determination and fire coursing through her veins. Austri's hand shot out and grabbed her arm, as the other dwarf in the space grabbed an axe and sprinted out the door.

"No, Revna," he shook his head, his light brown eyes pleading, "I cannot let you put yourself in harm's way."

She wasn't angry. Revna knew that Austri thought her capable of protecting herself, but the last time he'd let someone he cared for run off to battle, they'd never returned. She tried to soften her features and placed two hands on his shoulders.

"Austri, I won't sit back while our home is being attacked. I will not let other people fight battles in my stead." She thought momentarily of Havvar and his eagerness to see battle, at all the young men and women she'd sparred with and trained, panic eating away the calm she was trying to convey. "I wouldn't be able to live with myself. Please, do not stand in my way."

Before he spoke again, Revna saw his choice flicker across his face. He gave a solemn nod, then went to the wall of weapons to grab an axe of his own. When he turned back to her, Revna had a moment of regret. His grip was firm on the handle, his chin tilted in resolve. He would fight with her.

"Promise me that you will keep that axe in your hands," he said, gesturing to the beautiful weapon she still held in her grip.

"I promise."

Then they were running—up the stairs, down the moss-lit halls. With every step, Revna felt an urgency so palpable it felt as though it pushed between her shoulder blades. As they neared the main doors to the keep, Revna glimpsed a few warriors quietly guiding younglings to protective alcoves. There were no cries of alarm, no clash of weapons, only the breath-holding silence before a storm.

From the hall on her right, Havvar stepped out carrying a spear and shield, his face morphed into young and reckless determination. Revna slightly faltered in her steps, resisting the urge to grab him by the collar and lock him in the nearest closet with the younglings. One glance over at Austri, and she knew that he felt the same way.

"Havvar!" Revna called. The young Jotunn whirled and rushed toward her. "I need your help."

"I'm ready, Commander. I will fight by your side," he said eagerly.

Commander.

By now, most of the residents knew what she'd done in Myddheim, who she'd been. Fenrir, Hel, and Tyr often told anyone who'd would listen. But she hadn't been called that since she'd left Myddheim, and the feeling of hearing it squeezed at her heart, filling her with the familiar regret of leading those she cared about into harm's way.

"I'm glad to hear it, Havvar. Because I have one of the most important duties for you—one I can only entrust with one I can rely on. Will you do this for me?"

Havvar nodded, eager to please.

"I need you to go protect the younglings. Should we fall, you are my last line of defense. Do you understand? I need you protect those who can't protect themselves."

Havvar pressed his lips together, but something in Revna's gaze, in Revna's pleading tone had his stance bolstering.

"I will protect them with my life, Commander." He placed a hand over his heart and bowed his head, his long braid falling over his shoulder.

Revna would make sure it wouldn't come to that.

Thunder boomed overhead, shaking the entire keep.

The storm had arrived.

"Oh, Revvvna!" A familiar, vile voice called from outside, somehow echoing through the keep.

Warriors made their way to the front door, some taking the stairs that flanked its frame to take their positions on the parapet above. The quiet stillness of the entry hall gave way to the sound of boots on stone, blades being pulled from leather sheaths. She turned to Havvar one last time and gave him a squeeze on the shoulder. "Go."

Jogging the rest of the way to the doors, the warriors parted to make way for her, Austri close on her heels. She fought the instinct to ask Austri to join Havvar, knowing he would see right through her. That his answer would be a resounding *no*.

Outside and beyond the bridge, where the river carved through the forest, stood Thor and a retinue of golden-armored warriors. Revna moved in front of the keep's assembled force, her gaze darting to the wall above where archers were positioned, bows at the ready. On the banks of the river, other Vanaheim warriors waited, ready to strike.

"There you are." Thor's spit on the ground in front of him. "Odin wants a word."

Making a show of glancing around, Revna shrugged her shoulders. "So where is he? Too scared to leave his gilded halls to come speak to a mortal woman himself?"

Thor sneered, the action wrinkling his nose.

"By the way, how is your nose?" Revna poked, tapping her own. The more she talked, the more she could delay a fight. Fenrir and Tyr wouldn't be back until the early morning hours, but Hel could arrive at any moment. Perhaps the face of Death itself would be enough to send Thor and his warriors running.

"Better than your tongue will be when I carve it from your mouth, *girl*."

Girl. As if that word was an insult. As if she didn't owe everything she was to the girl she used to be. The girl who'd fought, the girl who'd held strong through so much pain and despair, never knowing if there was another side. The girl who'd tended to her cuts and bruises alone, but still always *hoped*.

That *girl* was her fighting, bleeding, unwavering heart. And Revna owed it to her to fight.

Thor took one step forward—one step—and Austri and several other warriors closed in, flanking her, tension thrumming through their bodies. Thor paused and smiled at the action.

One thing became perfectly clear to Revna in that moment. Vanaheim could not attack first. They could not rise to the provocation of drawing first blood and give Asgard and the Aesir any justification for retaliation.

Revna tried to sound bored and unaffected. "Deliver your message and then leave this realm."

Thor laughed, the sound stomach curdling. "I am not here to deliver a message. I am here to deliver *you* to Asgard."

"*Revna*." Austri warned quietly at her side.

She ignored him. "What makes you think I would willingly go anywhere with you?"

"My only order is that I don't kill you—that I don't give that mutt you married any reason to call in a debt on our laws of binding. There are any number of other options to persuade you at my disposal."

"And if I refuse?"

Revna knew what he would say before Thor spoke again, heard it as thunder growled overhead like a waiting beast. "I may not be allowed to kill *you*, but others may not be so lucky."

And there it was. The very heart of the worst fear she possessed, and he'd taken her measure so quickly. Piercing right to the very center of her. Revna glanced around, seeing all those beings who'd fled their homes for a chance at a better life, who'd treated her with kindness and open hearts since she'd arrived. Who had families and younglings. She knew her answer.

She took a step forward to stand in protection of Vanaheim.

Austri grabbed her wrist. "No."

"This is my choice," she whispered. "I will not abide anyone to suffer because of me."

"Then I'm coming with you."

She pushed against his sturdy shoulders as he tried to step forward, shaking her head. "I need you to stay here and speak reason to Fenrir. Tell him that I went willingly. Tell him ..." Her throat grew tight. "Tell him that I am sorry."

There was so much more she wanted to say, wanted to tell her husband, but she couldn't find the words. Instead, she concentrated on that place in her chest where she knew he felt her.

I'm sorry. Please forgive me, my wolf.

Shoulders back, Revna turned to face her fate. Thor shoved a handful of thin chains at the warrior to his left. "Bind her and take her."

The gilded warrior got all of three steps before an arrow pierced the gap in his armor at his neck and he fell to the ground. Whirling, Revna searched for the archer, her eyes landing on a familiar figure standing above the door.

Havvar.

No.

Thor smiled and thunder cracked overhead. "Attack! Bring her alive!"

The air erupted with battle cries as fighters from both sides charged forward. Revna spun, yelling at the warriors closest to the keep. "Close and bar the doors! Do not let them break through!"

With a single-minded focus, she sprinted into the fray. Across the bridge and on the river side, fighters were engaged in combat—a blur of gold, greens, and crimson and the sound of clashing steel. When the first warrior came upon Revna, he hesitated. His first and only mistake.

Her axe got its first taste of blood.

Perhaps she should have given more thought to the life she was taking, but she only cared about protecting the residents of Vanaheim, those being attacked rather than those attacking. The Asgardians avoided her, choosing to engage with everyone but her, so Revna threw herself between anyone she could, slicing them down with brutal efficiency.

Arrows whizzed past her ears. Thunder cracked so loudly overhead it made her skull rattle. Light flashed from her periphery, and she saw as Thor leaned idly against a tree, sending down bites of lightening to prevent anyone from coming near him.

Everywhere she turned, warriors fell. Their bodies hit the earth in screams of pain or in choking silence. Revna wanted to scream; she wanted it to stop.

"Thor!" she called over the wild sounds as she cut her way to him. "Call your warriors back and I will come with you. I will give myself up to you."

Through the chaos, she saw Thor smile, and then it fell from his face as he stared beyond her.

Revna whipped around to find Hel standing there with a look of fury on her face, sword in hand. Her draugr form ripped from her body as she turned and slashed through a warrior who was coming at Revna's back.

The draugr moved through warriors with an otherworldly speed, their bodies falling into heaping piles.

Revna turned to get back into the fight when an arrow grazed her cheek. Her hand went to the little cut as a pair of arms wrapped around her, twisting and pulling her to the ground.

The arms released her and she rolled out of their grip, axe at the ready.

But it was not an Asgardian warrior.

It was Austri.

With an arrow through his throat.

"*No!*" Revna scrambled on her knees through the dirt, setting the axe down at his side. She reached forward, pressing her hands to the flood of blood, the warmth of it seeping through her fingers in a steady river. "No. Please. *Please.*"

She didn't know who she was asking, who she was calling out to, but she couldn't stop begging as her hands became unrecognizable, coated in crimson.

Revna risked a glance up to see that Thor had fled, leaving his dead behind. All around her the world fell quiet as Hel took care of the remaining warriors.

Austri gave a gargled cough as blood sprayed from his mouth.

"You're alright—you're going to be alright," Revna tried to assure him even as great sobs wracked her body, hot tears coursing through the grime on her face. She looked up again, watching as Hel ran toward her. "Hel. Please, *please* help him."

The Goddess of Death knelt at his side and squeezed his shoulder, then gave Revna a sad look, shaking her head. Her power was Death, not Life.

"No," Revna gritted out, pulling Austri's head into her lap. His eyes started to fade as they met hers, but they still held such kindness. With a shaking hand, he reached up to cup her face, but his blood-covered fingers slipped on the smoothness of her cheek. She took her hand and pressed it on the outside of his, holding it to her face. "Thank you, Austri. You can rest now. I have you."

She wanted to say more, to thank him for more. Wanted to tell him that he'd healed a part of her that she hadn't known hurt. That in his quiet support, she'd found renewed strength.

A strangled choke had his eyes pinching in pain. Revna looked up at Hel, the request clear. The Goddess of Death smiled down at Austri, laying a gentle hand on the center of his chest.

A relieved sigh bled into a quiet death rattle as Austri took his last breath, the hand on her cheek going limp.

Revna placed his hand over his heart and bent forward, kissing his forehead, knowing to whom she should call.

"Freyja," she croaked out. "Freyja, please hear my call. Take this soul and reunite him with those he loves. Freyja, hear me. *Please.*"

Revna whispered the plea over and over, her forehead pressed into Austri's.

The sound of Hel standing had Revna lifting her head. The Goddess bowed her head and backed away as a golden, spectral boar approached Revna where she held Austri's lifeless body.

The boar spoke directly into her mind. *I will take him home, Revna.* She wanted to reply, to ask questions, to thank him, but found all she could do was nod.

A ball of shimmering light lifted from Austri's chest, his body sinking even further into the earth. The orb floated until it reached the boar's heart, flashing as it melted into its ethereal form.

Freyja's golden boar bowed to Revna before carrying Austri's soul away to be reunited with his family at long last.

Forty-Two

Fenrir

H E WOULD KNOW.

Fenrir would *know* if Revna had been hurt.

Even knowing that, even calling to the earth, he could not make his horse run fast enough. Fenrir gave everything he could to his mount, pushing it and rolling the ground to give it the speed he needed. Tyr kept pace, reaching out a healing hand to ensure that the horses needed no rest. But as dusk bled into night, their strength was starting to flag.

Fenrir didn't care. He would run the rest of the way on foot. He would crawl if he needed to. He would ...

Shift. Shift. Shift.

His body screamed at him to the point of pain. His ribs felt as though they might break, his spine threatening to bend and twist, contorting into the monster he so desperately wanted to be. If he could shift ...

No.

Fenrir didn't know what they would be riding into. His shifting may play into a carefully laid trap. It wasn't worth the cost. It wasn't worth the repercussions. The one hope he held onto was that Hel had arrived before the fighting started. Even the most formidable warrior wouldn't seek to incur Hel's wrath—to catch the cold gaze of Death.

With only mild relief, they exited the valley and entered the forest surrounding the keep. Fenrir kept his ears and nose sharp, letting his senses search for any signs of fighting. His ears strained past his own panting breaths, past that of his horse, but he heard nothing.

They had been riding hard for hours, and his body shook with exhaustion. Each agonizing moment snipped at the fraying threads of his mind. He reached up and rubbed over the spot in his chest, the warmth there dull and lacking the comfort he was used to.

He would know. He would know.

The unmistakable smell of blood hit his nose. The smell of death. The horses were finally too spent to gallop, but the keep was within sight, so he pulled his horse to a stop, Tyr following suit. Fenrir dismounted and sprinted on shaking legs. Through the trees, he could see the glow of lanterns and a small fire. He still couldn't hear any signs of distress. But that smell ...

Bursting through the tree line closest to the bridge, several warriors raised their weapons in warning at his intrusion. When they realized it was him and Tyr, they relaxed, but wouldn't meet their gazes. Panic roared in his chest, restricting every breath, every heartbeat.

"Where?" he panted, his eyes quickly scanning through all the people gathered outside the keep. His senses tried to search for the one scent he would know even in death. A cart full of dead Asgardian soldiers in bloody, gilded armor was pushed past him, the wheels squeaking under the weight. He whirled in a circle, eyes searching, searching ...

His gaze landed on three bodies of warriors from Vanaheim. Bokka. Eldnee. And ...

Dagmar.

It wasn't long ago that the Jotunn had showed him and Revna his scar. Made Revna laugh with unrestrained joy.

"Revna!" Fenrir yelled, the panicked sound deafening over the solemn quiet.

"Brother," the soft call of Hel came from his right and had his body tensing and whirling to her voice. Her draugr form stared down at a prone, lifeless body and ...

Revna.

Fenrir made it to her in three strides, dropping to his knees where she knelt with Austri's head in her lap, her eyes staring, unseeing, at his fallen body. A cloth had been draped over the dwarf's throat, drops of blood staining the delicate fabric. Fenrir tried to swallow back the grief that roared through him.

Grief for Austri. Grief for his wife, who clung to the dwarf who'd treated her as his own. Grief for Dagmar, Bokka, and Eldnee. Grief for his people, who now had to live with these losses and the memory of what took them.

"My *máni*," he implored gently, clenching his fist to prevent reaching for her. "Please look at me."

Let me see you. Let me see that you are still here.

She blinked once, then slowly met his gaze with swollen and bloodshot eyes. Unable to resist, he reached his hand and cupped her face, his fingers loosening the crusted blood on her cheek. He leaned in to kiss her forehead, inhaling her scent deeply.

She was still here. She was alive.

When he pulled away and met her gaze again, his body went rigid, the wolf under his skin nearly whining at what he saw.

In Revna's eyes lived anger and hurt so on fire that it threatened to burn the world down around her.

She returned her gaze back to Austri, and Fenrir finally looked back to his sister, finding concerned etched into Hel's features. Her draugr stood to the other side of Revna, staring at his wife with an unwavering intensity. Hel gave her head a little shake and Fenrir understood. The draugr wouldn't retreat until the threat of death was no longer present.

And Revna was murderous.

Fenrir understood the feeling all too well. Asgard had taken something irreplaceable from them, something that would leave a deep scar.

It could not go unpunished.

"This debt will be repaid, Revna," he promised her. "For now, we need to honor Austri. We need to put his body to rest."

Long moments passed before she nodded. Fenrir called to Tyr and a few others, asking for them to see the bodies of the Asgardians burned and to erect pyre rafts for Austri, Dagmar, Bokka, and Eldnee.

They worked tirelessly through the night. The air became cold and damp, causing Revna to shiver uncontrollably. Fenrir created a small fire behind her to keep her warm. He took a damp rag to her face and hands, trying to remove the stain of blood. But still, she didn't move.

When the rafts were prepared, he knelt at her side.

"It's time," he whispered gently. "Let us put him to rest, so he may complete his journey to Freyja's embrace."

Revna bent forward, placing one more kiss on Austri's forehead, and then gently slid him off her lap. He, Hel, and Tyr helped place Austri's body in the center of a raft, surrounding him with gifts and memories to take with him on his journey. Fenrir watched as Revna gripped her axe in both hands, grappling with whether she should put it in the boat.

"It's yours, Revna." He squeezed the back of her neck. "Austri would want you to keep it."

The dwarf had come to him not long ago, asking for Fenrir's input on the design. He was glad that he had given it to her before ...

With rafts on their shoulders, the residents of Vanaheim made their way to the fjord. Fenrir briefly looked for Jormun—trying and failing to not be angry at him for not being here. But Jor wasn't who Fenrir was most angry with.

He was angry with himself.

He never should have gone to see Freyja. He never should have left. The guilt sat heavily in his body.

Revna waded out into the water next to Austri's raft, her face tight and wan, her scent full of bitter despair. She reached up and smoothed back his hair, whispering something that Fenrir couldn't hear. She kissed Austri on the forehead one last time and then came to stand by Fenrir's side, hands clasped tightly in front of her.

The boats were pushed out, gliding on the water, creating great wakes of water and grief. Archers launched their arrows, setting the rafts ablaze. The fire reflected off the still waters. No one spoke—only the soft muffled sound of cries could be heard. A sound that would haunt Fenrir's waking and sleeping thoughts for many nights to come.

Slowly, people dispersed, exhaustion setting in, and likely craving the reprieve of sleep. Fenrir asked Hel and Tyr to escort everyone back. Revna stared, unmoving, out at the nearly burned boats.

The darkest part of the night came and went, Revna shivering under its cutting cold. He came up behind her and gently placed his hands on her shoulders, rubbing them up and down her arms for warmth. For a long time, she didn't move, didn't react. But he didn't care. He would stay out there with her for days if she needed.

But as the first hint of light hit the horizon, she took a step back, her shoulders barely pressing into his chest. With a deep breath, she turned and rested her forehead on his chest. Fenrir sighed in relief as he wrapped his arms tightly around her, burying his head into the crook of her neck. When her legs gave out, he sat on the ground and pulled her into his lap.

They said nothing as they watched the sun rise on a slightly darker world.

FORTY-THREE

REVNA

REVNA WISHED SHE COULD stay in bed for days. She wanted to drink a tonic that would make her blissfully unaware, and slide into the place between dream and awake where everything was dark and unchanged.

But she couldn't. She knew if she gave in, she might never resurface.

And she had a fucking debt to pay.

When she and Fenrir had finally returned to the keep, the sun had long risen, but the once verdant landscape felt cold and gray. Revna had tried to sleep, the exhaustion a living thing in her body. Each time she came close to being pulled under, her rest was broken by dark visions and distorted words. Whispers that snaked into her ears and darkened her mind.

Odin wants a word.

The knot in Revna's chest tightened its fist, the pressure almost unbearable on her broken heart. Asgard would not cease their pursuit until they had her. The threat of their return would loom like a blade overhead. And inside Revna rose every old, reparative impulse.

Surrendering herself seemed like the only way to prevent further loss. Vanaheim would only continue to suffer while she was here. But it wasn't that simple—not this time. To leave behind those she cared about, those she loved with an intensity that scared her. The thought of abandoning them ...

The walls of the keep seemed to close in, pulling the air from her lungs. She was caught in a web of impossible choices and devastating consequences. No matter what she did, no matter which path she chose, pain would follow.

Revna rose gingerly from their bed and stared down at herself. Fenrir had made her change, throwing her blood-stained clothes in the fire, but she still felt coated in death. Pulling Fenrir's tunic off, she trudged to the waterfall off her and Fenrir's room, letting the cool water run through her hair, down her body—willing it to take it all away. Fenrir had ventured down to the kitchens to bring back some food, knowing she wasn't ready to go in there just yet. Knowing the hollowness she would feel being in a space that Austri had occupied.

She took a step back out of the water and leaned her head against the rock, hand pressed to her chest, taking deep, measured breaths.

Revna wanted it to stop. All this darkness, all this chaos that drove this kind of disregard for life. She was so tired of fighting. So tired of trying to keep water out of the boat even while it sank.

Splashing her face one last time, she stepped out of the water, grabbing a weave to dry herself with. As she was ringing out her hair, Fenrir stepped around the corner, his expression soft.

"Come dry off in front of the fire and get something in your stomach, my *máni*," he said with an edge of a plea.

They hadn't talked since he'd come back—Revna couldn't seem to make the words she was thinking cross her lips. She felt a burning need to apologize, senseless though it was. But it was her very presence in Vanaheim that had spurred Asgard to act. It was because of *her* resistance that Austri was no longer here.

She followed Fenrir and sat in a chair in front of the fire, the warm flames drying her damp skin. A small plate with bread, cheese, and an apple sat on the table next to her with a pitcher of water. Such simple fare. Because Austri was no longer there to cook. Because the whole keep was in mourning and exhausted and scared from the previous day.

Revna's stomach revolted and her throat became tight. The thought of eating anything felt daunting. Impossible.

Fenrir poured them both some water. "Try to take a bite. Please."

Concern and exhaustion were so etched into his features that she had to try. Reluctantly, she picked up a piece of bread and tore off a hunk, putting it into her mouth, followed by a big gulp of water to get it down. She followed up with a piece of cheese, and a bite of apple.

"Thank you," she croaked, realizing she hadn't spoken at all since she pleaded to Freyja over Austri's lifeless body. Fenrir's eyes shuttered in relief. "I think I'm going to get dressed and head to the training yard. I need to …"

She wasn't sure how to finish that statement, but Fenrir nodded all the same. "I need to meet with Hel and Tyr, and check in with everyone. Will you join me? When you're ready."

The thought of rehashing everything made Revna want to disappear into the forest, but she understood Fenrir's intention. He was trying to make sure that she wasn't kept in the dark.

"Are you planning a retaliation?" she asked, her voice becoming stronger. Two sides were warring inside of her. One that craved the deep satisfaction of avenging the death of Austri, Dagmar, Bokka, and Eldnee. The side that wanted Asgard to suffer. The part of her that was so dark and full of burning hatred that she wanted those who wronged the ones she loved to choke on it.

The other side of her, the side that had stepped onto a boat to save her Maidens, who'd learned from the dwarf who had put out his fire and picked up a kitchen knife, knew that violence only produced more violence. If they retaliated against Asgard, many would get hurt. More would die. And nothing would be resolved. Violence and war were not solutions with an end, they were circles that continued over and over, feeding off generations of wrongs and hurt.

Fenrir took a deep breath, placing his elbows on his knees. "I want to, believe me. But I know the repercussions would outlast the momentary satisfaction. There is so much at risk, and we don't yet have the allies that we would require—"

"What happened with Freyja?" The image of Freyja's boar approaching Austri flashed in her mind.

"She *heard* you, Revna."

His words didn't take root for a few long moments. "What?"

Fenrir rose from his chair and came to kneel in front her. His dark hair was wild and falling into his eyes. Revna absently reached a hand up and brushed it off his face, his eyes closing for a moment at the brief touch. "She heard your call. One moment we were talking, the next ..." he shook his head.

Realization hit Revna at what Fenrir must have felt in that moment. Knowing that Vanaheim was under attack, and he was so far away, unable to do anything. Revna slid to her knees in front of him and placed her hands on his shoulders.

"I'm so sorry, Revna. I am so fucking sorry I wasn't here." He grabbed onto her waist and hauled her into his lap so that she was straddling him, burying his head into her neck. "I should have never left. If I hadn't—"

She yanked hard on his hair so that his eyes met hers once again. "Don't you fucking *dare* apologize. This is not your burden to bear."

Something in her eyes, the set of her jaw, must have given her away. "It's not yours either."

She didn't respond—couldn't respond. Instead, she gave him a soft kiss and slid off his lap. As she dressed, she could feel his eyes on her, but didn't dare look back at him.

Revna was feeling too much. It pounded against every corner of her body, begging for release. The only option was to keep moving. Keep breathing.

With a quick goodbye, she left the room.

The whole keep was quiet—a mournful hush that even had the moss dimming its glow. No talking or laughing echoed down the halls. No familiar sound of younglings running wild. It wasn't long ago that Fenrir had walked her purposefully through these halls, showing her how much life and joy lived within. But now it felt tainted. A blanket of grief and darkness had settled over everything, and Revna's chest felt tight.

When she reached the training yard, there was no one else there save for one person.

Havvar was taking a sword repeatedly to a wooden target, hacking and slashing with such unbridled ferocity that Revna's throat clogged at the sight. His breath was coming in great heaves and sobs. When the sword handle broke off, he tossed it aside and started punching at the wood, knuckles ripping and bleeding instantly on the splintered wood.

Revna ran to him. "Havvar!"

Undeterred, he kept on his strikes, the wood staining dark with each blow. When Revna reached him, she used her whole body to knock him aside, her hands grabbing at his forearms to keep him from swinging.

Unfocused blue eyes met hers, his face crumbling as he fell to his knees in the dirt. He bowed his head as a wave of sobs tore from his throat. Revna knelt in front of him, placing her hands on his shoulders.

"It's m-my fault. I-it's all my f-fault," he choked out. "Austri is d-dead because of me."

Her heart shattered into pieces. Tears that she'd withheld suddenly overflowed her eyes, streaming freely down her face. With gentle hands, she grabbed Havvar's face and tilted it up to hers, but his eyes squeezed shut, unwilling to look at her.

"Havvar," she said, her voice coming out steadier than she felt. "Look at me, please."

With great reluctance, his eyes peeled open, his chin trembling as he tried to hold back more tears.

So young. He was so young.

"Listen to me, Havvar, and know what I speak to be true. It is not your fault." He tried twisting his grayish-blue face away from her, but she held strong. "It is *not* your fault."

It's mine, the darkness in her mind whispered.

He tried to shake his head. "If I hadn't fired that arrow—"

"Asgard would have found another reason to attack," she finished for him. "It is not your fault."

"I'm so sorry. I'm so sorry, Commander." Havvar choked on a sob and leaned his forehead against her shoulder.

Revna couldn't take the apologies, couldn't stand letting others take blame for something that wasn't their burden. Fenrir. Havvar. None of it would have happened if she hadn't come here. If she'd gone with Thor when he demanded it. The guilt of it ate away at her like an insidious worm.

Over Havvar's shaking shoulders, Revna saw Tyr enter the training yard, his eyes falling on Revna. He gave her a concerned look before slowly approaching. Tyr sat on the ground between them, placing his hand on Havvar's back.

You alright? He mouthed to Revna. She gave a small nod, but no. She was not alright.

When the worst of his sobs cleared, Havvar lifted his head to see who had joined them, his face flushing when he saw Tyr. He opened his mouth to speak, but Tyr held up his hand to stop him.

"Let yourself feel and process this, Havvar," Tyr encouraged. "However you need to. But don't for one moment think you must do it alone."

He gave Revna a meaningful look—a look that said the statement was not meant for Havvar alone.

Exhaustion washed over the features of Havvar's face and body. Tyr and Revna helped him stand just as a group of warriors entered the yard. They took one look at the young Jotunn and pulled him into a group hug. After a moment, they all started walking him out of the yard, talking quietly.

Revna felt the beginnings of an appreciative smile pull at her lips, but it didn't fully form. Tyr came around to face her, and she could barely withstand the sympathy on his face.

"When I still lived in Asgard, I was witness to years of Fenrir's abuse." Tyr shook his head. "I watched as they collared him, caged him, fed him with one hand, while beating him with the other. I *watched*. I did nothing, and I regret it every day. But our realms are not set up to give strength and voice to those who need it most. I want it to be different. I am the God of Love and War, and all I want is for war not to rid the realms of love." He placed his hand and his arm on each of her shoulders. "I can see that you torturing yourself, Revna. And I meant what I said to Havvar, you don't have to bear this alone. The only way anything will change, the only way we will win, is by doing it together."

Unable to respond, Revna stepped fully into his arms and hugged him. Tyr's power pulsed through her body, alleviating all the aches and pains from the previous night's battle.

"Thank you, Tyr," she whispered. After a few more moments, she pulled away and took a deep breath. "Did you need something?"

"Actually, I came to find you and bring you down to the fjord. Jormun finally responded to Hel's call. Fenrir would like you to come meet him. Officially."

She nodded. Tyr slung an arm around her shoulders and together they walked out of the training yard. "What should I expect?"

"Oh, Jor is complicated and cunning. Honestly, I've known him for a long time, but feel like I barely know who he really is. He's reclusive and a man of few words. When he does speak, he has a biting wit." He smiled down at Revna. "You two are either going to get along *swimmingly* or hate each other."

Revna pinched at Tyr's side and smiled at his poor attempt at a joke. "There's only one way to find out."

FORTY-FOUR

FENRIR

FENRIR STARED DOWN HIS brother from the rocky shore of the fjord, knowing the anger he felt was misplaced. The sun hid behind a dense layer of slate clouds, casting the water dark and unyielding. Jormun stood waist-deep in the safety of the water, his white hair a beacon amid the somber fjord. Despite his best intentions, Fenrir couldn't help the needling irritation at not knowing where his brother had been.

He'd been making the rounds in the keep, checking in on the residents, when Hel's draugr had beckoned him to follow. He'd needed to stay in the keep—to be there for the residents—but when the draugr had led him toward the fjord he'd known what for. He couldn't decline the opportunity to speak to his brother, not knowing when he would resurface again.

Hel tossed Jormun a pair of pants. "Will you please come out of the water and put those on before our new sister gets here?"

Jor snatched the pants out of the air before they hit the water, his slit eyes impassive. He slowly waded to the shore and pulled on the loose trousers.

Fenrir crossed his arms over his chest in an effort to calm himself. "Where have you been?"

"There are a lot of other realms out there, brother. Many things to see and hear. I don't care to stay in one place too long."

Fucking non-answers, as always.

"Jor, we were attacked by Asgard last night. Did you *hear* any-thing about that?" Hel's question was laced with impatience. Fenrir glanced at his sister, as did Jor, surprised by her tone. Out of the three of them, she was always the most level-headed.

Jor's jaw flexed. "I did not. Are you both alright?"

Before Fenrir could open his mouth, Jor's eyes flicked to the space behind him. Fenrir smelled her before he turned. Revna and Tyr came down the wooded path toward them, and Fenrir's whole body felt as though it sighed, putting eyes on her.

She looked exhausted. So pale that Fenrir wanted to throw her over his shoulder and take her to rest. When she came to stand next to him, he noticed her eyes were reddened and could smell the slight brine of old tears. When he furrowed his brow in question, though, she gave her head a little shake and grabbed his hand. Placing a quick kiss to her temple, he turned to his brother, finding Jor watching them with disinterest.

"Revna, this is my brother, Jormun," he said, watching as Revna narrowed her eyes at Jor. "Jormun, this is Revna," he said after a short pause, considering her aggressive stance.

Jormun lifted one corner of his mouth in a sardonic smile. "Are you going to try to poke me with your little blade again?"

Revna looked him up and down. "The more you talk, the twitch-ier my hands will get."

Fenrir sighed and ran a hand down his face as Tyr gave a loud laugh. Then he watched as something unbelievable happened.

They fucking smiled at each other. Genuine smiles.

Fenrir barely withheld a shiver of fear.

But as fast as the smile came, it fell from Revna's face.

"You look sturdy for a mortal. I guess we will see how you fare in the realms of Gods and monsters," Jor tried taunting again.

Fenrir growled and took a step at the near-threat, but Revna yanked him back.

"You said you were in other realms," Hel tried. "Why?"

Jor's face morphed into one of seriousness. "The waters taste of something corrupt. I followed the deep current between realms, trying to find its source—"

"Myddheim?" Revna asked, taking a half-step forward.

Jormun's jaw flexed before answering. "There is blood in the water. Boats and bloated corpses line the bottom of their seas. Smoke chokes the air. It seems as if they are at war."

Fenrir felt as Revna flinched and then tightened her grip on his hand before turning to Hel. "Do you know anything about this?"

The accusation was clear in Revna's voice. Her people were dying, and no doubt Hel had welcomed new souls to her realm, ones that the Valkyrs and Otta had left behind.

Hel's mouth pinched into a line, but her eyes were soft. "I intended to tell you yesterday when I arrived."

But Hel had arrived to chaos. A small breeze blew along the fjord shore, filling Fenrir's nose with the smell of Revna's tangled and tainted emotions.

"What did Asgard want?" Jormun asked, his gaze fixed on Revna, though the question was directed to anyone who would answer it.

Asgard will want her, he had said weeks ago.

Fenrir had the desire to cover Revna's body with his, to shield her. If she'd let him.

"They want me," she said, taking a step forward. "According to Baldur, Odin believes me to be a sacrifice from Myddheim and says that I belong to Asgard."

From the few Fenrir had been able to speak with about what had transpired, they'd all said the same thing: Thor demanded that Revna come with him to Asgard at Odin's behest. That he wanted *a word*. That they'd waited for Fenrir, Tyr, and Hel to all be gone …

He felt his canines prick his lower lip.

"Speaking of"—Fenrir stepped forward so that he was next to Revna again—"is there anything you want to tell us, *brother*? About how Revna came to be here?"

Fenrir hadn't been able to confront Jormun since his mother's confession about her part in Revna being here. He wanted to hear it from Jormun's own lips, the part that Fenrir suspected he'd played.

"I may have assisted the tides that brought her here. But it seems to have had a happy ending." Jor pushed back the white hair that had fallen into his eyes. "Are you not happy with your new wife, brother?"

"Your actions have made us a target, Jormun," Hel snapped, her voice laced with death-like coldness. She seldom used their true names, always preferring to call them brother. When their given names were used, Hel was incensed.

Fenrir and Hel had never understood what hold their mother had on Jormun, that she could always twist him to whatever shape she desired. Fenrir was constantly caught between pity and anger.

Right now, anger was winning.

Revna's hand loosened in Fenrir's grip until she let it go completely, crossing her arms over her chest. Her eyes grew distant, and he could have sworn he felt her very energy retreat within herself—her scent going completely neutral.

It felt like losing her.

Broken and distorted images he'd tucked into dark recesses of his mind emerged, dragging claws across his heart. Revna, on a barren and burned landscape, dissolving under his touch. The words of the prophecy circled round and round just over an edge he couldn't reach.

Then break it. Freyja's challenge rang in his ears.

For the first time, he was considering it. Myddheim suffered. Vanaheim paid a steep price. War loomed, regardless of him doing his duty. Maybe his mother was right. Maybe it was time to remember who he was.

But he needed to talk to his wife first.

A sudden gust of wind whipped through the trees and Revna's gaze jerked to watch it dance in the branches. Fenrir furrowed his brow and turned to see what she was staring at, but her eyes remained unseeing on the branches. They suddenly cast to the ground, as if she was searching for something among the sand and stone. Then she turned and walked into the trees.

Tyr and Hel both cast him looks of confusion but he barely saw them, already turning to chase after her.

"I'll stick around for a few days, then I will be gone," Jor called out. Revna stopped in her tracks, Fenrir nearly running into her, as she cast one look back at his brother—her gaze completely unreadable. Then she turned back and continued into the forest.

Revna hiked on, her purposeful steps crunching leaf and branch underfoot, for a long while. Fenrir followed in silence, letting her take the lead. Instead of returning to the keep, she continued deeper into the forest. As the undergrowth thickened, and the branches blocked her path, Fenrir called to them, clearing the way. Revna cast a look of annoyance back at him, but still didn't say anything.

They walked on as the day faded, its retreat casting long shadows on the forest floor. Revna tripped over roots, exhaustion pulling her down, but still she pressed on, still he followed. At some point, their path circled back and lead them to the rune gate. Revna stopped and stared, breathing hard.

"Revna." Fenrir tried.

Finally, she turned to face him, tears running silently down her cheeks—face twisted in anger. He took a step toward her, but stopped as she retreated.

"Open the gate, Fenrir."

It took him a moment to understand what she was saying, to understand her intention. He growled low at her. "*Fuck* no."

"Do it."

"*No.*"

She closed the distance between them and shoved at his chest. "Please. Please let me do this."

"No."

Revna shoved again and again, pushing against him, begging him. Her heavy breaths morphed into sobs, and she collapsed against him. Fenrir's eyes stung with unshed tears as he pulled her down to the ground and pulled her into his lap. He held onto her, allowing the grief and anger to pass through him, through her scent, through their bind, in suffocating waves. Sharing in this moment of heartbreak.

When her sobs eased, she pulled back to look at him. Tears were now flowing freely down Fenrir's face, and it dawned on him that he'd never cried in front of anyone before. Revna reached up and brushed them away, kissing the stains they left behind.

She sighed and placed her forehead against his. "I feel so helpless." Fenrir understood this feeling better than most, but he didn't interrupt her. "Everything that has happened could have been prevented. It happened because of me, and I don't know if I can bear it. Because I freed you. Because I didn't take my place on that boat. Because I came to Vanaheim. Because I followed you into Jotunheim. Because I didn't go when Baldur came. Because ... because I begged Austri to let me go fight ..."

Revna's breath hitched and Fenrir moved a hand to sprawl across her chest, over the mark of their bind, willing her to take a deep breath. Everything he wanted to say to her became a tangle in the back of his throat, the words unable to form. He wanted to tell her how wrong she was, but it wouldn't be heard. He could tell by the tone of her voice that she believed in what she was saying. And it broke his heart.

She adjusted herself out of his lap until she was kneeling in front of him, grabbing his hands. "Please let me make this right. Let me go to Asgard. Let me *go.*"

Fenrir dropped her hands and stood abruptly, shoving his into his hair as the earth gave a slight tremble under his feet. What she was asking of him was the one thing he couldn't give her. The one thing he would selfishly cling to. Fenrir wouldn't and couldn't give Revna up—and he hoped that she wouldn't hate him for it.

"I can't, Revna." He looked down at her. "Not only because I am selfish, but because I can't allow you to take the blame for something that is not your fault. You say everything has happened because of you? And what about Asgard? What about Odin?"

She closed her eyes, looking so defeated.

Fenrir knelt before her again. "Please believe me when I say this is not your fault. Please hear me when I say I won't give you up, Revna. Don't ask it of me. I can't."

"Please," she whispered, still not opening her eyes. Everything within him shattered, the broken pieces puncturing his heart. Not long ago, she had asked him to promise they would face the uncertainty together. It was a promise he intended to keep.

He slid his hands into her hair, her gray eyes fluttering open. "I'll do it. But know this. If I open the gate, I follow. Wherever you go, I follow. Whatever you fight, I fight. And I will fight with you, fight for you, until the dark and burning end. In life and in death, there is not a place that you can go that I will not follow you."

He placed a hand over her heart. "You have been fighting for so long and I'm going to ask you to fight again. To fight for *yourself*. Please, stay and fight."

Revna studied his face for a moment, then reached her hands to thread through his hair at the base of his head. She nodded. "Stay and fight."

Relief washed through him, unclenching his jaw, untangling the knot in his chest.

Leaning in, she pressed a soft kiss to his mouth. His hands reached down to rest against her thighs as she took his mouth again, tongue sweeping across his bottom lip. With a small groan, Fenrir opened to her, tasting her, losing himself in the sensation.

"Fenrir," Revna whispered, desperation in her voice, her nails clawing at the skin on the back of his neck. "Please."

"Are you sure?" He wanted her with barely contained madness. He was so desperate to feel her, to hear her, to remind himself they were both here, but needed to make sure she felt the same.

"Yes. I need you."

Fenrir leaned in for a deep kiss and then grabbed at her waist, forcing her to stand. He looked up at her, pulling off her boots, then unfastened her belt with her daggers. With a tug, he pulled her trousers down over her lush hips. She placed her hands on his shoulders as he pulled them off. He grabbed one leg and draped it over his shoulder, wasting no time in licking her center.

He stared up at her, watching as her mouth opened on a gasp, her eyes meeting his. She reached down a hand to brush his hair back and he growled against her at the scrape of her nails on his head. Taking his time, he explored her with his tongue. Licking, kissing, sucking, until her leg started to tremble. Gripping her ass with one hand, he pulled his mouth away to slide two fingers inside of her. She moaned loudly as his tongue swirled around her most sensitive spot.

He wanted her to come, but she was going to do it on his cock. When he felt the telling tightening, he withdrew his mouth and fingers from her. She looked at him in confusion, but as he unlaced his trousers, understanding had her dropping down to help push them just enough for his cock to spring forward.

Grabbing her hips, he placed her straddling him. A hissing sound escaped from between his teeth as she grabbed him and positioned his head at her entrance. He watched her face as she lowered herself onto his hard length. Gripping her tightly, he gave his hips a thrust, fully seating himself. They stayed that way for a moment—breathing, feeling.

"Look at me." His voice was pure gravel and full of emotion.

Revna's eyes found his as she started to fuck him. Rising, lowering, grinding herself in controlled, maddening movements. As he looked at her, he felt desperate. He never wanted this to stop—never wanted to be without her. The thought alone …

"You are my heart, Revna," he rasped. "Together. Promise me will face all of it together."

She rolled her hips in a way that drove him to the edge. "I promise."

"I love you, my *máni*. I love you. I love you."

"I love you, my wolf."

A single tear rolled down her cheek and Fenrir leaned up to kiss it away, then her mouth crashed against his. Lips, teeth, and tongue grew more frantic with her rhythm. He was so close, and he needed her to go over with him. Together.

He snaked a hand between them, rolling his thumb, causing her to grip him impossibly tight. Everything within him was coiling with rich heat, the need for release coming faster than he intended.

"*Fuck*," he snarled. "Come, Revna. *Now*."

He leaned forward, biting the slope of her neck, and felt her as she fell over the edge. As she moaned his name, he followed her. Her movements slowed to a lazy grind, and she kissed him deep as they moved together through the end.

Fenrir couldn't shake the feeling that she was kissing him goodbye.

Forty-Five

Revna

A s they all gathered in the dining hall that night, Revna felt peaceful. She'd made a choice, and it was the right one. It had come to her in startling clarity as they'd walked back to the keep and she saw the still-disturbed earth of the previous night's battle.

Vanaheim had become her home, and the people in it, her family. They would get through this together—just like Tyr said.

And Fenrir ...

She loved him. *Fiercely.*

The thought of him hurting in any way was what made her choice so easy and so difficult. They would get through this together. Fenrir. Tyr. Hel. All the residents of Vanaheim. She had to believe that. She repeated it in her mind like an invocation.

Some of the residents had banned together throughout the day to get the kitchen back in working order, stating truly that Austri would not have wanted anyone going hungry. They'd prepared a magnificent feast, opened all the barrels of good mead and ale, and gathered to honor the life of the fallen with good food and drink.

The hall glowed amber under the candle and torch light and smelled of spices and memories of Austri. Roasted fowl with bowls and bowls of potatoes steamed on all the tables. Baskets of Austri's special bread lay under linen to keep warm. Vegetables and berries and cheeses, all the things that expanded in the stomach and comforted the heart.

At first, people gathered and talked quietly. Revna could still see the storms in their eyes, having not yet cleared. Then, the sound of younglings laughing had several residents joining in—capturing and clinging onto a moment of joy. After that, voices became louder, laughter flowed, and people honored the dead in the best way possible. With unrestrained life.

Since leaving the woods, Fenrir hadn't stopped touching her. Holding her hand, an arm around her shoulder, a hand on her leg. And if Revna was being honest, she couldn't stop touching him, looking at him, either. Needing reassurance and confidence.

Across the table, Hel eyed her, a suspicious tilt to her head. Revna offered her a closed-lipped smile and Hel returned it by narrowing her eyes.

Revna picked at the food on the table and drank sips of the mead, ignoring the Goddess's keen gaze. She couldn't stop thinking about what Hel had said to Jormun. *Your actions have made us a target.* Those actions being what brought Revna to their shores. She knew that Hel didn't mean it as an insult to her, but she still felt the weight of it. The truth of it. Felt the weight in her temples.

As if sensing her discomfort, Fenrir leaned into her. "Are you alright?"

"Just a bit of a headache." She kissed his jaw. "I'll be fine after I get some sleep."

He gave her a look of concern. "We can head back to our room—"

"Not yet," she whispered. She wanted him to savor this night. This moment of suspended normalcy. She tried, too, but as she looked around at the smiling faces, she felt removed from it all. Like life was happening around her, but she couldn't grasp onto it like everyone else. "I think I'm going to go to the kitchen to grab some tea. I'll be back."

"Let me go." Fenrir made to stand, but she pushed him back.

"No, I want to do this." Revna didn't want to go in the kitchen yet, but she needed an excuse to give herself a few moments of reprieve. He nodded and reluctantly let go of her hand.

She crossed the hall and passed through the doorway that led down to the kitchen, taking the steps slowly, trying to prepare herself for not seeing Austri. She felt her heart clench as she stepped into the space. A few others who'd always been in the kitchen with him bustled around the space. When they saw her enter, they paused, giving her small nods, but didn't say anything. She wondered if they blamed her.

On a small shelf in the corner sat a clay pot with a blend of feverfew and mint. Austri had made the blend for her headaches, the ones that crept in after being awoken by nightmares. Without fail, he had a cup waiting for her every day when she reported to the kitchen. Lifting the lid, she put her nose to the dried plants and inhaled deeply. She swallowed past the knife in her throat, past the urge to fall to her knees and break. Grabbing a mug, she sprinkled the blend in, pouring hot water on top. She would never make it as good as Austri, but it didn't matter.

Leaving the cup to steep, she ran up the other staircase and headed straight to the healing room. She knew she didn't have long before someone came looking for her, so she quickly gathered the supplies for a sleeping tonic. One that would allow for a deep, dreamless sleep. Revna silently thanked Ingrid for the invaluable knowledge she had imparted.

Her head gave a pulse at the thought of Ingrid and all the rest of the Maidens on Myddheim.

There is blood in the water.

Jormun's words from earlier were a constant ringing in her ear. She didn't know what had happened, what led them to war, but she knew the Maidens would have no choice but to get involved. Another way she had failed. Another wrong to be righted.

She tucked the small pouch into the spot between her breasts and exited the room.

Only to run right into Hel.

"I thought you were going to get some tea," she accused.

Revna's face remained neutral. "I am. But I also wanted to sleep tonight."

Hel's hand shot out and grabbed Revna's forearm. "There is a cloud of death surrounding you, *Revna.*"

"Perhaps it's because I held Austri in my arms as he died last night, *Hel.*" She ripped her arm away and watched as Hel's face morphed into one of sympathy.

"Whatever it is you're thinking, whatever it is you are feeling, you are justified. But please don't let it destroy you."

Too late, Revna thought.

Instead of answering she threaded her arm through Hel's and guided her back toward the kitchen to grab her tea. They didn't say anything else, but she could feel Hel's power thrumming the surface of her skin, the sensation oddly comforting, and abating Revna's headache.

Once back at the table, Fenrir swung one leg over the bench and pulled her so that she was between his thighs, her back to his front. She took a sip of the tea and sank into her husband, relishing in the warmth and comfort. Even for a moment.

Across the table, Tyr was talking with two light elves—Kaneff and Alfa. Hel sat next to them but kept her eyes on Revna and Fenrir. With a purposeful and exaggerated yawn, Revna leaned into to Fenrir's shoulder.

"Maybe I am ready for bed," she mumbled to him. He nodded and said his farewell. Revna wanted to round the table and give Tyr and Hel a hug, so grateful for their friendship and everything they'd done for her.

Instead, she said goodnight and told them she would see them in the morning.

Fenrir put his arm around Revna's waist as they made their way to their room. The solid feeling of him next to her made her heart fracture with each step. Each moment closer to loss. When he leaned down and placed a kiss on her temple, her knees nearly buckled in grief.

"Is your head in that much pain?" He stopped their walk, turned her to face him. He leaned in, pressing a gentle kiss to her forehead, and she heard his subtle inhale of him trying to decipher her scent, and the feelings likely trickling through their bind. To know what to fix.

"Yes," she responded, not truly lying. Her head was in pain, but so was her heart. "I just need you to hold me for a while."

"As my wife commands." He gave her a wolfish smile, then scooped her up in his arms, carrying her the rest of the way.

Once inside the room, Fenrir set her down and moved to sit on the bed, unlacing and pulling off his boots. Revna used the opportunity to pull the pouch from between her breast and dump the contents into a cup, pouring ale over it—hoping his senses wouldn't pick up the subtle smell. She poured a second cup and walked over to where he sat on the bed. He cocked his head at her as she handed him the cup but didn't question it.

"To Austri," she said, raising her cup. "He will not be forgotten."

Then she took a big drink, Fenrir doing the same. His brow furrowed for a moment as if trying to place the peculiar taste, but she distracted him by taking the cup from his hand and asking him to lay with her. He pulled his tunic overhead and then lounged back on the bed, opening his arm to her.

Revna undressed to her tunic and burrowed into his side. She rolled half on top of him, burying her nose into the crook of his neck. Nothing had ever felt as solid and real as Fenrir. Nothing made sense like he did.

He threaded his hand through her hair, angling her face to take her mouth in a slow and lazy kiss. She broke it before she faltered, but it was too late. Her chin started to tremble, and tears flowed freely from her eyes.

"Rev ... na?" he said in question, his words starting to slur. "Rev—"

"I love you, my wolf."

But she didn't know if he heard, as his eyes fluttered closed and his breath deepened. She clung to him for a long time, crusting his skin with the salt of her tears. Holding him. Feeling him. Mesmerizing his features, so relaxed in sleep. When she could wait no longer, she pressed one last kiss over his heart, dressed, and left.

⇥————⇤

As fate would have it, Revna made it out of the keep and down to the fjord with no interference. Not that it mattered—what lay ahead of her threatened to ruin everything. She had to convince Jormun.

As she reached the water's edge, she took a moment to admire the reflection of the moon off its still surface. Faint green lights tried to make themselves known next to the moon's full light, sharing the sky in soft harmony.

Unsure of what to do, she picked up a rock, throwing it out as far as she could into the water, disrupting the perfectly still surface.

"Jormun."

She waited, but soon the ripples faded back to stillness. She picked up another rock, tossing it again, calling his name a little louder.

Still no response.

Fuck.

With her concentration on the water, she jumped as a rock struck her back, whipping out her daggers. Jormun leaned against a tree, quirking a brow.

Meeting him earlier had done nothing to stop the shock of his appearance—so different from that of Fenrir and Hel. Fair skin, white hair, and shocking slit-like pupils that leaned more yellow than gold. His hair was shaved close on the sides of his head, but the longer white locks were pushed back on top. Delicate black ink that mimicked snakeskin decorated his forearms and the sides of his neck. He was perhaps half a head taller than Fenrir, but slightly leaner. Only just.

He was beautiful and fucking terrifying. The way his snake-like gaze tracked every slight movement. The way his body always seemed coiled and ready to strike.

"What do you want, *dearest sister*?" he hissed the term of endearment.

Though they had only spoken a few words, she had taken his measure, and Jormun appreciated directness. "I want you to take me to Asgard."

He didn't so much as flinch. "Why?"

"Because I refuse to let anyone else suffer because of me. I will no longer stand by while people make bargains or die. I am what Odin wants, and I intend to strike a deal with him."

Jormun narrowed his eyes further at Revna. "What makes you think Odin will be content with just you? And don't you think Fenrir will just come after you?"

"*You* will convince him not to. At least until I can do what I need to do." Revna knew that Fenrir would come after her, just as she would for him. She also knew that he would likely break his bind with Odin and shift. But she would do everything she could to protect Myddhiem, Vanaheim, and most of all, Fenrir. Do everything she could to end this pointless conflict.

Revna approached Jormun. "I think you owe me this. Since you and your mother schemed to get me here, now I call in the debt. Take me to Asgard."

Revna's only way to Asgard was with Jormun. She knew the gate could bring her there, but had no idea what the runic pattern was to direct it. She could end up in the land of fire, should she get it wrong. But Jormun ...

Jormun could travel easily through the many waters connecting the realms. He just needed to get her within Asgard's waters. She would swim the rest of the way if she had to.

"They will never forgive me."

Revna guessed the *they* he was referring to be his siblings, but noted that he wasn't saying no.

"You know, Fenrir asked something similar of me a few years ago." Revna tilted her head in question. "My brother asked me to bring him to Myddheim. He said he just wanted to see you. Make sure you were well. I refused."

Fenrir had never told Revna this, and her stomach gave a painful lurch. "Why did you refuse?"

"Because I couldn't let him torture himself anymore. Nor let him face the wrath of the Aesir should they find out."

And there it was. Jormun, without thinking, exposed his soft underbelly. A place of vulnerability that she could use. For all his severity and cunning, Jormun cared for his brother and sister.

"And that is exactly why you need to take me. Because if I stay here, Asgard will not stop until they get me, and your brother and sister may become collateral damage," she said, voice steady. "Please, Jormun."

His slitted eyes searched Revna's face. When he found what he was looking for, he sighed. "Fine. I hope you can hold your breath."

Forty-Six

Fenrir

F ENRIR GROANED AS HE rolled over to pull Revna closer, the absence of her warm body having woken him up. He reached out his hand and encountered nothing but empty cold.

He cracked open his eyes, feeling as though he'd somehow absorbed Revna's headache—improbable as that was. His temples throbbed, and his mouth felt dry. Hesitantly, he lifted his head and scanned the room for his wife. Early morning light blanketed the room, but there was no sign of Revna. Where her weapons usually leaned, there was nothing.

He sat forward, pressing the palms of his hands into his eyes. He'd slept so deeply that he hadn't even heard Revna leave for the training yard. Guilt swarmed him, wondering if he'd slept through one of her nightmares.

He threw back the furs on their bed and walked straight to the waterfall, letting the coolness rinse away the lingering vestiges of exhaustion. After he was dried and dressed, he went to grab a drink of water, noting a small pouch on the table sitting next to the jug of now stale ale. He froze. Fenrir brought the contents to his nose, all the blood draining from his face.

He knew this smell.

He dropped the small pouch and rushed over to where their cups rested from the previous night. He brought one, then the other to his nose. There was a distinct difference—one he hadn't noticed last night when his focus was so completely on Revna.

The smell brought him back to over nine years before. To a boat arriving. To spiking Revna's ale with ...

Fuck.

Fenrir dashed out the door, running toward the training yard, hoping he was wrong. Hoping she would be there. Raven-haired and gray eyes full of fire. Residents watched him in concern as he sprinted past them. Inhaling deeply, he searched for a trail of her scent, but he couldn't detect it. Couldn't detect her.

He rubbed at the center of his chest upon entering the training yard, only to be met by a handful of faces—none Revna's. He asked them quickly if they'd seen her; they all shook their heads. He was running again. Maybe the kitchens. Maybe the gardens. Maybe somewhere she felt close to Austri.

But each space he entered, she wasn't there. He felt his heart beating faster, his mind clouding over with every terrible fear he'd ever had. He was banging on Hel's room door when Tyr's flew open, Alfa and Kaneff walking out, their smiles disappearing upon seeing Fenrir's frantic face.

"Fen!" Tyr rushed to him. "What—"

Hel came from the other end of the hall, stopping mid-bite into an apple when her eyes fell on Fenrir.

"Where is she?" His voice came out barely above a whisper. Fenrir took a step toward his sister. "Where is she, Hel?"

Hel's eyes flicked over his shoulder to where Tyr stood with his night-time company. "She's probably in the training yard—"

"She put sleeping tonic in my ale last night."

Hel's eyes briefly closed, and her head fell forward. "I'm sorry, brother. She said it was for her. I thought because of everything, because of the nightmares, she wanted a night of reprieve."

Fenrir stared at his sister as fear crept up in spine.

He should have known.

He stalked past her, making his way through the keep to the entry hall, trying to find any trace of her. He could hear Tyr and Hel close behind him, muffled by the sound of his pounding blood in his ears.

Just outside the keep, Fenrir came to abrupt halt as he noticed Jormun pacing just on the other side of the bridge. His brother stopped his pacing and pursed his lips.

"What are you doing here?" Fenrir asked. Jor hardly ever came this close to the keep, preferring to stay near the water, where he could shift and swim away quickly.

"I—" Jormun cleared his throat. "I have a message for you. From Revna."

Fenrir's whole body went cold. Power thrummed so close to the surface of his skin that the earth gave a violent tremble, though Fenrir's body remained eerily still.

"Where is my wife, Jormun?"

"She asked me to tell you that she is sorry, and to please forgive her."

"*Where is my fucking wife?*" Fenrir yelled, roots crawling across the shaking earth.

"She asked that you don't go after her. Said that this is her choice," Jormun ground out.

Fenrir slowly stalked toward his brother, watching as Jormun took a defensive stance. "And why did she tell *you* this, Jormun?"

"Because she asked me to take her to Asgard. And I did."

Fenrir attacked, launching himself at his brother with claws that had been withheld for long years. Root and thorny vines shot forward, wrapping around Jormun, restricting his body and breath, pulling him to the ground. But his brother also pulled from the earth. Leeching it of all its moisture and water, dumping it in a relentless torrent onto him. Fenrir tried gasping for breath, but he couldn't rid the water from his face. The force of it had him dropping to one knee.

A blast of gold had Fenrir whipping his head up to see Tyr standing in front of him, a shield of soft light blocking the water. Then the torrent stopped and Tyr lowered the shield. Fenrir wiped his face and stalked back to his still-bound brother, canines fully descended.

"Let him go, Fenrir." Hel's voice came out as dozens, her powers rising to the surface. She stood between him and Jormun, her draugr close at her side. "Let him *go!*"

Fenrir glared at his brother over Hel's shoulder. "If I ever lay eyes on you again, I will fucking kill you."

Jormun gasped as he released him, blood trickling from the cuts and scrapes of Fenrir's assault.

Fenrir needed to get to Revna. Before it was too late.

FORTY-SEVEN

REVNA

R EVNA'S BOOTS MADE A loud squelching sound as she was
pulled through the polished halls of Asgard. The humid air
proved useless to dry her waterlogged body.

Traveling through the rune gate was much preferred. Jormun had
created a pocket of air around her head and told her to hold on as he'd
shifted into his large sea serpent form. She'd nestled herself between
two large spikes on his back and held on so tightly that the muscles
in her hands and arms were still painfully contracted. Once close
enough to shore, he'd surfaced, and she'd swam the rest of the way.

Where she was greeted by guards in gilded armor.

Every instinct begged her to fight, to wrench her arms out of their
grasp and stick her daggers deep in their necks, but she'd resisted.

When they'd made it up the path on the white-washed cliffside,
Revna's eyes had been assaulted by the shine and opulence of Asgard.
Jewel-encrusted walls and impossibly sculpted stone—there wasn't
a surface that wasn't embedded with riches and abundance. Now,
large domed ceilings covered in vibrant mosaic designs had Revna
craning her neck back at a painful angle. Even the smell carried a
sickly sweetness that made her nose twitch.

It was overwhelming, and it made her ache for home. For Vanaheim. For the man she'd left behind.

The guards yanked her through an archway that led to a courtyard full of meticulously placed plants, streams of water, and chairs set in a semi-circle. Behind the largest chair at the center was what looked like the root of a tree so massive that it could only be Yggdrasil.

Entranced by the tree, Revna didn't notice the figure sitting in the chair. The guards shoved her to her knees, her bones immediately bruising against the hard marble. She shot them a glare before she turned back, this time training her gaze on Odin.

As she gazed upon him, she felt the need to scoff. He hadn't changed since she'd seen him in Fenrir's memory. The same ash-colored hair, the same eye patch. The same displeased set of his mouth. He was so unremarkable. But Revna knew better than most not to assess danger on appearances alone. She stared him down with an unflinching gaze.

"Your dog tried this tactic when we first met." His voice came out commanding and at odds with his appearance. "And look where it landed him."

Revna remained silent and Odin studied her with a cruel, glaring eye. "Why are you here, mortal?"

"You tell me. It was you who requested my presence."

A sneer briefly crossed his features. "I'll ask again, why are you here?"

Revna took a deep and calming breath, focusing on the warmth at the center of her chest. Holding onto the feeling of her wolf, letting it bolster her.

"I am here at your request and in good will." She swallowed down the bitterness she tasted. "And in that good will, I ask that you leave Vanaheim alone. That you stop plaguing Myddheim with the desire to fight one another for whatever twisted pleasure it brings you."

It was Odin's turn to remain silent. Revna watched as his jaw flexed and his eye narrowed. Then, to her surprise, he asked all of the gilded guards to leave.

Revna stood, no longer willing to kneel before this man who'd tortured those she loved.

He stood from his chair and looked down at her. "Have you ever heard of the moon kissed raven?"

Revna stiffened, her blood running cold, but didn't respond.

"Long ago, after dreams plagued me for many months, I went to the three sisters for knowledge of the future. I received the prophecy that told of the moon kissed raven. Wings white as bone, flying over the realms teeming in darkness, searching—a wolf running below, slinking between the shadows. A serpent hiding in murky depths. And death always waiting, watching. When the raven finally landed on a branch, its once pure feathers bled to black, ridding the realms of the darkness."

Odin paused, shaking his head. "But that was where the prophecy stopped. No indication of where this darkness came from, or of how to mitigate its effects. No idea of when it would come. Desperate, I gave my eye to Yggdrasil and hung myself from its branches for nine days and nine nights for the power to *see*. But still, it wasn't enough."

Revna's head was on fire, as if the phantom flames were trying to smoke out something from her mind. The words of her prophecy trying to reconcile with the images of his.

Odin turned and walked to the root of the Yggdrasil. Reluctantly, she followed. They trailed along the root until they were no longer within the confines of the palace, but outside in what looked like a lush green valley. All the while, Odin talked, and Revna's mind burned.

"I asked Freyja to join us in Asgard—to teach me her ways of divining. But the power never spoke to me like it did her. The witch cursed it to turn to ash in my hands. So, I tricked her with her own foolish heart to keep her within Asgard, to keep her with her *beloved*." He gave Revna a knowing, mocking smile. "After all, those in a *Hjarta* bind can't be separated unwillingly."

Fate will always call us back to one another. Revna believed that to the very core of her soul. As excruciating as it was to leave, their bind still burned bright. She sent a pulse of love to the center of her chest as Odin continued to speak.

"But the bind was somehow unable to fully form, and Freyja figured out the love she thought was real was nothing more than my manipulation. She killed her husband, so I imprisoned her. Then, I gave her a choice: relinquish her power ... or *burn*."

Revna nearly relieved him of his other eye when he spoke next. "She burned. And burned. And burned. Three times, and still she refused. She escaped and we went to war for many years. With each year of war, something took root."

They came to the base of the root where it met the trunk, the size an impossibility that Revna could barely fathom. It was so wide she couldn't see around it. The gnarled and twisted tree reached high into the sky, disappearing behind a dense layer of clouds.

"Yggdrasil began to rot. It took on a sickly darkness that corrupted all nine realms. I knew that the moon kissed raven prophecy was upon us. I knew that an evil had been born into the realms that would one day become its destruction. When I found those *monsters* hiding in a cave in Jotunheim, I knew it was time to search for the moon kissed raven that would rid the realms of its darkness. In that endeavor, I had the assistance of a certain *sister*."

An image of the future-weaving Norn flashed in her mind's eye. The marking on her chest—a marking of a bind. *Skuld.*

"As both a keeper of the future, as well as a Valkyr, she had much at stake. Many sisters to protect. She searched the future for that prophesied raven, of where it soared, and what she found was astounding. This raven, this healer of darkness, was a mortal. From Myddheim."

Revna swallowed, her damp clothes suddenly seeping cold into her very bones.

"But Freyja thought she was cunning, trying to thwart our attempts. Her power obscured who this mortal was. After the Aesir-Vanir war, she fled to Myddheim, as though she could hide. There she dwelled for many years, though I cannot fathom why. But before she left, before she returned to Vanaheim, she used her power to create a protective barrier around Myddheim. Nothing could leave or enter, save for *one* day."

Sacrifice day. One day a year.

"With her interference, our progress slowed. The tree continued to rot, and I had to use all my strength to shield it, so that it went unnoticed by all. Going so far as sending an ancient power to its roots, hoping to slow its progress." He tilted his head up at the tree, a look of resentment on his worn face. "When I brought those three *monsters* here, I thought I could stall the things that plagued me. I separated them, thought to train that mutt, but he was too defiant—"

"Why not kill them?" Revna interrupted.

Odin leveled her an impatient look. "To kill them would acknowledge their power. To control them only bolstered mine." His face morphed from irritation to one of arrogance. "Besides, the wolf had another use for me, and that, foolish mortal, is where you come in. Everything that has happened *is because of you.*"

"Get to your point," she seethed. She held enough blame on her shoulders. She wouldn't let him add to the weight.

"With powers and fates working against me, we could never truly discern what this moon kissed raven looked like. We chose at random, plucking names from the tree that had an air of fate about them, names that shone differently on the web."

All those people, all those sacrifices.

"But with each failure, my frustration grew heavier." A terrifying smile spread across his face, pulling his eye patch tight, sending ice prickling along her spine. "Until I had a thought. Most believe that I banished the wolf to Myddheim as punishment for biting off the hand of my son, but no, I banished him as *bait*. Because where there are *wolves*, there are *ravens*."

Hearing the echo of Urdu's words made Revna feel dizzy. The ground spun as loose threads fastened themselves into neat little knots. Fenrir had been her fate all along, and she his. Each other's fate, each other's doom.

"Fate can sometimes be quite literal, *Revna*."

Odin waved his hand and the clouds overhead dispersed, revealing high winding branches—bending and sagging under ...

Bile rose in Revna's throat as she looked up into a sight of pure evil.

Hundreds of bodies protruded from the tree. Their bones were stripped of tissue and sinew, speckled with dark, sappy blood. As if sludgy darkness oozed from their hollow pores.

All those sacrifices over the years, bent and twisted and eaten by the tree.

He gestured up to the morbid branches. "I tried to diffuse the growing darkness, allowing it to absorb into the bodies of the sacrifices, but it only corrupted it further—spitting out the bones of anyone who wasn't the moon kissed raven."

Revna was circling the truth, afraid to look it straight in the eye. She needed to understand everything.

"Why make the deal with Fenrir when he returned? Why intentionally stop the sacrifices?"

"Because when the wolf returned, he was the immediate threat. But one I could use it to my advantage. I knew, one day, he would bring the raven to me. That he would bring *you* to me."

Something itched at the back of her mind. Something whispered to think, to remember. The pressure of it pushed aggressively on her skull. It was clear that Odin had received *a* prophecy about the moon kissed raven, but not *her* prophecy.

Revna walked to the root and hesitantly reached out her hand. Her finger barely touched the surface when she felt a tremble radiate through her arm. Placing her palm flat against the root, Revna could feel a heartbeat. Whether it was her own, or the tree itself, she couldn't discern. Odin was saying something, but she ignored him.

Yggdrasil began to whisper. Began to thrum. Revna felt her body lock, her mouth fill with a bitter taste, and then she was screaming.

The earth was a scorched, dying thing. Everywhere Revna turned, there were little fires and bodies. So many bodies.

Bodies covered in ash.

Bodies unmoving.

She ran, looking for anyone who could be saved. Anyone who was still here. She ran, the ground starting to rise until she was running uphill, breath heaving and catching in her throat as she inhaled smoke. The earth shifted and moved until she was crawling, nails gripping and ripping against the rough surface.

As she reached the top, she clambered back to her feet on shaking legs and tried to understand what she was looking at.

From her vantage point, she could see all nine realms—or what she assumed were the nine realms. Nine massive worlds circled around a giant tree. Yggdrasil. But the tree was burning, and its heavy black smoke shrouded all nine in darkness.

Everything was gone—completely destroyed. Devoid of life. And she felt destroyed with it.

Revna turned from the impossible view and found a crook of the root, sinking to the ground, unable to hold herself up any longer. She lay down, placing her cheek to the ground, willing herself to burn. To drift away.

As her eyes began to close, she heard an agonized howling from some-where in the distance. Some part of her knew the sound, but it only made her cry.

Fighting to remain conscious, her eyes watched as a wolf—her wolf—appeared. But it was too late. His nose nudged her body as a high-pitched whine sounded in his throat, and then she was gone.

Revna sucked in a sharp breath as she came back to herself, releasing her hand from the tree, pulling it close to her chest. She was shaking and felt as though she might be sick, but she swallowed it back.

Odin stood to the side, staff in hand, staring at her with his emotionless eye.

"Do you see now?" Odin questioned. "Do you see how the Yggdrasil's corruption is bleeding into the lands? Do you see how the realms will suffer? You think your precious Myddheim and Vanaheim suffer because of me?" He scoffed, gesturing to the tree. "Do you see?"

Revna glared at Odin. "I think it's you who needs to *see*, Allfather. Things do not rot under proper care. Things do not corrupt unless touched by a blight." She took a step, pointing her finger at him. "*You* are the plague on the realms. It was *you* who demanded the knowledge from Yggdrasil, who tried to take what wasn't given. It was *you* who demanded Freyja's power. It was *you* who took children from their home and treated them like animals. It was *you* who took, and took, and *took*."

His answering smile sent a wave of coldness through her bones. "It is my duty to ensure there is a balance of harmony and chaos, light and dark. This is your fate. Denying it will have severe consequences. It would be you now, Revna, who condemned the nine realms, condemned everyone you care for, should you not embrace your destiny."

Before she stepped foot in Asgard, Revna had made her decision. She would do whatever it took to protect those she loved, protect those who couldn't protect themselves. When she had first arrived in Vanaheim, she had made a promise to herself that she would find a way to help Myddheim.

Fate was cruel.

"And what, *Allfather*, do you believe my fate to be?"

Odin gestured above his head to the bodies in various stages of decay. "To bleed the darkness."

He was asking her die.

FORTY-EIGHT

FENRIR

"**B**ROTHER!"

Fenrir could hear Hel calling, but he couldn't answer. His focus was wholly on reaching the gate, on getting to Revna.

"Fen, please!" Tyr called. He just pumped his legs faster. Rolling the earth, moving branches, compelling everything to stay out of his way.

He should have known. He should have fucking realized how quiet she was during dinner. Should have realized when she'd kissed him in the woods and it had felt like goodbye. Because it was.

No.

He refused to believe she was gone. Fenrir would know—he would feel it. Wouldn't he? He pressed a hand over his bind mark, feeling the frantic thump of his heart. The one hope he clung to was that if she had gone to Asgard to make some kind of bargain, he could intervene. Whatever the cost was, Fenrir would pay it. Even if it meant spending the rest of his days locked in a cage.

His steps faltered a bit as he thought on the worst outcome.

If she was gone, Asgard would fall at his hands.

Shouting echoed from behind him as the gate came into view, but he continued to ignore it. Once he was within reaching distance, a shield of light dropped in front of him and he ran right into it, almost falling back on his ass. He whirled and looked incredulously at Tyr.

"You think to keep me from her!" he boomed.

"Of course not," Tyr said, raising his hand. "Let us help you."

Hel walked slowly to him. "You will do Revna no good if you storm into Asgard—it may even make things worse. Please tell me you understand."

Fenrir shook his head to dispel the thoughts of violence threatening to overtake him—of razing the entire realm—and took a deep breath. He nodded and squatted down, shoving his hands in his hair.

"The gate on the other side will no doubt be guarded," he finally said, trying to formulate a reasonable plan. "We need another way to enter."

"Jor—" Tyr tried.

A low threatening growl was pulled from his chest at the mention of his treacherous brother. "No."

"Mother," Hel muttered.

Fuck. She was right, of course. But it could turn out to be a complete waste of time. His mother had conspired to bring Revna to the realms of Gods and monsters, but what if this was also part of her plan? Revna sacrificing herself, forcing Fenrir to act, forcing him to shift.

Because he needed to be reminded of who he is—what he is.

His mother's words had floated around his head nearly every day, a prophecy waiting to be fulfilled. But he found that he no longer cared. If he needed to become the monster they thought him to be to save those he loved, he would do so. Gladly.

Fenrir stood and walked to the gate. "You two stay here and make sure Vanaheim is safe. Just in case—"

"No."

"Absolutely not."

Both Tyr and Hel spoke at the same time. He didn't have time to argue with them, so he woke the gate and pressed on the runes for Jotunheim.

Once they all stepped through, Fenrir took off running again, calling to his mother in his head. He hoped that whatever magic and power she possessed, she would hear the call of her child.

After far too long with no sign of her, he stopped and turned to his sister.

"Hel," he pleaded, and hated himself for it. For asking this of her.

For all those long years in the dark, dampness of their childhood cave, their mother had forced Hel to study with her. Made her stay awake for days learning spells, bindings, and ritualistic blood magic. He knew Hel had never wanted this knowledge, but also that she could use it to call to their mother.

His sister lifted her chin and gave a small nod. She knelt to the ground, drawing a circle around herself, placing a rune at its head. As she began to chant, she withdrew a dagger from a sheath across her chest, cutting into her hand, dripping the blood on the rune. Her eyes hazed over and her draugr stepped from her body, turning to protect her back.

Guilt swarmed Fenrir, knowing what this was costing Hel. That he was asking this of his sister ...

He took a step forward with the intention of telling her to stop, that they would find another way, when his mother appeared.

Hel stopped her chanting and stared emotionlessly up at their mother. "What—"

"Revna is in Asgard, and I need you to send me to her," Fenrir said, interrupting her question. Her face remained unaffected and, for a moment, she reminded him so much of Jor that he clenched his fists.

She shrugged. "Perhaps this is her fate."

"If you care anything for my happiness, you will do this for me. This one chance to prove that you care about me—about us." Fenrir gestured between himself and Hel.

Something akin to an emotion flashed in her eyes. "Maybe it is because I care for you that I should not do as you ask."

"You wanted me to remember who I am," he seethed. "I fucking remember."

Angrboda began pacing, and Fenrir resisted the urge to scream in frustration. Every moment wasted was another moment that Revna could be suffering.

"Have you thought about what you will do to get her back, my son? What you are willing to do? Who you are willing to become?

She wants to know if I will shift—finally set the wolf free. He didn't respond, but he let her see the intention on his face. He would do whatever it took to get his wife back. Because he was selfish and loved her more than his very being, yes, but also because he could not allow her to take the weight of this blame. That she might die believing herself to have caused all their troubles? It was an unbearable thought.

"Brother." Hel came to stand before him. "We will get her back, but you must also have care for your life. For those who love and need you."

"I can't lose her, Hel," he whispered.

She searched his face, then placed a hand on his cheek, nodding. Then she turned to their mother. "Please."

It was only one word, but coming from Hel, and full of layered emotion, their mother looked like she'd been stricken. It was the most motherly look she had ever displayed.

And that was all it took, one look from the daughter she, in her own, terrible way, cherished. Angrboda dipped her head in conciliation and to work. Fenrir pulled Hel into a one-armed hug and kissed the top of her head in thanks, words too far out of his reach.

"Do you have anything of hers? Clothes? Weapons?"

Without a second thought, Fenrir walked over to his mother and took out a dagger. He pulled his tunic down to expose the area above his heart where their bind lay and ran the dagger across it, drawing blood.

"I am hers." He handed her the dagger. "Wholly. By love and bind."

His mother nodded, understanding the power of the binding that he and Revna completed. Within a few moments, a door appeared on the side of a boulder.

"Thank you," he said, meeting his mother's gaze.

"I am glad that you three have each other, at least."

Fenrir swallowed down the foul taste that rose thinking of Jormun, but didn't correct her. There was no time.

Without another word, he stepped through the door.

Forty-Nine

Revna

R EVNA FELT AS IF she'd been split in two.

Half willing, understanding—the other unwilling, revolted. Caught between the pull of fate and the cold grip of dread.

She knew she was the moon kissed raven, but hadn't accepted what it meant, some part of her mind protecting her from connecting that part of the prophecy with all the darkness that followed. Hearing it spoken aloud by Odin felt as though her mind itself was peeling back its layers, revealing an ancient truth that had been locked away.

The air seemed to tighten around her, pushing and pulling at her heart and mind. The tree loomed, the wind between its branches a whisper she was trying to understand. Revna couldn't rid herself of the innate feeling of wrongness.

Revna peered over to where Odin stood, leaning heavily on his spear, jaw tight. For the king of the Gods, he looked weak, he looked ...

Powerless.

Not completely, she realized, but waning rapidly. He had demanded power from Yggdrasil, and it had enervated him in return. Trying to take back what it lost. This wasn't just about restoring balance to the nine, it was about restoring *his* power.

But did that matter?

Revna knew that the realms suffered, that they would continue to. She had seen it; she had felt it.

Looking up at the gruesome limbs, though, she realized it couldn't be that simple. Odin's past attempts had been wrong for many reasons—his tragic attempts had lacked the balance he claimed to be a steward of.

"Since you have an affinity for bargains and binds, I should like to make a deal with you," Revna said, crossing her arms.

"Is it not enough to restore the realms? It is your fate."

She gave him a saccharine smile. "Oh, but it's not only the realms that suffer, is it *Allfather*?"

His answering silence was all the confirmation she needed.

"If I should help temper the darkness, you will leave Myddheim and Vanaheim alone. You will let them live their lives in peace."

"I will have no need to take action against the realms," Odin replied.

She swallowed before speaking her next demand. "And if I asked you to break the bind with Fenrir? To free him?"

Revna knew in her bones that Fenrir would break his bind with Odin when he found out what she'd done. She had known it when she'd made her decision to give herself to Asgard.

He had shackled himself to protect her, to protect so many that he cared for. And now, twisted though it was, she would try to free him before he had to make that choice, take that risk, himself. To protect him with everything that she could in the hope that it would lessen the destruction of her actions and all their repercussions.

A flash of anger crossed Odin's face briefly before he answered. His one eye narrowed at her. "No. The bind with the wolf still holds. Should he shift, any civility or peace we have fostered will be no longer. Our deal, as well as yours and mine, must stand for the safety of Vanaheim. But, as we agreed, I can give you my word that Myddheim will remain untouched."

Revna chewed on her tongue. "You truly fear him?"

Odin's hand gripped his spear a little harder. "True wisdom comes with equal parts apprehension and courage and knowing when a fight is not worth having. For years my dreams have been plagued with my death at the maw of that monster. It would be foolish of me not to have him within my grasp."

She paused, staring at this man who feared his death enough to sacrifice the realms for it. A defeated chuckle escaped her throat. She was ensnared in a web that she couldn't be free from. The more she struggled, the tighter it became.

War. Chaos. Destruction. It was inevitable.

Fenrir would fight, no matter if Odin forced her into this useless bargain or not. He may be on his way to Asgard already. May have realized what she'd done, and why.

How could she save the realms when she knew to the very bottom of her soul that the very act Odin proposed would lead to suffering? How could she save her husband? Revna had never felt so sick or helpless.

Out of habit and looking for comfort, she reached for the daggers at her waist. The familiarity of the worn leather in her grip soothed something inside of her, even as a loud buzzing sound filled her ears.

Keep them with you. Always.

Austri's words, never getting to explain why. That they were imbued with—

Revna's breath caught in her chest as searing clarity slammed into her, burning through her.

A moon-kissed raven, shadows in wake

With unbound chains, the darkness break

The chains that had once bound Fenrir, now forged into something new, but still imbued with the power of ...

The prophecy. *Her* prophecy.

These roots and wings, fates intertwined
A cov'nant sealed, both power and bind

She was Revna. The Raven. Her fate was bound to Fenrir's, but also to Yggdrasil's. Her thoughts drifted to an earlier time. To a talk of binds.

Galdrloka.

The buzzing in her head abruptly stopped and something within her sighed.

Baldur had said none knew of its true power. That the Gods went mad in their attempt.

But she was no God.

As discreetly as she could, she pulled her right blade out of its sheath just enough to slice into the tip of her finger. Instinct had her pressing her fingertip into a score in the root. Revna watched in awe as the blood absorbed, and then oozed black.

She understood now.

Somewhere in the back of Revna's mind, she'd realized that Odin's blatant honesty was coming from a place of surety—knowing that whatever he told her would die with her. He thought she was already dead. And that gave her freedom. *Power.*

The sound of Odin's voice snapped her back.

"My patience grows thin, girl. Are you willing to accept your fate? You must be *willing.*"

Revna's stomach twisted as she realized the weight of what he said. All those that had been hung above her had done so of their own volition. Sadness threatened to bring her to her knees, but she steadied herself. "And how did you convince them?"

"When they arrived here, they already half-way believed their fate was to be a part of a greater sacrifice. I gave them the final push. They died knowing it was for the good of the nine."

And in a twisted way, he had convinced her of the same thing, pulling strings in her life from his vaulted halls. And she had allowed it.

For many long years, she had tried to account for the wrongs. For her master beating Helga to death in her stead. For Fenrir sacrificing himself. For Myddheim suffering worse and worse every year after. For the giant being killed in Jotunheim. For Asgard's attack on Vanaheim. For Austri.

She was tired. So tired of feeling like she was unable to do anything.

Only now, she could.

Her purpose, her fate, wasn't to sacrifice herself. It was to meet her fate and claim it, giving those she loved their best chance.

Revna turned and hoisted herself up on the root, walking its length until she reached the base. Yggdrasil hummed underfoot, and she had the oddest desire to comfort the tree. With a few deep breaths, she followed her instincts. Taking out a dagger, she sliced deeper into her finger. She knelt on the uneven surface and started to draw with her blood. As she stared down at the bind rune that mirrored the one on her chest, she hoped that she was right.

Yggdrasil began to shake in earnest, as if awake, as if excited. Gripping a dagger in each hand now, she looked down at Odin one last time.

"What are you—" he started to ask, panic paling his face.

Revna smiled. "Fuck you, Allfather."

With all the strength and fury she could muster, she stabbed both daggers into the hard wood of Yggdrasil.

For Ingrid, Asta, Ellika, and all the Maidens.

For Gunnilda.

For Tyr and Hel and Jormun.

For Austri and all of Vanaheim.

For Fenrir—her wolf.

She focused on the warmth in the middle of her chest, sending all the love she could through the bind.

A pained hiss escaped her as her hands started to burn on the daggers, a scream slipping free from her throat.

"Revna! *No!*" Fenrir's voice howled, the sound coming from too far away.

She wanted to turn to it. Wanted to tell him to run, but her body was locked in an invisible hold. The ground began to shake and her body with it.

Then, darkness exploded.

Fifty

Fenrir

THE GROUND GAVE A violent tremble as Fenrir entered Asgard—the door dumping him in the courtyard near Yggdrasil's root. Hel and Tyr stumbled through a moment later, weapons at the ready.

Fenrir took a deep inhale, searching for his wife. She was here. She had been here.

The earth trembled again, and a heart-stopping cold crept through his veins to surround the bind mark on his chest.

"Is that you, brother?"

"No—"

A blood-curdling scream ripped through the air and Fenrir felt his body prepare to shift at the agonized familiarity of it. He took off running toward the sound, following along the root and out of the palace, until there was nothing but wilting grass.

Up ahead he could see Odin, furious and frozen.

Another scream had his eyes looking up, and for a moment he thought he might be sick.

Revna was up on the root, near the rising slope of the trunk, hands gripping her daggers and stabbing into Yggdrasil. He sensed it this time, before the earth gave a violent lurch, making Revna's whole body shake violently.

"Revna!" he screamed. "No!

He was running again when power and darkness erupted.

His body landed with thud, making every part of him scream in pain. Blood trickled down his temple and his ears rang with a high-pitched whine. Peering around, he tried to see through the smoke and dust. He could just make out Hel's draugr and the glow of a shield that held Tyr and Hel underneath.

Pushing to his feet, Fenrir swayed and looked toward the tree. Looked for Revna. But he couldn't see her.

"Revna!"

As the smoke began to abate, the surrounding land was left covered in ash—absorbing all sound.

Yggdrasil was no longer visible, and with a horror that turned his blood to ice, he could see why. A shimmering shield of gray light encased the entirety of the tree. Smoke was so thick inside the protective barrier that there was no sign of his wife. He sprinted up to the shield, only to be knocked back.

Scrambling to stand, he pounded against the barrier, screaming, "Revna!"

A bloody hand broke through the smoke and smacked up against the shield. He would know that scarred palm anywhere, know those calloused fingers. As if willed, the smoke from inside the barrier cleared, giving Fenrir a full view of Revna.

He dropped to his knees on a bellow as she tried to lift her head. Black tears dripped from her eyes, and black blood ran from her nose and the corners of her mouth.

Fenrir took out his sword and struck the barrier repeatedly, but to no avail. The blade broke against its indestructible surface. He tossed it aside and started punching at the surface—it broke his knuckles like the strongest stone.

The muffled sound of his name broke through his desperation, and he watched as Revna tried to drag herself up, placing her forehead against the barrier and panting, more blood falling from her mouth. Her eyes drooped, the dark tears running down her cheeks.

"Hang on, Revna. Please hang on," he begged her as tears started falling from his own eyes. "Fight, my *máni*. Fucking *fight*."

She looked to him then, her gray eyes dimming with each blink, and Fenrir let out a sob followed by a frustrated scream.

A sound from behind had him turning his head to see that Hel and Tyr were standing barrier between Fenrir and a retinue of Odin's warriors.

Anger and fear coursed through him. He dug his fingers into the earth, calling to it, trying to call to Yggdrasil—begging it to *let her go*.

There was no answer.

Fenrir leaned his head onto the barrier right where Revna's forehead rested.

"I love you," she choked out.

He pulled back to look at his wife, only to see a large black mass heading straight for her. It looked like a root but moved like smoke. Before he could warn her, it stabbed through Revna's back, right through her heart. Her spine arched on a sharp breath, black pouring from her mouth.

Whatever hold that Fenrir had kept on himself broke in that moment. He grew larger, his fangs and claws snapping into place. Flesh and bones, muscle and sinew, stretching, cracking, breaking, and reforming. And with a long-repressed howl that burned his lungs, his wolf broke free, looming and full of fury.

He barely felt the painful snap of the bind with Odin breaking and ignored it.

Looking down at Revna through new eyes, he watched as more black spears of smoke pierced her body. He let out a growl and began to dig, his large claws tearing through the earth. But it didn't matter. Because as sure as he was digging deep, the barrier only followed.

Collapsing down, Fenrir nudged his nose near his wife, emitting a high-pitched whine. Her head lolled before her eyes found him. Her face crumbled as she took in his wolf form. A shaking hand reached to his face.

Fenrir recalled his wolf and shifted back, placing a hand over hers just as another coiling black wisp reached out and wrapped around her ankles, dragging her away. Revna screamed in pain, and Fenrir felt as though he was going to die at the gutting sound.

He punched, clawed, and kicked against the barrier, but it was no use. The earth surrounding the tree started to shift and roil, and with one swift tug, the darkness pulled Revna down until her lower body was eaten by the earth.

Wide, unfocused eyes stared over at him, the blackness that fell from her eyes, nose, and mouth covering most of her beautiful face.

"Fenrir," she called. He could barely hear the word but knew what his name on her lips looked like.

"Revna!"

But with one final tremble of the earth, the darkness pulled her under. And she was gone.

Fifty-One

Fenrir

The barrier disappeared. Fenrir crawled to where Revna had just been pulled under and dug his hands into the earth, tears still blurring his vision. He dug and dug, but the earth was unforgiving and solid. He needed to reach her, he needed to follow her. He had promised ...

Wherever you go, I follow. Whatever you fight, I fight.

There was no trace of her, no familiar smell, no drop of her blood. Only cold emptiness.

She was gone.

And Asgard would feel his pain.

On a bellow, he shifted back into his wolf form and turned to where Hel and Tyr were engaged in battle. Fenrir launched himself forward, his gigantic body only needing one leap to reach them. Then he stood over Tyr and Hel, letting out a roar that would be felt through all nine realms.

Fenrir lowered his head and bared his teeth, watching as several warriors turned and ran—he snapped at their retreating forms.

But they were not his prey.

All he wanted in that moment was Revna back.

And to kill Odin.

The Allfather was nowhere to be found. He roared his rage into the sky once more, then leveled his face on the remaining combatants. For now, Odin's remaining warriors would have to do. He swung his snout wide, knocking several aside, uncaring if they got up again.

"Brother!" Hel's voice commanded, coming out in dozens of over-layed voices.

Lumbering back, he glanced down at her, her eyes full of tears. He had no time, no space in his own grief, for her sadness. Instead, he lifted his head again, searching for Odin, searching for a fight. A growl pulled back the skin on his nose, and he sent a wave of his power into the earth, knocking retreating warriors off their feet.

Hel grabbed onto the fur of his leg and tugged, trying to get his attention.

"I think I know where Revna is!" she screamed.

His ears perked at his sister's words, and he dipped his head and whined in question, the control of staying still making his whole body start to shake. He could tell she was reluctant to speak.

"We need to go to the gates of my realm."

Fuck.

Fenrir's stomach sank into a fathomless pit in his body, the feeling unending and torturous.

His wife was in Helheim, the one place he couldn't follow.

He'd have to find a way.

He stood, his body already aiming before his brain could catch up to where they'd need to go. They hadn't considered how they'd get back when asking his mother to open a door for them, and Fenrir instantly regretted the oversight. They would need to make it to the gate on the other side of the palace.

He would take out anyone who dared get in his way.

Fenrir dipped down and nudged Hel and Tyr to climb atop his back. Once they were settled, he took off running.

He crashed through the courtyard, knocking aside anyone who didn't move fast enough. Veering left, he kept them to the outside as much as he could, until he could no longer fit through the spaces. He felt an arrow pierce his leg and he let out a strangled cry, but still, he kept running. A faint glow surrounded him—Tyr had put up a protective shield.

They came to an opening that would lead them into the hall, but Fenrir wouldn't fit in his wolf form. He knelt, letting Hel and Tyr slide off before shifting back to his human form. After years of not shifting, he felt weak and slightly dizzy from the back and forth.

He didn't care, didn't let it stop him.

Fenrir ran down the hall, the gate within sight. He was almost to the runed arch when a bolt of lightning struck down in front of him, blocking his path.

All three of them whirled to face a sneering Thor.

"You are going back to your cage, dog," Thor spat.

Fenrir made a move to charge him, but Tyr stopped him with an arm and pushed him toward the gate. "Go." He nodded for Hel to go, too. "Both of you, go. I'll hold him off."

"I won't leave you, Tyr," Fenrir said, trying to push past him.

Tyr gave a small chuckle. "My friend, you aren't even wearing trousers." Fenrir glanced down, completely forgetting that aspect of shifting. Tyr's face turned serious. "Go find Revna. And bring her home."

Tyr gave him one more big push before turning and running at Thor. Thunder growled overhead and lightning struck down atop Tyr's shield, the sound rattling his teeth.

As if sensing his hesitation, Tyr turned back one last time. "Go!"

Hel tugged on Fenrir's arm and quickly tapped the runes on the gate to Helheim.

———

The gate dumped them out at the barren and craggy landscape at the entrance of Hel's realm. A cold spectral breeze raised his hair in warning.

Fenrir was not dead, nor was he a lost soul, so he could not enter Helheim. But he wouldn't let that stop him if that's where his wife now resided.

"Where is she, Hel?" he asked, looking around. There was no sign of life. Nothing but barren rock.

Fenrir had never been to her realm before, but he could feel Hel's power only strengthened the closer they walked toward the large stone doors. It thrummed from her and, for a moment, Fenrir was intimidated by his sister.

"When she was pulled under, I felt something cross into my realm." Fenrir's stomach sank, but she continued, "it didn't feel like the way the dead usually enter. It was deeper. Darker. Down to a place I would usually dare not go."

"Is she dead?"

Hel turned to him, and he watched as tears spilled over her lower lids and her mouth pulled into a sad smile. She loved his wife, too.

"I'm not sure."

Fenrir felt removed from her words, his mind and body unwilling to cooperate or reconcile with the possibility. He ignored the searing pain in his body and took a step closer to the doors.

His sister's hand shot out, stopping him.

"You cannot go with me," Hel said, her voice apologetic but hard as stone. "You won't be able to leave."

"I am going with you, Hel," Fenrir snarled at his sister.

Cloudiness overtook her eyes and something in the air pulsed. "No, you're not. I do not permit it."

He ignored her, trying to step around her when invisible ropes tied around him, slamming him to his knees. His muscles felt weak, his head light as Death tightened its hold on him. He gave his head a shake and growled at his sister.

"Do not keep me from her, Hel," he pleaded.

She knelt in front of him. "I will not sanction your demise, Fenrir. You need to listen to me and trust in me. This is *my* realm. If you enter, you cannot leave. And there are others who need you. Do you understand?"

What did that mean for Revna? How would she leave? He opened his mouth to ask the questions but couldn't form the words. His heart was shattering into pieces and each shard made breathing painful.

"Take a breath and focus," Hel gently commanded. "Can you feel her?"

He did as his sister asked, trying to clear his mind, trying to feel past the pain. Just on the inner edges of all that pain, he felt it. Dull and wavering, but he felt it. The warmth of his wife at his very center. He held onto it and nodded at his sister.

"Wait here and I'll be back as soon as I can."

Hel reached for him, squeezing his shoulder before walking right through the stone doors. The ropes holding him released and he fell forward, his hands catching on the rock.

He shoved down the urge to chase his sister again. To find his wife.

He had to trust Hel, like he always had before. Had to believe Revna wasn't lost to him.

Not wanting to be himself anymore, Fenrir shifted back into his wolf form and laid down before the gates of Helheim.

And there, he waited.

Alone.
Alone.
Alone

Fifty-Two

Hel

S WEET DEATH WRAPPED AROUND Hel as she entered her realm. The cool and comforting feeling settled into her bones, strengthening her, singing to her.

Her sentries bowed quietly in greeting, their onyx armor catching in the blue torchlight. Purposeful steps echoing off the cavernous entry hall, she made her way to the giant yawning chasm in its heart. Great obsidian stalactites bit down from overhead like monstrous teeth, hot liquid dripping from their sharp points. Rusted fire pits with blackened skulls burned hot, surrounding the dark pit in the middle.

Everything was meticulously crafted to inspire fear. To feed on it.

Hel peered down into the inky darkness of the chasm before stepping onto its ledge. Arms wide, she tilted over the edge, falling into its depths. Letting darkness surround her in its suffocating hold. When she felt herself nearing the bottom, she positioned her body and sent down a wave of power, landing on her feet.

Her eyes adjusted, taking in the perfectly circular chamber with three doorways. One led to the wastelands of Niflheim. One to the bowels of Helheim, which she reserved for the truly vile.

And the other ...

Hel had placed a stone and steel door in front of it, in fear of what lay behind it. She took a torch off the wall and approached the door. The closer she got, the more the torch seemed to dim. With all her strength, she pushed the door aside and immediately felt every hair raise on her arms as she peered down into the darkness below.

Lifting the torch, she was able to make out roughly hewn stairs that wound down, down, down. With a death-laced breath, Hel took the first step.

The torch in her hand only allowed her to see as far as the next step in front of her. She carefully followed them for what felt like hours. The lower she went, the colder the air, the harder it became to breathe.

Hel loved Revna as her own flesh and blood sister, and she was terrified of what she may find at the bottom of those steps. Terrified of what would be left of her friend.

When the stairs finally leveled out and there was only flat ground, Hel paused and lifted the torch to the unending darkness. It came at her from all sides, surrounding her, compelling her to *give in*.

But she was the fucking Goddess of Death, and darkness was an extension of her. She closed her eyes, sending out a pulse of power, searching for a soul—living or dead. Somewhere beneath the coldness, beneath the bitterness, she felt something.

Two somethings.

Fury and fear burning through her, Hel lifted her torch and her chin higher, gazing into the awaiting darkness.

"Give her back," she snarled, a thousand voices echoing through the unending gloom.

A deep, rumbling growl answered in response.

Epilogue

S HE'D HAD A NAME once.

She had existed.

Hadn't she?

Somewhere in the darkness, she searched for a name. Any name. Anything to feel.

She thought she heard the faintest sound. A howl ...

But there was nothing.

Only the low, rumbling growl of the beast that had wrapped itself around her and pulled her under.

And she had allowed it.

Because she didn't have a name anymore. She did not exist.

She was alone ...

And there was only darkness.

Acknowledgements

Holy shit, I'm writing my first-ever book acknowledgments. This book has been a long time coming and would not have been possible without the help, love, and support of some really special people.

To my husband, Jasen: Without your unwavering belief, listening ear, and unlimited supply of hugs, I wouldn't have made it. I am so beyond grateful for your unconditional support, patience, and reminders to eat something. Thank you for being my self-appointed CFO/CTO/CSO and cheerleader—especially when technology tries to get the best of me. This year was quite the journey, and I wouldn't want to do it with anyone else. I love you. Like, a lot.

Big hugs to my family, whose excitement and pride fueled me on days when my energy wavered. You've believed in me since day one, and I don't take that for granted. Thank you, thank you, thank you. I love you to the moon and back.

To my in-laws: If you've made it this far in the book, we don't need to talk about the spicy chapters. Ever. Thank you for your support and for clapping for me even when I get embarrassed about it. Love you guys.

To my editor and champion, Kearstie: This book wouldn't be what it is without you. I can't thank you enough for holding my hand and the constant reminders to be gentle with myself. You are more than just an editor; you are a wonderful friend and stuck with me now.

To Heather, my co-wife for life: Your friendship and encouragement have meant so much to me over the last couple of years. Thank you, from the bottom of my heart, for everything. This year is going to be the year that we finally get to hug in real life. I can feel it.

To Ali, my soul-sister across the pond: You are such a source of sunshine in my life. Thank you for your limitless hype and Pedro Pascal pictures/videos. You have a wonderful heart, and I am so grateful that I get to call you my friend. Te quiero, mi amiga.

To Amber, my Hoa Hoa Hoa girl: Thank you for cheering me on so loudly. You were one of my first Booksta friends, and I am so glad we slid into each other's DMs. You are an amazing person, and I am so grateful for you. Belllar.

To Lex, my twin in so many (scary) ways: I wouldn't have made it through the end of this journey without you. Thank you for the hours and hours of phone calls and voice memos—for the encouragement and understanding. Your friendship saved me this year. I can't wait for the day we unite the powers of Brian and Dane to write together. (Kears, you were right about us.)

To Elyse, proofreader and VA extraordinaire: You literally saved me from pulling my hair out, and I am forever grateful. Thank you so much for your support.

To the Bookstagram community: You all are the reason I was finally able to stare down my imposter syndrome and say, "Fuck it, I'm going to do it." Watching this community share their love for books, writing, and shedding years and years of shame around sex has been such an honor to be a part of. Never stop. You're fucking awesome.

And, lastly, to you, dear reader: Thank you for taking a chance on a new author. You have made my dream come true.

Rachel's love of books and writing started when she experienced the high of attending the school book fair, and she's been chasing that feeling ever since. She enjoys writing spicy fantasy romances with intriguing worlds, complex characters, and a dash of darkness. When not slamming her head against her keyboard, you can find her on the hiking trail or burrowed on her couch. She lives in Southern California with her husband and all the characters constantly swirling around in her mind, who have yet to pay rent.

Email: rachel@authorrachelnharker.com
Instagram: @author.rachelnharker
Website: www.authorrachelnharker.com